THE SAVAGE PLACE

THE SAVAGE PLACE

Leon Arden

FOR MY FATHER

so that my life (which liked the sun and the moon)
resembles something that has not occurred:
i am a birdcage without any bird,
a collar looking for a dog, a kiss
without lips; a prayer lacking any knees
but something beats within my shirt to prove
he is undead who, living, noone is.
I have never loved you dear as now i love.

—e. e. cummings

TABLE OF CONTENTS

ONE

1

THE WIND tore at him with hungry hands, pulling at his clothes and hitting his face. The speedometer needle danced at eighty. A hill came rushing forward, and the young man felt everything rise and fall as it passed beneath him. Up ahead, two men of the Guardia Civil stood idly watching from either side of the road. Each wore an ankle-length green coat, a three-pointed flat black hat, and a long rifle. In a moment they were behind and disappearing. Their presence without bicycles in the middle of that wasteland meant the next town was still far ahead.

Five hours of steady driving into the wind had made him numb to it. Only when he stopped along the straight Spanish road did the young man sense how still the land was. And only then, feeling the heat and the silence, did he discover how fast he had been going.

He rolled and lifted the heavy German NSU back and onto its stand, the front tire off the ground and turning slightly. Leaving it there, he did deep knee-bends and ran along the empty road stretching his legs. Then he took a sip from an almost empty bottle of wine, spitting out bits of cork, after which he unwrapped and ate a piece of soft chocolate. He stood and suddenly listened to the incredible quiet and tried to feel whether the warm air made even the slightest stir against his skin. Then he started the motor with the foot crank, worrying that perhaps too much time had already been wasted, picked up and put on the silver crash helmet, adjusted the goggles over his eyes with both hands, and drove away, feeling the wind again and watching the speedometer climb.

Forty-five minutes later he was motoring down the luxuriously wide Paseo Recoletos toward the even wider Paseo del Prado and looking for the Calle de Alcalá and the address of a small hotel that had been given to him by his friend D. J. Jones, who had been in Madrid the year before. To the young man it seemed now deathly slow to be moving through these streets at only a quarter of the speed he had been hitting for over six hours. It felt as if he were dragging weights, and he was needled by the temptation to throw on the speed. But gradually his attention became absorbed with the late afternoon congestion and especially with the police. Nowhere, at any time, had he seen more police stationed in the streets simply to guard the traffic against itself. It gave him an uneasy feeling.

At first he had trouble locating the address and he had to stop several times to examine the map, but at last he saw the sign: RESIDENCIA ALBINA, and all at once the search was over. D. J. Jones had sent him to this place for several reasons. First, the rates were cheap. This was always important. Next, Señora Albina, who owned the rooms, was a charming, middle-aged woman whose knowledge of the capital was complete. There seemed to be few people she didn't know, and if you asked a favor of her, no matter how difficult, she would simply make a few quiet phone calls to people who appeared to be old friends, and in a day or two the job was done. On top of that, she somehow always knew just what was going on of importance around the town and would often share these tips with her guests. All in all, for someone in a strange city she was definitely a good person to know. Yes, D.J. had spoken highly of her; but more than that, he had even displayed a quiet, almost awed respect for her, and this was odd, because from him, respect of any kind was rare. And there was still another attraction to the Residencia Albina, for working with Albina was a beautiful black-haired Spanish girl. D.J. had taken a great deal of pleasure and time describing her to him. The young man now recalled some of the details and felt desire stir within him. "But there's one trouble," D.J. had said. "She's typical Spanish. I mean *real* Spanish. You can't touch her. She has a set of cemented morals, like if you put some dynamite under them and

set it off, you'd kill *yourself* in the blast, but *she'd* still be standing....
I know—I tried.... What a blow!"

The young man remembered D.J.'s words very clearly. There
had been a time when hearing such reports about a girl would have
immediately disappointed him, but now he was no longer sure what
he thought. He had come a long way and left much behind him,
and one of the things he had left was the innocent trust he had
once had in the future. He had learned several years ago that one
can be sure of absolutely nothing—not even change.

Anyway, now he was very tired. With his clothes pack removed
from the cycle and hanging over his back, and with his helmet in
his hand, he stepped into the elevator and rode to the fifth floor.
The small landing had only two doors and on one of them was
the sign RESIDENCIA ALBINA. He pressed the bell with the hand that
gripped the helmet and then waited. The uneasiness he always felt
just before meeting strangers had already taken hold of him. He
was about to change the weight of his clothes pack from one hand
to the other when the hurrying of high heels approached the other
side of the door. The last moments were prolonged as someone
fumbled with a turn-lock.

The sudden beauty of the girl who stood before him overthrew
his pretended calmness, and for a moment he tingled with confusion. He looked directly at her, but in the swiftness of the moment
he saw very little. He was aware only of the darkness of Latin hair
and skin and the elegance of a girl dressed for an evening out. But
he did notice the incompleteness of only one earring dangling
against her neck and the thick scent of newly applied perfume cutting a little too sharply through the air. It was obvious she had been
interrupted in the last stages of dressing.

"May I speak with Señora Albina?" he asked.

"*Momentito*," she said, and with a smile, drew him in. The girl's
heels hammered lightly across the bare floor until she reached a
room at the other end of the short hallway. She leaned in and spoke
a few words of Spanish and then walked off out of sight back to her
mirror.

Almost immediately Señora Albina appeared, and with a polite, experienced smile spoke to him in an accent he did not recognize. "You please sit down."

He went to the couch while she chose one of the two wooden chairs that faced him on the opposite side of a low, glass-topped table. The young man had already left his clothes pack and helmet in an empty corner.

The Señora was dressed well. Tasteful clothes and jewelry seemed as much a part of her as her slightly graying hair, whereas the young girl who had answered the door had been decorated only for the occasion of evening. The Señora had an inner calm that made silence natural and desirable, and she even had a way of sitting in a chair as if it were a throne; to accomplish this she did not have to pose, stiff and regal. She could cross her legs or slouch back, and yet the effect would not be lost. Across her face—over every line and curve of bone and texture of skin—there was still being fought the battle against age. It had started late and would go on for many years, but even down to the end there would always be that reminder to others of what she once must have been.

"What can I do?" she asked.

He began a little uncertainly, believing that perhaps after all he might be in the wrong place, speaking with the wrong woman.

"There is a letter…"

He hesitated, but her face revealed nothing. "I sent it to you about the bullfight and the…"

"Oh, yes. I have it." Then, pointing with her finger: "Your name is…ah…" For the moment she paused at the verge of recall. She was almost excited.

"Andrew Williams." He smiled.

"Ah, of course. I was wondering since Wednesday where you were."

"I hope I'm not too late for tomorrow?"

"No, no. It is all arranged."

"Good. That's a relief."

But Señora Albina leaned forward. "You know, there may not be anything good tomorrow. Nothing special."

"God, I hope not. I've come a long way for this."

Albina nodded in sympathy. Curling her fingers, she studied one of her long red nails.

"Anyway," she said, looking up. "I have the letters of introduction for you. Everything is ready."

"You know, it is very kind of you to go to all this trouble for me. Someone you hadn't even met."

"It is nothing, please. And I am arranging for your trip to Valencia, too. But one thing. That boy who recommended my place. His name again, what is it? Can you tell me?"

"D. J. Jones. He stayed here last summer."

Her face began to remember.

"He's a big, frightening guy," he added. "Loud and funny."

"Ah, yes, I recall. A wonderful boy. We laughed so much at him. And how is he…your friend? Such a funny name."

"D.J.'s fine. Nothing changes much with him except maybe he gets louder."

Albina bubbled a gentle laugh. Then she noticed Andrew's belongings in the corner of the hall.

"What is that?" she asked, indicating the helmet.

"It's for riding a motorcycle."

"You come on motorcycle?"

"Yes, ma'am."

"From where?'

"I bought it secondhand in Paris. But it's a German machine."

"It must be wonderful." In that moment her eyes seemed younger than ever. Then she added: "But you are careful?"

"Very careful." He smiled.

And at that she decided he was the handsomest American she had seen in quite some years.

The time had come to ask about the cost of the room. As they talked, her manner had somehow given him the impression that he was an old friend back from a long trip. It was a feeling he had not had in some time, and for the moment he did not want to lose it. To talk of money might shatter this illusion of friendship which had suddenly been created, and he was surprised to find himself unwilling to take the chance. He decided to let her bring it up first. In the meantime he would at least ask if she had a room at all.

"By the way, you have a place here for me?"

"Don't worry." She laughed. "Five people, they move out this morning. My beds they are almost all empty. Would you like to see your room?" She leaned forward ready to rise at the first sign of his agreement.

"You say the room is nice?"

Albina seemed puzzled. "Yes."

"Then let me take your word for it." He smiled.

"Don't take my word," she said with a good-natured frown. "I show you."

"But this way will save me time, and I can go down and get a drink."

The Señora got to her feet. "Come," she said, in the manner of a command. "I *give* you a drink."

Without looking to see if he had accepted the offer she led the way to the door through which she had come. But she stopped short before she got there and turned around.

"The room, it will cost sixty pesetas, yes?"

She asked this softly, as if implying that the amount would certainly be lowered if he thought it was too high, and that he should not hurt himself with worry over it.

"Fine," he said. "Fine."

The room into which she brought him was very small and comfortable. It was decorated to the ceiling with wall rugs, floor lamps, table statues, tightly filled bookcases, paintings, and photographs. There were two comfortable-looking armchairs and there was a day bed covered with scatter pillows. The one small window was covered with sheer drapes, and all three of the lamps were turned on. Alone in the room, lounging proudly in one of the chairs, a plump, well-fed man sat and waited. He held a cigar in one hand and a drink in the other, and it struck Andrew at once how unfortunately the man's face resembled a hog.

"Andrew Williams," the Señora said, "this is Leopold Mueller." And she sat down on the couch to mix him a drink. With considerable effort Leopold leaned forward out of his chair and extended his hand. It was chubby and soft, but he shook hard.

"A pleasure," Leopold said loudly. Then he slid back and slowly put the cigar into his mouth. "Make a strong one, Albina. He looks like a drinker to me." And he followed this with loud and raucous laughter.

"How long you stay in Madrid?" she asked, giving Andrew his drink.

"About three days or so. Perhaps more."

"Oh, there is so much to do."

"Yar," Leopold agreed, "Madrid is all right. But the best place of all is right here in Albina's." Gallantly he held up his glass as if offering her a toast.

"Leopold is sweet," she said.

"Do *you* have a room here?"

"As a matter of fact, I do," Leopold answered. "I checked in the day before yesterday."

Andrew studied the man with dim displeasure. He looked about thirty, but could have been less. The thickness of his face seemed unsupported by any bone structure underneath, and the heaviness of his cheeks almost swallowed up the rimless glasses encased in his flesh. His nose was turned up at such an extreme angle that his nostrils were almost vertical, and his hair had been cropped short. On his heavy body his clothes either stretched ungainly or bulked in the wrong place. A thin black tie was knotted snugly around a crumpled collar, and a large part of his shirt had crept up unnoticed from under his belt. The resemblance his face had to a hog now seemed stronger than ever, and Andrew wondered if Leopold ever thought this when he looked at himself in a mirror.

"How do you like Spain?" Albina asked.

"Best of all."

"Leopold doesn't." She smiled, looking slyly in his direction.

Leopold answered slowly, rolling his cigar in his fingers. "No, what I mean is…there are some things I like, and some things I don't like." He allowed a pause for this to be thought about. "Take the food, for example. Now, I like my sauerkraut." Pause. "But it's just no good out here. I ate some good sauerkraut in Paris. But in this town they just don't know how."

"*That's* why you don't like Spain?" Andrew said.

"No. I mean, there are other things." He leaned forward and lowered his voice a little. "The government," he said. Then he paused to let this register. "The government." He leaned back.

Andrew didn't know which of many retorts to use first. He hesitated too long.

"Now, mind you, Albina," Leopold began once more, "this is nothing against yourself. You understand? Know what I mean?"

Albina, seated gracefully on the couch, kept her eyes on her drink and put forward a face of polite attention. But to Andrew her expression was a little too motionless, a little too rigid.

"Now to me it's loathsome to be living under a dictatorship. I mean, it's something we have never had in the States, and I find it loathsome. Back home we would never put up with it."

"Does it bother you so?" Andrew asked. "I hadn't even noticed."

"No. I mean, it's the principle of the thing."

"Of politics I know nothing," said Albina. "Really…. Anyway, things are not so bad. You get used to things. But did you like Barcelona?"

"Very much," Andrew said.

"I think it a wonderful city," she agreed.

"Now, you see, Barcelona was much too quiet for my tastes."

"I saw a wonderful bullfight there last year," Albina said.

"Now there!" Leopold said, pouncing in. "There's something I really can't see. Really. I think it's loathsome. I mean, I can't fathom how people sit and watch it."

"A funny thing," the Señora remarked thoughtfully. "Some people they get so…so shocked. Others they like it. You can never tell ahead, you know? I once send some people from your country and they come back so angry at me. A lady with them, she faints. They have terrible time." But her lips gave way to a private smile.

"No. I mean, it's more basic than that." He shook the cigar in the air as if it were a sixth finger. "To my mind you've got to possess a certain brutality before you can enjoy…"

But the maid had stepped into the room, speaking several fast phrases in Spanish. Andrew decided she was about to leave. The girl wore both earrings now, and her lipstick and eye shadow had been applied boldly.

The Señora turned to Andrew. "This is Bianca, my maid and critic." She looked up at Bianca and then laughed, for the girl didn't understand. Then, as Albina talked, Andrew heard her speak his name. The girl looked at him and smiled.

"*Buenas tardes,*" Bianca said. She was a model of politeness.

"*Buenas tardes,*" he repeated, unable to keep from smiling at this attractive girl leaning nonchalantly, almost comically, against the doorway.

"She is going to meet her young man," the Señora explained. "She says she is late."

"Well, send her off then," Leopold boomed. "Hurry, hurry!"

A few words from Albina and the maid nodded slightly and backed off.

"*Hasta la vista,*" she said to the two men. Then she was gone.

"Now Albina must sit and wait until she come back," the Señora explained. "Until then I cannot eat." She took a sip from her drink and smiled sadly.

"How come?" Andrew said.

"Someone should be here always. You know? We take turns. When she goes, I must stay. But she will be back at eleven. Leopold has kindly asked me to dinner and he says he doesn't mind waiting." Then to Leopold she said: "Is true?"

"As long as you keep supplying the liquor, Albina." The air in the room, now filled with cigar smells, was shaken with his laughter.

The Señora put her hand to her cheek. "Oh, he drinks so. I never see such a thing."

"I just like my whiskey, that's all. Good for what ails you." He laughed again.

"You wish to eat with us?" Albina asked the young man.

"Yes, I would like to." He smiled. "But I don't think I can wait till eleven."

"Oh, of course. You will be too hungry." She said this as if she had committed some great stupidity.

"Thank you, anyway."

"You hungry now?"

"A little."

"I know a place it opens early. Real Spanish food, you know? Right near."

She gave him the name and explained that it was close enough for him to walk. And then, so he would not get lost, she made one pencil mark on the map and then another to show where the hotel was.

"Or, if you like German food, that also is near. The Idelweise."

"That's where I didn't like the sauerkraut," Leopold said. Mention of the restaurant seemed to surprise him.

Albina said nothing. She looked at Andrew questioningly, waiting for his preference.

"All right," Leopold conceded after a moment. "Try it. See if you don't agree."

"Which is nearest?"

"The first one," she said.

"Can I go there now?"

"Yes, is just opening."

"Dressed like this?" He looked down at his traveling clothes doubtfully.

"Oh, is all right. Just put on a jacket. Don't worry."

"Well, then," Andrew said, getting to his feet slowly and putting down his empty glass. "I guess maybe I'll go, then. O.K.?" He wondered if perhaps it was impolite to leave so quickly.

"Yes, of course, you are hungry," the Señora said. "Tomorrow we will see you, yes? Remember, if anything I can do, you please tell me .... Really."

"I will. Thank you."

"Eat hearty," the voice boomed after him, "and watch out for señoritas."

2

ANDREW WILLIAMS stopped under a lamppost to unfold and examine the map. After guessing his way down the last two streets he had decided he was lost. In the dim cobbled road he stood and studied the confusion of lines and names until he found where he was. Next he had to find where he was to go. The little penciled circle that Albina had made on the map to mark the restaurant was, he discovered, just two streets away. He had been walking in the right direction after all. With a smile he took this as a tribute to his good sense of direction.

A bald-headed man and a girl, both well dressed and walking in swift, perfect steps, went past without giving him a look. Their eyes were on each other as they walked and their lips were moving in conversation. Andrew watched the couple until they rounded a corner. Then he turned and went slowly down the dark cobbled hill toward the oasis of lamplight at the bottom.

Albina's hotel had pleased him. Its hint of respectability without great expense was just what he wanted at the moment. For a long while now he had succeeded in thinking mostly about other things, and not about himself. At times this was not easy, but for the last couple of weeks he had been almost calm and confident inside. There was nothing to worry about, he kept telling himself. Nevertheless, the maid, Bianca, must be kept at a distance. For the moment he was taking no chances. Above all, he wanted no more humiliation, no more failures.

Of the Señora, he recalled how with only a gentle gracefulness of posture and a few simple sincere words she could put across a stronger feeling of femininity than could young Bianca with her full breasts and small waist. Only Leopold spoiled the picture. The young man admired Albina's ability to cover up successfully the annoyance she must feel toward him. But then again, this was her job. It certainly would not do for a hotel owner to show that she preferred one guest to another.

He passed the door of the restaurant three times while searching for it. There was no sign, no unusual lights, only a small beer ad of cardboard standing in a dark-curtained window near the door. Inside, all the tables except one were empty, and this gave Andrew a moment's indecision about where to sit. A grinning boy of seventeen, who wore a filthy white apron around his waist and a pencil behind his ear, was in charge. When the boy discovered that Andrew was an American, he let loose an enthusiastic display of newly learned English, but Andrew found it almost unintelligible, for the boy's vocabulary, which was mostly mispronounced to begin with, kept failing him and in desperation he had to resort to Spanish words. His enthusiasm brought him to a point of excitement that made his speech breathless.

"You fith?" the boy asked, pointing meaningfully at Andrew.

The customer's face showed his puzzlement.

"You … *fith* … *fith*." And he held his hand straight and vertical and wiggled it through the air.

"Oh, fish!" Andrew said, greatly relieved. "Certainly, let's have some."

"Fish, fish," the boy repeated in a gush. Then he held up his hand, spreading out the five fingers. "Five … minutes," he said with effort and a great deal of doubt. Then, when he saw that the American understood, he beamed and hurried off.

Andrew held a match to the tip of his cigarette and felt the heat of the flame near his fingers. Seated in a quiet, pleasant restaurant, a bit hungry, waiting anxiously for a good meal, deciding to order some beer, pleased with his hotel, pleased with Madrid, he realized with a little surprise that he was genuinely happy. For a moment he had forgotten himself.

Waiting for his food, and having nothing else to do, Andrew became interested in the only other people in the room. They were seated at a table not far away—two young women and an old man. But it was not until one of the women gave him a long, unabashed look that he began to grasp what he saw. They were not his daughters, these two, nor were they relatives of any kind, or even friends. The two young women were in their middle twenties. One was a slightly overweight redhead with light skin and freckles, while the other was a trim attractive brunette with a practiced, devastating smile. The old man was completely bald except for the little hair he had left on the sides of his head, and his eyebrows were thick and dirty-gray. He must have been over sixty, yet he still looked as though he were in good condition, as do many army men his age when they retire.

The women at the table, in a happy mood, were not concerned that the man with them took little part in their gaiety. They laughed at the brief little stories the man solemnly told them, but the humor that was aroused was immediately turned against the old man with veiled derision. This was done carefully and subtly, and if he understood he did not let on. Mostly he kept himself above the gaiety at the table as a father would with his two silly daughters. The brunette, more than the other, gave full rein to her frolicking spirit, and occasionally, when the old man had commented on something and the two women had agreed with a shake of their heads, the brunette would look over at Andrew and wink or shrug her shoulders as if to say: This poor old bastard; I don't know what the hell he's talking about. The redhead was much less expressive with her face, but when the old man wasn't looking she would suddenly bring up her arms and make a quick comic gesture with each hand as if rolling up her sleeves in preparation to hit him, dropping her arms again just before he looked up from his food and giving him a smiling nod of her head as if all the while she had been completely engrossed in his speech.

This performance continued as Andrew ate his way through dinner. The brunette's eyes kept meeting his with brief, naked glances. This was dangerously done right under the old man's nose, and when a particularly long and penetrating look was fastened on Andrew, he felt as if his chest and back had been splashed with hot water. At one point the brunette even brought Andrew into the conversation at her table. "Now," she was saying in perfect English, "that young man over there looks to me like a North American. What do you think?" And the man turned and looked with nearsighted eyes that struggled to make out Andrew's features. He returned the old man's searching stare and saw for the first time how old he really was. Then they both turned away and Andrew stared at his plate, wondering what kind of justice awarded this man two women when he had none. It seemed a strange waste, a humorless parody, and yet he envied the old warrior's quiet, patient confidence—a confidence that concerned the two women and the bedroom ability he would use that night—while for Andrew, who was about a third this man's age, there was nothing but doubt and past humiliations.

Intent on his food, as if he were all alone, the old man sat and worked clean a piece of white chicken bone with his mouth. He seemed to be waiting, biding his time, putting up with the ridicule hidden behind each ripple of laughter, putting up with the wink the young waiter received and gave back to the hard-faced redhead as she sipped her coffee, putting up with the weight of his own years, with the very strengths and weaknesses of his life, biding his time, waiting patiently until later in the evening, until the time would finally arrive when he could deceive the years and become a man again like other men.

At one point, while Andrew was taking his dessert, the eyes of the pretty, well-dressed brunette became so bold that he was frightened for a moment that she might get rid of the old man and come over to him. This fear made her performance no longer enjoyable to him. Only a moment ago he had thought of taking out a roll of pesetas from his pocket and flashing the bills so the brunette could see them and understand that he too had money enough to buy her. He would have done it just to see what would happen, but now he sensed it would be a foolish risk to take.

When the old man finally climbed to his feet and motioned the two women to follow him, Andrew felt relieved. The group walked past his table, heading for the door, and this gave him a chance really to study the tall brunette as she strolled by. She had the elegant figure needed to fill out her snug knitted dress and he watched the wool slowly tighten and loosen again over the lower parts of her body as she walked triumphantly on display. She passed so close to him that he could have stood up and taken her suddenly into his arms, and yet at that moment, and despite the smiles she had thrown so carelessly in his direction, he felt that she was impossibly beyond him, farther from his body than from any man's in the world. He felt himself grow weak. The reality of her loveliness made him catch his breath, but when she reached the door, being the last in line, she turned to look at him with possessive eyes and hesitated for a moment. Once again Andrew felt the hot water of fear splash over him. It was as if he could breathe once more when finally she left.

He finished his dessert, but with a blank mind. His mouth did not taste the ice cream at all. He knew only that it was cold. The flurry of happiness he had felt when he had first come in was now entirely gone. He, too, climbed to his feet, and after paying the check, walked to the door, deciding he had better get plenty of sleep that night, for he discovered that a surprising fatigue rested heavily on his shoulders. But outside he was startled to find the old man and the two girls still there, standing at the curb. They had been trying to hail a taxi, and now finally one was coming for them. As it drove up, one headlight beamed dimmer than the other. The redhead jumped in first, getting a push from the old man, who quickly followed. Last was the brunette, who waited a moment for the other two inside to slide over and then lowered her head and made the high step into the taxi, pulling a slimly curved leg in after her. In the rear window, as the cab pulled away, Andrew saw the silhouette of the old head, tall and proud and motionless as the two old arms reached out like wings and pulled the two young women close to him.

Losing a woman after only a glance can often be more painful than losing one after many years. But to lose a woman one might have had if only one had been man enough to take her—this seemed to be worst of all. Andrew could still see the probing eyes that understood all that went on in his head, the soft, smiling mouth that effortlessly spoke two languages, the curve of hip in the woolen dress; all these things he remembered bitterly, for the woman was now gone forever. As he walked out of the dark side-street toward the brightness of theatre lights and the ambling crowds, he tried to forget.

But he had already begun to remember. His condition was supposed to be funny, but this only taught him that people laugh at the wrong times and at the wrong things. It was psychological, this condition of his, but to him this meant only that he had no way of dealing with it. Was he to be a washout for good? Was a bed to be nothing more to him than just a place to get eight hours sleep? With a very special effort he forced himself to drop these thoughts and to turn his mind to other things.

On the corner was a newspaper stand with a selection of unfamiliar magazine covers. A police officer saluted a man who approached from the middle of the street to ask a question. On a theatre marquee the word *HOY* appeared in tall red letters. Two men of the Guardia Civil, each with a rifle slung over his shoulder, strolled the boulevard together, their manner of casual disinterest unconvincing. In a restaurant window a man sat alone, yawn-tapped his mouth with the thumb side of his fist, and for several fading moments his image remained photographed on Andrew's mind. Everywhere there were noises.

Andrew lost himself among the strolling tides of people. Some were heading for dinner, others strolled aimlessly, while still others walked briskly toward some special theatre or movie. But everyone was moving; no one stood still. There are few things as universal as a crowd, and accustomed as he was to the multitudes of Manhattan, Andrew felt at ease. To one brought up in the scramble of a large city, it is better to walk through a forest of people than indulge in the self-pity of your own room, or worse, the emptiness of a hotel. He walked and saw the faces, and occasionally the faces saw him. Somehow, there was comfort in this.

The young man was surprised, but not startled, when an arm entwined his. It had slipped in so gently, as if it belonged, that he simply turned to see who it was. A girl's face appeared, inches from his shoulder. The mouth was opened and held with the lips curled back to show the teeth. Andrew didn't know at first what it meant, then, as the girl pressed closer, it dawned on him. Her suggestive, challenging leer had been used so often, displayed without feeling in so many cafés and on so many street corners, that it had become just a meaningless contortion of facial muscles—a horrible grimace conveying nothing more than the sexual deadness behind it. Only for fear of hurting her feelings did he restrain himself from pulling away. He was certain she knew how she looked. Then the girl spoke to him, but in Spanish, and he didn't understand.

"*No habla español*," he ventured, hoping this would put an end to it.

The girl stopped walking and pulled him to a halt. Her look of interest was almost authentic, and then a smile appeared that put a little life into her face.

"*Americano?*"

"*Sí.*"

"*Me alegro.*"

She giggled then, realizing he did not understand. But she followed with a stream of Spanish anyway, using a voice so warm and lazy that it was not hard for him to guess what she wanted. His face must have seemed puzzled, for she threw back her head and forced out a laugh. Meanwhile her appearance began to register on him. She must have been twenty-six, or even older, and the beauty of which she once must have had a great deal was now terribly marred. The corners of the mouth were pulled down to such an extreme that it seemed almost a joke she was playing. The jowls sagged slightly as if terribly tired of holding up the dead expressions that did not really belong there. The hair was frizzled and ugly. Only her eyes seemed alive, but they appeared blank and neutral, just watching, not taking part in anything that the face or body did. Although her eyes were alive but inactive, the rest of her was active but seemed dead. He was talking with a corpse. Nothing about her had the appearance of flesh and blood.

"*Tengo calor*," she said, and rubbed against him with a counterfeit smile.

Oh, now wait a *minute*, Andrew said to himself. What *is* this—Halloween?

She pressed further into him and he pulled away and tried to walk on, but the woman caught his arm again. She spoke several phrases, slowly and carefully, hoping he would understand.

"*Mañana*," he said, tugging to get his arm free.

"*No mañana. Esta noche.*"

Several times the young man tried gently to release himself, but he could not. Then, just as he felt himself growing desperate, she suddenly let go and stepped back. Her smile puzzled him. It seemed to have roots of pain beneath it and it hurt him to watch.

"*Es temprano*," she said. "*Hasta la próxima vez. Adiós.*"

Afraid to look back, Andrew lost himself in the crowd. His stomach unwound slowly with relief. But the memory of this encounter did not leave, and without intending to, he began to think of what her life must be, and it chilled him. She had been born into the same world as he, into the same world as his sister, and yet it was luck and nothing more that allowed his sister to lounge in her new bathing suit on a beach-chair in their backyard, slowly eating grapes and listening for the phone, while this bleak and dried-out girl who had just approached him in the street must endure every day and its night and the endlessness of living. It was that strange insanity of justice that inflicts punishment before the crime has been committed.

What he really wanted to do now was just walk. He saw marquee lights blazing on both sides of the boulevard but he was not tempted by any of them. He felt the loneliness that can come to a person far from home and all alone. Five minutes later he realized that walking was no good. The streets were filled with prostitutes, and a young man walking alone was always the first to be singled out. He became tense with precaution, for they seemed to be wherever he looked—strolling in the crowd, leaning waiting in a doorway, or standing together in twos on the corner. But wherever they were, they were always watching him. The ones in the streets were almost all poorly dressed and unattractive, for the streets are the last stop for a whore in Spain. Her career begins in the best houses or in bars or in dance halls and then moves to the worst houses and, finally, to the streets. This all takes years. But the streets are patient, and they wait.

Passing a bar, he saw that inside it was bright and crowded and he decided to go in and escape the street. In the back it was a restaurant, but all the white-clothed tables were empty and waiting for customers, and the presence of the two waiters standing idly among the tables made the place look even more deserted. But up in front was the bar, and this was filled. Andrew worked his way in and asked for a cognac. The babbling of voices around him, though he couldn't understand them, gave the place a sound of friendliness. Not knowing the language and yet watching the people speak, gave him insights that normally he might have missed. He saw how unemotional the Spanish were when they spoke, hardly ever using their hands, and yet they did not, as did some Americans, seem plagued by boredom or the false calm of sophistication. They did not laugh often, and if they did, their laughter was rarely loud and out of place. More often he saw them smile in a knowing, pleasant way, as people do who have seen far too much to be able to forget it all in a loud burst of laughter.

Andrew finished his drink fast, ordered another, and held it in his hand. Relaxing against the bar, he thought about nothing. Lighting a cigarette, he watched with pleasure the slowly exhaled, ghostly undulations of the smoke. Its winding, spreading, fading designs absorbed him. For the moment he felt not happy, but, somehow, released and untroubled. Gradually the eye of the photographer opened up within him again. He began to look about him as if his Rolleiflex were there ready in his hand instead of in his clothes pack up in his room, waiting for tomorrow and his next job. Among the maze of table- and chair-legs he saw a woman scratch the ankle of one foot with the bare heel of the other. A half-empty glass stood upon the table where it had been picked up and replaced many times, leaving several circles of rimmed beer. Two men standing side by side, each with one shoe on the railing, lifted their drinks to their lips, threw back their heads together, drank, and at the same moment firmly replaced the two glasses on the bar and stared at themselves numbly in the mirror. Outside, the rear wheel and fender of an automobile came to a stop at the curb. Feet could be seen climbing from the opened door. Then the wheel and fender moved off again, exposing the street. Andrew exhaled smoke, sending it into another adventure of light. But afterward, as he was about to drink up, he noticed for the first time what he would rather have not seen at all.

Men, mostly, stood at the bar. The few women in the place sat near by at wooden tables talking with the men who brought them. But among the men at the bar, separate from each other, each perched on a high stool, alone, not having any attention paid them, were two women of a completely different type from the sweethearts at the tables or the girls working out on the street. The two women were well dressed and attractive; and there was even a touch of class about them. One had seated herself on the first stool by the door and remained quiet and alone, as if waiting patiently for a friend who would arrive at a precisely given time and not a moment sooner. In front of her was a small shot-glass filled with liquor and untouched. Andrew was puzzled. What could she be doing here, he wondered as he took a sip from his drink. Then, as if in answer to his question, she turned and looked right at him, picking him out from among all the men standing nearby. The message in her eyes, without the eagerness of necessity to ruin it, was self-assured and almost strutting in its confidence.

It was Andrew who turned away. Good God, he thought, what *is* this? You've got to fight them off with a stick. As he turned from her his eyes ran right into those of the other woman who was also sitting alone and unattended at the far end of the bar. Now he turned around completely in a dramatic effort to avoid them both, but he felt their eyes burning his face. He tried to ignore it. He held his drink near his belt, placed his back against the bar, and gazed at the tables before him. It was only then that he saw still another woman staring at him with interest from one of the tables. She was sitting alone by the window and was looking at him as if she had been watching for some time. At once he felt trapped. To make sure he wasn't imagining things he glanced around again; no question, there they were, sitting like vultures, waiting for the resistance inside him to die. So what he had heard about Madrid was unfortunately all too true. It *was* a wild town. But damn it, he had not come as a tourist. He had come to work and then move on to work somewhere else. But it was a crazy town and inside of him the unrest had all started again. Andrew could take it no longer. He paid for his drink and made for the street. As he passed the woman who had started it all—the one seated on the stool by the door—he gave her a quick, guarded glance but discovered he no longer existed for her. She was staring at her drink, a woman waiting for a friend, and between her and the young man now leaving, nothing had taken place at all.

Out in the street Andrew felt more hunted than ever, for he didn't have the protection of a plan of action. What to do next? He was lost. Going back to the hotel was no good, for Albina and Leopold would still be there. Besides, he didn't want them asking him why he wasn't out enjoying himself. The hell with it, he thought. He would walk the streets, anyway. But his interest was gone, and he knew it. There was only one thing to do.

He walked hurriedly down José Antonio, his eyes searching carefully into each shop window.... Once inside the store, he had a little trouble because the owner kept bringing out bottles of bourbon instead of rye, but at last he spotted and pointed to just what he wanted, and the sale was made. From there he made straight for a movie across the street, the weight of the pint of rye in his side pocket pulling at his jacket as he walked. He bought a ticket and entered the dark, quiet theatre and hunted himself a seat. There he sat, not giving a damn about himself or the city or the job coming up the next day, lifting the bottle in the darkness to take in a long, stinging swallow, and watching Groucho Marx fluttering his eyebrows, tapping his cigar, and talking in a long stream of rapid, dubbed-in Spanish.

3

IN THE vacuum of half-sleep a voice was searching about like an anxious bird trapped in a sealed room. It echoed loudly and seemed to be calling to someone. The young man's brain listened just as it would have listened to the wind, without trying to understand or remember, perhaps not really listening at all. Then the voice began to register. But not because the voice spoke in English, but because it was southern, Andrew woke up. This did not happen quickly, either, the waking up. His head was filled with rust, his eyes felt like open wounds, and even before he could sit upright and focus through the blur of light to where he saw his clock, he knew it was afternoon. On the table and next to the clock, which now seemed to be ticking for the first time, stood the bottle. There was not enough liquor left to fill a thimble.

He lit a cigarette.

"Man, we're having a great time," said the voice in the hall. "Hop down here. Hell, man, it's only a day's ride.... Me and Greco...Yar, we came down together.... Come on.... So go awol.... Come on."

The sink water was shockingly cold, but it didn't go in far enough and clean out the rust in his head. Andrew dabbed at his skin with a rough towel and his eyes felt as if a layer of tissue had been peeled from them.

"...Greco *said* you wouldn't come. He said you were chicken!...Yar...Yar, this town's great.... Full of women? Hell, man, our *room's* full of women!"

Standing barefoot on the dusty floor, the wood feeling cool to his feet, he climbed into his pants, one leg at a time. As he pulled on his shirt he looked into the mirror and decided he could get by without a shave. The face that looked intently back at him, somber and motionless, was a handsome one—too many people had told him that for it to be untrue—but to him it seemed thickly stupid and uselessly grotesque. He watched as his lips blew a thin ghostly stream of smoke at himself.

"Give Sergeant Sloane our love. Tell 'em we're never coming back!"

Andrew put on his shoes and went to the mirror again to brush his hair. Some strands in back would not go down, and he had to wet the brush and work on the unruly hair over and over until he felt the cold water reach his scalp.

When finally he got to the door and opened it, the conversation at the wall phone had ended and a tall blond figure was prancing down the hall as if the floor were painfully hot, his loud bare feet moving swiftly and his body wearing nothing but white undershorts. With a bolt he disappeared into a room several doors away. Andrew followed him, deciding to walk past and just casually look in. But as he got there, Albina was coming out and they nearly ran into each other.

"Sleep well?" she asked, her eyes searching to find the answer herself, her voice warm and friendly and for a moment, in this whole world, she was, strangely enough, concerned only with him.

"I don't remember."

"Then you sleep well," she laughed. "Come, meet two new people. They come last night, very late."

He followed her into the room, the cigarette hanging limply from his mouth. He was introduced first to the one called El Greco. The man might have been twenty-eight or twenty-nine, but the short cropped hair and the energetic, happy expression made him look much younger. Lounging on his bed, he wore a pair of pants but no shirt, and his body as well as his face was knotted and muscular. Because the man was lying down, it was hard to tell, but to Andrew he seemed very short. Standing between El Greco's bed and his own was the almost naked boy whose voice fifteen minutes ago had prodded Andrew from sleep. He was the handsome Adonis-type, his body ivoried and completely without hair. His name was Bruno, and he shook hands politely across the bed. On the other side of the room Bianca was busy making the empty bed.

Bruno scratched his groin. "Where you from?" he asked.

"New York," Andrew explained, removing the cigarette from his mouth.

Bruno snatched up a bottle of cognac from the floor. "Glad to meet you," he said. "Have a drink."

"Maybe later. I still have a stiff head from last night."

"Ah," Albina put in, "you do the town last night." She laughed pleasantly.

"You in the service?" El Greco asked.

"No, just passing through."

"Here, sit down," El Greco offered, pushing himself over. "You look tired."

"What are you two doing today?" Albina said.

"We don't know," replied the man on the bed.

"Hunt us up some women," said Bruno, speaking at the same time. Then he poured more cognac into his glass. As he did this, he gave Bianca a growl. Her lips tightened to keep from smiling.

"You want some cognac?" Bruno asked his friend.

"You hunt women like that?" Albina laughed. "You'll catch cold." Then she shook with even more laughter, as if she had noticed for the first time how scantily Bruno was dressed.

"Hell, this is the best way," Bruno answered. Then looking at Bianca again he said, "Ain't it?...Huh?" He pretended to make a rush for her and tricked the girl into jumping away.

"Toledo good to see?" El Greco asked.

"Is wonderful," the Señora told him. "So old and beautiful." Then she spoke briefly to her maid, who answered with a nod and a few words.

"Bianca agrees," the Señora explained happily.

"Sightseeing!" Bruno pronounced the word with derision and distaste. He bounced down on the empty bed, scratching his shoulder and balancing his glass. "They always get me to go to places like that. Every damn time I go, and every damn time I'm sorry."

The hallway echoed with the ringing of the phone.

"Ach," Albina said, "excuse me." She hurried out.

"If it's women," Bruno called after her loudly, "tell 'em to come on up. We're ready."

"You from the Southwest?" Andrew said.

"The big D."

"Where?"

"Dallas, Texas," Bruno said, without a hint of pride.

"Big men come from Texas," El Greco said. "And damn, he's big."

"Five-eleven, only? Ah, to you everything looks big."

Bruno glanced at the maid for a moment. She was fluffing a pillow and watching them at the same time. He turned away with a smile.

"But I can show *her* something big," he said. "Mucho grando." And he laughed at Bianca in a strained voice that rang more with triumph than with humor. But during those moments, no matter what he did or said, it was hard not to laugh with him.

"Mucho, mucho, grando," he said as he gestured.

El Greco's voice joined in with laughter while Andrew, to his surprise, found himself grinning. The girl tried to control her mouth with squeezed lips, but it did not work, and her shocked delight was suddenly revealed for all to see. After the first moment of his surprise, Andrew was about to become embarrassed for her, but in the end it was the look on her face instead of what Bruno had done that finally shocked him.

"You going to give her a heart attack," El Greco said.

"Ask if she understands."

"She understands all right. Look at her."

"Ask her," the Texan insisted. But his enthusiasm got out of hand and he began questioning her himself in the language she didn't understand: "Do you? Huh? Do you?"

El Greco spoke quickly to the girl in Spanish.

"*Si*," she answered, blankly.

"She understands."

"You bet she does." He took a drink from his glass. "Think she puts out?"

"No," Andrew said.

"Why?" Bruno asked him.

"I just don't think so."

"Sure she does, man." Then to the girl Bruno said: "Do you? ... Huh?"

He was standing now and went over to the dresser for a shirt. Bianca moved away a few steps as he went pass. He turned his head to look at her over his shoulder. "Do you? Huh?"

"Why don't you try her out?" Andrew said, trying for humor, and aware that he had not come up with any.

"He will, don't worry," El Greco said, slipping a cigarette in between his lips.

Bruno looked at the girl as he put on his shirt. "Boy, what a dressful!" He pretended to lunge at her like an animal. Again she was tricked and jumped away with a giggle. Bruno laughed his laugh of triumph and turned to the others on the bed to encourage them to join in.

But Andrew was thinking more of the Texan's strange restlessness than anything else. Even when Bruno had been sitting relatively still on the edge of the bed, fingering his glass and twitching his entire leg up and down nervously as he balanced it on the ball of his foot, he had seemed anxiously awaiting some excuse for movement. Also, this strange young Texan acted completely unaware of the fact that he lived in a world where people constantly observe and pass judgment on others. Here was a person unable to grasp the idea that there might be someone who disapproved of him or of what he was doing.

"What've we got planned for today?" Bruno asked his friend who was sprawled on the bed.

"I don't know."

Neither of them seemed particularly concerned.

"Christ," Andrew said suddenly, getting to his feet, "I've got to leave. It's getting late."

"Where you headed?" El Greco asked.

"To work. I've got to shoot a bullfight this afternoon."

They both looked at him, puzzled.

"I'm a photographer." He stepped to an ash tray and put out his cigarette. "Free-lance work, mostly."

"What magazine you work for?"

"I don't. I work through a photo agency."

"Make good money?" Bruno wanted to know. For a single moment his voice was tamed by respect.

"Soso. But it keeps you moving."

"That's it." El Greco pointed to his buddy. "We'll go to a bullfight."

"Too brutal." Bruno pushed the idea away with his hand and made a face. "I saw one once."

"How about Toledo?"

"I tell ya I won't like it. I just know."

Bianca left the room with an armful of used sheets.

"Hey, where you going?" the Texan called after her.

"I think I catch on now to what he likes," Andrew put in with a slight smile.

El Greco stretched out and folded his hands behind his head. His voice was sober. "How'd you ever guess?" he said.

Out in the hall again Andrew met the Señora, who was coming to hand over some mail that had arrived for him from the States. She also gave him two additional letters that she herself had written—letters of introduction in case he had any trouble at the bull ring. He thanked her several times, but she only made light of it, as though regretting she could not do more.

Back in his room Andrew opened his clothes pack and selected two rolls of 120 color film along with eight rolls of black-and-white, and pocketed them. He removed the sky filter and the yellow filter from their strap case and cleaned them, and then gently dusted both lenses of the Rolleiflex with a small camel's-hair brush. As he worked, sitting on the unmade bed, he could see, distant and miniature through his window, the pale-gray suburbs of Madrid and, beyond them, the flat, brownish plain. Shouldering the camera, he picked up his crash helmet and left. Behind him in the hallway as he was about to open the front door he heard Bruno's voice yelling, "Look out! Here I come!" And then Bianca's startled squeal.

Andrew walked down the five flights to the street for the elevator, because of the city-wide electricity conservation, was not to be used by people returning to the ground floor. The fresh, sun-warmed air touched his skin and invigorated him. But he was still angry at himself for having been so dull in the presence of the two new guests. He had wanted to talk more and say something funny, but had felt a strange tension when he was with them; he had been ill at ease. He wondered why this had happened. The hell with it.... Besides, he liked them.

His intention had been to sit in the saddle of his machine awhile and read his letters there, but several children had gathered in the street to watch him drive away. Some of them seemed to have been waiting for some time. Reluctant to disappoint them, he rolled the motorcycle partly away from the curb and started the engine. It took several pumps of his foot before the motor caught. Lowering his helmet onto his head, he buckled the strap under his chin firmly. Next, using both his hands, he fitted the goggles to his eyes. He noticed once again that the plastic lenses were badly scratched, and once again he promised himself to get new ones. Got to stop this blind flying, he told himself; definitely unhealthy for cowards. Then, with a smile for the children and a loud warning rasp of his horn for no one in particular, he roared away from the curb and down the street. The children shouted and ran with pleasure trying in vain to keep up with him.

He drove for several minutes in no particular direction until at last he found himself in a different part of the city. By now his curiosity about his mail was overwhelming. He stopped beneath the tall-stretching trees of the Paseo Recoletos, pushed down the stand, cut the engine, and pulled the letters out of the inside pocket of his jacket. Two were from his parents visiting relatives in Los Angeles. One, addressed in pencil, was from D. J. Jones. One was from *Graphic Globe*, and the fifth, he was surprised to find, was from his sister. She had not written since he had left. For a brief moment Andrew was hurt at the thought of several of his friends from whom he had expected letters. It was strange how important an unwritten letter could be. Ah, but good old D.J.! He never fails.

The letter, as usual, was badly typed. Words had been penciled out and others written in. There were misspellings and faulty grammar. But through all this, like a slap on the back, Andrew could feel the presence of his friend.

DEAR WORLD TRAVELER:

How are you doing, Boy? Making out? How is Madrid? Great? Boy, do I wish I was there with you. This soda-jerking all summer is killing me. How is Albina? Give the old girl my love. Isn't she great? Full of Old World charm. And how about Bianca? Built, huh? I told you. I told you! Damn this drugstore. I'm dying of envy. Guess who dropped in yesterday? Pauline. She didn't know I was working here and sat down without seeing me. What a blow! Did I shock her! I mentioned you were in Europe. She said, "Oh? Really?" You know. It was like, "Well, what else is new?" I don't know what you did to that girl but she sure hates you. Showing no mercy (in typical D.J. style) I asked her if she wanted your address. For a minute I thought she was going to throw her cherry soda at me. I even asked her for a date. Nothing. I didn't even get a tip. But she looked great as usual. Same old Pauline. Guess what? I'm thinking of selling my cycle. If I go back to school this winter I'll have to leave it in the garage like last time. As it will only rust there, I want to get rid of it. Do I hear any offers? How's the photo work coming? How is your NSU holding up? Christ, I wish it were a year ago. Man, how's that for a wish? Us whipping around the country over the weekends, Pennsylvania, Connecticut, New Hampshire, zoom, zoom, zoom. And all the guys on their machines like a small army. Speaking about that, guess who I met a few days ago? Big Mo Schwartz. He's taking his basic at Dix. Seems everybody is, these days. Nobody's around to ride anymore. We got to talking about the times when you and he used to compete for beers. Drag racing, control racing, hill climbing, any damn thing. But most of the time you kept beating him out. Remember? He used to burn rubber all over Long Island but he still ended up buying the beers. Big Mo and me, we got loaded one night just talking about it. Were we depressed! You know something? He called you the best damn cycle rider he ever met. And he wasn't very loaded when he said it. Told me not to tell you. You know Mo. But coming from him that's something. Said he had more fun riding against you than anybody. Me, he placed second. Well, I told you he was drunk at the time. Ah, the hell with it. Just writing about it gets me mad all over again. Well, what do you say? Want to buy my cycle from me? Get a fleet started. Otherwise the machine goes on the open market. And you know what that means. Old D.J. gets robbed again.

Keep having a ball, fella, and grab every girl in sight. D.J. is eating his heart out.

Your buddy,
D.J.

He read it over twice, smiling in the same places and feeling sad in the same places. Once more he wished he could escape back to the days he remembered when he had been happy and envied and young among his friends; when he had been the teller of funny tales, laughing easily at the humor of others, getting little time to himself, when he had been far too young and aware of it to be anything but modest.

But the Harley-Davidson he rode to school each day attracted attention, and soon everyone knew who he was. While changing classes, he returned dozens of greetings as he passed through the hall. He even began to get smiles from girls whose names he didn't know. Yet he wasn't the only one at high school who owned a cycle. There were D. J. Jones and Mo Schwartz and, of course, the Taylor twins. Andrew recalled that he had been the youngest among them. But because they all felt as close as brothers, believing themselves happy and brave together, and because he handled his cycle better than they, Andrew found that he had become the elder brother to each of them.

The years moved on; college was next, and then he went to work. But somewhere along the line the fun had all ended. D.J. went to Cornell, Mo Schwartz went to work for his father, Ike Taylor gave up cycling entirely after he broke his leg one night while riding through a heavy fog, and Ike's twin brother Sid got married the same month and took a job in Detroit. That was the year everything seemed to break up or drift away, and before he knew it, the person he had once been, and the gaiety and confidence he had once owned, had also drifted away....

Each time he came to Pauline's name in the letter, he felt himself wince. His eyes stopped at the same lines, and he could not move them. "*I don't know what you did to that girl but she sure hates you.*" His anger affected his breathing. Her name didn't belong in this letter. He hated the name because the name hated him, and it was wrong for her to intrude upon the cherished words of a friend. It reminded him of the shock he had felt when he had first understood what was in Pauline's mind and why she hated him. It almost made him feel sick. But he had other letters to read and they kept him from thinking about this.

The one from his sister was perfectly typed and beautifully blocked and margined, but the professional perfection of it did not bring to mind her secretarial skill. Instead, somehow, it seemed to bring to life Dominique herself. Letters often have a way of representing not just the people who have sent them, but the feeling of their presence to such an intense degree, that what you have in your hand is more than a written message; it is the very mood and memory of the person suddenly brought to life. The one from D. J. Jones had such an effect on Andrew, and so did Dominique's letter.

ANDREW:

Since I have not heard from you for two months, except that postcard when you first arrived, I cannot know very well where to send this. Mother said in her last letter that you were heading for Rome, but I remember you mentioning going to Spain first. To be safe I'm sending a copy of this to Rome too.

The reason for such concern about reaching you is explained in the following: I am no longer working at camp. I quit the job several days ago and came home. The life there was just too dull for words. I was going out of my mind. Since you know full well how Mother feels about me staying home alone, even for one night, you can well imagine what would happen if she found out that I'm now going to be home for a full month. It is important that she doesn't find out. I wrote to Mother saying I can get her mail a lot faster and safer if she and Father send it home instead of to camp. She knows I come in every Saturday afternoon anyway to see if everything is in order and then go back that same evening, so actually it makes sense. Well, anyway, Mother agreed to this without too many questions and so that's that.

The trouble developed with the owner of the camp. There was a counsellor at the camp who quit about the same time I did. The owner became suspicious because Derek had been dating me all summer and because we both live in New York. He also knows that Mother and Father are in California and he kept asking me where I was going to stay and did my parents know about it. I told him that my parents are letting me stay at home because my brother is staying there too. You see, he doesn't know that you're in Europe. I didn't want to say I was staying at a neighbor's for a whole month because it wouldn't sound right. The old bastard is just trying to cause trouble anyway. I think he'll be convinced once Mother's mail stops coming to camp.

And here, my dear brother, is where you come in. I know that there is probably no chance at all that you will send me a letter. But just in case you do, *don't send anything to camp.* If the miracle should happen and you do decide to write, don't mail it anywhere but home. And for God's sake don't mention to Mother what I have done. *Remember, she still thinks I'm at camp.*

I know you are having a good time in Europe. You will have plenty to talk about when you come back.

Your sister,

DOMINIQUE

The signature held his attention for a moment. Written in green ink, the letters were beautifully large and boldly marked. But the gigantic D was almost grotesque and completely dwarfed the other letters of the name. Andrew folded the paper inside the envelope and put it away into his coat pocket. Before he began the two letters from his mother, he straightened up in the saddle and curved his spine in as far as it would go, trying to lose a knot of pain that had developed just under his right shoulder blade.

He looked up in time to see the ritual of the changing of the traffic light. The signal was red and a line of cars was waiting quietly. Then the light turned to green. Nothing moved. Like a fire alarm, a painful clanging of bells came from a small box on the signal post. This kept up for several seconds. Next, the police officer blew loudly and long on his whistle, but when this was over the traffic still had not moved; after pausing a moment, dramatically, he gave a majestic wave of his hand, and the waiting autos, bunched and ready, sped away.

The two letters from Andrew's mother were like all the ones he had ever gotten from her before. They spoke to him of being careful and of not getting hurt; they told him to eat well and get plenty of sleep; above all, they reminded him to write, scolding him for not having written more in the past, and asking him to turn over a new leaf in the future. As Andrew went through both letters swiftly, nothing caught or held his attention, yet he was surprised when there was no more to read.

In the last envelope was a note from Ted Olson, the salesman at *Graphic Globe*. There was also a check for two hundred and twenty-five dollars.

DEAR ANDREW:

Those six rolls on the Mardi Gras were just fine. Everybody here is just crazy about them. Even the Old Bastard couldn't find anything to criticize. I already got the *Mirror* to take 5 shots (2 color) for the Sunday Supplement and *Vue* took 4 shots. The Old Bastard told me to tell you not to miss that Valencia festival. It seems he heard that *Photo Star* will also have a photographer covering it. He says for you to do a real good job. He says you should mail back the rolls fast. In other words, like you've been doing all along. The check is for the Lido Club story and for as much of the Mardi Gras story as I have sold so far.

Lots of luck,
TED

P.S. The Old Bastard said not to forget the bullfight story. Shoot at least 12 rolls, he said. Look, I'm just telling you what he said. I just work here.

This also he folded and put away with the others inside his coat. Then he took out his map and spread it over the handlebars so he could plot the way to the Plaza de Toros. When the direction was firmly fixed in his mind, he quickly went through the mechanics of preparation: the fitting on the head protector, the adjusting of the goggles, the pumping of his foot on the starter, and the gunning of the motor with its mean, powerful roar. He turned the throttle and the cycle carried him away from the curb and down the street. But with all the thundering of the engine and the movement of traffic around him, the presence of his sister, delivered from across the ocean, was as vivid and disturbing as ever, almost as if she were riding in the seat behind him, her eyes on the back of his neck.

So now she had the house all to herself. She had always hated the way her parents watched her, guarded her, prevented her, claiming all the while that she had their complete trust, but, nevertheless, checking and cross-checking to make sure their trust was justified. Even during a long Sunday afternoon or an empty evening when their parents were away in the country or at a movie and he was up in his room studying for school and she was down in the living room watching television or entertaining a boy friend he somehow had the feeling that he, too, was in the way.

The rule of the house was that she had to be home from a date no later than two o'clock, and her mother always questioned her carefully the next morning. The questioning was always conducted under the guise of genuine interest, as if her mother really wanted to know about the movie Dominique had seen, or the party she had been taken to, and where she had gone afterward for a midnight snack, and how long she had stayed there; but Andrew understood the real purpose of these sessions, and he listened to his sister patiently answer each question with a dry, absent-minded voice while he said nothing. They were asked simply so that his sister would have to account, hour by hour, for all the time she had spent during the night, and in this way the daughter would not get a chance to hide from the mother what the mother had once hidden from the grandmother and the grandmother in turn had hidden from *her* mother.

Actually, he knew very little about his sister. He realized that her evenings out were not entirely platonic, for when she came home at night her lipstick was always a little too freshly applied and her hair too newly combed. But except for these clues he could only guess. Even his friends knew more about Dominique than he, for most of them belonged to that small loyal army that Dominique always referred to as her "many, many admirers," while he, because of his closeness to her, must always remain far away. Well, at least now she would not be able to call out her army. She was in hiding and she would have to be careful. But then there was Derek. Yes, she could manage one easily enough without getting the neighbors' attention, but he would have to be careful not to be seen. Yet, somehow, Andrew got the feeling that Derek was the careful type. Good old Derek. Anyway, it was not like Dominique to suspend her social life for a month just because she was hiding from her parents. It was too great a waste, especially when all it took was a little coolheaded gambling to pull it off. Good old Derek, Andrew thought. I bet he wears taps on his heels and sideburns down the side of his face. He tried to visualize him, but all he could see was the vague image of the two of them alone in the empty house, and all he learned was that hate is a poor cure for a man jealous of his own sister. He thought of them dancing in the living room or perhaps eating together in the kitchen, enjoying the valiant pleasure of secretly defying the rest of the world, and for a moment he wished he could chain his sister in her room so that she could not roam wide and free and do whatever she pleased with whomever she chose, while he, though traveling abroad, could never, it seemed, roam in the same way.

As he drove toward the bull ring he remembered he had not eaten. Why was it he so often forgot all about food? Well, he would just have to wait. It was too late to stop now. Increasing the gas, he felt the wind whipping up a fury against his face. The excitement of speed, like a tonic, quickly brought him alive. He was actually on the road again and soon he would be at work once more. Happily he leaned into the wind.

4

To The traveler, Sunday is like any other day. Occasionally, when it catches him by surprise with all the shops closed, it can be a treachery. But, generally, traveling is a month without Sundays. Yet in Spain things can be different. For there, if you are an *aficionado*, Sunday means only one thing: four o'clock at the Plaza de Toros.

The streets approaching the bull ring were crowded in all directions. Automobiles and taxis moved bumper to bumper as they came into the shadow of the high round wall of the arena. But the main cause of the jam was the mobs of people on foot. They were so numerous they overflowed into the streets. Andrew left his cycle and carefully made his way through the throng. A man stood on the sidewalk facing the tide of movement, trying to sell imitation *muletas, capas*, and *banderillas* which hung from a large wooden board that he held upright with his hand. After the fight there would be men selling real *banderillas* that had been used that very day, the dried blood still on them.

Following Albina's directions, he made his way into the plaza with a ticket of admission which she had secured for him. Knowing almost no Spanish, he went to the first important-looking official he could find and watched his face as he read the letter of introduction. The Señora had told Andrew to withhold the second letter until he got to a man called Vincente Marcial. But he was sent to three other officers before he was finally shown into a room where several men were smoking cigars and arguing. Señor Marcial, in a shabby white suit, was seated behind a cluttered desk looking tired, hot, and unfriendly. But after one glance at the second letter, which was also written in Spanish, he looked up quickly with a face that for a moment had suspended its anger to take on a blank stare of interest. Then he placed Albina's letter on the desk top, scrawled a few words in ink at the very bottom and dashed off his signature.

Ten minutes later Andrew was standing in the hot sun on the hard dirt floor just behind the wooden fence called the *barrera*. He had come into the arena awed at the circle of humanity that was spread out above him. The excitement of the crowd kept warning: the trumpet is about to sound, the trumpet is about to sound. The ring was empty and waiting. It was actually too late in the afternoon for using color film, but he decided to have at least one try at it. Kneeling, he quickly opened the back-bottom section of his camera and wound in a roll of daylight Ektachrome. As always when working, he had left his brown leather Rollei case back in his room, for it made fast changing of film impossible.

One time at *Graphic Globe* he had casually made the statement that a good photographer under ideal conditions should be able to change film in a Rolleiflex in about ten seconds. Immediately someone took him up on it. Most of the people in the office didn't think it was possible and there was a good deal of wagering on the outcome. Ted Olson, the salesman, was appointed judge, and using a darkroom time clock, he officially recorded Andrew's winning time during three tries as 11½, 9½ and 9 seconds. But such speed was hard on the camera and Andrew used it only in emergencies.

Most of the photographers from the Madrid press stood together in an enclosure that was housed against the wall. This gave them added height from which to shoot and added safety, should a cowardly bull jump the *barrera*. But most of these men had telephoto lenses mounted on 35 mm. cameras, and Andrew did not. He chose, therefore, to stand up against the fence, which was a good six feet or so closer to the action. The *barrera* was too high for him to sight downward through the ground glass, so with his finger he pushed through the front wall of the foldable ground-glass box to erect the eye-level sports finder. Placing the bottom of the Rollei on the top of the fence, he could now aim easily into the empty ring. After mounting first the pink sky-filter and then the black lens shade, he studied the light. One roll of color and one only would be all he could get to use this day. The sky no longer had any of its noontime brightness. The trained light-meter of his eye told him to use £3.5 at 1/60th, so he turned the crank, set the lens opening and shutter speed with the twin dials, focused on "infinity," and waited.

He had come too late to see the ritual of the horses and the hats and, afterward, the grand procession of the three matadors and their men marching in uniform together with the music. But he didn't care. It would have been good to have had it on film, but if the rest came out the way he wanted, it wouldn't matter. At almost any time now the gates would open and the bull would rush forth to live out the last angry minutes of his life. In fact, there it was.

The trumpet.

Slowly the doors were opened and pulled back. Everyone waited. A man leaned over the wooden gate and looked into the blackness. He slapped his hand twice against the gate. Then he pulled his hand away and leaned backward. The bull was coming now, and everyone waited. They roared as he entered. Immediately he stopped and the huge shoulders and neck turned as he looked back. He ran off to the left, for something had caught his attention. He stopped. He turned again, angrily and in a hurry. Searching. Fierce. Puzzled. Indignant. All eyes were on the menacing horns. From behind an opening in the fence a cape was thrown and pulled back. He saw it and charged. He went across the entire ring, gaining speed slowly. He reached the fence and rammed a horn against the wood, the noise going up into the crowd and making it roar. Across the plaza another peon immediately stepped out and waved a cape and the animal ran after it.

The excitement continued for almost ten minutes. The picador, seated high on the padded horse, leaned on his lance, the point deep in the bull's bloodied shoulder. As the horns fought to upset the horse, Andrew took several shots. The action was taking place on his side of the arena and he had been at a perfect angle to photograph the last charge. Next his camera caught a man holding in each upraised hand a *banderilla* with its harpoon point. The man circled toward the bull, side-stepping in a graceful, almost bowing movement as the arms came down to place both points into the huge shoulder. Through all this the feeling of excitement remained, but when the first matador, a huge, stocky man with blond hair, went through his opening series of passes, Andrew saw at once that he was going to cheat. At no time did he stand his body near the horns. He would thrust out with the red *muleta* as if he were fencing, bending his leg and leaning safely forward at a right angle to the charge of the bull while the whole stadium remained coldly silent. Even at the end, when he ran at the bull with the sword, he stayed clear of the horns and drove the weapon easily between the shoulder blades. Three times he did this and each time the animal grew weaker. Andrew continued to expose film but he did so regretfully, and only when the angle was such that the man's cheating would not be detected. The matador's men, each with his waving cape, ran the bull in circles. Finally, using the cross-bladed sword against the helpless neck, the matador, while the animal stood still, successfully cut the spinal cord and the bull dropped in a sudden lump, the huge body making a hollow thump against the ground. But everyone had lost interest long before. Two mules, running chop-legged, dragged the slaughtered bull from the ring, and the attendants came out and raked the sand.

The next fight was not much better, but it was interesting, for the matador was a handsome young boy who tried to make up for his inability to handle the bull by standing foolishly close. Several times he was thrown off balance and knocked down. Andrew watched through the view-finder but did not shoot. Everyone knew that it was luck and not skill that was saving the young matador from the horns. When it came time for the kill, Andrew felt relief, for now it would soon be over. The matador held the sword handle near his eyes, the blade straight ahead. He bent his leg at the knee, slowly went up on his toes, came down with the other knee bent, waited, and then ran at the bull, holding the cape down and the sword high. But something went wrong. He was lifted off the ground by the powerful neck and horns, bounced, and then pitched away, landing awkwardly on his back. The sword had not gone in. It lay in the dust next to him. The bull was distracted by the other capes, and the young bullfighter got quickly to his feet, his legs and neck stiff with embarrassment. Andrew hardened with concern. He had missed the one good shot of the last five minutes, but his only thought was for the young boy. However, he detached himself from emotion and waited. The air surged with excitement. The spill was thrilling, but when it happened on the second try it was even more so, for this time, though he did not want it to take place, Andrew was watching for it, and when the horns caught the matador and yanked him off the ground, his legs kicking and wide apart, Andrew felt himself stiffen and shoot. But again the matador was unhurt. In a few minutes, and with a red face, he prepared himself once again. The crowd shrieked louder than ever as the horns, catching him still a third time, threw him away like a rag doll rolling in the dust. But in a moment the boy was on his feet, waving his handlers away. The bull and the matador stood watching each other. The sword was buried deep between the bull's shoulder blades. The young fighter waited. Suddenly the bull seemed to forget how to use his legs. He struggled to work them properly, stumbling through a cloud of death, unable to find his way. The staggering became more desperate until all at once the animal fell and lay still, a cloud of dust settling around him.

There was only one shot left in the Rollei and so, in order to be ready for the next bull, he snapped a view of the crowd and then changed film. The sky was becoming overcast, and for a few moments he and many others looked up and considered the possibility of rain. After loading and adjusting the camera for black and white film, he waited.

Once again the trumpet blew.

This fight disappointed Andrew even more. A tall arrogant man with a serene, hawklike face and a walk like a king was pitted against a bull who just would not fight. When the animal first came out, it proved itself a coward by trying to jump the barrier, and later it charged the picadors once and then refused to do anything more. All the while the audience was putting up a tremendous display of displeasure. They shouted and waved handkerchiefs at the official box high on the plaza and they hissed and booed and demanded a recall of the bull. But no signal came from the president, and so the fight had to continue. Slowly the disorder died away. The matador used every trick he knew as he tried to incite the bull to charge and keep charging. He kicked it and occasionally stuck it lightly with his sword point, but the bull refused to lose itself in anger, and it finally died easily and without emotion after one thrust of the sword. Arrogantly the tall matador walked off in disgust.

With the fourth *corrida* Andrew had about given up. It was the heavy blond matador again, and he repeated his first performance. Immediately the audience began to complain because he was not trying and because they remembered him. Andrew resigned himself. He was almost certain he would get no brilliant photo-story that day; in fact, he was sure that he was fated to see in this one afternoon everything that could possibly go wrong in a bullfight.

At this point the doors opened again and the fifth bull escaped into the prison of the ring. There were only two fights left. But when he saw that the matador who was to fight now was the same handsome boy who had escaped from, rather than killed, his first bull, Andrew knew that this *corrida* at least, would not be dull. Yet at the beginning, this, too, was wrong. He moved along behind the *barrera* and readied his camera. Again the youth failed to control his animal and every move became a struggle. He would destroy the beauty of each pass by stumbling against the bull, backing away at the last minute or, occasionally, even losing his cape on the horns. Then the animal got stubborn and refused to continue charging and recharging. As a result, the possibility of a series of passes with momentum and rising emotion was lost. Again everything was going to pieces.

Andrew was barely paying attention when it came time for "the moment of truth." But a rare thing was to happen and luckily he was to get most of it on film. The plaza settled into silence as the matador readied himself with his sword. The time had come. They ran together, the youth and the bull but the great animal did not play his part, and the huge neck and horns lifted at the last and worst moment, and the matador was jolted high into the air. On the ground the horns found him again and rolled him like a log for several feet. When the bull was finally drawn away and led to another part of the arena, the youth got to his feet without help. There was dark blood on the front and side of his costume, but it might have rubbed off from the bull. No one knew. The boy walked slowly to the barrier. Several of his men were next to him and speaking to him but he didn't answer. He looked disappointed. At the barrier he placed his forearm along the top and looked off into the crowd. Then he slowly lowered his head, his mouth open, his eyes closing, until his brow rested on his arm, and then everyone in the plaza knew that the blood was his. Before he had a chance to fall, they lifted him and passed him over the barrier to men on the other side who had run to help. He was held high by the strength of many arms and was carried along between the barrier and the wall toward the exit to the hospital on the opposite side of the stadium. Meanwhile the bull stood by himself in the center of the arena, six *banderillas* like the ribs of a broken fan jutting in all directions from the hump on his neck.

The job of killing now went to the next man in line. His eyes watched the *muleta* as it was handed to him. He adjusted it so that the stick stretched the cloth and held it properly. Then he took the sword with his left hand and with a magnificent gesture turned and slowly walked toward the bull. The other men left the ring and only the two enemies remained. But before it could begin, a local cheer sounded from the other side of the stadium where a matador was trying to climb the barrier into the arena as others worked to hold him back. He struggled in a frenzy, as if some great danger lay behind him, and only in the ring could he be safe. It was the youth who had just been gored who was causing the disturbance. With a vicious pull of his arm he broke free, cleared the fence, and landed on his feet in the dirt. The entire plaza sent up a cheer because it was seeing something rare. The boy trotted across the ring, oblivious to the bull, and retrieved his sword and cape. He could not move with ease and there seemed a knot in his stomach preventing him from standing straight. The dark red stains on his costume were of no concern to him, as if the clothes belonged to another man. The lines of his handsome face were clenched, and he had the appearance of one who had annoyingly and accidentally stepped into some excrement. After a few passes to get the animal into position, he quickly prepared himself for the kill and without hesitation rushed in, offering the sword to the bull and his body to the horns. This time the maneuver was executed faultlessly. The boy stepped away and watched the bull jump and twist as he tried to fight the long blade of steel buried in his back. Death was near. The animal used up its strength as it struggled, moving in a circle and chasing the targets of several elusive capes. Then it slumped into a lying position, as if suddenly tired of standing. A peon, holding a dagger crept up from behind and struck the bull vigorously in the neck. The bull bounced with a reflex action and rolled dead on his side. Only then did the blood-stained matador allow himself to be led away.

Beneath a bleak and fading sky the crowd waited silently for the last bull. The long afternoon had been a failure for them, yet what they had just seen had momentarily welded them together and blown away the discontent that had hung heavy in the air. There was one bull left, and everyone had hope. Meanwhile, Andrew had captured enough action on film so that the people at *Graphic Globe* would be able to put together a fairly adequate story. Much of what he had exposed on the five rolls he had already taken was uninteresting, because most of what had happened that afternoon was second-rate. There had also been the usual number of times when he had pressed the shutter release too soon or too late, freezing the scene in an awkward and forever unusable moment. Each time this occurred, he knew it—he didn't even have to see the prints washing in the large water tank. But when his finger released the shutter perfectly, the frozen beauty of the action would be photographed on his memory as well as on the film, and he would remember the picture in his mind for days thereafter, and often longer. There had been enough of these "right" moments today to wrap up the job, and now what he hoped for was a really good fight. And though his camera was still ready, he wanted this fight more for himself and the people in the stands than for the hypo tank back in Manhattan.

Kneeling in the center of the empty ring, the tall matador waited for the last bull, his hawk face expressionless and sad. Out of the blackness came the animal, his horns cutting the air, his magnificent anger almost too strong to hold. The matador, down on both knees, did not move. The huge animal came at him with a fierce grunt. The cape flicked out, the dangerous horns rushed past, and the crowd shouted with pleasure and fear. Now there was no longer any doubt; it was to see, at last, what it had waited for with such patience and understanding through the death of five bulls. When the picadors had come and gone, and the crowd had loudly booed these villains on horseback, the stage was set once more. They screamed for the bullfighter to place the *banderillas* himself, for they had seen this man many times before and knew what he could do. On his feet now, with a smile, his body moved with that beautiful arrogance which seemed right only for a man in his profession. They were demanding a one-man show and he came forward in answer.

With a *banderilla* in each hand and his body bent backward like the shaft of a drawn bow, his arms up and out, he sprang up and down on stiff legs like a man trying to look over a high fence. The movement caught the eyes of the bull. Man and animal came at each other slowly. Suddenly the animal charged and the horns hooked at the man's body, but the man, in a beautiful dance, as if he had all the time in the world, sucked in his stomach so that the horns barely missed. Before the bull had passed, two *banderillas* had been placed perfectly in his back. The animal swirled and came at the man again. Now there seemed no escape. The crowd roared without letup. In a slow, unconcerned trot the matador made for the fence. He cruised in half circles and the bull, in furious confusion, followed. The matador reached back as he ran and with his hand touched the horn as if to test its sharpness. A smile broke his lips. At the wall he timed his steps, and with the precision of a trained athlete he vaulted over it with leisure and grace. The bull was suddenly alone on the other side and ran along the barrier as if trying to remember a dream.

Twice more the *banderillas* were placed, with the bull following the man to the fence, but each time the animal found himself alone. Andrew braced against fear with each lunge of the horns, but he found himself, the camera dangling from its strap, applauding with stinging hands and watching the matador with strange affection. Then quickly he changed film.

The man with the hawk face appeared again. *"Huhah, Toro! Huhah!"* The cape was ready and again the bull came, this time grunting with rage. The matador leaned in, slowly dragging the red *muleta* low in front of him, as if it were extremely heavy. The horn slipped past and found nothing and the crowd yelled, *"Olé!"* Several times the matador did this, and after each charge the crowd cheered louder than before. Finally he held the cape as a target without looking at the bull at all but staring off into the stands, and the bull thundered by doing all the work himself.

Each series of passes brought the excitement closer to the breaking point. Again and again, as if in slow motion, the bull and the man came together, blended, and gradually parted. Rocking back and forth, blending and parting, with unbearable slowness, blending and parting, no longer with anger, no longer with danger, but with incredible beauty, with stinging excitement, a ballet of animal and man, of horn and cape, to the music of thousands of voices, under a darkening sky, blending and parting, blending and parting, and then finally, with one grand sweeping pass, the bull seeming to run right through the man—so close, in fact, that his own assistants, watching from behind the barrier, were themselves knifed by fear as they saw death come close. The bull turned sharply and became riveted to the sand, watching the matador kneel in front of him, his back to the horns, the sword and the muleta thrown away with a brazen gesture, the horns inches from the costumed back, the arms outstretched, a strutting smile on his face.

All at once, everything was motionless—the bull, the man, the crowd, the stadium, the sky, the earth—all hung suspended, waiting, the air vibrant—and then the matador climbed to his feet and walked slowly away, the bull watching him go as if it would never move again, and everyone's ears were filled with the thunder of voices.

The handle of the sword was in the matador's hands. The crowd cried, "*No! No! No!*" but the matador lifted the blade and aimed it. The animal was about to die; the end was about to come. The spectators wanted the action to go on forever, and they shouted to him not to kill, but death could not be escaped, and the beauty was about to be made perfect by the ending of it.

A sweep of wind dipped into the plaza and pulled at the edges of the cape. The matador waited for the wind to stop. Then, when he had readied himself, it came again, and the cape was blown against his body. He stepped back and walked to the barrier. From a jug, water was poured along the edge of the cape to weigh it down and protect it against the greatest enemy a bullfighter can have. Once more he was ready. The bull was worked into position and the sword came up. This time even the wind waited, and the matador ran at the bull and thrust the sword home. The animal danced with the blade hilt-deep in his back as a few drops **of rain** began to fall. The crowd, by way of celebration, started to pile into the ring. A thousand arms were preparing to lift and carry the matador in tribute from the plaza into the streets. They were all waiting, but first the bull must die. Andrew straddled the fence for the best angle.

The animal stopped dancing and studied the man who had injured him. The hawk face glared a command to the animal to fall. But the animal only stared back. Then the bull was rushed into a circle by moving capes as three peons tried to run him, exhausted, into the ground. The rain had increased. The bull grunted and tried to dance the sword out of his body. Then he stood still and watched the matador again. But he would not die. People up in the stands began moving back to shelter, away from the rain. Some drops struck his face, but Andrew didn't notice them.

The sword was removed and the bull was positioned once again for the kill. The matador ran at the horns a second time and bent his body over them as he thrust the blade home. The bull danced away, the sword halfway into his huge body. Kicking and twisting, he lunged his horns at the rain, but he would not die. The wind swept up a cloud of dust and moved it into the stands at the south end, making people squint and turn away. But the fine rain quickly dampened the ground and the dust did not rise again. The matador made two more tries with the sword. He had great difficulty keeping the wind out of his cape. He gave up running at the bull and resorted instead to the cross-bladed sword which is used when the bull is weak and standing still.

The part of the crowd that had climbed from the stands into the ring gradually closed in, giving the bullfighter only a fourth of the arena to work in. The people enjoyed this great stroke of luck, for most of them had expected to see the animal dead by the time they had gotten over the barrier. Now here they were, crowding about the matador as if he were giving a speech, having a better view of the action than from any seat in the house. It was like a picnic. The loudspeaker droned a warning to the crowd. The bullfighter made a sweeping gesture with his sword to move them away, but his heart wasn't in it. This only gave him a moment to breathe before having to plunge back into his nightmare. The arrogance was still there— even the last man in the last row could see it—but the matador was perjuring himself with bold postures, for the truth had drained out of them and disappeared into the sand. The arrogance was like a smile one tries to hold forever, and which in turn becomes no more than a bloodless wound.

The rain continued. More people began to leave their seats and move back through the exits. The first horn blew. The matador looked up at the slowly diminishing crowds in the stands and drew his arms out slowly and let them drop, slapping his sides. Then he held the sword high and waited for his assistants to trick the bull with their capes into lowering his head. Then the matador struck once more. But the bull wouldn't die. Again he tried, and again the bull refused to die. Now the bull was so weak that the assistants lowered his head by simply grasping the horns, pressing them toward the earth and holding them while the matador took another cut at the neck. At one point the bull surprised everyone by wrenching himself free from the spot where loss of strength had pinned him and ran blindly into the crowd, scattering it. The animal ran in no particular direction and at no particular person. Perhaps he saw no one at all, but had just felt death slowly coming and had tried to escape. The bull did not run far and finally just stood in the rain and looked straight ahead at nothing and waited. The crowd gradually came together again, and seeing that it was unhurt, decided that it had enjoyed itself.

Again the bullfighter stood in front of the animal with sword uplifted. His hawked face was masked with stiffness. The crossed blade chopped into the bull's neck and the animal backed away but would not die. The man chopped again, desperation making him sloppy. He stuck the point into the bull's snout to make him lower his head, and then he hurriedly chopped again at his neck, but the bull only watched him. Now the rain began to fall heavily and the people in the ring began to climb out. The aisles became jammed. Andrew closed up his camera and protected it with his jacket.

Hardly anyone was watching now. Only those stayed on who were content to cover themselves with newspapers or cushions, or who had been thoughtful enough to bring umbrellas, for it was not the rainy season and that morning the sky had been an open blue. As the raindrops struck his clothes, Andrew kept his eyes on the matador and did not move. Many rows were completely empty and the seats were filmed with rain.

Once again the matador struck with the blade. Then, for the second time, the horn sounded. There were sounds of surprise from those who had remained as they realized how gradually and completely the performance had come apart. But the matador kept at it with self-punishing deliberation. Gone was the glory, and even the desperation, for now he struck at the mighty neck as if striking at himself. The rain soaked his hair and disheveled it. He stood facing his enemy, sword high, waiting for the head to lower, fenced in by a crowd of strangers who, while braving the rain, stood stupidly by and watched with the insatiable eyes of people who knew they had no right to be there. The scene had all the loneliness of a street fight, of two men battling each other as well as themselves, while the merciless onlookers stand and patiently wait for the execution of a man's dignity.

Once more the assistants worked the animal into position and the matador lifted his sword. Again, at the proper moment, the cross blade landed heavily. The animal pulled away and blood flowed through the hair of the neck. The matador wiped the rain from his face with his sleeve, listening to a few words from one of his men, but the hawked face showed no signs of understanding. The palm of his hand was wet and he rubbed it against his suit under his arms. Up went the blade again. He waited. He jabbed at the bull's nose, then, angrily, he jabbed at it again. The head went down. The arm quickly up again, paused, then went down hard as if trying to drive the sword straight through the enemy and into the ground. Again, he did it. Again and again, but the bull would not die. Finally, with the sword ready once more, the horn blew for the third and last time and the matador lowered his head and turned away. The nightmare was over. He went to the barrier and handed over his sword and took a drink from a wine sack. The gates opened and several tame bulls came out and led the wounded one away. The matador did not watch. Silently the people filed out of the stadium. In the rain the matador walked across the ring, disgrace heavy within him. His men trailed behind and said nothing.

Andrew, alone in the rain, watched him go. The bull ring seemed terribly large now and it was a long walk across it as the thin mist slowly blanketed the city. Andrew felt water gathering on his scalp and beginning to stream down his face. The rain seeped through his shoes and finally reached the skin of his feet. The matador had almost disappeared behind the curtain of rain. He was only a few steps from the dark exit through which he had come three hours earlier, a brave man flaunting his arrogance and hiding his fear. Now he was disgraced, and all who saw him in the stadium that day or read about it in the papers the next morning, would know. But the time would come again when the matador would bury his shame under the glory of future Sundays, and eventually this dim afternoon would be forgotten … and there would be nothing for him to hide. If only it were this easy for others, Andrew thought. If only one really had the chance to wipe out the permanence of disgrace. As he stood now in the rain, holding his camera, he wished in sudden grief to change places with this shamed Spaniard; he wished, as he stood in his private desert of longing with its giant drifts of sadness, that escape could only be his this easily.

When he finally reached the street, the rain had stopped. Two small boys, their clothes torn by age, were each sailing their left shoes in a large puddle by the curb. The shoes were caked with mud and overuse, but they stayed afloat. Feeling thoroughly wet, Andrew wiped dry the saddle of his NSU with his handkerchief, and then wondered why he had even bothered.

5

A LOVELY sunset had colored the sky, and as he drove he kept turning his head to watch how it stained and bled the clouds. But the early evening crowds, heading home from work, overflowed the wet sidewalks, and riding on the cycle became slow and tedious. He wound his way carefully through the congested streets, and at every traffic light that stopped him he would turn slightly in his saddle and stare spellbound at the sky behind him until the angry blowing of auto horns announced to him that the light had changed again. When at last he arrived in front of the doorway that led up to the Residencia Albina he climbed off the cycle with great relief. He pulled out the key to kill the motor and left the cycle standing and locked. As he removed his helmet and was scratching his head, a familiar voice called to him from the sidewalk. There he saw Leopold lounging leisurely against the building. He looked as though he had been there for some time, cigar in hand, letting the hours roll endlessly by. He pushed himself away from the wall and came forward. His eyes were studying the machine silently. At Albina's he had heard some talk about Williams that very afternoon. In fact, they had all been quite impressed with the young cyclist. El Greco had thought him a bit of a mystery. To the Señora, he appeared to be unusually accomplished. Even Bruno, who seemed to respect nothing, was somehow slightly in awe of Williams. The best thing to do, Leopold decided with a twinge of jealousy, was to reserve decision.

"Whatdoyasay, Leopold, old boy?"

"You been traveling all over Europe on this thing?"

"Pretty much. Why?"

"I mean it's very dangerous, isn't it?"

"Oh, I don't know."

"Actually, it is."

"So is a knife, I suppose, or liquor."

"Ah," Leopold roared, "you're wrong there. Liquor hasn't killed me."

"No, but a knife might." And Andrew stabbed an imaginary dagger into the bulging stomach. This earned him a slap on the back and another round of laughter.

"You're quite a card, my boy."

"True," said Andrew, "true." He headed for the doorway.

"Where are you going in your almighty hurry?"

"Upstairs."

"No. There's no point to that," said Leopold mysteriously.

Andrew knew he had something up his sleeve, but though he waited for an explanation, none came. He decided that games of this sort greatly annoyed him.

"All right," he finally asked, "why?"

Realizing he had the attention of his listener, Leopold took even more time. He grinned hungrily and then said slowly: "Nobody's up there."

"Nobody?"

"That's correct."

"How come?"

"You want to know?"

"Go on."

"Well, they went shopping. Albina took the two boys out a few hours ago. After that, like little bunnies, they're going straight to dinner." He jammed the cigar into a corner of his mouth. "But that won't stop us, will it?"

"They won't be back before dinner?"

"Definitely not. They're probably eating right now. But let me ask you something." He removed the cigar. "Listen. How about you and me grabbing some grub together? We've been deserted on all sides. Might as well join forces, don't you think?"

"Dinner, huh?" Andrew said, stalling for time.

"How does the idea strike you?"

Andrew paused just a little too long, his mind racing for an excuse, so Leopold spoke again. But this time his voice had lost that shouting quality it always seemed to have. "What I mean is…supper…that's all…what the hell!"

His large pudgy face waited for an answer. One eyebrow lifted gradually and his mouth had come partly open. The look was strangely desperate, and the racing in Andrew's mind came to an embarrassed halt.

"First I must get rid of my helmet and camera."

"Know just the place," Leopold declared, holding up one finger for attention and then pointing it with an extended arm at the entrance of the building. The janitor, he said, was a personal friend of his. They had spent many an hour talking together and he was certain that Joe (who was really an Irishman) would hold the things for them in the little room behind the stairs, where they could pick them up when they returned. Andrew agreed, and in a few minutes they were on their way to eat.

Leopold had in mind a special Italian restaurant, and during the fifteen-minute walk to get there he spoke of nothing but their many fine desserts of ice cream and cake, describing each one in detail. But he failed to notice that Andrew wasn't listening.

"How does that sound?" Leopold said proudly.

"Sounds great," Andrew replied as he stared through the thickening darkness at the people passing them in the street. "Just great."

They walked on.

"Say, you been in the rain? Look a little wet."

"Yar," Andrew said, and kept walking.

Suddenly, in the middle of a dark street, Leopold grabbed him by the arm and kept him from walking any further. With a pompous smile he pointed up at a sign that Andrew had missed. It hung above a narrow, undistinguished doorway and simply spelled out in dull dirty letters the name PIAMONTESSA. Not wanting to give

Leopold a chance to speak, Andrew hurried in. At that moment, to hear his voice seemed unbearable.

The street floor had a bar and a room to check coats. Leopold left a crumpled raincoat with the smiling, middle-aged woman and followed Andrew up a narrow, winding stairway. Above them could be heard the mumbling and tinkling of a prosperous restaurant.

They followed the waiter in a winding path toward an empty table in the back. As Andrew casually glanced about him, a familiar face sprang out from the vagueness of the crowd. This was followed by another face, and still a third. Leopold noticed them too. The invitation of a charming smile called them over.

"Hello, hello," Albina said. "How was the fight?"

"Interesting."

"You didn't like it?" Bruno asked.

"Hello all," said Leopold.

"*I* liked it." Andrew smiled, realizing his voice had sounded flat.

"You don't seem enthusiastic," El Greco said.

"This is Alice," spoke Bruno in his most polite manner as he indicated a thin-looking blonde at their table. She said nothing. But whenever anyone spoke, she kept her eyes on him until he had finished, and whenever anyone laughed, she quickly and politely joined in. Yet it was her politeness that made her seem ill-at-ease.

The headwaiter was standing a few feet away, his arms folded across his chest. Andrew noticed the servile, businesslike tolerance on his face.

"Very pleased to meet you," Leopold was saying to the girl.

"We've got to go," Andrew explained to his companion. Then to Albina: "Would you excuse us? I think we're holding up traffic. We'll see you later, O.K.?"

"Oh," she said. "Of course. Please eat."

To Alice he gave a special, separate smile because they had just met. Then he and Leopold went to their table. When the waiter finally came for their orders, Leopold was still examining the menu. First he wanted to know what was good, and then he ignored the waiter's suggestion and asked him to describe several of the dishes, listening to each one carefully and then afterward sitting in deep thought while the waiter stood patiently next to him, pad and pencil in hand. Andrew became annoyed and gave his order with extra haste. It was always uncomfortable for him to be with someone who gave the waiter trouble. Embarrassment crawled over him. He turned away and tried to disassociate himself from his companion as much as he could.

"Let me see," Leopold began, "let me see…Give me…give me…give me some shrimps *marinara*. Are they good? I mean, they're good, aren't they?"

"Anything first, sir?"

"Oh, yes." He searched the menu once again. The waiter pointed with a pencil to the list of appetizers. "Let me see…" Then, to Andrew: "You ordered fruit cocktail, didn't you?"

"Right."

"No…no, give me a crabmeat cocktail."

Albina's comfortable laugh whispered above the vague noises of the crowd and the young man looked across the room at her table. From what he could tell, they seemed to be enjoying themselves. The blonde appeared to be in her early twenties, but to Andrew she looked only slightly pretty. She seemed too thin and her skin, as well as her short, chopped hair, appeared dull and without luster. He could see she was now loosening up a bit, for he watched as she said something with quick darting lips, her eyes coming alive, and she leaned forward and laughed. Bruno joined her, struggling with a mouth full of food. He was the only one there who seemed to concentrate on the meal. The rest of the table seemed overly concerned with politeness, and there was a mood of words being carefully chosen.

"Wonder where they got the blonde from?" Andrew said.

Leopold's face soured. "They shouldn't have brought her."

"Why?"

"It was in bad taste. I mean, to bring her here with Albina."

"I don't get you."

"I mean, she's obviously a whore."

"The blonde?" He turned and looked at the girl again and examined her expressionless face as she listened intently to someone talking. "What makes you say a thing like that?"

"Oh, you can tell," Leopold said, buttering a piece of bread.

"I don't think so."

"Who is she, then? Where did she come from? They must hare picked her up while shopping. If so, then that means she's a whore. You don't pick up any other kind in this country."

"She could be a friend of Albina's."

"No," Leopold said, dismissing the suggestion completely. "She looks more scared of Albina than anything."

The young man glanced at Alice again. But nothing was happening at that moment; they were all eating. He turned away, irritated, for he had a strong feeling that Leopold was right.

"Albina could be acting as a chaperone," he said stubbornly, knowing even before he said it that this was impossible. But he felt it important to defend the girl, especially against such certainty of opinion.

"No, I mean, the chaperone has to be the girl's mother or aunt or something. They have to know each other." Leopold tore off a bite of his bread. "Anyway, she looks familiar to me. I might have seen her in a bar somewhere." His throat filled with laughter. "But then I frequent so many."

Once again Andrew looked at the girl. Now that he watched her with doubt he seemed to see a lot more. She was listening as El Greco was talking to her across the table. At everything he said she nodded politely and kept listening, but afterward when the Señora broke in to add something, the girl quickly turned her head away from El Greco and gave the woman complete attention. It was a little too complete. It was steady, motionless, and totally unmarred by understanding. She wasn't really listening at all. Instead, though observing the Señora very carefully, she was not measuring an opponent's beauty as one woman might another's, but instead she was studying something far different. She seemed to be wondering what the Señora was thinking of her.

The waiter stood at Albina's table handing out menus again, then he stepped back, awaiting their orders for desserts. Silently his eyes settled on Alice. She was glancing at the selections and leaning over as if about to confer with Bruno. Forgetting for a moment that others might be watching him, the waiter's face sagged slightly with the secret weight of disapproval. At that moment someone at the table indicated he was ready and the waiter came alive again and stepped forward with pencil poised and eyebrows raised. The Señora gave her order first and then sat back, rearranging the napkin on her lap. Her eyes lazily wandered about the room until she noticed Andrew looking at her. She hesitated, turned to see if the others at her table were watching, and then quickly gave him a bold wink.

"What do you think of that?" Leopold said triumphantly. "Did you see that?"

Andrew crushed a bread crumb against the tablecloth with his fingers. He felt like having a cigarette but told himself to wait. Leopold's face hung unavoidably before him. Its puffed, overweight features seemed filled with intolerable self-satisfaction. The collar points of his shirt were curled upward, and the thin narrow knot of his tie was loose and off center.

"Well?" said Leopold.

"Well, I'm not sure what I saw." But the doubt he displayed was in his words, not in his heart.

The wink she had given him seemed to proclaim her innocence of something. It enabled her safely to escape all incrimination, for it lifted her to the level of playful superiority.

"I mean, it was as clear as day."

He understood now that the proper thing for him to do was to keep still. He knew of no attack to launch or of any defense to offer. But silence would mean he was conceding. He found himself not brave enough to back down.

"There's no way of telling," Andrew said angrily. "We could be imagining the whole thing."

One fruit cocktail and one crabmeat cocktail were placed in front of them. Leopold began eating as soon as the waiter's hand had left the cup. Several quick forkfuls and then he sat back to rest. A little sauce clung to his chin. He removed it with the back of his hand and then he dabbed at it with his napkin.

"Of course, Albina seems as relaxed as ever."

"That doesn't mean anything," said Andrew, still feeling the smart of his antagonism. "You can't tell." He was about to sip from his water when another idea occurred to him. "You can't tell what the hell she's thinking. She's not the kind of person to embarrass anyone by noticing their mistakes. She's too big a person."

"That she is, that she is. But did you notice how extremely polite she's being with the blonde? Politeness is something you watch out for. Mark my words."

"If you're right, the boys have done a terrible thing."

"That they have."

Andrew's voice spoke softly, as if he were alone: "They must be blind." He seemed to notice on the Señora's face a touch of polite sorrow. "I suppose she's stuck with them the whole evening."

"Well, my boy," Leopold said, patting his mouth with his napkin, "that's life."

Andrew grunted, for he had taken his first spoonful of fruit. Not one to let a silence go unchallenged, Leopold began a slow, detailed report of his recent stay on the French Riviera and why he felt it was the most beautiful spot he had yet found in Europe. When those at Albina's table got to their feet and began to file out, he was still on the subject. Albina and El Greco waved and Andrew waved back. They were too far away to speak to, he thought, so he just smiled a farewell.

"Have fun," Leopold called in a booming voice.

Disturbed by the noise, several people looked around, but Leopold had returned to his food and it was Andrew who received the glances of disapproval.

Leopold looked up suddenly. "You're from New York, check?"

"Check."

Leopold lowered his face over the dish again.

"What line are you in?" he asked, the food still in his mouth as he talked.

Andrew told him. But when he did so, his dinner companion gave an almost imperceptible frown, because to be involved in such a business as free-lance photography immediately divorced Andrew from the fraternity of professions that Leopold understood and therefore accepted as respectable.

"What magazine do you work for?"

"I don't," he answered and then explained about the agency he was connected with.

"That's all you do, right? Photography."

"Right."

"Good. Glad to hear it. I'm sure you make a lot of money."

"What makes you so sure?"

At first Leopold looked more puzzled than ever. "Ha, ha," he boomed. "You're quite a joker, my boy, quite a joker."

For a moment there was nothing.

"I sell insurance," Leopold spoke suddenly as if he were answering a question.

"Oh?" Andrew dug his spoon into his food.

"You from New York, right? It's good old Yorkville for me. How about yourself?"

"Queens."

"Ah, yes. Queens." Then, as an afterthought. "Good old New York. Greatest city in the world. In the whole world." He lifted his glass and delivered a toast to Andrew. "Comrade!" he almost shouted, his face valiant and beaming.

Embarrassment twinged Andrew's back. A defenseless smile crept into his face, and at the man sitting across from him he laughed weakly. "Comrade."

When they were finished with dinner and waiting for the check, Leopold leaned back with a cigar and studied the room. A gray thread of tobacco smoke hung in the air above his head. The dishes had been removed and the table brushed clean, but in front of him, where he had eaten, the white cloth was stained with food.

"Ever go to the Pasapoga Club?"

"No," Andrew said.

"The best in Madrid."

"Never been there."

"You ought to go. It's one of the places to see in this city. What say we take it in tonight? "

The racing started again in Andrew's head as he began reaching desperately for an excuse.

"No, I don't think so," he said. "I'm not in the mood for a night club tonight. But if you want to, go right ahead. Don't let me keep you."

"Well, what *are* you going to do?" Leopold asked with a frown.

"I don't know. First I want to go to the hotel. If Albina's there with the rest of them, perhaps I can rescue her. Otherwise I'll just take a walk or just drop into a bar or something. I really don't know. But, as I say, if you want to go to the Pasapoga, go right ahead."

"No, I mean, I'm not really that keen on it. I guess I'll string along with you—up to Albina's place, anyway—and see what gives. That is, if you don't mind." His large forehead frowned again. The importance of the answer for which he was waiting hung in the air and seemed to frighten him.

"No, not at all," Andrew said slowly. "Not at all."

Inside the Residencia Albina all was dark and deserted. The problem was whether to explore further or give up right then. They stood together in the darkness, not knowing what to do.

"They didn't come back, I guess," Andrew whispered. Then, after a moment, he added: "Which brings up the question, why am I whispering?"

"*Someone* should be here. Maybe Bianca is asleep."

"You're whispering, too," Andrew's voice said. "Come follow me." He led the way through the darkness, walking carefully so as not to bump into anything. When he turned to check whether Leopold was behind him he saw the glow of a cigar tip inches from his face.

"Careful with that thing."

"They aren't dangerous. They're like motorcycles!"

Andrew smiled. "Remind me never to speak to you."

The man behind him nearly choked as he fought down his laughter. Slowly they worked their way around a corner, and there, from an open transom, a rectangle of light fell across the opposite wall. Without looking, Andrew knew immediately what room it came from. As they moved closer, voices were heard. Andrew listened carefully. He identified Bruno's and then El Greco's, and then came a laugh that he decided belonged to Alice. This was followed by a period of silence. Thin lines of light outlined the door. Behind him the breathing presence of Leopold was very strong. He was beginning to feel foolish. Inside the room the conversation started again and for the first time Andrew heard the Señora's voice. He couldn't catch the words, but there was no mistaking it.

"Let's go," Andrew said softly.

"Right." Leopold had heard it too.

But just as they got to the turn in the hallway the door to the room suddenly swung open and they saw Bruno, dressed only in his undershorts, come out in his bare feet and head away from them down the hall toward the bathroom. The door had been left open, and the loud delighted laughter of the women inside came to them clearly from the bright room. Leopold and Andrew listened silently. Afterward, when they were once again in the freedom of the lighted stairway, Andrew felt a heavy depression settle on him.

"You know of a good bar near here?"

"That I do, that I do," Leopold said. "Now you're talking my language."

They climbed down several flights in silence. It was Leopold who finally spoke.

"Quite a surprise up there, wasn't it?"

"Something like that."

"I see you don't like to barge in on people."

"Yar."

"I noticed your hesitation."

When they were almost down to the street it was Andrew who broke the silence.

"She seemed to be enjoying herself, no?"

"Hard to tell," Leopold explained. "As I say, politeness is something you should look out for."

6

ANDREW WILLIAMS watched the blood appear on his face. He felt the sickening thinness and penetration of the cut. As soon as it happened, he knew his hand had been moving too fast. Leaning closer to the mirror, he saw the blood grow on his chin and start to trickle in a line down his neck. Cursing, he blamed the razor, but he knew the fault was his own. He wanted to shave and dress quickly and catch them before they left. He thought he remembered El Greco's saying that they might go to Toledo and he wanted to catch them and talk to them first. But not about Toledo. In fact, he didn't know exactly what he wanted to speak to them about. All he knew was that he felt a strange need to be once more with the Texan and the little Greek.

He rummaged in his case until he found his styptic pencil. He rubbed this over the cut after he had washed the blood away and it burned and the new blood dirtied the whiteness of the pencil. Torn between his haste and his wish not to cut himself again, he finished his shaving with much discomfort. He had a headache, also, and he promised himself for the third time that morning to go a little easier on the liquor. Been drinking too much the last couple of days, he told himself. Thinking of this, he smiled. Certainly a twist for one who never could stand the taste of liquor.

Andrew whistled as he put on and buttoned his shirt. Gathering up his camera equipment, he placed it all in a saddlebag to take with him. The clothes pack he would leave behind, because after the job in Valencia he would be back. When he was at last ready, he marched down the long hall to the door where, the night before, he had stood listening to the voices. It was wide open now, and leaving the saddlebag outside, he stopped and looked in. Sitting on the bed near the wall and smiling with approval when she saw him, was Alice.

"Come on in," she said cheerfully, for she had been hoping to see him again. "*Hello!*" Her accent, he decided, was definitely German.

Bruno and El Greco greeted him. Bianca, standing and changing a pillowcase, smiled pleasantly. El Greco was lying on the bed again. He had on a corduroy shirt and pants, but no shoes. His hands were folded behind his head and he was staring dreamily at the ceiling. Bruno stood at the closet, his hands quickly going through the pockets of a jacket. He wore a white shirt, tie, and huge cuff links. He had not yet put on his pants.

"That's all the money I got," Bruno said. "You see, I told ya."

"Where did it all go?" Alice asked.

"It was gone before we got here." El Greco smiled at the ceiling. "It was gone years ago."

"You shouldn't spend your money so."

"Didn't you have some last night? " Andrew put in as he lowered himself into a chair.

"That was the last of it," said Bruno, turning around.

"Really. Except this." El Greco held up a few pesetas.

"Well, I'm still hungry," Alice said.

"Me, too," El Greco added.

The blonde got to her feet. "Let's put together what we have. I got some money."

The Texan teased Bianca by reaching out for her while pretending to keep his attention on the discussion. She bit her lips with a smile and moved away.

"You want some breakfast?" Andrew was asked by the blonde.

"If you let me pay my way."

Bruno moved closer and Bianca moved further away.

El Greco broke in. "People who pay their own share not allowed."

"Oh, quiet," she said. "Who wants hamburgers?"

"Hamburgers in Spain?" Bruno asked. "You're crazy." Balancing his weight on one leg he began putting on his pants.

"*I* can get hamburgers," she said, her eyes widening with insistence.

"Where?"

"Right next door. It takes five minutes."

"They better be good," said Bruno, pointing his finger at her and holding up his pants with his other hand.

"I'm paying," she said, putting her hands to her waist. "You don't complain."

"They better be good, that's all."

"Now, who wants hamburgers?" One by one she took the orders, speaking to Bianca in Spanish when it came her turn.

"Bring some Cokes."

"Yar, some Cokes," El Greco agreed.

"How much cognac we got left?"

El Greco reached under the bed and pulled out a bottle. "Almost all gone."

"Get some," the Texan said to Alice as his hand started to roam again toward Bianca.

"Where am I going to get the money for all this?" asked the blonde, slightly annoyed.

"*You've* got money," El Greco insisted, and he leaned over the bed to return the bottle to the floor.

"Here," Bruno replied, handing her the money in his hand. "Here's money."

She counted it. "This all you have?"

"We told you," El Greco said as he lay back on the bed again. "We poor people."

"Ohhhh! What a dressful."

Bianca squealed.

"Here," Andrew said, taking money out of his pocket. He peeled off several bills. "My share. The liquor, too."

"No, no," Bruno protested. "The liquor *we* pay for. Just for the food you give."

"That's silly."

"We insist," Bruno replied with great finality, and again there was that tinge of respect in his voice.

"So where's the money for the cognac then?" the blonde asked. She had turned to look directly at the Texan.

"You've got money enough."

"Not for everything."

"Hell, woman, you're lazy," Bruno said. "You've got to walk the streets more."

"You're so kind," she hissed sarcastically.

Bruno was walking past her as she said this. He was on his way to get the bottle of cognac under the bed. But he reached out and with his full hand he squeezed her bottom. Andrew expected her to explode and unconsciously tensed himself as he waited for it. But the girl merely swiped at the Texan's arm, her face squinting with annoyance, but she didn't even turn to look at him. He pulled away with a grin, grabbing the bottle from under the bed at the same time.

"Easy on that stuff," El Greco said.

"Hell, man, we're getting more."

"With what money?" Alice asked, her arms folded.

El Greco raised himself on one elbow and glanced at Andrew. "I think this woman nags, you know?"

"I think this woman hungry." Andrew smiled.

"Anyone want a drink?"

"How am I supposed to buy," the blonde asked, bending over and looking right into El Greco's face, "if I haven't got the money?"

"You got the money," he answered.

"Look," Bruno said, collapsing on the empty bed, "you're always crabbing about money." He glanced up at the blonde as he worked the cork out of the bottle. "Will you split with me if I get you a job?"

She looked at him. "What do you mean?"

"If I get you a job?"

"Up here?"

They were looking at each other carefully.

"That's right."

"I guess so."

"Yes or no?"

"Yes."

"All right, get out of here and get the breakfast. Lay out the money and I'll get you the job later."

"Who you going to get?" she asked.

"What the hell do you care?" Bruno said as he took a glass off the table between the beds. "Since when are you fussy! This mine?" he asked his friend, holding up the glass.

"I think so."

"Half?" the blonde said.

"That's right." He patted the bed next to him and then motioned for Bianca, who was folding a blanket with her hands and chin, to join him. She smiled and shook her head No.

"Anyone want a drink?"

El Greco said a few words to Alice in Spanish. They were spoken softly and she nodded her head.

"Yes, I go," she said quickly and she made for the door, where she nearly bumped into Albina. They laughed together at the near collision. Alice kissed the Señora on the check. "I'm getting some food," she asked, "Would you like some?"

"Oh, no, dear, thank you. But I eat already."

When the girl had left, the Señora questioned Andrew about what he had done the night before. As they talked, she watched his handsome face with that special middle-aged longing which only a woman of her years could feel for a youth whose looks and manner excite her fancy.

"Went to the Pasapoga."

"You like?"

"Not too much."

"Yes." She smiled. "It is not real. You know?"

"But the women … beautiful."

"Ah, yes," Albina agreed, and she raised her eyebrows in warning. "But best you stay away. They not safe."

"Really? You mean sickness? But they looked so good."

At this Albina leaned back and let herself go. " 'But they looked so good,' " she laughed, repeating his words gleefully.

"What place is *this*?" the Texan asked.

"It's a night club we went to."

"Say," El Greco said, "that Alice better be clean."

"Ah, she is," Bruno nodded, and then he dismissed the whole idea with a wave of his hand.

Andrew leaned forward in his chair. "Would you like to sit down?" he asked the Señora.

"Ah, you are kind. No, I just come for Bianca. She must clean my room. But she is always here cleaning, you know?" Her laugh rippled quietly. "She is always here. I think she is fascinated." She glanced across at her maid and her eyes had the look of a mother.

"*Diga, Señora?*" Bianca asked.

Albina explained to the maid what she wanted.

"*Aaaaaah,*" Bianca said.

"Aaaaaah," everyone repeated.

The room filled with laughter and Bianca escaped through the door, blushing.

Albina got the greatest pleasure of all, but her face quickly sobered, because above the sounds of their enjoyment, she heard the ringing of the hall phone.

"Again," she said. "It never stops."

Bruno called after her, "Hurry, hurry."

Andrew reached out to detain her, but she was gone. He had wanted to remind Albina of the letters of introduction she had promised to write for him, because today he was to leave for the big job in Valencia, but then, deciding there was still plenty of time, Andrew gave in to the desire that had brought him to this room in the first place—that odd need of his to watch these strange people in action. He would not leave their company just yet, though he knew he should.

"It rings all day," El Greco explained, listening to the phone.

"Maybe it's broken," Andrew suggested. It was an attempt to be funny, but immediately he hated himself for it.

"It rings all night too," the Texan said, staring at his friend with a grin. "I found out, remember?" And for a moment they shared the delight of a secret, unspoken memory. Bruno finally dissolved his smile as he emptied his glass. For some unexplained reason Andrew became afraid that they might, somehow, be laughing at him.

"Looks like you guys had some fun last night," he said.

They smiled again.

"Well—" Andrew said, trying to draw an explanation from them, "as long as you get what you want."

"We never got to look far," El Greco said, and they laughed once more while Andrew watched.

"How'd you happen to hook that blonde?"

"We met her in a store."

"She was giving him the eye," El Greco said, "so he just took her by the arm and said, 'Come on,' and she come."

"Crazy broad," Bruno added, as he reached under the bed for the bottle again.

"How did Albina get along with the blonde?"

"All right, but if it wasn't for Alice, we'd be nowhere."

"Stupid broad," the Texan said. "Pays for everthing."

"Why does she?" asked Andrew.

Bruno shrugged.

"She complains an awful lot," Andrew suggested.

El Greco fell back full length on the bed. "She makes a lot of noise. But that's all."

"Stupid broad," Bruno said.

El Greco's forehead wrinkled. He was thinking. "I don't know," he said. He folded his hands on his stomach. "She's been around too much to be that stupid."

"Maybe she likes what we give her," said the Texan.

But El Greco kept talking as though he didn't hear, as though still deep in thought.

"You know, I was talking to her just before. The blonde. She told me the Señora used to be the wife of some big bullfighter. And she thinks that John Barrymore used to be friend of hers too. The actor, you know? People like that she hung around with. Christ, she used to live on the Riviera and everything."

"You sure?"

"The blonde knows. I don't know how she knows. She just told me."

"John Barrymore maybe, huh?"

El Greco changed his position on the bed. He didn't answer.

"Jesus," Andrew said with dull envy, "she really must have lived."

"She's older, that's all," the Texan complained. "We ain't had enough time."

"You got something planned?" Andrew said.

El Greco smiled. "He ain't planned a thing his whole life."

"Man, we ain't done nothing yet."

"Yar, you've been moving real slow," Andrew said. "You disappointed me. By now I thought you'd have Bianca knocked up three times over."

"Ah," the Texan said with a wave of his hand. "That's not as easy as you think. You know that?"

"Think she's a tough nut to crack?"

"I mean any broad," Bruno said. "It's not as easy as you think. Back in Texas, before I went into the army, I spent a year and a half trying to knock up this redhead I was shacking up with. I was really trying." He began walking up and down between the twin beds. "Ever try to knock up a broad?" Andrew shook his head. "Christ, man, it ain't easy." As Bruno said this he looked puzzled. "A year and a half and nothing." He stopped. "Can you beat that? A year and a half."

"Why try?"

The Texan shrugged. Then he looked at Andrew and waited for him to say something. He waited to hear some word of explanation from this well-traveled photographer, this quiet stranger who had, he noticed, attracted both the attention and the silent admiration of several of the women. He watched Andrew with a puzzled air of cautious interest, and though he did not realize this himself, it was a real indication of esteem.

"Means nothing," Andrew said.

"That's what *I* told you," said El Greco.

"She could have been sterile or something. Forget it."

"Hell, I'm not worried," he said, walking once more. "I don't give a good God damn!"

"You've got years yet," said Andrew. "Forget it. How old are you, anyway?"

"Nineteen."

"That young?" he said with surprise. "Really?"

"Yar."

"You've got no kicks coming."

"Why, how old are you?"

"I just thought you were older, that's all. I'm twenty-four."

"Greco, he's twenty-eight. Now *he's* the guy who don't look it."

The strangely battered and boyish face on the bed said nothing.

"*Gentlemen*," a voice interrupted. "Now tell me—what's all the commotion about?"

A slight grin was embedded in the heavy face that was watching them from the doorway. The apparition from yesterday took Andrew by surprise. The pug nose and the rimless glasses now carried with them memories, old and ugly, that the long, dull evening had slowly and mercilessly dredged up. So far that morning he had been successful in forgetting the night before. Sitting in this room, listening stupidly to the entertaining ramble of words, had helped him. But when Leopold walked in he brought the night with him.

"Well, look who's here," the Texan spoke up.

"Hello," said El Greco and he let himself fall back on the bed.

"Have a drink," the Texan suggested and he climbed to his feet searching for a glass.

"I believe it's a bit too early."

"I thought you were a drinking man?" He washed out a glass at the sink.

"That I am."

"Well, show us," El Greco replied to the ceiling.

When the drink was ready, no amount of protesting could hold the Texan off. The drink was placed in Leopold's hand and he was told to sit down; El Greco shifted his feet to make room. The bed gave slightly under the added weight. Leopold looked very uncomfortable. As usual his clothes either sagged ridiculously or were stretched in some places as tight as a drum. He was seated facing the doorway, but he had to lean back and support himself on one hand so he could turn and see the rest of the room. When Leopold finally took a sip, Bruno seemed relieved. He fell lazily onto the empty bed.

"What did you give him?" Andrew asked. "Hemlock?"

"What's that?"

"Poison," El Greco explained.

"No," the Texan said seriously, "the drink's O.K."

"It better be," said the little man on the bed. "We've been drinking this stuff for two days."

The bottle was still in the Texan's hand. He held it up. "Just a drop left." He lifted it to his mouth and pointed the bottom of the bottle at the ceiling. "*Now* it's dead." He rolled it under the bed, where it gently hit against another hollow bottle.

"You boys have a good time last night?" Leopold asked.

El Greco slipped his hands behind his head. "We always have a good time."

"You said it, man."

"How'd that little blonde gal treat you?" inquired Leopold.

"You like her?" the Texan asked, leaning forward and scratching his leg.

"The blonde?"

"Alice. The one eating with us last night."

"What about her?"

"Do you *like* her?"

"She's all right."

"I mean, would you like to bed down with her?" Bruno insisted.

"Such indelicacies, my boy, such indelicacies!"

"Well, would you?"

"Why do you ask?"

"I think I can fix you up, that's why. She'll be up here in a minute or so."

At this Leopold looked at Andrew, who simply shrugged his shoulders.

"As they say in the trade, what's in it for you?"

"Nothing," Bruno answered. "Just thought I'd let you in on a bargain."

"How much?"

"Five bills."

"I appreciate it," Leopold said, with a knowing look. "Maybe some other time."

"Man, you're missing out on something."

"How do you know? You had her?" Leopold's face became doubtful again.

"We both did."

"She knows her business, all right," El Greco joined in.

Leopold waved them away with his hand.

"If you like her," Bruno said, "this is your chance."

"We talked her price down and everything."

"Thanks, but count me out."

"How about it?" Bruno asked.

"No."

"Huh?"

"I said no. Not interested."

At that moment Alice came in carrying a package of bottles and a large box of food. She walked around the first bed and dumped herself and her things next to Bruno on the second. El Greco swung his legs out and sat up, his knees nearly touching Bruno's.

"I'm hungry."

"You bring the cognac?" Bruno asked her, looking into the bag.

"Hello," the girl said to Leopold.

"How do you do?"

"Want some hamburgers?" she asked him, breaking the string on the box.

"Do you have enought to go around?" Leopold asked.

"Yes, but you got to donate."

"Love to, my dear," he said proudly, "love to."

Seated next to Bruno, with the cardboard box balanced on her lap, the girl reached in and began handing out the hamburgers to everyone within reach. An extra portion she handed to El Greco who rolled back on the bed and extended it in turn to Andrew. Meanwhile Bruno uncapped the bottles and doled out the drinks. Everyone except the blonde wolfed down his food with great energy. She ate slowly, taking tiny bites and touching her lips with a napkin each time.

"I think I'll call up my black friend," Alice said casually, "and have her come up and join us."

"Who's that?" Bruno asked, his mouth full of food.

"My black girl friend."

"A nigger? No. No niggers."

She turned to Andrew. "But he'd like her. My black friend and I, we always go together."

"No niggers," Bruno insisted, a fierceness deepening his voice.

Alice watched him quietly for a moment and then stared blankly at her lap. As Andrew watched her he decided she was more attractive than she had first appeared at the restaurant. He no longer noticed her unhealthy thinness, but became more and more aware of the energy of her expression and the touch of wit about her lips. The scar on her cheek fascinated him, but somehow all it made him think of was his own silence. He had been secretly hating himself for it, hating the weight of flesh and bones that was himself piled worthlessly into the chair unable to speak, or, once speaking, unable to say anything worth hearing. He had been searching for the reason without much success, yet from the very beginning he knew it had to do with Bruno. There was an unchallengeable strength in this handsome Texan that threw Andrew into a respectful silence.

"Excellent," Leopold said to the girl, holding up his Coke bottle in a toast. "You should get us food every morning."

"Let it digest first," Andrew said. "Don't commit yourself."

"Yar," El Greco said, "you might not live until morning."

But while they teased Leopold about the food he had just eaten, Andrew noticed the Texan whispering secretly into the girl's ear. His arm was around her shoulders and she listened with a taut, suppressed grin. When Leopold glanced their way, Bruno turned his head away with a poorly acted nonchalance. A moment later he returned his mouth to the blonde's ear and when he finished, she shook her head up and down and leaned away from him. She sat as if waiting, her eyes on Leopold in a concentrated stare. Then, during a moment's quiet, with a mute, open-mouthed smile, she sprang from one bed to the other, pushing Leopold down and almost spilling his drink as she pinned him against the mattress. El Greco pulled his legs away just in time. At first Leopold appeared really frightened, but he made no sound.

"I *like* this chubby one," Alice said, and she shifted more of her weight on top of him making herself comfortable for a long siege. As she moved about for the best position, she accidently kicked El Greco in the leg.

"Ow!" he yelled, pretending more damage than was actually done. "Take it easy, woman."

The girl smothered Leopold with a long kiss. Her fist held down his head by clutching his hair while her other hand wandered lingeringly over the mountain of stomach. He looked more ridiculous than ever. Andrew had to laugh. Leopold's free arm was held up straight and stiff, as if grotesquely offering a drink to the ceiling. Andrew was overcome with comic pity and climbed to his feet only long enough to remove the drink from Leopold's grip and then sat down again. The kiss showed no signs of ending and its fury held the room in silence. The attacked man made several polite attempts to get her off his chest, but at last, when it looked as if she might stay there forever, he gathered his strength and made a determined effort, forced her away, and the kiss was broken. He sat up with a face tinged with red. The front part of his shirt had come almost entirely out of his pants and he began tucking it in again. But the girl was not through, and he made the mistake of taking his eyes from her a moment. She dumped herself onto his lap and tightened her arms around his neck while Leopold floundered to regain his dignity. He was completely at a loss as to how to meet the challenge. Alice began to remove his glasses and he had to stop her by grabbing her wrist. But he was not fast enough, for she had already released the stem behind his left ear and the glasses came loose and hung stupidly across his face.

"I think he's afraid of me," she said. "He won't even talk."

Leopold worked his hand across the top of his head in an effort to arrange his hair. Since the girl remained on his lap, he now tried to pretend that he enjoyed having her there. But noticing this, she quickly turned her attention away from him and began running her hands up her leg to straighten her stockings. As she did this, working first on one leg and then the other, her skirt got lifted up in the process to where, darker than the rest, the tops of the rayon could be seen. Then, as she examined a garter clasp, there was a sudden flash of white skin. Andrew watched, aware that his were not the only eyes that followed her quick, expert hands as they worked with familiar haste on her own clothes. He could not help worrying that perhaps sometime she might try this very trick on him. He began to feel the wish to leave. He hoped it would not be very long before he could get his hands on those letters. Perhaps now was the time to go to the Señora and ask. He wanted to get out.

Bruno and El Greco, on the other hand, were watching with foolish grins. At that moment Leopold was again caught off guard, for as he lost himself in the study of the girl's stockinged legs, she suddenly grabbed and kissed him. Over backward they went, but this time he fought with real purpose. The girl's strength surprised him, for now she clung to him as if her life were at stake. Their struggled kiss parted and rejoined again as they wrestled. Finally the man halted all resistance. An arm curved gradually around her waist.

Bruno was on his feet.

"Come on," he said, "that's enough for free."

He leaned over the bed trying to pull the girl off. Placing one leg on the mattress to get more leverage, he yanked the blonde away.

"No," she breathed, "let me go."

"That's enough," he shouted.

Alice pulled herself free and pounced once again onto her victim. The three of them struggled, each for a different purpose, while El Greco sat Indian style, watching with the pleasure of one who has a grandstand seat. Bruno placed his knee on the bed again, but this time, when the weight of the four of them became too great, a loud crack was heard and with a thundering thump the entire bed fell in. Bruno was pitched forward and everyone was dumped to the floor, their legs dangling over the edge of the bedframe. Alice squealed, Leopold grunted, and El Greco, with a wrinkled monkey-face, lay on the collapsed mattress in a helpless fit of laughter.

When El Greco gained enough control of himself to get up and survey the situation, he immediately called for nails and a hammer.

"Albina must have some," Bruno said, studying the broken bed-spring support. Beside him, Alice, who had stopped laughing only because everyone else had, looked as if she could be set off again at just a touch. Andrew was on his feet, where he could observe the tangle of people piled inside the bedframe. He had jumped up and stood watching, but afterward, when he went back to sit down again, he found Leopold using the chair, rubbing lipstick from his mouth with a handkerchief and looking as if three men had just jumped him and taken all his money.

"We need a hammer and nails," El Greco repeated.

"Come on," Andrew said, putting his hand on the small man's shoulder. "Let's ask the Señora."

Together they went to Albina's room and found her working at the small table by her bed. They asked her for the tools but teasingly wouldn't tell her why they wanted them.

"But why?" she asked, examining their faces to see if perhaps she was missing some joke. They only smiled at her questions, and finally she told them to look for the tools in the bottom of the drawer in the hall dresser. Again Andrew was about to speak to the Señora about her promise of the letters, but now she had returned to her work and looked exceedingly busy. Then, too, he felt it would be wrong if he didn't help them with the bed. Anyway, there was still time. They searched the drawer and selected the better of the two hammers. But though they rummaged noisily for nails they could find none at all.

"Forget it," El Greco said. "We'll use the old ones."

When they returned to the room, only Bruno was there. A childish grin smeared his face and he had sprawled himself contently across the remaining good bed, reveling in silent celebration. He sprang up when he saw El Greco and bounded across the room, grasping his much smaller friend by the shoulders.

"He took it!" the Texan said, with explosive joy. "The fat kraut took it!"

Throwing his head back he let go his laugh of triumph.

7

EL GRECO stood motionless, the hammer hanging from his hand. "Well, my God," he said.

"Bianca!" the Texan bellowed, cupping his hands around his mouth. "Bianca!" He was beaming with pleasure.

"What did he say?" Andrew asked.

Bruno rolled face down on the empty bed. "The kraut? He said, 'A guy can change his mind, can't he?' " He rocked with laughter. Then into the pillow he yelled, "Bi-an-ca!"

"Where'd they go?"

"He took her to his room."

El Greco pulled the mattress from the ruins of the broken bed and then lifted out the spring. Andrew came over and held it for him.

"*Bi-an-ca!*" the Texan called. "Damn it, woman, where are you?"

"Let's stand this thing against the wall," Andrew suggested.

"No, just hold it. I'll be through in a minute."

He stepped over the bedframe and knelt beside the damage. The maid hurried into the room and stopped with a gasp at the sight of the disassembled bed.

"*Qué pasa?*"

"Nothing *pasa*," Bruno said. "Come here and scratch my back."

But Bianca insisted on knowing what had happened, and El Greco finally explained it to her as he pulled some nails out of the wood.

"Tell the broad I want my back scratched," Bruno said.

El Greco translated and the girl giggled.

"So come here, damn it."

Bianca silently followed orders, but it was obvious she was pleased with the novelty of the request. She seated herself next to him and worked her long fingernails into his shirt-covered back. Bruno purred like a kitten, causing her to giggle all over again.

"How's it coming?" Andrew said.

"I'll get it," El Greco explained with a labored voice as he yanked out a nail. The sudden momentum rolled him backward into a sitting position.

"They must be at it by now," the Texan said as he looked at the wall that separated Leopold's room from his. "Go, man, go," he shouted, trying to penetrate the wall.

"Shhhh!" El Greco said. "You don't talk like that."

Just then, and to everyone's surprise, in walked Alice.

"Didn't he start yet?" asked the Texan.

"He finished."

"That was fast," Andrew said. She looked no different than when she had left.

"Yar," agreed El Greco as he yanked out another nail.

"It was all over before he touched me," she explained, lowering herself into the chair and fishing a mirror from her pocketbook.

This sent Bruno into an orgy of laughter, and for a while Bianca stopped scratching his back. El Greco enjoyed it, too, but he simply chuckled to himself without interrupting his work on the bed. A thin veil of pain quickly spread across Andrew's face and then vanished. But it left his features tired-looking and somber. He wanted to get out.

"He still ain't said a word. He just smiles," she said, enjoying for the moment their strict attention and quick response.

"Fat kraut." Bruno laughed and punched the mattress.

"Damn it!" El Greco roared. One of the nails was giving him trouble.

"Hey, he paid you, didn't he?" Bruno asked.

"Don't worry."

"Two hundred pesetas."

"Yes."

"All right."

"Look," the blonde said, after a pause. "I want to call my black girl friend, all right? You'll like her."

"That nigger again?" said Bruno.

Alice examined herself in the reflection of her compact mirror. "My black friend and I are always together."

"Well, not this trip," the Texan said, resting his head on the mattress, his face toward the wall.

"Yes," she added, as if to herself. "I think I'll call her."

Bruno's head shot up again. His voice was desperate. "Tell her, will ya?" The tendons in his neck bulged like stone. "In America we don't *like* niggers. That's all."

The blonde accidentally touched her lips with a finger and smudged the lipstick. "Ah," she said with annoyance, "I messed this up. Where's the bathroom?—*I* remember." She hurried out.

"What if she brings that nigger here?"

"Don't worry about it." El Greco began hammering the nails back into the broken spring-support.

"I don't *like* niggers," said Bruno in a little-boy's voice. He looked around at Bianca as she worked on his back. "Do I?" he asked. "Huh?...Only white girls...Huh?"

The girl smiled vaguely. The Texan rolled over and growled at her like an animal about to spring. Slowly her mouth opened with anticipation.

"Look out!" Bruno yelled, and one of his hands swiftly grabbed her. She pushed his hand away and jumped up, but her face was only pretending anger. She leaned over preparing to swing her arm at him but he hid his head under the pillow. A little smile took control of the ends of her mouth and gave her away.

"Good God!" Andrew said. "Can she be made, too?"

"Why not?" El Greco answered. His hammer drove in the last of the nails and then rang against the wood.

Bruno spoke to the girl. "Just a matter of time, isn't it? Getting ripe for it, aren't you?" Then to his friend: "Tell her some guy's going to come along someday and she's going to get it. Go ahead, tell her."

El Greco translated the message to Bianca and when she gave her answer he smiled.

"She says yes, but it won't be you."

"Well, she hasn't known me long enough."

"Maybe she knows you too long," El Greco replied. He stepped out of the bedframe and signaled Andrew to lower back the spring, while he waited with the mattress. Alice returned and dropped her pocketbook into the chair. Then she stood and watched the operation. When the mattress was put back, the sheets and blankets were in complete disorder, and the two women began to arrange them. But Bianca made certain, before she bent over to smooth the sheets, that Bruno was well out of reach.

"I just called my black friend," Alice said and she lifted an end of the mattress to tuck in the blanket. "She'll be up sometime late tomorrow. She couldn't come right away."

"God damn!" Bruno yelled, and in anger he sent an empty, crushed cigarette pack to the floor with all his might. "What'd you do that for? You *called* her? *God damn!*"

"But you'll like her," Alice protested, looking first at El Greco and then at Andrew.

Bruno could no longer remain seated.

"We're getting out of here, Grec. Shove it. I ain't going to be around when she comes. We don't want no niggers."

"Wait awhile," El Greco said, helping with a blanket. "We can always get out."

"You'll like my friend," the blonde was saying.

"The hell we will, man. Is she a whore like you?"

She turned on him savagely, but held her tongue.

"Look, take it easy," said El Greco and he tested the bed he had just fixed by sitting down on it with great care.

Bruno's agitation faltered for a moment. Then it took a different turn.

"Say, where the hell's that money the kraut gave you?"

LEON ARDEN

"I have it," she said, pointing to her pocketbook.

"Half of that's mine," he said, moving toward the chair.

Alice, saying, "Keep your hands off," got there first and snatched it up. "I'll give it to you. Just wait."

"Come on, woman, I want my rake-off."

She removed a small roll of bills and dropped the pocketbook onto the bed.

"You should get only a third," she said, " 'cause I had to do the work of talking him into it."

"You little bitch. That was the easiest money you ever made. I think I'll take two-thirds. How about that?"

"No."

He reached out, but the blonde made him miss by pulling her hand away. The Texan grabbed again. This time he caught her and they began to struggle. Having moved to the other side of the room to get out of the way, Andrew sat down next to Bianca. Her face was placid, but her eyes were wide with concern. The struggle on the other side of the room was mute and grim. The blonde's face was twisted with effort but she hadn't the strengtth to keep herself from being thrown down on the bed. El Greco hopped to his feet as soon as she landed.

"Look out!" he yelled. "Christ, I just fixed it."

The Texan heard nothing. He twisted and bent her arm but the fist that held the money would not open. The blonde was sprawled face down, her arm bent behind her back and her features sculptured with pain. She kicked her legs with such strength that her shoes flew off. With her free hand she gripped the bedcovers so desperately that they tore free, and she twisted and rolled so hard on the mattress that her skirt worked up to her waist, but she would not let go. The arm got bent further and further behind her back until Andrew thought it might break. All at once she stopped resisting, pressed her forehead into the mattress, and hunched up her shoulders in pain.

"Ieee."

Andrew could take no more of this and abruptly got to his feet to stop it just as the little white fist that held the money opened wide like a starfish and the roll of bills dropped out. Bruno snatched it up and walked away, counting. Behind him on the bed the girl lay as she had been left, the straining of her breath moving her ribs in and out.

"Just take half," Andrew cautioned.

"She doesn't deserve it."

But finally he threw at the motionless girl half of the money in his hand, and the bills sprinkled over her like the dead leaves of a tree. The half that Bruno kept he held in front of Bianca's nose and waved up and down.

"How much? Huh? You little piece. How much?"

El Greco reseated himself gingerly on the bed and reached for the bottle standing on the floor.

"We haven't had a drink in a long time."

"Good idea," Bruno said. "Drinks for everyone."

The Texan, seated next to the maid, was still waving the money at her. She proved she understood by lifting her nose in comic defiance and turning her face away.

"Huh? How much?"

Slowly Alice sat up. The money that had been thrown on top of her fell off, but one bill still remained, clinging precariously to her tangled yellow hair. She pulled down her skirt with foolish suddenness. There had been tears on her cheeks but she had rubbed them off on the blanket with a twist of her face before getting up. When Andrew saw that she had been crying, he suddenly felt as if he had watched some unspeakable crime. There seemed nothing he could do. She had a proud control over her face, and only the wateriness of her eyes and the grimness of her mouth gave her away. As she turned to pick up the stray bits of money he noticed that the scar on her cheek had turned red.

Someone was talking to him.

"What?" he asked.

"Some cognac?" El Greco said, handing him a drink.

As the blonde bent down to pick a few of her pesetas from the floor, the paper bill that was perched on her head fell off.

El Greco held out a glass to the blonde. "How about you?"

She reached for it without a word and took a long swallow. Her pain and the tears it had brought had gone completely unnoticed by the others in the room. El Greco was mixing drinks with the slow care of a chemist. Across from him, his arm around her, the Texan was kissing Bianca steadily on the mouth. The flat of his hand slid persistently along the curve her dress made over her thigh, and, just as persistently, she kept pushing his hand away. It was clear that these three were paying the blonde no sympathy and this wounded Andrew, for he was aware that there were words that should be spoken. But the things he wanted to say all remained inside him, and far away a girl with thin white arms and a scar on her cheek sat staring at her drink while she crushed in her fist some leaves of paper money.

"We don't drink enough, you know?" El Greco spoke quietly, leaning over on one elbow. "On a vacation we should drink all the time."

"Well, keep it coming," Bruno answered, his mouth muffled against Bianca's neck,

"We spent a week in the Alps once," El Greco said to Andrew. "We didn't stop drinking the whole week. Nearly killed ourselves skiing. Remember, Bru?"

The Texan grunted.

"Where are you stationed?" Andrew asked Bruno, trying to keep the conversation on a safe topic, but El Greco answered the question.

"Paris. But I only work for the army. I'm not in it like Bru. That's where we met—Paris. Only there we got the best setup of all." The Greek's face began to wrinkle. "I got to tell you sometime."

"I was in Paris once," the blonde said. "When I was thirteen."

"Did you like it?" Andrew questioned.

Her face became beautiful with enthusiasm. "Oh, it was wonderful."

"Yar," El Greco said. "We got it great in Paris. There's only one trouble. It's expensive."

Bianca gave a little shriek and they all turned to look. Her hand was spread over Bruno's face and she was pushing with all her strength. She burst into a little giggle, but she kept pushing until his arms came loose from around her waist and she jumped up.

"What happened?" Andrew asked. "You hit a nerve?"

"The little bitch!" Bruno reached for her, but she slipped away and walked around the foot of the bed and stood there.

"Guess she's a cherry after all," Andrew said, smiling at the Texan's expense. Yet his mood was sober, for as the girl leaned against the bedpost he noticed how the round ripeness of her figure threatened to burst the dress that held it. The familiar tremor of appreciation came over him. Bruno seemed about to go after her and tension quickly filled the room, for one never knew what went on inside of him. At that moment Andrew decided that the time had come. He would get out, and he would do it now. Once again he climbed to his feet.

"I hate that kind," the Texan explained, standing up and blocking the way. "She's moral, all right, but that don't stop her from letting everybody have a free feel and giving everybody the wrong ideas."

"It's called being a nice girl," Andrew replied.

"Some guys have another name for it."

Leaning her stomach over the bedfoot, Bianca watched him with a promising smile.

Bruno looked desperately at Andrew. "Lend me the key to your room, will ya?"

Reaching into his pocket, Andrew handed it over.

"Room eight, isn't it?"

He nodded, "What are you going to do?"

Bruno did not answer. Taking the blonde by the wrist, he pulled her to her feet.

"Come on, you."

He made for the door, pulling her behind him. She stumbled along, fighting to keep her balance so as not to spill her drink. At the door she was resisting like someone on water skis, leaning back against the pull of his arm.

"Come on, huh?" he said with annoyance.

She pulled against him now with all her might, the drink dancing precariously in her hand. With a yank he overcame her strength and she almost ran into him.

"Let me get my pocketbook, will you?" she yelled. "Wait a minute." And with the hand that held the drink she reached over to the bed and, with great effort, using only two fingers, she lifted the pocketbook into the air, where it dangled and swayed as if it would fall. Bruno yanked her by the arm again and together they disappeared from the room.

8

H<small>E MOUNTED</small> a hill and came down again, feeling everything rise and gently fall as it passed beneath his cycle. A scrawny little tree appeared in the distance and began to inch closer. Then, though his speed did not change, the tree began to move more quickly. After a while it came right at him, growing steadily in size and coming faster and finally rushing up and vanishing behind him as he went on. He was riding away from that place in Madrid, from Bruno and from the unhappy person he had been while he was there.

Even the time he had spent waiting impatiently for the Señora had been wasted. This he discovered as he went out to pick up his saddlebag. Glancing down the hallway at his room into which Bruno and the girl had disappeared, he noticed for the first time the very letters he had been waiting for Albina to write. There they were, thumbtacked right on his own door, where they had probably been all the while.

But now at last he had ended all thought involving the Residencia Albina or himself. There was distance to be covered, and a big job to be done; and as he continued to move into the wind, rushing along in peaceful solitude, he became dimly conscious of a small and growing measure of contentment.

The road to Valencia had not yet begun to wind its way down to the Mediterranean. Mostly it was flat and dry and strangely ravaged-looking and mute. White hills far off seemed speckled with pepper, but as the road wound and headed toward them, what looked like pepper became scrubby little dark-brown bushes growing like a three-day beard on the face of the plain. He could see the road winding ahead of him through the stunted hills, appearing and disappearing for miles as it curved its way along and out of sight. At the bottom of one of the curves was an overturned truck with bales of cotton dumped and scattered along the road. The driver was sprawled on several of the bales reading a newspaper and waiting. He didn't bother to look up as Andrew slowed down and drove by.

Andrew passed through a lonely village whose faded building-fronts had once been painted blue. The road continued through the empty black-and-white land and came upon a wide deep bed in the earth at the bottom of which trickled a small stream that had once been a river. It was the third such stream he had seen in the last couple of hours. Now the road worked its way downward, gradually edging off the plateau, lowering itself slowly after many hours and many hills and towns. Occasionally Andrew would stop and lift the NSU back onto its stand and run along the ground with that odd feeling in his legs as though they had not been used in weeks. Then it was back on the cycle and away again, but not until he had paused in his running to savor the silence and the empti-ness around him, and not until he had looked at the few puffs of clouds hanging low and flat in the sky with their shadows slightly purple on the speckled hills.

Night had closed in by the time he reached Valencia, and the buildings made the noise of his machine sound like thunder. Almost everything he saw appeared shabby and poor, and the empty streets of the city looked nothing like Madrid, or even Barcelona. Perhaps it was just a trick the darkness was playing. Anyway it was good to leave the bad roads behind him, especially those just outside the city, and to travel on solidly paved concrete again. But looking about him, it seemed impossible that here on these desolate, age-worn streets there was to be a festival, the magnificence of which he had heard so much about. The more he saw, the more he feared that the Fiesta de las Fallas would not be worth the time nor the film.

But he decided not to worry about it now. The day had taken a lot out of him, and all that mattered was the finding of food and sleep. The hotel that Albina had recommended was not far off **the** main square. In searching for it he lost his way many times because the street signs on the buildings had all worn away with time, or had never been there in the first place.

His room had a window that looked down on a silent, empty square. There was something very somber about it, and he remained at the window several minutes with his hand holding the curtain aside. Later, when he went down to eat, the hotel restaurant was crowded. By tomorrow, he thought, nearly all available room space in the city would be taken. After finishing dinner, he felt the need of sleep more than ever, but he no longer felt any of the soreness that the full day of traveling had given him. Sipping his coffee, he absent-mindedly watched an old woman at another table. She was eating her food with very small bites, touching the napkin to her lips after each swallow. Only that morning Alice had eaten her hamburger in the very same way. Remembering this, his mind raced back to Madrid for a moment and he wondered what they were all doing that evening. Then it occurred to him that here in Valencia he knew no one. He wondered why this thought should bring with it a tremor of lonesomeness.

He climbed back up to his room and studied the empty street once again through the open window. A shabby mongrel halted under the dim lamplight to sniff at a piece of newspaper in the middle of the road. But a sound in the darkness made the dog bolt in fright for several yards and then lope less swiftly out of sight. Climbing into bed, Andrew unfolded and studied a large map of the city which the desk clerk had given him. There was comfort in plotting out just where he was on the map and in studying the areas where he would probably be working tomorrow. But this did not hold his attention for long, and finally he lost all interest. More than anything, he wanted sleep to come swiftly and for night to pass. He would be shooting all day tomorrow, and there would be plenty happening, and much to see. Tomorrow he would be happy.

Turning off the light, he rolled over. But he was much too anxious for sleep to come immediately, and for a while he just lay still in the darkness and waited. Later, finding himself still awake, he grew impatient, though actually he had been asleep for two short snatches. At last his fatigue won out and he began to sink away. He felt himself going slowly, but as always, he dropped off before he could catch himself at it.

A loud explosion went off much too close to his window. He stiffened from the shock and opened his eyes to the light. It was very early—he decided it was about six or six-thirty. What could possibly have made such a noise? ... Then he fell asleep again. When it happened a second time he jumped up and hurried to the window. But as he looked out, he completely forgot the explosion. What he saw was the face of a giant. It had an idiotic smile and a winking eye. The eye was the size of Andrew's face, the head was as big as he was, and the smile seemed wide as his arm. This giant caricature of a man, multi-colored and moronic, stood three stories high in the center of the square. The giant was bulging his belly, holding his hip, and thumbing his bulbous nose with a monster hand. A few people in the street, looking like midgets by comparison, were staring at it from many yards away. But the men who had assembled the giant during the night had already gone. A string of fireworks was going off around the corner. The Fiesta de las Fallas had begun.

After breakfast he hurried outside and strapped the saddlebag with the film to the motorcycle. A little girl was squinting into the sun as she held a brimming pail of milk. She was watching a man on a ladder stringing a line of fireworks across the street. Andrew wasn't ready—the hood of his camera wasn't open—but he aimed blindly and snapped. The little girl heard the sound of the shutter and turned to look. She stared at him, wide-eyed and motionless. Opening the hood, he aimed carefully at the man on the ladder. The girl called out in a tiny voice of warning, but the shot was taken before the man could look around to discover what was happening. He gave a puzzled smile as Andrew cranked the film. The little girl continued to watch, but she now used both hands on the handle of the heavy pail of milk.

After taking several pictures of the towering giant standing in the street with his thumb to his nose, Andrew climbed on his cycle and rode toward the center of town. Before setting to work, he wanted to give the letters of introduction to the proper people so he could get permission to work from the balcony of one of the official buildings overlooking the Plaza del Gaudillo. He understood that it was in this plaza on the final night that the huge climax of the fiesta was to take place. As he rode in that direction he came across many statues standing in small cross streets, each structure different in size and color from the last.

One of the letters Albina had given him was addressed to a man who worked at the Spanish Tourist Bureau. The other was to an uncle of hers who held a job somewhere in one of the government agencies. As it turned out, he did not have to use the second letter, because more than enough help was offered at the Tourist Bureau. Among the odd bits of information he picked up were the facts that there had been over one hundred statues constructed throughout the city (each one a satire on some national or international topic or person) and that the entire festival was dedicated this year to Salvador Dali. He was told that each day at twelve noon and at twelve midnight a special display of fireworks was to be held in the Plaza del Guadillo, and when he asked for permission to use one of the prominent buildings from which to photograph this display on the final night, an official pass was given to him immediately. Afterward, as Andrew was about to leave, the man whose name was Barenta brought the conversation back to the subject of Albina. As he did when Andrew first came in, he asked once again about her health and about her new activities, if any, these days. Andrew tried to fill in as best he could, but to the greater part of the questions he had to admit unhappily that he did not have the answers. He finally left with Señor Barenta standing in the doorway saying that he wished he had been told earlier of Andrew's coming, for then he would have been able to do much more for him. Andrew wondered what more he could possibly have done.

Walking from the Tourist Bureau into the main plaza Andrew now gave his attention to the principal statue of the festival. He could see that this one was larger than all the others. In a grand, surrealistic manner it announced the general theme of the festivities. High in the air was a huge bird-monster with great outspread wings and the savage mouth of a serpent. Extending from a rod just above its back were the three blades of a helicopter propeller, and suspended from the claws was a life-sized bull with sword and *banderillas* deep in its hump. The bird-monster was supported by an odd-looking column of broken rock several stories high. On the ground stood a uniformed matador with a pair of tremendous butterfly wings attached to his shoulders. An assortment of vultures was suspended in the air, and off to one side, rising fifteen or twenty feet from the plaza, loomed the headless, grotesquely mustached mask of Salvador Dali. All of this was encircled by a strange brick wall. Here and there replicas of human figures could be seen breaking out of the wall as if from a prison, each figure struggling to freedom in a painful posture of suspended animation.

Andrew used up half a roll on this display alone, getting a variety of close-ups and long shots. Then he spent the rest of the morning photographing about fifteen or so of the dozens of statues he came across, limiting himself only to those that seemed outstanding as he rode through the city. In some of the poorer parts of Valencia, the presence of these colorful displays seemed painfully incongruous. Suffering lurked in these streets, and the erosion of poverty had put the look of death in every window. But perhaps only a block away and among identical buildings and streets all caked with layers of dust and grime there would be a startlingly tall, brazenly painted structure of happiness and wit that seemed entirely out of place.

And then of course there were the children. Dismounting to examine one of the statues, Andrew heard some giggling behind him. A group of small boys had been following at a respectful distance, watching him with great interest. They were dressed in colorless, half-ragged clothes that probably had once been worn by their parents. They called to him to take their picture and then giggled again, for they didn't really believe he would. But Andrew surprised them, for he turned with a grin and carefully began focusing. The children frantically pressed together, forming a hasty line four wide and two deep. With all their might they tried to hold a proper posture of military attention, but their joy upset their formality, and their military manner kept breaking down into a waving, smiling disorder of self-conscious happiness.

It was almost noon when he returned to the Plaza del Guadillo. The square was filled with people. Working his way into the throng, he reached a roped-off area behind which the winged serpent was supported by that broken column of rock. Wooden poles had been erected, with strings of explosives strung out from them and hanging ready in the air. On the ground were rows of cannon-like funnels sandbagged firmly into position to propel objects into the sky. The roped area was about the size of four boxing rings placed together to form a perfect square. The crowd was allowed to stand right up against the ropes.

The plaza was packed now and the people stood waiting quietly while several workmen checked the last of the fuses. Andrew braced the camera against his chest and planted his legs wide apart. He didn't know exactly what to expect, but he was ready.

There is a single, quick deep thumping sound. A missile trailing white smoke is sent up five or six stories high. It explodes with a blast that for a moment makes him feel sick. But the crowd is an army of deaf mutes. Andrew's nervous system coils for the next blast. What if his eardrums cannot stand it? High above the houses a lazy ball of white smoke is drifting away. He waits, and the air seems to threaten him with its brittleness. At once there is another quick thump and a second missile flies upward. It trails smoke as he watches it in the ground glass. Again there is violence in the air. Its force tightens his finger, accidentally triggering the camera. He is shaken by the noise, but this time he knows what to expect. Disappointment comes with the realization—too late—that the picture just taken is no good. Just a pointless puff of smoke against a cloudless sky. When the third blast comes, he has grown accustomed to it. Then a string of fireworks goes off like a savage drum roll. A dozen rockets fly upward, going off all at once and leaving the blue sky spotted with puffs of white smoke. Again it isn't a picture. Now the rockets and firecrackers keep up while other explosions begin. Finally, too many things are happening at once, and everything blends into one continuous sporadic thundering belch of sound. Great clouds of smoke fill the plaza until most of the people are lost from sight. Long, thin reeds keep falling out of the air, along with bits of ash. Andrew has to cover his head several times. At that point there is a brief pause and he waits for the eruptions to continue. But the pause lengthens and a deep silence descends on the plaza and he realizes it is all over.

The crowd began to disperse. Several people next to him were talking, but their voices came from far off and seemed muffled, and there was a persistent ringing in his head. He felt depressed, as though the effect of much drinking had suddenly worn off. The smoke had spread out in all directions, settling evenly in the air, and people were calmly going about their business again. The only excitement was displayed by a group of children as they climbed into the roped area to see if they could find any explosives that had failed to go off. The plaza seemed covered by fog. Beyond fifteen feet or so, nothing more could be seen than the vague outlines of people fading into the distance. On the ground were several reeds that had struck him when they fell. At his feet he noticed a small roll of burnt-out cardboard. It was still warm inside where the gunpowder had been.

Now for several hours there would be nothing to do. In the ground glass he inspected the image of some people moving off into the smoke; he decided against taking it. Children were still rummaging through the debris. He moved closer to the rope and peered down into the camera hood. No ideas came to him. The smell of gunpowder was very strong. As the smoke lifted, people could be seen walking away down many of the streets. No one was standing alone now except for a scattering of stragglers. The lifting smoke made the sky dull and overcast when he looked up. The ringing sound in his head was fading. Everything was colorless and dead.

But suddenly the gloom lifted. A voice called out to him and he turned to find himself face to face with an old photography friend. Looking like a pack camel, Ben O'Connell was shouldering a huge gadget-bag, a strobe light, a battery case, and two cameras, and there was a tripod hanging from his belt. His hair, as always, was uncombed, and no matter how bright his smile, he always seemed a little sad. But now he was so overcome by surprise that, instead of shaking hands, he gripped the top of Andrew's head and shook it gently.

"I can't believe it," he said. "I just can't."

They had always been friendly, though not the best of friends. Of all the people Andrew knew, he considered Ben perhaps the kindest and most considerate. But he was also the one for whom Andrew had the most pity. Even now, in that wonderful moment of unexpected meeting, he could see in Ben O'Connell's eyes that old look of troubled confusion and vague fear. They had met at *Graphic Globe*, where Ben had been working on salary for almost ten years. Photography was never more than just another way for Ben to sweat out a living. Always apprehensive, he went about his work with that misdirected zeal which often did nothing more than tangle him up. He was constantly trying too hard, and as a result, bad luck never seemed to desert him. One day he was given a rather important color assignment involving a new Broadway musical. Because of a light leak in his camera which ruined almost every roll, he found himself suddenly out of a job. He had a wife and two children, with a third on the way. He was desperate. The next morning, on his forty-first birthday, he took up free-lance work again. But the going was slow, and several times he had had to borrow from friends. Finally he had moved himself and his family to Florida, where the competition wasn't so stiff, and that was when Andrew lost track of him. But now in Valencia, of all places, he suddenly pops up again with the same tousled hair and the same melancholy smile, as if he were suffering some recent bad luck.

"So you're here in Europe, too," said Ben. "That's wonderful. I'm glad for a fellow like you, unmarried and on his own." He had always liked this boy who seemed to have talent enough to accomplish whatever he set out to do, and to do it while he was still young.

They went to the circular wall of an empty fountain to sit for a while and talk. The novelty of meeting each other passed, but unexplainably Ben O'Connell remained nervous and excited. Seated by the fountain, he did not bother to take off the heavy equipment hanging like so much lead from his back.

Andrew pulled up his feet and folded his arms around his knees.

"Your wife—did she come over with you?"

"No, no, she's back in the States with the children. I figured if I worked in Europe for about a year I could make a lot more money for the family and work off a few debts."

"You're selling to *Photo Star* these days?"

"That's right."

"You know, I heard that *Star* had a man here to cover the festival, but I had no idea it was you. Funny, you and me competing. I get a kick out of that."

A scramble of children suddenly ran past. A boy holding an unexploded firecracker was out in front with the others chasing him. Ben snapped his head around to watch them and then he jumped to his feet, lifting all his camera equipment with him.

"Was that a roll of film in his hand?" he called, excitedly. He took a few steps forward, straining to see better.

"I don't think so," Andrew said, confused by his friend's behavior.

"That kid over there. The one running away. See him?"

"It was just a firecracker."

He looked around as though surprised to find Andrew seated behind him.

"Huh? Sure it wasn't film?"

"What's wrong, Ben?"

The man sat down again on the fountain wall. He tried to smile. "Ah, you know me. Always a hassle." Making a grimace and shaking his head, he punched himself in the thigh.

Andrew waited.

"You see ... you see ... My film has been stolen."

"Your exposed film?"

"No, every roll I had."

"Good God, when did that happen?"

"At the railroad station this morning. It was all in a small valise. I put it down to check on some information at the window, and the next time I looked it was gone. I reported it to the police. They took it all down, and I signed it. Very polite. But a waste of time."

"*All* the film, huh?"

"I had a few extra rolls in my gadget-bag, but I used those up today. Now I'm all out. I won't be able to shoot the rest of the festival. And there's the bullfights this afternoon and tomorrow. I'm sunk."

"Wait a minute. What's your problem? Just take some of mine."

Ben shook his head. "Don't be silly. Then what will *you* do?"

"I have enough for both of us. And besides, I have more coming from New York. Wait here. I'll be right back."

Ben called, but Andrew didn't stop until he had crossed the plaza to his cycle. Opening the padlock, he took out ten rolls, which was all the film he had in the saddlebag. He carried them, smiling, back to the fountain and placed them in the hands of his friend. Ben started to protest, but Andrew cut him short.

"Take them and shut up, or I'll change my mind."

For a moment Ben didn't know what to say. "Well, at least you've got to let me take you to lunch," he insisted, after the film was safely tucked away. He was ecstatic over his good fortune. "And that motorcycle! Have you been riding all over Europe like that? What a man! Say, do you know of a good restaurant around here? And what hotel are you staying at? Oh, hell, we'll talk about all that later. Come on, give me a ride on that thing. Let's go!"

It took Andrew almost two hours to break away. Not until well after lunch (which was followed by several more drinks) did he get the chance to explain that he wanted to go to his room to rest before the bullfight. But instead, when he returned to his hotel, the first thing he did was to check out. The ten rolls of film in his saddlebag that morning would have been just enough to last him through the photo-story. To give Ben only five would leave them both short, so Andrew gave him all he had. There was more in his room in Madrid, but that meant a long trip back, missing some important events of Las Fallas. He would then have to spend the night at Albina's and return to Valencia in the morning to catch what was left of the festival. He had been aware of all this while he was giving his film away, but now that the enthusiasm of his generosity had worn off, it left him with the uneasy feeling that perhaps he had acted the fool.

At the gas station, while having his cycle made ready, he thought of Albina again and wondered whether her guests were still there. Several minutes later he pumped the engine until it roared, placed the silver helmet back on his head, and started back to find out.

9

For Hours the light had been growing thin, as though being fil-
tered gently from the air, and even now, as it failed and began
dissolving into darkness, the process was so gradual that no one took
notice of it. The sound of high heels in the hallway brought an end
to the lazy silence that had numbed the room. Albina appeared and
stared at them through the semi-darkness with puzzled eyes. She
was dressed in a beautiful red gown with a high collar and molded
hips, and her hair, in an upsweep, was held with a large comb. She
had peeled away ten years as if they had been an old coat she had
taken off and hung away for the evening.

"How do you see here?" the Señora asked as she walked in. "I do
not understand."

Bruno turned on the light. "Say," he yelled, "do we look
beautiful!"

"I don't know if *you* are," she teased, "but I try hard to be."

To avoid offending him she quickly added: "I only make joke,
you know? You are handsome. Really, I am ugly, I think."

"No, you are beautiful."

"Yes," Andrew agreed.

"You are all polite and kind," she said, and then to Andrew she
added: "So soon you are here?"

"Just to get more film. I go back in the morning. But your letters
work like charms, and the festival is wonderful."

"Oh, I am so glad," Albina said, wishing she had been there
with him to watch him work. Her regard for him had grown from
liking to admiration, from simple attraction to a sort of repressed
idolization.

Bruno finished a long swallow from his glass. "We are all polite and kind," he said with a slightly inebriated flourish. "But with *me* you are not safe."

"Food," El Greco broke in as he saw Alice come in the door of the bedroom carrying a large boxed supper.

"Who is not safe with him?" Alice asked.

"Looks like no one is," said Andrew.

"Ohhh. Again food?" The Señora laughed, putting her hand to her cheek. "Are you going to spend the rest of your days here? It is two days already, I think. You want to see Madrid, no?"

"I'm seeing Madrid," the Texan said, throwing his arm around Alice's waist. Then he roared at his own humor.

"What time?" Albina said suddenly.

"After seven," said El Greco, examining his watch.

"Ah, again I must go." Then looking at the Texan. "You do a favor for me? A favor, no?"

"With pleasure," Bruno said, breaking the string on the food box.

"Bianca must go to sleep early…" And she let her voice fall and her request became an unspoken one. She looked at them pleadingly.

"You want us to be quiet? Right?" Then Bruno cupped his hands to his face. "Quiet everybody … everybody quiet."

"Qui-et!" El Greco followed up.

"Everybody quiet," Andrew echoed, loudly.

"Quiet, everybody," Alice shouted. She was enjoying the game like a little child.

El Greco reached into the box and pulled out a chicken leg. The blonde slapped his wrist but let him keep it.

"Ohhh. You people," Albina said with pretended disgust, as if she were giving up all hope for them. "You are all crazy, I think." And she laughed a delightful, loving laugh. She was shaking her head with hopeless enjoyment as she vanished from the room.

Many hands reached into the box where the warm pieces of chicken were buried beneath dozens of crisp fried potatoes. Andrew joined the others, his fingers quickly becoming covered with grease as he picked out a chicken breast and held it firmly so he could tear at it with his teeth. Alice had given up all attempts to make an orderly distribution of food. At first she had hoped to disgrace their greediness by putting on a determined look of disgust, her hands clamped to her waist. But soon she had to abandon this and join in, for the food was going fast. They drank the usual cognac and Coke, and for dessert Alice had brought four jelly tarts, one for each of them.

Andrew noticed the Texan watching him.

"You don't talk much," Bruno said. He poured some Coke into Andrew's glass.

"I've been eating."

"I mean usually."

"He's the silent type." Alice smiled, her voice echoing into her glass, for she was about to take a sip. She too had been watching him. She had never met a photographer before and she was sure they were different from other men. Certainly this one was. He had come all by himself from across the sea, living a free life, working on his own … and yet there was something strange about him — at times something almost like fear. But she loved his smile and, deciding he was rather handsome, wondered what he was really like. Then she got an idea that she thought might help her find out.

Andrew studied the bleak, thin chicken bone he held in his hand. "The silent type? I guess so," he said.

"No more potatoes?" El Greco asked. He was sitting on the bed, Indian style. Smudges of dirt could be seen on the bottoms of his bare feet.

"No more," Alice said with sad finality.

Also on the bed, Andrew continued to eat. The trip back had not been as exhausting as he had expected, even though now, after the many hours on the road, he felt hollow and numb and properly tired. Bruno had grabbed him the moment he walked into the hallway. Offering him a drink, the Texan had promptly pulled Andrew into their room. El Greco was still reclining, and Alice had just gone to get some food. It was as though Andrew had never left. He couldn't stay very long, he told them, for he planned to get plenty of rest that night and make an early start in the morning. The earlier to bed, the better. In fact, he decided that as soon as he finished eating, he would leave.

All that prevented him was a silly jelly tart that sat in the palm of his hand. When he had eaten this he would be through. The contract would be null and void. In two enormous, tasteless mouthfuls he consumed it all and then washed it down with some long gulps from his drink. But it was all done too fast, and a hard lump of pain started moving slowly down through his chest; he leaned back on the bed and waited for it to pass. It was a stupid thing to have done, especially when he wanted to get up, excuse himself, and leave. But when the pain in his chest was at its worst, something took place that made him completely forget it. Alice let out a sudden, happy yell. She put aside the box that had remained all this time on her lap and jumped to her feet. Then she ran across the room to greet someone standing at the door. Andrew turned and saw a tall, silent, beautiful Negress looking at them. She smiled faintly at Alice's enthusiastic greeting, and the two girls briefly slipped their arms about each other's waists and pressed themselves together with a hug.

"Aw, hell," Bruno said in a soft but savage voice. He turned away with disgust and went back to his eating.

"This is my friend," the blonde said, taking the newcomer proudly by the arm and leading her into the room. "Andrew," she said with an introductory wave of her hand. "Carlotta."

"*Me alegro de conocerle,*" said Carlotta shaking hands.

Andrew jumped to his feet and put on his most pleasant smile. "Do you speak English?" he asked, startled by the closeness of her lovely face.

"No." And with a smile she gave a sad and apologetic shake of her head.

El Greco shook hands with the girl and then spoke to her for a few moments in Spanish. This gave Andrew a chance to watch her.

She was dressed very conservatively in a tasteful blue suit, but it was the tranquil beauty of her perfectly proportioned face that made her presence so disturbing. The command she had over herself indicated good training as a child.

Bruno moved further back on the bed until his head rested against the wall. His turn to be introduced was coming next and he looked like a trapped animal.

"*Buenas noches*," Carlotta said to him.

"Whatdoyasay?" Bruno answered, greatly ill at ease. The Negress did not attempt to shake his hand.

"*Haga el favor de sentarse*," El Greco said, moving over to make room.

"*Gracias*," she replied and carefully sat down.

"Now that my black friend is here," the blonde said, "I'm happy."

"Drinks on the house," El Greco said, lifting the bottle like a banner of war.

"Drinks on the house," Alice shouted with a burst of enthusiasm. She ran to the sink to get a glass for her friend.

"*Decoro*," Carlotta said to Alice in a gentle but scolding voice.

"Damn it," Andrew said, his eyes searching for his own glass, "I'm sober. We haven't been drinking enough." As he hunted the room like a beachcomber, the memory of his decision to leave was suddenly washed ashore. But just then he saw a glass on the floor behind one of the legs of the bed and he snatched it up and elbowed the memory away. There was only one thing he wanted now: a drink. And besides, there was Carlotta. She was something new. As he held out his glass to be filled, he enjoyed the smooth and rich brown color of her skin. He wondered if she ever really smiled or let herself go.

"Let's sing," Alice said, with a happy face. "I feel like singing."

"Come here," Bruno said lazily. He caught her arm and pulled her down on the bed beside him.

"What can you sing?" Andrew asked her.

"I know some English songs," she said, allowing Bruno to lean her against him.

"Like what?" the Texan said.

Alice lifted her face toward the ceiling and began to sing:

"When the Saints
Go marching in,
Oh, when the Saints go marching in."

"What G.I. taught you that?" Bruno asked.

The blonde smiled but kept singing. Everyone but Carlotta joined in. The Negress listened politely and smiled faintly at what she saw.

"I want to be in that number,
When the Saints go marching in."

One song followed another as they sang, for now that they had begun, it seemed a shame to stop. Anyone had only to start a song and it was immediately snatched up by the others and carried along in the vigorous, disjointed chorus. Andrew's voice was loudest of them all. He lay back and stood his drink on his stomach, his hand holding it steady. The coldness of the glass sank through his shirt and touched his skin. The singing was making him happy and he didn't want it to stop. The more he put into each song, the happier he felt. He closed his eyes and bellowed at the ceiling.

"Yankee doodle, keep it up,
Yankee doodle dandy;
Mind the music and the step
And with the girls be handy."

Several minutes later, his eyes still closed, he felt the shifting of weight on the bed. There, right above him, and poised on hands and knees, he saw the blonde. At first Andrew couldn't imagine why, but then he remembered what had happened to Leopold. Was she going to pounce on him too, hoping to make him one of her customers? But to push her away meant taking the chance of seeing her face sour with hurt feelings. It was fear of this that kept him from moving. Then, just as she seemed about to pounce, she changed her mind. Her eyes became timid, and a certain wariness made her pause. But having come this far, she knew she must do something. So she simply leaned down and for a moment placed her mouth against his. Caution had stolen almost all sensation from his body. He felt the dark edges of his world begin to curl with nausea.

"*Decoro*," Carlotta said.

The weight of her face was gone and the brief little kiss was over. They looked awkwardly at one another. She had come very close to making a bad mistake and she knew it. To jump on him as she had on Leopold would have been much too crude. Perhaps she had gone too far as it was. She climbed off the bed.

"You want her?" the Texan asked. "Go ahead, don't let us stop you."

Andrew thought it strange that they should talk about her as if she weren't there.

"No thanks."

"Why not?"

"I've never paid for it in my life," Andrew said, borrowing words he had heard other men use. But could it really be that some men pay nothing? Most of them, he felt, pay with more than money. And often those who are so sure they are spending the least, end up spending the most. They pay with money and time, deceit and flattery, lies and banality, pretense and posturing, degradation and false gaiety. For women bring out the worst in men because men have discovered it is the worst in them that gets results.

"Like us." Bruno laughed with the gusto of companionship. "He pays for nothing."

"Who wants to get paid?" Alice said, but now, because Andrew did not want her, he won her deepest respect.

What the blonde had said broke them up, but Andrew joined in the laughter with the stiffness of one whose mind was far away.

"Drinks on the house," Bruno yelled with a sudden wave of his hand.

"Drinks on the house," Alice repeated.

"Hey," El Greco complained, "I haven't finished this one yet."

"Can't wait for stragglers," Bruno said, snatching up the bottle.

"Let her go," El Greco said, downing his drink and then holding out his glass.

"Drinks on the house," said Alice again, and she too emptied what was left in her glass.

10

H<small>E H<small>AD</small></small> been drunk and then asleep, but for how long, he did not know. When the awareness of the room had finally returned to him, he felt foolish and angry. He had been left alone on the bed, undisturbed and abandoned, while around him others were awake and enjoying themselves. It reminded him of how his mother would always make him lie down every afternoon for a nap when he was a child. He would do so just to please her, planning to lie still for just the required hour and then quickly go back to play, but sometimes sleep would trick him and he would come awake hours later completely alone in his dim and quiet room knowing he had been betrayed. He was sure that his mother had looked in on him several times, smiled, and then closed the door quietly, letting him sleep on and on. This stung him and made him turn his anger of the moment against her, for when he was a child it had never occurred to him to blame himself.

As he lay on the bed facing the wall he estimated he had been unconscious for over an hour. It surprised him that his head did not hurt. He rolled over slowly away from the wall, expecting the headache to begin at any moment. The room was lit by one dim lamp and night had painted the windows black. Near Andrew's feet was Carlotta, who had taken off the jacket of her suit, which left her in a white sleeveless blouse that revealed part of a rounded shoulder and the length of a brown arm. The Texan sat next to her, his hands lazily pawing her clothes.

"Hey," Andrew said, swinging out his legs and sitting up. "You shouldn't have let me sleep. I'm taking up your bed."

"Don't be silly," Bruno replied, "stay there. We're taking turns with Alice. She's in Leopold's room." He thumbed at the wall. "She never gets a chance to get out."

Andrew glanced at the plaster and unfortunately he seemed able to look into the next room and see them there. Quickly he shut out the vision until there was only the wall before him.

"But why this?" He nodded at the Negro girl. "I thought you didn't like Negroes?"

"It's here, ain't it?" The Texan grabbed part of her as if to prove it. "That skinny blonde aint enough for both of us, anyway. This is how I keep busy between shifts." He looked at Carlotta. "You keep me busy, don't you?" He waited for an answer. "Huh?"

Andrew rubbed his face with his hands. For Carlotta's sake he wished to give some dignity to the conversation, even though he knew it wouldn't work.

"She's got real class."

There was a silence while Bruno thought this over.

"You want her?" he said finally. "Why don't you take her?"

"Why don't *you?*" Andrew returned.

To keep the conversation going was all Andrew wished. Make noise with words, keep filling air with sound.

Again Bruno paused before he spoke.

"Naw, I don't want her now. Maybe later. But if you want to— hell, man, go ahead."

"No, no, I ..."

"Go on!"

"Later maybe," Andrew replied, putting on a smile and hoping that Bruno would recognize his own words thrown back at him. He didn't.

"Well ... okay ... but don't stand on ceremony."

In a moment he was pawing Carlotta again, but she sat with the same stoic face whether she was being handled or not.

Now Andrew had no one to talk with, no one to help him fill up those terrible silences, no one to rescue him from having nothing to do. The bottle found its way into his hand again and he lifted it against the lamplight. There was only a fourth left. His great dis-appointment was his inability to stay drunk. Glass after glass had gone unrewarded, and then all at once it had come, a thick roll-ing wave that lifted and carried him, smudging the night into an Indian summer of colors and laughter and injecting into each of his carefully labored thoughts a joyful, roaring flourish. But then it had rolled onward and left him there staring at the shadow of himself against the wall. His arm rested on his knee and the bottle dangled between his legs. He was trying to decide whether to start again. At the moment it seemed like too much work. Leave, he said to himself. For the last time: *leave.*

His eyes accidentally caught sight of how Bruno's hands cov-ered the surface of Carlotta's hidden body, trying, in a lazy way, to be everywhere at once. He looked at Carlotta carefully. Her style of dressing was to hide, instead of reveal. Perhaps, then, to undress her might not be a disappoitnment for him as it had been with most women. Could he be right about this? His senses tin-gled with the dull pleasure of frustration. But though he itched to touch her, too, it would not be with hands as rough and cruel as Bruno's, but with gentleness that had respect, with hands that appreciated, as well as used. He wished he had unlimited time to spend and a wonderful place to go, for then he would take her there and see if he could make the beautiful brown mask smile just for him.

He wished he could get drunk again and stay drunk for a long time and then fall asleep and in the morning remember nothing and have no headache or regret. The bottle was in his hand, but he did not lift it to his lips. He did not bother with it at all, for to be drunk was really not what he wanted. At such times liquor was no good, and even a sea of it would not have helped him. The bottle slid gradually from the grip his fingers had around its neck until it noiselessly touched the floor.

El Greco came into the room. He looked gnarled and unattractive.

"Okay, Bru, she's all yours."

The Texan took his arms from around the Negress and stood up. He removed the cigarette that had been dangling all this while from his mouth, and ground it out in the bottom of an ash tray on the table as he blew one last cloud of smoke into the air. El Greco slumped down next to Andrew, smiling like a child.

"The cigarettes?" he asked.

"Mine are over there," Andrew said as he pointed across the room with his chin. El Greco rose to get them.

"How do you feel?" He smiled, and Andrew realized the Greek was talking to him.

"Okay."

"You were sleeping like a baby."

"I sleep the only way I know how."

"Me too," the Texan laughed.

Andrew felt the bed sag as El Greco sat down again. The cigarettes were in his hand and he was grinning. "Hurry up, Bru, a quickie."

"Drink your beer," Bruno's voice said as he went through the door.

"But you're holding me up."

"Suffer."

El Greco laughed as he lit a match, and he was still shaking slightly as he held it to the tip of his cigarette. With sudden surprise, Andrew noticed a small line of numbers burnt into his skin along the inside of his right arm. They struck him with horror. He had never before seen the brandings of a concentration camp. El Greco noticed him staring.

"Oh, I'm sorry," he apologized, offering him the package of cigarettes. "Help yourself."

"What? Oh, yes. Thanks."

The package was offered to Carlotta, but she declined it with the bare thanks of a smile. El Greco's match was still burning and he held it out to Andrew to be used.

"If you're in a hurry," Andrew said, after he had blown some tobacco specks from his mouth, "why don't you take Carlotta to my room?" The need to talk again had become desperate.

"I would," said El Greco, "but this is a contest. She was bragging she could take it longer than we could."

"But she probably can. What happens then?"

"In that case," El Greco said, "we lose."

The accidental humor of what he had said hit him all at once, and he fell back with a wrinkled face and laughed noiselessly. Andrew glimpsed the row of numbers again.

"Tell me," he said, beginning to speak without knowing what he intended to say, "where … where … uh … were you born anyway?"

"Athens."

"Really." Andrew smiled. "I didn't think *anyone* was born in Athens any more."

"Sure."

"And you met Bruno in Paris?"

"That's right."

"You were going to tell me about some kind of setup you had, remember?"

"Oh, yar," he said, and then laughed at the thought of it. "I knew these two women, you know? They both lived in the same building." He stopped and grinned for a moment. "I spent all night with one and then all day with the other. In the morning I say to one, 'Well, so long, baby. I got to go to work.' Then I go down to the floor below and walk in on the other one and say, 'Hello, baby, back from work.' Like that I did it for two weeks." His face broke with wrinkles again.

"It must have been great."

"Yar."

"Where was Bru all this while?"

"He was up on the top floor spending all his time with a third woman he was trying to knock up. He's been trying now for half a year. He says the bitch must of had something wrong with her.

"But that's life," El Greco added, picking up the bottle and holding it up to the lamp. "Almost empty."

Andrew grunted.

"Goddamn stuff goes fast."

"Next time," said Andrew, "we'll buy a case."

117

El Greco leaned over to him whispering: "You mean *she'll* buy a case." The monkey face wrinkled. "That dumb woman," he wheezed, "she's paying for everything."

"Why is that, do you think?"

"I don't know," El Greco said, reaching to the table for his glass. Then he shook his head from side to side as if it was all too incredible for anyone to explain. "Dumb woman."

"Hop to it, man," a voice said, startling them with its loudness, "and keep the ball rolling."

It was Bruno. He stood before them like a colossus, and with a sweep of his hand he snatched the bottle and lifted it to his mouth.

"Christ, take it easy! What's your rush?"

"Ah, I thought you were ready to go," Bruno said.

"This guy's a monster."

"Come on, come on."

"Well," El Greco said, getting slowly to his feet, "back to the old grind."

Holding his thumb over the opening of the bottle, Bruno dumped himself into Carlotta's lap. Her face flickered with surprise but soon it returned to its stoic neutrality. He draped his arm around her neck and went to bite her ear, but she pulled her head away.

"Come on, Grec," he shouted at his friend, "let's see some action. Alice says you're getting too tired to lie down."

"Like hell I am," the Greek answered as he stumbled from the room.

Bruno held the bottle by its neck and balanced it on his knee. He wiped his mouth with the back of his other hand and tightened the ring his arm made around Carlotta's neck, pressing her head against his shoulder.

"You don't look like you're having fun," he said to Andrew.

"Don't worry about me. I'm all right."

"Ah, but hell, you ain't. Come on, take Blackie, here, and have some fun."

Carlotta's head turned slowly and Andrew saw her looking at him. He wondered just how much she understood. The thought went in and out of his mind and was gone.

"Look, I'm not killing *your* fun, am I?"

"That's it. You are," the Texan said. "It's like drinking. I hate to be in a crowd when someone's not drinking. You know what I mean?" He climbed to his feet. "Come on." He took Carlotta by the wrist and pulled her over until she was sitting next to Andrew, her weight against his shoulder. "Go to it, man."

The handsome naked animal stood before him and did not move, the bottle like a club in his hand. His two rock-green eyes burned Andrew with their insistence. Andrew felt weak. If he kept saying no, the rock-green eyes would begin to look at him as if he were a freak; he almost felt it already. Carlotta was waiting for him when he turned to look at her. How many times could he refuse a woman who looked like this? Who waited as patiently as she was waiting? Whose dark, quiet beauty was so infuriatingly available and yet, at the same time, indifferent? How many times? With all his heart he did not want to fight.

"Say, you ain't got anything against niggers, have you?"

"No, nothing against them," he said softly.

"Well, what's holding you?"

"Because," he said, knowing it was not the truth, "because I don't want to pay."

"Who's pays?" the Texan said. "Nobody's paying. Hell, man, she's all yours."

"I guess so," Andrew said with a foolish little laugh. He hated his voice. It was constantly being caught naked and unprepared. The abracadabra of his emotions danced in a blurred circle. Everything was as still as a floating vulture.

"Go to it, man, and tell us how she is."

The Texan's hand struck Andrew's shoulder twice. The young man looked at Carlotta's increasingly sensual face, but there was no answer to be found there. He took her hand and climbed to his feet.

"I'll use *my* room," he said pointlessly.

She followed him up, and with a backward roll of her shoulders, her breasts thrust themselves against her white blouse, the perfection of her posture adding new beauty to her figure.

"Go, man, go!" the Texan yelled as he happily dumped himself onto the bed they had just vacated. His thumb was over the opening of the bottle to keep it from spilling. "Come on, Grec. A quickie."

11

THE AIR had been imprisoned too long and it was dry and dusty to his lungs. A window should be opened, but he knew he wouldn't bother. The crumple of bed sheets showed him that strangers had been in his room. He looked fearfully to see if any telltale marks or stains had been left to show what had taken place. His careful eye saw none and yet he did not want to go near it. But it was his bed—no one else's—so to keep himself from staring he went over and sat down. The bare sink looked pitiful with the pipes exposed beneath it. The mirror on the wall was cracked in the lower left corner. Three light bulbs together in the ceiling filled the room with a merciless light that made his hands look the color of dried white plaster.

She was humming. He turned and saw Carlotta undressing near the wall. He watched for a few moments, but this was a mistake. It was a mistake he always made. Don't watch, damn it, he thought and turned away. Why is it that so few of them know how to undress? He stared miserably at the floor.

Sitting as if in a trance, he slowly unbuttoned his shirt. He put all his attention into the removing of his clothes, as if this were the most important thing he had ever had to do. Every movement was painful. Yet it astonished him to find how quickly his clothes came off. His pants and shirt hung lifeless and crushed over the back of a nearby chair. They would get wrinkled, but he didn't care. Not until he had slipped off his shoes did he really feel naked.

His mind was dancing strangely. He knew he was on the outskirts of panic, for he had been there before. Sometimes it can come and you don't know that it's happening until it's all over. It was a strange feeling. He grew feverish, like a man on **the** beach who has sat too long in the hot sun and who begins to feel the bubbling of heat which seems to come from inside him, rather than from without, and who begins to wish, lazily, that he were no longer in the sun.

Two brown thighs moved past him. Carlotta had walked by to turn on the lamp at the head of the bed. She went to the door, made sure it was secure, then turned off the ceiling light. Everything fell into the gloom and shadow of half light. Making a graceful turn she smiled herself into a pose and held it as she studied his face. The lamp gave depth and roundness to her body, and he found it even more ample than he had expected. The thighs that had seemed so appetizing when revealed beneath her skirt by Bruno's hand were now simply the upper parts of two legs. His eyes watched hers, but he couldn't get himself to smile. The effort only made him wince.

She walked up to the bed, climbed around him and stretched herself out. The weight of her head sank into the pillow. She waited; her body was like a black work of art. As Andrew leaned back on his elbow he saw she was studying him. What were those eyes saying? With great patience the motionless figure of dark marble was waiting to be touched. Was she hard or soft, he wondered? She looked beautiful, the way a statue looks beautiful, but her clothes were gone, and with them, the urgency he felt for her had gone, too. When he had watched Bruno molding her leg with his hand, a slithering warmth had worked its way into him, but now everything was oddly cool and tranquil. He reached out. Her skin was neither warm nor cold. It felt inhospitable. This was all he could think of. It seemed foolish. But where would his hand go now? To decide was an effort, and actually he didn't really care. The spreading fingers moved up the curves of her body, and as he watched his hand on the unfamiliar skin he realized that what he was really doing was waiting.

The mattress moved as Carlotta moved. She lifted herself until she was almost in a sitting position, her weight resting on her long arm, her hand pressed into the bed. There was no expression, only the threatening emptiness of her face. But since she must be thinking of something, Andrew found himself trying to read meaning into her steady eyes and her gently separated mouth. What he thought he found there frightened him. The Negress leaned forward and transferred her weight against his body. He surrendered himself onto his back, his head cupped into the pillow.

There were cracks in the ceiling and yellow smudges where the plaster had fallen off. Some of the old paint had peeled and curled into the air and hung as if any moment it might drop. He wanted to reach up and tear the pieces off. But the ceiling was too far away. He could lie on the bed and stretch forever and he would never be able to reach high enough. Even if he stood on the bed, he thought, he might not be able to extend his hand high enough. There was no way unless he jumped or threw something. That was stupid. Why was he wasting time thinking of such things?

His hands had been moving over Carlotta's skin all this while. Her forehead was pressed against his shoulder. The moments passed, one after the other, bringing with them neither relief, nor pleasure, nor pain. His mind was so clenched against thought that only the thinnest and most meaningless ideas got through. It was as if he had become suspended in a soundless void. And somewhere behind him, where he could not see, he felt someone was observing him with scorn.

It was quite some time before Carlotta gave up. She rolled away to get a better look. Her eyes examined his face as if she had never seen it before. But there was no reproach. There was no anger. There was nothing. Yet Andrew was certain he knew what she was thinking. Even masks say something. Then he discovered that his mind had been working all along, in fact, it had been working with great diligence, and suddenly he realized that his old, invisible wounds which he had been trying so long to heal had now all opened again.

He sat up and dropped his legs over the side of the mattress. To move again felt good. But it was just a flicker of feeling in a senseless body. He sat leaning forward with his elbows on his knees and he watched as his toes moved some dust on the wooden floor. Two gentle fingers nipped his ear lobe and he turned around and found her smiling at him. What she was attempting to do now was something completely different, but this too failed. She was trying to keep him from feeling bad, and though he couldn't smile in return, he patted her hand as it rested on the crumpled bed sheet. Then he looked away.

The getting dressed was the worst of all. It had a terrible significance, for it seemed endlessly to prolong this ritual of worthlessness—an irrevocable announcement of shame, an act he was made to perform while some hidden enemy with whom he could never come to grips smiled and looked on.

Standing, he cinched his belt around his waist. Then, with his hand, he felt for his billfold, to be sure it was still in his back pocket. From his clothes pack he counted out enough film to conclude the festival and stuffed it in his pockets. This accomplished, he was aware that there was nothing more for him to do. Meaninglessly he glanced about the room as if to assure himself about something, but his shame exposed his posturing and made him sick of pretending. Escaping, he moved toward the door and undid the latch. With his hand on the knob, he looked over his shoulder. Carlotta was dressing at her own speed. With lazy indifference she rotated her skirt on her hips until she located the front. Her white brassiere was buckled with a black clasp behind her back, and her body seemed to have regained its potency now that it was no longer naked. He pulled open the door and walked out. From the time they had entered until the time he had left they had exchanged not a single word.

A dim light hung at the other end of the passageway, but his thoughts had so distracted him that he did not see Bruno leaning with one outstretched hand against a closed door. His head hung as if his neck could no longer hold it.

"Shhh," Bruno said, putting a finger in front of his lips.

He was completely undressed and stood barefoot on the wooden floor of the hallway. His nakedness made Andrew feel out of place.

"Shhh," Bruno said as Andrew approached. Then the Texan bent down in front of the door and peeked in through the keyhole.

"What are you … ?"

"Shhh."

All of a sudden Bruno had a key in his hand and he was slowly and gently placing it into the lock.

This time Andrew prepared himself for speaking. Softly he said, "Where'd you get that from?"

"The kitchen…. It's the skeleton key."

Bruno grinned, and then he could hardly keep from giggling. Andrew thought this over, but could find nothing in it to amuse him. Perhaps he had missed the point. Maybe he was slow.

"So what are you … ?"

"Shhh!"

The sound was like a whiplash. He felt as though he were a little boy in school, frightened again into stupidity by the threat of reprimand.

With a voice soft and dead he asked once more: "So what are you doing?" This time he got it right.

"Man, don't you see? I want to get her while she's sleeping."

"Why?" he finally asked.

But the answer must have been obvious, for the Texan ignored it. The key was in the lock now, but instead of turning it, he pressed his ear against the door and listened. From where he stood Andrew listened too, but he heard nothing. The waiting was getting on his nerves.

"Who do you want to get?"

"Shhh!"

Little lumps of fire moved through Andrew's blood

In a forced whisper he tried once again. "Who do you want to get?"

"Bianca."

Of course. It was Bianca's room. Andrew couldn't understand why he hadn't noticed this before. There was a slight click and he realized that Bruno had turned the key. The Texan prepared himself. His face had become grotesque with grinning. He was about to rush his way in.

"Ready?" the Texan asked.

"I don't think you should…"

"Shhh…. Here we go."

Bruno hunched himself as though ready to run a hundred-yard dash. He seemed to be waiting only for the sound of the gun. Any moment, now. But Andrew stepped forward to stop him. He couldn't allow this, he thought angrily to himself. He must stop this maniac. Andrew placed his hand on the warm flesh of the Texan's shoulder. The hardness of muscle surprised him. But Bruno had chosen that very moment to lunge into Bianca's room. As he did so, swinging the door open and lurching into the darkness, he pulled Andrew right in after him. Bruno's long arm reached out through the blackness, his hand fumbling along the wall. The elbow swung against Andrew's mouth and a tooth cut its way into his lip. Then the room exploded with light, and its sudden brightness seemed to trap him. Now was the time for action, but Bruno did not move. With squinting eyes, Andrew peered over the Texan's shoulder. His lips were opened slightly, forming a little bubble in front of his blood-speckled teeth. There was perfume in the air, but not the kind Bianca wore when first they met. All at once thoughts of his sister came to him, because it was the perfume that Dominique herself used. And now this girl, surprised in her own bed, even looked like his sister with that same sudden wild hair of Dominique's when she let herself become careless in her own home because no one of importance could see her.

Bianca's face cradled a strange ugliness. She was bare to the waist, but in place of the straining blouse her chest was as flat as that of a young boy. Andrew turned away, not from what they had seen but from what they had done. They hurried out and closed the door, leaving the light still on in the room. The girl had covered herself up and was spitting at them.

From down the hall where he happened to be standing came El Greco on the run.

"Hey," he called ahead of him. "You don't do that." El Greco took hold of his friend. "Cut it out. Remember what Albina said. Grab him, huh?" El Greco said to Andrew. "Come on."

They both started pulling the disenchanted Texan back to his room. Andrew had hold of an arm by the biceps and his hand felt as if it were grasping a rock. But Bruno came along easily. Down the hall Alice stood watching with a blanket around her.

"What is it?" she asked. Then, seeing it was all over, she disappeared. When they got to their door, she was peacefully in bed. Without warning, Bruno ran in and dumped himself on top of her. She screeched as both she and the bed were given a precarious jolt.

"Meat," roared the Texan.

El Greco had a fit. "Christ Almighty, you're going to bust it again!"

The bed quivered but held.

El Greco sank into the chair, exhausted. Meanwhile Bruno was kissing the blonde in a bearlike crush.

"He's a monster," Andrew announced quietly, watching from the doorway. He didn't want to go into that room again. He had decided to leave for Valencia now and not wait for morning.

A long gust of air escaped El Greco's half-closed lips. "You haven't seen the half of it."

"I got to be going," said Andrew.

"How was Carlotta?" El Greco asked, suddenly remembering that Andrew had been away.

"Hell, yar," the Texan agreed, forgetting the blonde and sitting up. "How was it?"

"My black friend is good, isn't she?"

Andrew put his hand on the doorsill.

"She's all right," he said. His voice could hardly be heard. "I got to be going."

"Man, she give you a good ride?"

He pulled some paint from the doorsill and examined it.

"Well…"

The room was still. Even Alice was watching him. But Andrew had come to a fork in the road, and in neither direction was he able to go. At that moment Carlotta walked in past him and the sickness of fear returned to him as if it had never been away. She primly seated herself with her hands clasped politely in her lap. He was aware that her presence was not a rescue and that the nakedness of exposure threatened to fill the room with unspoken ridicule and invisible laughter.

"She don't look like she had a workout," said the little Greek.

Alice and Carlotta were exchanging words in Spanish. Andrew's stomach felt a flash of pain.

"Ask her how he was?" Bruno said. "Is he any good?"

The two prostitutes exchanged some more words and those in the room who understood Spanish, smiled.

"What she say?" asked the Texan. "Huh?"

The blonde looked at Andrew and grinned before she spoke.

"She says you were the best she had in months."

Andrew glanced at the Negress and discovered her eyes waiting for him. She studied the relieved and puzzled look on his face before turning away. But her expression, in that quick moment, said to him: Did you think I would not understand?

Bruno spoke and his voice sounded odd now that it had been touched with real admiration. "He was the best, huh?"

But his hesitation lasted for only a moment.

"Well, that's because you ain't had me yet." His good-natured laugh put a smile on everyone's face. Despite himself, Andrew's grin was the brightest of all.

"Tell her," Bruno said to Alice. "Tell her how good I am."

"Oh, go away." She waved her hand at him.

"Go on, tell her."

"Just soso." But she had difficulty keeping a straight face, and when he grabbed the pillow and tried to smother her with it, her face nearly burst from grinning.

"That's because you ain't had *me* yet," he said to the Negress. "Look out," he added to Andrew. "I'm going to do better than you."

Carlotta was grabbed by the wrist and up she came. He pulled, and they headed for the door like a stumble of puppets. Andrew stepped aside in amazement.

"*Decoro.*"

"Look out," the Texan yelled, and his triumphant laugh echoed down the hall.

When it was quiet, El Greco motioned to Alice to reach under the bed and get him the bottle of cognac.

"Jesus Christ," Andrew mumbled as he headed for the street. "Jesus H. Christ."

12

A NIGHT journey makes for a totally different experience than traveling the same road by day. If an uninhabited stretch of land at noontime has a lonely vastness about it, at least the empty panorama reveals a speckled row of hills, a faithfully guiding road, and the sky. But when darkness comes, it brings with it a chilling, unseen desolation which is all the more powerful because it is mostly imagined. A distant pinpoint of window-light seems no closer than the face of the moon. On either side of the road the darkness is filled with bottomless drops of land, with secret hills and invisible valleys, and with an occasional cluster of huts sealed up for the night. And then, to remind the traveler how far he is from others, should he ever be in need of help, there appears every now and again, many hours apart, the phenomenon of a passing car. But to Andrew, all these distractions were welcome, for they kept his mind from the thought that what he was doing was running away.

Dawn was coming up out of the sea as he reached Valencia. But it was like entering a city under siege, for every so often a distant explosion was heard going off in one of the streets. The same grotesque statue, still thumbing its nose, loomed out of the sickly, early morning light as he halted his cycle and climbed off. But inside the hotel there was now not one room available. Andrew finally made it clear to the night clerk that he wanted him to recommend some other place where he could sleep, and he was sent to another hotel further from the center of town. While standing outside and pounding a door that no one answered, he began to think of what to do in case there were no rooms anywhere. The accumulative fatigue of the last two trips began to engulf him. Of the last twenty sleepless hours, he had spent fifteen on the road, and it would not have been difficult to doze off right there in one of the doorways. But morning had come and this stopped him, for he knew that on this, the final day of the festival, the streets would soon be filled with people.

At last the pounding of his fist was answered, but to his surprise the person who came to undo the latch was a small boy. A few feet away, inside the door, he could see the cot where the child had been asleep. The only place the boy had to offer was a room normally used for storage. To take advantage of the great influx of travelers, it had been equipped with a bed and a table. Pushing open the shutters, the boy yawned down at the empty street. He was certain that this American would decide against taking the room, as had all the others, but when he turned around, Andrew had already removed his shirt and was hanging it on the bedpost. After the boy left, Andrew closed the shutters again, removed the rest of his clothes, and went to bed. Sleep floated him away in a matter of seconds.

Sudden painc took hold of him when he finally came awake. He sprang from the bed and swung open the shutters. Outside, it was night again. How much had he missed? He looked at his watch and saw that it had stopped at seven minutes after three. The sounds of the festival were constant now, as though a great battle were taking place. In no time at all he was dressed and down in the street, adjusting the dials of his camera. He rode toward the sounds of the festival until the crowds became too thick, forcing him to continue on foot. The disjointed conflict of a third-rate band was marching toward him up the street. There were great crowds of people everywhere. He thought for a minute of Ben O'Connell and wondered where he was. Perhaps they would meet. All about him he heard the joyful exclamations of a language he didn't understand. The band marched into the lamplight and he ran and knelt in their path to snap the puff-faced horn-player encased in the coils of his tuba, while at the same moment the trumpet player next to him was examining some dirt in his mouthpiece with a face of great disgust. Andrew danced out of their way, and then, as the last of the players were marching away, he caught in the ground glass several boys prancing behind in imitation, holding their invisible instruments with grotesque postures and puffing their faces in comic mimicry.

Down the far end of another street he could see one of the colored statues standing in a flood of lights. Many people were watching as a vine of fireworks was being wrapped around the giant's head and body. Andrew ran to get closer. Suddenly, overhead, a festoon of low-hanging firecrackers stretching down the entire length of the narrow street burst with the repetitive violence of a machine gun. Andrew and the others near him were surrounded by exploding air. There was no way to turn. He ducked and covered his hair for fear it would be singed. The explosions worked their way from directly above him to points farther on down the street, until at last they reached and set off the fireworks on the statue. Andrew stood dazed with delight and amazement while the others around him only laughed and began walking again.

Many times in the next couple of hours he was startled by just such a rampage of explosives. Yet he grew more accustomed to each new assault of sound until at one point he surprised himself by remaining unperturbed when a sudden string of them burst along the ground between his legs. The sporadic commotion of violent noises, or the silences that followed, threatening new eruptions—all this provided him with a missing element of life. His existence up to this evening had not seemed real. Except for occasional moments on the cycle, or when he was good and drunk, his life appeared blank and flat. He had been deceived into believing that all the many subtleties of life somehow made up for the ferocity and turbulence of real living. This revelation appeared before him now for the first time. The Spanish air was vibrant with its secret.

His eye sprang from one object to another in swift contemplation. Nothing of the essence of what he saw eluded him. Or so it seemed. To his photo-conscious eye, the greatest picture was always the one he was not quick enough to capture. Now the world was filled with such visions. A child's fleeting look of astonishment in a dark and noisy street. A sudden dance to safety of a man with a vine of live fireworks falling onto his shoulders. Someone jumping to see above the heads of others. Multiple flashes of exploding light. Running feet that vanish into the crowd. In fact, almost all he saw showed the toyful turbulence and ferocity of the Spanish at play.

Time now came to a halt inside of Andrew just as earlier it had come to a halt inside his watch. The dimensions of the universe extended only as far as the festival, and he wandered happily through the many streets as though night would never end. But then something happened to remind him that the night must end, and with it, the celebration. He was also jolted into remembering that he had a business here besides his own enjoyment. The jolt came soon after he found himself in the neighborhood of the hotel where he had spent his first night.

Several blocks away he saw the grotesquely pot-bellied giant standing in the street light thumbing his nose. A display of fireworks strung around the giant's body was in the process of going off. It was all louder and more sustained than ever. There were also burning flares hanging from strings that dropped shimmering sparks to the pavement. More people crowded the statue than usual. Andrew thought nothing of this and simply forced his way into the throng to get closer. Then, as the display of fireworks was coming to an end, he finally saw what was happening. Smoke appeared first, because the small flame down at the base was shielded from his sight by the crowd. But slowly and steadily the brightness grew and then the smoke was gone and it was all flame. The statue was burning.

Andrew readied his camera and tried to work his way forward, but the crowd had grown too thick and he couldn't get through. Placing his back to the throng and facing away from the statue, he lifted the camera above his head and held it upside down like a periscope. Looking into the ground glass he could see and photograph the fire without trouble. Señor Barenta of the Tourist Bureau had told him that at twelve midnight the statues throughout the city would all suddenly be set on fire. But had the hour already come? Had the evening really gone so fast? The legs of the statue were burning fiercely in the night and it lit up the surrounding buildings like a great bonfire. Andrew could see people watching from every window—people he had never known were there. The flames licked their way into a huge torch. Its heat grew so intense that the crowd was forced to give ground. The swirling flames warmed Andrew's neck and hands. The street swelled with daylight. Out of the corner of his eye he noticed several people watching him use the camera.

Enveloped by fire, the giant suddenly came alive. He no longer thumbed his nose at the people watching him burn. A murmur spread through the crowd. They backed further away. The giant bent still more and thumbed his nose at his own feet. He seemed to be slowly kneeling to the ground as the flames covered him like a blazing cloak. Andrew discovered as he turned the crank that there was no more film left in the camera. But now it was all over, anyway, for the statue finally toppled over into the street, scattering a segment of the crowd. Night had closed in again. Now he had to change film. As he knelt near the gutter to do so he became aware, amid smells of gunpowder and burning wood, of the faint odor of dried urine.

People began moving away, but all in the same direction. It was a mass migration toward the center of town and the Plaza del Gaudillo. There was mostly silence now. Andrew knew he had just half an hour to get ready for the grand finale. He ran for several blocks, walked for a while, and then ran again. Most of it was broken field running, so thick was the crowd. It seemed that the whole city was advancing together on the plaza. There in the semi-darkness the flying monster with the bull and the face of Dali were still standing.

The uniformed guard leaning against a wall at the front entrance of the main building hardly glanced at Andrew's pass before allowing him to enter. A bottle of wine and a piece of cheese wrapped in newspaper were hidden behind one of the large pillars near the door. The guard returned to them as soon as he was alone.

Climbing a spacious stairway, Andrew found himself in a long, empty hall. No one was in sight, so he continued to climb. There were statues of marble on the third floor and everything was cool and still. All the noises of the main square were sealed out, and the slight tapping of his own footsteps was all the sound needed to give dimension to the silence. Soon he came upon a row of doors that looked promising. Selecting one on the left, he opened it carefully, but the room was dark and quiet. Closing it again, he tried another. As he opened this door he heard the sounds of the street. Across the room, the windows of a balcony were wide open. There were several people sitting in the darkness, talking and waiting. Andrew nodded, went past them onto the balcony, and looked down at the flying monster and the bull.

Below him was a scene resembling Times Square on New Year's Eve. But there was less noise and light, and here too they were waiting. Nothing could be seen clearly; only the stars were sharply defined. Andrew sat on the cold concrete wall of the balcony and wondered about Ben O'Connell. Was he down there in the crowd, or was he up in one of the other balconies? ... Afterward, people came out of the room and stood against the wall. Andrew asked the time, and one of the men said it was thirty minutes past midnight. Andrew set his own watch. Any moment now it would begin. His camera was ready.

In the darkness, a rocket shoots across the plaza, strikes one of the buildings, and breaks into a cascade of shimmering sparks. Colored rockets range into the black sky and curve and slice in all directions. Then, turning night into noon, they burst into a waterfall of multiple lights. Darkness closes in again, but more rockets go up, and then still more. Finally they begin coming without stop. Several rockets go flaming in the direction of the balcony. At the last moment they dart over the roof and disappear, but one of them, flying a little lower than the others, sails into the brick wall and drops a cloak of sparks onto the balcony. Several moments later, as Andrew is winding the film, the rockets suddenly come at the balcony again. This time everyone can see that they won't miss. A woman screams. Andrew and the others duck away. Two rockets fly against the concrete railing. There is a flood of colored flame, sparks, and then the darkness again. Andrew moves to the wall once more, but the others stay carefully back. While he peers into the ground glass and arcs the camera to follow a new flight of rockets towering upward, something strikes heavily against his wrist. At his feet he finds the burnt-out end of a rocket which has just fallen from the sky.

Below there is excitement, too. A rocket-launcher goes faulty, and a flaming ball drives into the throng. A hole in the crowd suddenly opens to give it room. One man does a hurried dance as the rocket swirls blazing at his feet. When an explosion in the sky lights up the plaza again, Andrew sees a mother in the crowd holding a sleeping baby. Particles of light fall to the ground, but mostly people pay no attention. Rockets continue to bounce into the sides of buildings or against windows. Another ball of fire lands right on a man's head and he jumps and swings his arms in the street, shaking off the sparks. When he is finally free, he grins foolishly at his smiling friends. Andrew smiles, too, just as the burnt-out end of a rocket strikes him on the shoulder. But he disregards it, leaning over to take another picture. Another rocket falls into the crowd. The people around it run as if a bull has been turned loose in the street. No one seems worried about the danger. They all laugh at themselves and at others, as if this were the happiest day of their lives.

Abruptly, everyone's attention is diverted from the sky. Explosions are heard near the statue of the bird-monster. They continue for several minutes. Finally this last structure also begins to burn. Dozens of rockets built into it now sail forth as the flames reach them. The fire works its way slowly. Human silhouettes at the front of the crowd move back, giving way to the heat. The flames reach the bird and spread out along its belly and across the bottom of its wings. The blaze begins to hypnotize the crowd. An odd silence settles over the plaza as the sound of crackling reaches the balcony. The face of Salvador Dali begins to be transformed in the dancing light. Flames are climbing down the claws of the bird, onto the hump of the bull. Soon it all becomes one enormous living flame and the whole structure is lost in it and begins to crumble. Andrew is transfixed. He is lost in the wonder of it, frozen by the dancing silence of it, paralyzed by its overwhelming, yellow beauty....

When it was over, Andrew found himself in the street. All the clocks in the world had slowly begun to move again. The sluggish crowd gradually left the plaza and he worked his way against the tide, his camera hanging dead from his shoulder. Everyone was heading home. The suddenly vanished excitement had left him numb and depressed. He stood by the fountain for a time looking for Ben O'Connell. Several young couples straggled along behind the crowd while loneliness, like an old enemy he had tried to ignore, began pulling at his sleeve. Afterward he moved with the others until he found his cycle again, and then he drove slowly through the throng to his hotel.

The next morning he tried once more to find his friend. He went to the hotel where Ben was staying, but Ben was not in his room. After a leisurely breakfast, he tried once again, only to be told that Mr. O'Connell had checked out. Quickly Andrew drove to the hotel where he had spent his first night in the city but where he had later been unable to get a room. Sure enough, there was a note waiting for him. In it, Ben explained that he had taken the morning train to Barcelona and that he was sorry they had missed each other. He thanked Andrew once again for the film and suggested that they get together in Paris. Andrew rushed to the railroad station. The train to Barcelona had gone.

Now the only people in Spain whom he knew and could go to were back in Madrid. Also, many of his belongings were still in his room at Albina's. But even if there had been no other reason to make the trip, he knew he would have gone anyway because, though part of him rebelled at the thought of returning, there was another part that hungered to be with familiar people again. It did not matter how unlikely they were as companions, or how much distress they caused him. Today he needed people. Tonight he might feel differently. Tomorrow he might even wish he were alone again. But now there was nothing more important than to be with others.

Returning from the railroad station, he stopped for a while in the plaza to watch some men cleaning away the debris of the night before. Then he gunned the engine and headed back.

13

IT HAD rained in Madrid that evening and the streets were still wet. Everywhere could be heard the hiss of wet tires. Climbing off his cycle in front of the building, he felt it was good to stretch his legs again. Removing his helmet, he bent his head back and looked up at the windows of Albina's small hotel, but he did not go up. He would put it off for a while. He wasn't quite ready. Taking his camera and crash helmet inside, he left them with the superintendent on the main floor and started off on foot. Might as well eat first, and get that over with. But where to go? He seemed always to be asking himself this question. Then he remembered the restaurant to which he had gone on his first night in Madrid. The boy with the dirty apron and the gushing broken English, the two prostitutes and their proud, stoic old man—he remembered them all.

He had crossed the main avenue and was now heading down a series of dim streets. A short man with a black briefcase had been walking some distance ahead. Only now, when the girl stepped out and blocked the man's way, did Andrew really take notice of him. Standing in the man's path, she began the smiling, hurried monologue of the desperate solicitor. Annoyed, the man tried to step around her, but she prevented it. Finally, when his anger showed signs of erupting, she gave up and moved out of his way. But they both stepped in the same direction at once and collided. In a sudden rage, he flung her away from him and her thin body bounced off the building wall, then stumbled back against it as she almost fell. The man continued on, and the woman, without bothering to turn her head to glare at him with hate, simply brushed the dirt of the wall off her dress and began walking again. Only when they got closer to each other, with Andrew wondering if he should cross the street to avoid being approached, did they recognize each other.

"Did he hurt you?" he asked.

"Ah," she said, and her disgust dismissed him as someone not man enough to hurt her.

"I thought you didn't walk the streets!" He spoke with annoyance. "I thought you worked in a bar, or something!"

The light from high on the lamppost caught her skin and turned it a dead white. How thin she looked!

"I don't. But I got an hour to kill before I have to see this old man I know. I see him every Sunday."

Andrew had begun to scold her, for a reason he did not understand, but he caught himself just in time. Actually he was as glad to see her as if she were an old friend.

"Where are you going?" Alice asked. It was a simple, friendly question, and he could tell that for a moment she had forgotten the obsession of her job.

"Just to eat."

"Oh."

The mention of food had been a mistake. He could tell by the expression on her face.

"Have you eaten yet?"

"Ah," she snorted, as if the subject were beneath her. "These are my slave hours. Now I work."

"I didn't ask that."

"When you work you got to apply yourself." She rambled on. "My only thought now is work. Some of the other girls are always..."

"Hey—" he said, "hey!"

She looked at him.

"Have you *eaten* yet, I said."

"No."

"Then come on, you're going to have dinner with me."

He took her by the arm and led her down the dark street. She continued to protest, saying that he was very kind but that these were her working hours.

"Look," he finally said, stopping and facing her. "You work to make money, right? And what do you use the money for? To eat, right? Well, I'm taking you to eat. So what's the problem?"

She studied him as if she hadn't heard his words.

"I'm busy later," she said with a worried and apologetic face. "I have to see this old man."

For a moment he almost didn't understand.

"No, no, just as friends. No strings attached."

"This is very kind of you," she said, but despite the conventional tone of her voice, there was surprise on her face. He could see that a dinner without obligations was something that did not come her way too often.

When they entered the restaurant, Andrew half expected to see the two prostitutes and their old man still seated where he had first seen them. But now even the young boy was gone. They were served by a thin, chestless man with a slight mustache and a grim mouth. With Alice translating the menu for him, he ordered a full dinner and made her do the same. This time she agreed without an argument, and he noticed that she kept her selections well within the price range which he himself had chosen. When the waiter left for the kitchen, she smiled her thanks again. Feeling uncomfortable, he started conversation by saying something safe.

"You know, you speak English extremely well."

"I learned it in school in Vienna. Also, my father spoke English."

"Is that where you were born? Vienna?"

"No, Barcelona. But my father was Austrian."

He wanted to ask her what she was doing here in Madrid walking the streets, but he knew he should not. Yet after a little silence (and before he could catch himself) he said: "How's business?" This sounded so wrong that he quickly added: "I mean, are you making any money?"

"You can make good in my profession. A man once give me a dress and a sweater for one hour." Then to impress him with the wonder of this she repeated: "Just for *one hour!* That's why I work for myself. A house is no good. You have to give a hundred and fifty pesetas out of three hundred to the madam. Streets are no good either. The bars are the best."

The coming of the waiter interrupted them. Two shrimp cocktails were placed on the table, and some bread. The blonde immediately began to eat, but with leisure and care. Poverty had not taken its toll of her manners.

"I see you finally left Albina's. Is Bruno still there?"

She was chewing and did not hurry to answer.

"That guy's a no-good son-of-a-bitch!" she said.

He was not being very clever today. The food was tasteless as he chewed and swallowed.

"Are all Americans like *him?*" she asked, after an odd silence.

"I'm an American too." He smiled.

"Are they mostly like him, or you?" She appeared indifferent to the answer, as if she were not really waiting for it. Her mouth was serious. Her eyes watched her food.

"Like neither, I hope."

But he could not get his smile to spread to her face.

"You'll meet more of them soon. They're coming over because of the deal the U.S. made with Franco for airfields."

She grunted and ate another shrimp.

"Are they mostly like him, or you?" she repeated calmly, after a moment of thought.

"Maybe a little of both."

"Carlotta was in North Africa during the war. She's Spanish-Moroccan. She told me they're all like him … that pig."

"Tell me: if you hate him so, why did you stay?"

"I don't like old men."

"There are plenty of young men besides Bruno."

"All the young men are poor."

"But Bruno gave you nothing."

"I didn't want anything."

"In fact, he used *your* money."

"For food, only."

He waited a moment.

"Well, at least they should have paid for half."

Still simmering and filled to the brim came the bowl of soup. It was too hot for his lips, so he began cooling it with a rhythmic lifting and spilling movement of his spoon, while clouds of steam climbed into the air. But Alice seemed to have no trouble with the soup. She drank a spoonful right down after blowing on it.

"They *had* money," she admitted. "I knew it."

"Is that why you're mad?"

"No, I don't care."

"You hate him, then, for the way he treated you?"

"The son-of-a-bitch," the girl whispered to herself.

Feeling the discomfort of being close to anger that he could not calm, he busied himself with the job of getting the soup down. It was so hot he couldn't taste it.

"He kicked me out," she said suddenly. "He had one more day before going back. He even said so. But the no-good pig—he kicked me out."

For the first time he realized how far apart they had been all this while.

"Well, you're going to see that old man tonight," he said, trying to comfort her. "At least *he* won't kick you out."

"Old men!" She grimaced the words with great distaste. "I just can't stand old men. They're so sickly sweet and gentle. I hate it."

She took several long swallows of soup, one right after the other, and then, as if it had been some magic fluid, she became herself again.

"I went to a wedding today." She smiled, and then she rambled into a long, detailed description of the ceremony and how everyone looked and how beautiful everything was. She did not stop even when her dish of roast pork was placed in front of her. But Andrew heard very little of what she said. He was too fascinated by the look of near ecstasy on her face as she talked about the wedding.

"I'm going to be married myself soon," she said abruptly. Her statement surprised him, for with uncanny timing it answered a question that had just flitted into his mind.

"Oh?"

"He's going to send me money so I can go up to London and marry him."

"Soon?"

"In a month or two."

He thought: Is this the same old line? Salvation just over the next hill? Marriage, the savior of princess and prostitute?

"Oh, but the wedding was beautiful," she said as she worked her knife and fork. "Some people are just lucky. That girl who got married. She went through the whole thing a year before. A wedding just as nice. She had been divorced, you know."

"In *this* country?"

"Oh, the church allowed it."

"The Catholic Church allowed it?"

"Yes, it was annulled. Something was wrong with him ... I don't know ... It seems that in bed he was no good."

He was aware of time moving with great slowness. They were sitting across from each other at the table casually eating, but impatience began silently to threaten him.

"He wasn't a homo, either," she said.

"How do you know?"

"A friend of mine knows them both well."

"What happened?"

"I don't know. They stayed together for a couple of months before she couldn't take it no more. She told her priest even before she told her mother. He said for her to try again, but she just couldn't any more. The priest had a talk with the boy and I don't know what happened, but they finally got the marriage annulled."

"I mean, what happened? They tried for months and they couldn't work it, huh?"

"He kept saying she wasn't good-looking enough. Things like that. When I first heard about it I felt so sorry for her."

She broke off some bread and buttered it with her knife.

"Does she hate him for it?" he asked quietly as his finger pushed at the ash tray.

"They say she will not speak of it. She never mentions his name."

Into the room came a warm silence that made him feel a little sleepy. There were three other people eating there besides themselves. Seated against the opposite wall were a mother, a father, and their young son. The little noises that knives and forks make when people are in a restaurant had no effect on the silence.

"Your food is getting cold," Alice said.

"Yes, so it is." And he cut slowly into the meat. He was aware that her eyes were on him, so he purposely worked on and achieved a smile.

The streets were now a patchwork of wet and dry. The fall of footsteps sounded almost metallic across the cracked concrete of the sidewalk. She was close beside him, her hand gently holding his arm.

"I'll be late if I don't hurry."

But she made no move to increase their pace.

"Let me ride you over on the cycle."

"The what?"

"Motorcycle."

"Go on," she said, as if being teased. But he simply nodded his head, and she added, "Really?"

It took him a while to convince her that he would actually take her for a ride.

"Is it dangerous?"

"Terribly," he said.

"Good."

Once, while Andrew was in Valencia, Alice had heard Bruno and the others talking about the motorcycle. El Greco, who appeared interested in its make, asked if anyone had actually seen it. The Señora offered the information that Andrew had done some racing with it in North America. Everyone seemed impressed, and now she was actually going to ride on it herself.

After they walked a few steps, the thrill of what they were about to do came over her as a delayed reaction and she swiveled, clapped her hands together and, with a beaming face, said, "Ohhhh!!" And then, a moment later: "Really?"

The cycle was waiting in the street where he had left it. For a moment he worried that Bruno and the rest of them would come out while he and Alice were there at the curb. But he decided they probably had all gone to dinner some time ago. The blonde needed no coaxing. Men occasionally showed fear of riding with him, but never women. Though she wore a dress she straddled the rear passenger seat with ease and clasped the rubber ring firmly with each hand without having to be told. He knew he should go and get his crash helmet, but he was too lazy. There were two pairs of goggles in the saddlebags. One pair he gave to her. Beneath the rubber and plastic that now encased the upper part of her face her mouth beamed like that of a happy child.

"Now my friends should see me."

"They wouldn't know you," he shouted, starting the engine.

Carried along swiftly, they felt the wind paste their hair flat against their heads and work with feverish little fingers at their clothes. The damp side-streets of the great city echoed like little canyons to the roar of the machine. On the dry main boulevards he opened it up to give her a thrill. At one point he heard her squeal with delight. She directed him by first tapping on his shoulder and then shouting into his ear. Occasionally, when he looked back, her smile was still there beaming into the wind.

At last they approached an imposing building and she told him to stop. The ride was over, and the look of a child that had been on her face was now gone. She climbed off and silently removed her goggles. This left a rim of red across the white skin of her forehead. With a quick, careless hand she made an attempt to arrange her hair. Andrew looked at the tall building and wondered behind which of the many windows that sent light itno the darkness sat the old man.

"He lives on the top floor," she said.

At the very top and on the extreme left he saw the window.

"Who is the bastard, anyway?" he asked, looking at the tiny light.

"Just some fogy. I see him every Sunday."

The motor idled uselessly, puffing wisps of thin smoke from the exhaust pipe.

She looked at her watch and said, "I really have to go."

"Well, go then. I'm not keeping you."

Immediately he was sorry for the way he had spoken.

"You know how to get back?" she asked gently.

"Yes, I think so."

"Thanks again for the meal."

She looked so sad. But as soon as she left, he knew why. She waved once before she disappeared. Behind the curtained inner door of the apartment house he caught a glimpse of stairs going up. Then his own loneliness appeared from out of the shadows where it had been lurking, waiting for the first moment it would find him alone.

14

THE WRINKLED face looked like that of a drunken monkey. In a fit of laughter, with mouth open, lips drawn back, and eyes tight shut, the face showed a row of twisted, partly blackened teeth, as if revealing a deep personal secret. The head bobbed helplessly on the shoulders, while the rest of the body, scantily covered with sagging underwear, shook rhythmically.

"Phew," El Greco said.

"Christ," Bruno said, and then he started to laugh too. Like little boys, they hunched over and giggled together. El Greco leaned weakly against the wall while Bruno slapped his bare leg triumphantly.

"Jesus."

"Huh?" Bruno asked, with an upward pitch of his voice.

Then they both fell to giggling again, and the sound cut through the hallway.

"Shhh!" the Señora warned. "... Bianca." Smiling, she was standing in a pair of men's pajamas.

"Ah, she's a cherry," said Bruno waving off the warning. "All cherries sleep well."

There was a sudden conspiracy of hushed laughter.

It was Bruno who first noticed him. The young man was standing a few feet away with a look of vague displeasure on his face, watching them.

"What happened to you?" the Texan asked.

"What?"

"Where have you been for crysake?"

"Oh … traveling," he said. His tongue seemed thick and lacking in practice, and he had to chew each word, doubtful about its success until each syllable had actually been spoken. He was terribly drunk.

"The hell with that," Bruno said. "Have a drink."

"No. It's O.K."

"Have a drink, anyway." The Texan spoke sternly.

Andrew lifted a fifth of whiskey out of his side pocket and dangled the bottle by the neck. "It's O.K., see?" he said.

The Señora chuckled softly. "We all drink tonight, I think."

A voice called from inside the bedroom. Albina answered in Spanish, a whiskey smile clinging to her lips without her knowing it. In the dark bedroom two legs swung off the bed to the floor and a woman who was introduced as Lola came out into the hall. She was more drunk than the rest. She went into a little dance, kicking her dress high with her knee and loudly humming the music of the cancan. Albina joined in. Out of breath, Lola stopped. In a brief effortless movement the top of her dress came open and one of her ample breasts was resting in her hand. "Much spaghettis," she said, "much spaghettis." At this the Señora exploded with laughter. Lola casually buttoned her dress again.

With the slow-witted understanding that was familiar to him after too much drinking, Andrew realized that his upraised arm was still exhibiting the bottle of whiskey, his fingers holding it by the neck. He put the mouth of the bottle to his lips and tossed himself a swallow. He had intended to come back late, when they were all asleep. But he had not come back late enough and so had landed smack in the middle of it. Stupid! Three cheers for stupid Andrew. The dance of the cancan swirled briefly along the edges of his mind, but suddenly it was gone. Three cheers for Andrew. Thoughts rushed through his head like film in a movie projector that was being run too fast. Only the bottle was his friend and he clutched it tightly. He wanted to go to his room. Just him and his bottle in the room. He began to walk.

"Where you headed?" Bruno asked. "You got to have a drink."

Andrew held up the bottle.

"Hell, man, that's almost dead."

It was the truth. Holding it up, Andrew peered inside and found it was almost empty.

"We got to get you a *man*-sized. drink."

Albina said: "We drink too much, I think."

The Texan put his arm around Andrew's shoulder, watching him pour the last drop into his mouth.

"Them bottles ain't big enough," he said. "Hell, you never should buy it that size."

"Phew," said El Greco, still leaning against the wall.

"Ah," the Señora said. "*Here* it is."

They all swung around and saw Leopold studying them sheepishly from inside a grotesquely wrinkled and high-collared raincoat. He said nothing, but his face bore an alcoholic grin. The nose jutting upward was flushed red, and the rimless glasses were definitely off center.

"You see," Albina announced, as if proving a point, "we *all* drink."

"How long you been here?" asked the Texan, as if a trick had been played on him.

"Come," said Albina, extending her arms to Leopold in a motherly gesture, "you look sad."

"No, he doesn't," Andrew heard himself say.

"Much spaghettis," said Lola.

In answer to her call, Leopold came over and put his arm around Albina in a grandfatherly gesture, his eyes dim and stupid with cognac. After a while his free hand gradually began encircling Albina's waist, but she only smiled and pushed it away.

"Look at her," Albina said pointing to Lola. "I never see such a thing. I am small, you know? But she is something."

The muffled sound of a flushing toilet came to them from behind several walls. Down at the end of the hall the bathroom door swung open and from around it walked another woman. Seeing her coming toward them, Lola once again became filled with energy.

It sent her into another dance and she tried to hold a knee high while making circles with her foot, but the cognac had given her gaiety without ability, and she almost lost her balance. Grace, the newcomer, seemed embarrassed and smiled at everyone politely.

"Where you been?" Bruno asked her in English, though he knew she didn't understand.

Grace did not answer.

"A quickie," Bruno announced and promptly dragged her off into the bedroom.

"Shhh," Albina said with worried eyes.

The Señora and Lola exchanged a few words and then both laughed. Albina turned to Andrew. "I ask her if she finished. She said—" pointing to El Greco—" 'He finished, not me.' "

The Greek, still leaning against the wall, grinned absent-mindedly.

Leopold whispered into the Señora's ear and she smiled, but shook her head.

Andrew noticed a bottle of bourbon on the floor. Good grief, I'm drunk, he thought. There was that familiar roar in his ear again, and he could do nothing without grotesque exaggeration or abruptness. But he was worrying about the letdown. He looked again. The bourbon was still there. He bent over and took hold of the bottle. Then he stood up and reeled like a wounded giant at the novelty of height. I should ask first, he thought. I should be polite, because the whiskey is not mine. But the lecture he gave himself did no good, and he lifted the bottle and drank. It stung his throat and reminded him how much he disliked bourbon. He took a second swallow and that burned, too. I should have asked first, he repeated to himself, pointlessly.

Behind him people were talking and moving about, but he had turned his back to the world. Somewhere muffled drums seemed to be thundering a tribute to him. The sound inspired him as he stared at the wall. It needed a coat of paint. The whole hallway needed a coat of paint. Three cheers for Andrew, the observer of walls. He heard a noise. The loud stamping of a foot on the wooden floor. He turned, then reeled slowly with the novelty of turning. El Greco looked confused. He had Lola by the hand and was trying to pull her to the door. She was resisting and stamping her foot.

"She wants *you*," said Albina, smiling at Andrew.

El Greco seemed relieved by what was happening.

"Come on, man, give her a good time." It was Bruno, standing in his white shorts like a Greek god. He had appeared suddenly from nowhere. He spoke loudly to Andrew over the roar that the whiskey was making in the air, telling him to take Lola to his room because he, Bruno, wanted her himself, but that Andrew must go first. He was quite emphatic.

Where was El Greco now? He was gone. It was all very confusing.

"Come on, man," Bruno said. "Move it, huh?"

These words slowly pushed their way through the many layers of cognac and whiskey until suddenly they hit a nerve.

Andrew was surprised by the savage sound of his own voice. "I don't want the job, damn it! Leave me alone!"

"She's waiting for you. Christ, man."

"Look, I'm just not interested!" And as he shouted the words, listening as if they had been spoken into his own ear, he realized that there were fears even whiskey could not help.

"Sounds to me like you're scared."

Andrew lifted his voice above the roar of muffled drums. "Don't be stupid!"

"What's with this guy, anyway?" asked the Texan, his arms spread wide.

They were standing further down the dim hallway now and Andrew was trying to remember how they got there. A weight tugged at his arm, and he discovered he was still holding the whiskey bottle. There was a babble of confused voices all around, but he had difficulty understanding. The roar inside his head was almost too loud. Albina spoke against the voices in hushed, quieting tones. Time after time she reminded them to speak softly because Bianca was asleep. Bruno looked angry, while Lola alternated her moods between giving Andrew a coquettish smile and then stamping her foot in protest at his inaction.

The crazy swirl of sound seemed to have nothing to do with him. Andrew leaned against the wall and swallowed another sting of whiskey. But, strangely, there was one voice he did hear clearly. It was Leopold, lying on the bed in his room, calling to Albina. He was still wearing his raincoat. Andrew reached out, touched her on the shoulder, and pointed into the other room. Without even looking up she gave a little grin, indicating that she too had heard.

"I don't dare," she said.

Then the chaos took a playful turn. Half-carried, half-pushed, Andrew found himself slowly being transported toward his own room. Lola was on one side and Bruno on the other, but the Texan was doing most of the work. Behind him he could hear the Señora softly laughing. At first it was fun. He tried to hold his ground by digging in with his feet and throwing back his weight, but slowly he was forced to give way. The Texan's arm was bruising his back, and when he tried to escape its semicircle, the arm closed like a vise around his waist. Suddenly it was no longer fun. But he had to continue the pretense for fear that anything else he did would make him look like a fool.

Gradually they worked him closer and closer to his door. As the three of them struggled, the bottle in his hand struck his own knee accidentally, and for a moment he felt pain, as well as anger. He caught a glimpse of the Texan's face. It wasn't smiling. This startled him and it was then, at that moment, as the door to his room came within reach, that he suddenly knew he was going to fight. It was as if a decision had been made for him somewhere miles away and he had only to wait patiently for it and finally it would come. The message surprised him, for he had come to expect panic, but instead came only anger.

He did not mind the noise now. What the hell did *he* care? He was going to fight. To free his right hand, he shifted the bottle to his left. He was ready. He would have liked to have taken another swallow first, but there wasn't time. He hoped he was not too drunk, and at the last moment before he stopped thinking he realized why it was he felt so good. It was because he no longer cared at all whether or not he would make a fool of himself.

In one violent moment, concentrating all his strength, he tore himself free and landed against the wall. Bruno stared at him with surprise, his mouth open and ready to smile. Stepping back from the sudden display of masculine strength, Lola studied them with annoyance. "Shhh," Albina said from the other end of the hall. Bruno stepped closer, his hands ready to take hold again.

"Stand back, you dumb bastard," Andrew heard his voice say.

He clutched the bottle to his chest as if it were the whiskey he was trying to protect. He lifted his right arm and clenched his fist. Bruno was halted by surprise, as if he had just opened a familiar closet and found a dark stranger waiting inside.

"What the hell's eating you?"

"Game's over. Stand back."

The gleefulness drained from Bruno's eyes. He was staring as though at a leper. It was a look Andrew would never forget.

"Come on. Come on."

"I said I'm not interested, damn it! She doesn't attract me."

The Texan's face went blank. This idea was new to him. He struggled briefly to grasp its meaning, and then dismissed the whole thing as odd and unnatural.

"What's the matter, you queer?"

A foot stamped angrily on the wooden floor. There was a flash of Spanish, and Lola marched away. Neither of them noticed that she had gone. Bruno's mouth seemed about to smile again and his hands reached out. The upraised fist meant nothing to him. The powerful hands grasped Andrew by each shoulder and pulled him away from the wall. He was turned like a puppet until he faced the door. The fist that hung like a warning in the air did not move. The game was about to start again. Then he heard it.

But it seemed to be so far away. First that awful, splintering sound, then the heavy fall, and the dim passageway was quiet again. Odd, Andrew thought, as he waited for something more to happen. Bruno was speaking. "What the hell...?" Everyone turned in the direction of the sound. For a moment there was nothing to see. Then a door opened quietly and El Greco came out. He was barefoot and wearing only his white cotton shorts. His face was a mask of sleepy boredom. He looked up to find them all watching him.

"I need more nails and a hammer," he said.

15

AFTER HE took another drink (which he didn't need, because the happy insurrection in his head was going full tilt) he worked his unsteady feet forward toward his room. Once inside, he slammed the door and leaned hard against it. Now, for the first time that evening, he felt safe. The room was dark and he left it that way. He did not need light. The shade was drawn and roped tight, and a faint glow from the dim hall lamp drew a thin long line under the door. He found the bed and sat on it, hearing the creak of its spring. He held the whiskey close to him and stared into dark space. The universe, it seemed, waited for him to start thinking. The universe had great patience, and it waited, and he stiffened himself against it.

He lay on the bed, the bottle standing on his stomach like a monument held between both hands. He decided it was time to drink again. He put the bottle to his mouth but forgot that he was lying down and spilled some on his face. Liquor, the perfume of the timeless. Three cheers for Andrew! The lurching in his head carried his thoughts off in the strangest directions. He had heard it said that liquor would keep a man from killing himself.

Once, years ago, an old man living down the street from Andrew's house had killed himself and shocked the entire neighborhood. He had not really known this old man and had never talked to him, but over the years he had seen him too often to think of him as a stranger. They said he did it because he was ill, but they couldn't explain why, if he was so ill, he never failed to go for his evening walks. Andrew remembered seeing him many times, passing slowly through the dark streets, always alone, never seeming to go anywhere, just aimlessly walking. Sometimes Andrew would meet him miles from home, moving as if in a dream, bundled warmly against the winds of winter, or wearing a sweater on the warmest nights of summer. He never walked fast, and his eyes rarely turned to notice the life around him. Andrew would always marvel at what had led the old man on that bitter journey of sixty years through all those twists and turns of life, through good fortune and bad, closer day by day to that last moment when, with his children and grandchildren out to an evening movie, he placed a Colt .45 into his mouth and blew the back of his head, like the guts of a cat, all over the cellar wall.

He let himself think about all this because he wanted, desperately, to avoid thinking about something else. In the dark, Andrew took the glass monument from his stomach and brought it to his mouth. Another bubble of whiskey warmed its way down his throat. He peered up at the ceiling he could not see, and he seemed to notice sparks of light in the air. But when he tried to see them clearly, they suddenly vanished. Then a crescendo of lurching silences whirled and roared with him through space while he lay quietly on the bed and dared not move.

There was the stealthy sound of a knob turning slowly, followed by a long pause. Then the door swung casually open, someone came in, and with a gentle rattle the door swung shut again. Now there was a rhythmic breathing in the room, but it was hardly audible, and as he strained his eyes against the darkness he was aware only that someone stood there. He could see nothing more.

"Who is it?" he asked, realizing that he had not kept his voice casual.

The darkness waited.

"Who *is* it?"

This time he spoke angrily. He listened carefully, but could hear nothing. He was seeing sparks again, sharp and white, but when he tried to see them in detail, they disappeared. The darkness waited with great patience. Everything had patience. It was incredible how much patience there was in the world. And yet he seemed to have none. Then he heard the key turning slowly in the lock, the metallic click that fastened a door, and then the sound of a key being carefully withdrawn. He felt a shiver slither over his skin. It was like a slap of cold water. He placed the bottle on the floor next to his bed. Reaching for the table lamp, he fumbled so badly trying to find the switch that he half expected his phantom visitor to laugh at him. Then he found it. The lamp belched light, caught him in the eyes, and then the room went dead. Slowly the blackness returned and as he lay on the bed he cursed the bulb for blowing out. He swung his leg over the bed and sat up, lifting his dizziness with him. The whole thing seemed so stupid. He tried to get to his feet secretly, but the creak of the bedspring gave him away. The silence waited for someone to speak, but no one did. Then there was a new sound, and he was aware that someone was moving closer. He placed his feet apart, bent his hand into a fist and got ready. The scent of weak perfume moved vaguely toward him and sank into his lungs. Slowly his fist unfolded while his arm went down to his side. But now fright began to take over. The silence continued. Then a strange hand, which somehow knew its way in the dark, was suddenly, gently placed on him. He doubled up slightly as if he had been struck. In sudden panic, he bolted past her and with the flat of his hand sliding along the wall, he searched for the switch by the door. The ceiling light went on. He watched Lola coming toward him, clutching the key behind her back.

You're so silly, her face seemed to say. It's *because* you are shy that I like you so. Andrew turned the knob and rattled the door, but as he had feared, it was locked. Standing, half-turned with indecision, he noticed the shadow of himself trapped against the wall.

Señora Albina sat down. She was exhausted. Her two guests had gone home. At last the moment had arrived when there was nothing more for her to do. Everything had come to a halt as soon as the two women had departed. El Greco lay on his bed, his eyes hypnotized by the ceiling.

"Phew," he said, after a long pause. "I'm glad *that's* over."

Near him sat the Texan, his head hanging between his knees, as if he were trying to look under the bed. He did not move. Andrew had climbed up on the table near the window. His legs dangled in the air. Like Bruno, he too stared at the floor, as if in a trance. No one risked using the bed that twice had collapsed. Only the small lamp was on. It threw into deep shadow half of everyone's face. The silence seeped in through the walls and cast a pall over them. It was as if a great battle had just been fought and they were all trying to regain strength. With his back inches from the open window, Andrew felt a surprisingly cool breeze push through his shirt and finger his skin.

The Señora was the first to speak. "She is funny, no?"

"Who?" Andrew asked the ceiling.

"Lola," she said, and smiled.

El Greco politely agreed, but now the Señora was chuckling softly to herself and did not hear him.

"You had a good time?" she asked a few moments later.

"We always have a good time."

"He—," she said, secretly indicating the Texan, "did he have a good time, you think?" The question seemed important to her.

The little Greek looked at his friend and turned away. He held up his hand to Albina and nodded his head quickly. There was uneasiness in his eyes and his whole manner seemed to say: Yes, yes, but now we must be careful.

"And you?" said the Señora. Andrew looked up slowly and found her eyes holding his. Her face revealed nothing, but it was too intense to be neutral. He felt the chill of disapproval.

"I...I did just fine."

Silence.

"What happened to Leopold?" asked the Greek.

With a grin, she said, "Asleep." He understood and smiled.

Pulling the collar of her pajama top closed, Albina threw her shoulders forward as if chilled. No one moved.

"The worst meat I ever had," Bruno growled softly. His head still hung loosely at the neck, his eyes on the floor. "I hate old meat." His head sprang up like an animal sensing danger. Then he was on his feet, heading for the closet. The small light played dimly on his naked body, coloring it yellow. His voice was strong now but he seemed to be talking to himself. "The worst I ever had. Where's the good meat at? Ain't there no good stuff in this town?"

Silence, while they watched him climb savagely into his pants.

"Worst I ever had."

"Be nice," the Señora begged.

"Where you going?" El Greco asked. He was sitting up now and his eyes had suddenly cleared.

"*Out!*"

"You're going out?" Albina asked, not able to understand. "Why?"

"Because the meat here stunk."

"You don't talk like that," El Greco pleaded.

Bruno quickly buttoned his shirt. His hands tried to hurry.

Albina said: "You didn't have enough?"

"Hell, no."

"I cannot believe this," she said, looking around the room for help.

Bruno was on the bed now, swiftly putting on his shoes and socks. He grumbled angrily, as if he were protesting a great injustice. The Señora eyed him with the enchantment of a child seeing a village juggler for the first time. Her face became young with reverence, and Andrew watched the transformation with envy.

The colossus stood up and announced his battle cry. "Women!" he shouted. Then he put on his tie.

Both Albina and El Greco cried, "No!" without realizing they had spoken.

"How can he do this?" she asked. "I don't understand."

"First a drink," Bruno shouted. He left the room to hunt for a bottle. The little Greek climbed wearily to his feet. His pants and shirt had been hung over the point of the bedpost and he removed them slowly and put them on.

"I never saw a guy like this one," he said. "He never stops. He's been at it all night. I see it with my own eyes. Now he wants more." The little Greek shook his head. "I never saw such a thing. Never. But I must go with him. I can't let him go alone. I don't want a woman, but I'll go with him. I can't let him go alone."

"Why does he do this?" she asked.

"I don't know. Nothing satisfies him. He is always hunting. And afterward he is more hungry than before. I don't understand. I am his friend and I don't understand."

She turned to Andrew. "Why?" The question was in her and had to be answered.

Andrew knew, without looking up, that she had spoken to him.

"He knows he won't find what he's looking for, that's why he's looking so hard."

"For what is he looking?"

"To disprove a weakness."

"But he is not *weak*, certainly." And she almost laughed.

"Then why is he not happy?"

"Oh, maybe he is weak in other places."

"I think we are weakest where we seem to show the most strength."

She stared at him for a moment as he sat on the table gazing at the floor. She turned away and looked at El Greco as he buttoned his shirt. She began asking more questions, but Andrew was no longer listening.

Bruno returned with a bottle of cognac in his hand. "Who wants?" he asked, holding it up. No one did, so he put the bottle to his mouth.

"Let's go," he cried. And he marched out, carrying the bottle with him. Something drew them all after him, and in a moment the room was empty. In the dim hallway Bruno whirled and pointed his arm at them like a sword. "You!" he said, "come with us."

Andrew took a step back and put up his hand as if stopping traffic. He felt himself flush with surprise.

"No, no," he said. "You go ahead."

"Come on, man. We're going to hunt us up some meat."

He leaned forward and grabbed Andrew by the wrist. Like a trapped animal, Andrew tried to pull away. Bruno's eyes were blank and faraway. But his grip was steel. It reminded Andrew of another fist, one with a key in it, and of a devilish smile that had turned his room into a prison.

He would always remember. Like two children they had wrestled for the key as if it were a game. Fear chased after him, but it gave him purpose. It is good to have a purpose. They struggled for the key and both fell to the floor. He felt foolish and worthless. But he kept struggling. He twisted cruelly the skin of her wrist with all his strength. Her hand opened finally and stayed open like a starfish and the key clattered to the floor and he scrambled for it. Then he saw her face. The smile had gone and in its place there was a hint of tears. Had *he* done this? He watched with opened mouth, unable to speak, unable to explain, as her face filled with loathing. He felt the sag of hopelessness, having heard the hollow sound a blunder makes as it echoes and re-echoes through a man's mind. He hated himself more than she or anyone could possibly hate him.

"Let's go, man."

His arm was being pulled out so far that he feared it might leave his body.

What was happening to him, anyway? Was he the only sane one in this madhouse? Oh, God, the last thing in the world he wanted to do was to make love to Bruno's hungry, smiling women. Where was the love he had heard so much about? And when did sex alone ever cure the loneliness of a single human heart?

He was being drawn toward the door and for a moment felt completely powerless. But he knew that he must make himself free, must isolate himself forever. He borrowed strength from fear and with a gritting of the teeth he tore himself free. The momentum sent him reeling to the opposite wall. Bruno turned around and his eyes gleamed.

"Leave him," El Greco warned and he pushed his friend toward the door. "Forget him."

"More damn queers in this filthy town," the Texan complained bitterly.

He stood and watched Andrew for a moment as if he had found a great ugliness there.

Then they were both gone.

"Be careful," Albina called. The noise of their laughter echoed in the stairwell of the building. He listened until the sounds slowly grew distant and dissolved. His weight was still pressed against the wall. He didn't move. The two of them were alone. Albina turned, and for a moment she stared at him as if he were a slide under a microscope. Then she went into one of the empty bedrooms, her slippers shuffling across the floor, and swung open the French windows and leaned out happily and waited for them to appear below her in the lamplit street.

TWO

16

THE HISS of automobile tires on wet pavement reached him again through the window. Each gray morning he had slowly come awake to this sound, listening for it, yet hoping not to hear it. Now he lay there suffering his luck and thinking that soon he would have to go out into the drizzle, mount his cycle, and continue on his way. It had already rained for three days and for three nights, and he was sick of it. On this fourth and final morning it was still raining.

Each day he had to put on a large, black rubber cape which hung down around him, covering even the handle bars. A pair of special black rubber pants protected his legs, and motorman's gloves covered his hands. On his head was the silver crash helmet. Though the only part of him exposed was the lower part of his face, he somehow managed, during those three days, always to get soaked at his ankles and sometimes even around his neck. Also, his goggles kept steaming up and had to be wiped constantly. Beneath the layer of rubber that covered his body it got so warm that he often felt the perspiration glue his shirt to his back.

A week spent in Madrid had made him forget just how poor the Spanish roads were and how good had been those of the French. It took just a few minutes of riding to remind him. Motoring north from Madrid, he worked his way past Segovia and Burgos. Near Bayonne he crossed the border and turned east, heading for Toulouse, then the Riviera, and finally, beyond that, Italy. That became his goal. Bruno and the Señora were being left further and further behind.

As he traveled day after day over the good roads and the bad, he discovered that he had developed an obsession. The obsession was saving time. Up at dawn, eat quickly, keep going, get gas, keep going, save time. And all the while holding him back, slowing him down, was that damned rain. He grew to hate it. This too became an obsession.

There were also those strange gaps in his mind that had to be filled with thought. He tried to think only of the rain or of the road passing beneath him, but his mind would not behave. He felt the old, familiar pressure of worry. No matter how fast he drove, he couldn't seem to get away from it. The trees were passing him in double, regimented rows, disappearing swiftly on either side. He tried to concentrate on the memory of a bright and carefree day long ago. But unwanted thoughts crowded him menacingly. Once again he found himself on a furious merry-go-round, rehashing a problem that seemed to bother not one of the other men he knew. All such bitter thoughts he silently tried to shout down. His head was filled with wild denials. Then, when it seemed he had tormented himself to the limit, he began the agony all over again, as though his appetite for pain was unquenchable. Meanwhile, the rain kept lashing his face, but he did not feel it, the trees continued to rush by, but he no longer saw them.

There was movement around him. He didn't understand. Didn't care. Whiteness. He sensed the motion of something white. It was large and close to him. There were several of them and they were moving and he didn't care. He was sitting up. It was rather easy. One leg was stretched out and the other was bent at the knee. He was leaning on his right hand. It was very easy. People in white costumes were moving about him. They were talking, but they said nothing. Something was being done to his neck. If he turned his head he would be able to find out what it was, but he didn't bother. They were all friends and very close to him, although he didn't know who they were. He didn't want to know. It was the feeling.

The feeling was everything. He felt something on his shirt. It was soaked through. He could tell by the way it clung to his chest. It was all over his rubber pants, too, but the rubber prevented him from feeling it. And it wasn't water. It looked like a stain. What could it be that had stained him? He tried to think. They were still moving around him, the strangers he almost knew. Odd, that nothing was clear, that nothing stayed together in his mind long enough for him to get a good hold on it. He was trying to think. It wasn't easy. He looked at himself again. Blood! That's what it was. Blood. And it was *his* blood! *His own blood!* Oh, God. An accident. He must have been hurt in an accident. But this couldn't happen. This was supposed to be a vacation. Had it really taken place? Oh, God. All his clothes had been stained with his own blood and he had been in an accident. He had been hurt. Oh, God.

"How did it happen?" he asked.

A nurse was securing a bandage around his neck. It felt tight. Another nurse was standing by and watching. No one answered. He was seated on an emergency table, his feet out in front of him. He was still trying to think. There were so many things he did not know. Could he remember how it happened? He tried, but it would not work. He attempted to move his mind back into the past, but it became cumbersome and didn't behave. He could recall rain falling on the streets, the rhythmic, vibrant movement of the cycle, and the wind stroking his nose and mouth. He could recall the wet shining roads and on either side, as far as he could see, the strong, silently rooted trees. All that was easy. It came to him repeatedly, always remembered in the same way, as if it were on film. But he could recall nothing else.

"How did it happen?" he asked.

This time someone answered him. She spoke clearly and calmly, and he listened with wild attention. But when it was over, he knew nothing of what had been said. He kept listening, even after the words stopped coming, hoping that understanding would arrive soon afterward. But it did not.

"God damn it," he said.

His blood was all over him. God, how could he have bled so much? So it had really happened. Jesus Christ. It was beginning to scare him.

"God damn it," he called loudly.

No one answered. When he spoke they didn't even bother to look his way. Suddenly fury at his bad luck took hold of him and he erupted with a string of angry curse words. They seemed not to hear.

Someone was speaking, but not to him. A swift, unemotional command, and then one of the nurses left the room to do something. The words that had just been spoken hung in the air and he studied them. Once again they had no meaning. They just hung there. Then all at once he knew. Of course.

They were speaking French!

He must really have gotten it on the head, he thought. Must be getting punchy. Four years of it in school, and then suddenly you don't know what the hell it is. Well, here goes. He looked up at the nurse standing near him and spoke to her in cautious French.

"Good afternoon."

"Good afternoon." She smiled back.

So far, so good.

"I desire to speak with a person English."

Was that right? Is that the way French sounds? He was beginning to wonder if he were all there. But still, his words seemed to work. The nurse didn't laugh. She didn't even smile. She simply nodded her head and replied: "Yes, in a moment."

Ah, he thought, if only good old Mr. Bartlett back in high school could see me now.

It was then that he became aware of a doctor working on him close to his left side. He must have been there all along. Slowly his left arm was being placed into a sling and then moved so that it would rest across his chest. A warm, dull, friendly pain began moving through his elbow. The young man almost enjoyed it, and as the doctor worked, silently moving the arm, the patient sat and watched the operation with interest. It was the only thing he could be sure of, this pain—the only thing that had no mystery. But all at once came a different pain and it knifed up the center of his arm to his shoulder. The young man hunched up and his body became rigid. Only afterward, when he saw that the doctor was aware of the pain he had caused, did the young man loosen up again. Before they could get his arm fully in front of him and hanging freely in the sling, the brief wild pain returned twice more, but each time he was ready for it and it was not as bad.

The next thing to do, it suddenly occurred to him, was to ask them in French if they knew how the accident had happened. As he was phrasing the right words, forcing into action his rusty knowledge of the language, someone entered the room and, with a friendly voice that was anxious with concern, said to him in English: "For heaven's sake, my child, what has happened to you?"

It was the language that did it. The surprising sound of those familiar words filled the room and returned his tongue to him. He was a mute no longer. Now he could say all of the things he wanted to say and ask all of the things he wanted to ask. But the sudden realization of all this struck him dumb again. The concern and understanding and pity that he found in that voice flooded him with weakness and confusion. His eyes began to fill and he knew that if he tried to speak he would begin to cry.

The one who now stood before him—she who had just spoken—was an old-faced, black-robed nun. He avoided her eyes. Then noticing the window for the first time he saw that outside it had suddenly become night. Where had time gone? An entire afternoon had been stolen from him.

"Are you badly hurt?" asked the old nun, preparing herself to share his grief.

After pausing a moment to try to collect himself, he ventured a sentence or two, steering them carefully through his now treacherous and uncontrolled emotions.

"I don't feel much pain .... I don't think so."

"Good, good. And tell me. Is there anything you need?"

"I don't think so."

"Now, tell me," she asked with concern, "how did all this happen to you?"

The young man paused for another moment and then shook his head. Seeing how she stared at him, he was aware for the first time of what an awful sight he must look.

"I don't really remember."

The nun turned and spoke to the doctor in French. The young man was too busy trying to control himself to follow. This constant threat of tears was beginning to anger him.

"Well, it seems they don't know, either," she explained, turning back to him. "They claim they'll have all the facts tomorrow." She spoke as if she were apologizing.

"My arm," he said. "Ask them how my arm is."

Immediately, she turned to the doctor.

"They say it is not broken. But only badly sprained."

"I see." Then all at once he was himself again. He grinned. "Well, listen, you can't have everything."

She responded warmly with a slight smile, but she was really concerned less with what he had said, than with the fact that he was able to say it.

"I'm glad you're in such good spirits," she said. "Ah, but I see that they wish to take you to your bed."

She bade him good-by. But at the door she stopped as if she had forgotten something. "Now, do you realize that I don't know your name?" She seemed to be scolding herself.

"I'm sorry. My name is Andrew Williams."

"Ah, yes," she said, as though by some mystic appointment she had been expecting him all along. She smiled and left.

The hallway through which they wheeled him was dark and ominous. The air seemed heavy with the presence of sleep and everything was broodingly quiet. One of the wheels of the movable table to which they had transferred him squeaked incessantly on the linoleum floor. He was brought into a small room where there were two beds, one of which was occupied by someone deep in sleep.

They removed both of his shoes and from out of them, onto the table, poured two small mounds of what looked at first like sand. But it sounded metallic, and when he looked closer he saw that they were pieces of finely broken glass. Two nurses, with the help of an attendant, lifted him into bed and removed his clothes. When he saw his underwear, he realized that he had also bled from the lower parts of his body. A needle jabbed his right arm and then he saw that they were hanging a bottle of plasma high at the head of his bed. A long rubber tube hung down in the darkness to join with his skin. He realized suddenly that he was very tired, and that it was a great effort for him to pay attention to anything. He tried to remember if they had given him a pill. Yes, he remembered, they had. But where had they put his clothes? He had forgotten to look. And his cycle? How badly smashed was it? Was it stolen? And his money? He recalled that it was still in his saddlebag. And his camera? Were they lying out there somewhere in the night? Tomorrow. He'd worry about it all tomorrow. Now he would sleep. It was good to sleep. It was very good.

17

THE WINDOW shade rolled up with a start and a harsh, bright light suddenly flooded the little room. The young man turned his head on the pillow and squinted at the door. It was open. Had someone come in? Then he saw a woman moving away from the window. It was a nurse, fat and matronly. She was smiling as if this were to be the luckiest day of her life.

"*Bon jour.*" She laughed and asked him how he was. He was fine. She was glad to hear it. Then she looked at the man in the other bed, studied him silently, shrugged her shoulders, and went out.

Andrew was stiff with sleep. He noticed a clock on the metal table: 6:05 A.M. Had there been a mistake? Slowly, interest in what the day would bring took hold of him, and fatigue gradually left him. He began to test his body. The more he moved his limbs, the more they ached; and the more they ached, the more he found that was wrong. Both knees, his left shin, his entire left arm, his left shoulder, his chest (especially when he took a deep breath), and his neck (stiff, as well as painful). On top of all this he also had a headache. A lulu of a headache.

He was considering going to sleep again when he heard a dull thumping in the hall. It was like the sound of a broom handle pounding heavily on the floor and it seemed to come nearer with each rhythmic stroke. Finally, when he thought it could not possibly get any louder, and while he was wondering what the hell it was, a large bearded man with a checkered bathrobe and a wooden leg came into view. He glanced at Andrew with an inquisitive look and then marched resolutely onward.

Breakfast came in on a wagon. It was rolled in by a friendly nurse whom he recognized as one who helped undress him **the** night before. A bowl of warm milk was placed on the little table next to his bed, along with two pieces of stale bread and a metal cup filled with wine. The same was placed on another table beside his roommate, but all that Andrew could see of him was the back of a half-pillowed head.

"Breakfast," the nurse said, but the head didn't move. She stood looking at the bed for a moment, then shook her head and went out. Right after breakfast she returned, though, with a pair of white cotton pajamas for Andrew to wear. Together, they gingerly undid the sling and carefully and slowly slipped the bad arm into the sleeve. Next came the ritual of the thermometer, for which Andrew had to roll onto his side facing the wall. Afterward she jotted the information down in a little book, placed Andrew's empty breakfast dishes into the food wagon and then, almost reluctantly, turned to the other bed.

"Well," she said, as if straining against fatigue, "are you eating?"

No answer.

"It is getting cold."

No answer.

Andrew thought that perhaps the man was asleep but the nurse, as if from experience, seemed certain that he was not. Holding the thermometer doubtfully in her hand she moved toward the bed.

"Time to take your temperature."

No answer.

"Look, it's my job."

Then, carefully, she placed her hand on the covers. But as her fingers touched the bed they set off a violent movement. There was an angry wild grunt and the covers were savagely pulled up over the patient's head. The nurse also reacted with brisk anger, but all she did was to turn from the bed with disgusted finality and push the food wagon from the room.

Afterward, Andrew noticed a change in the bed across the room from him. The man who had covered his head when the nurse came close to him was now lying on his back, his face exposed. He was staring with a long, melancholy silence at a crack at the ceiling. His delicate, almost feminine features were those of a man of about twenty-six. The face was tranquil, undisturbed, almost beautiful.

Andrew waited for what seemed to him a long time. He was anxious for someone else to come into the room, for something else to happen. Yet when it did, his mind had wandered off so he was taken by surprise. In rolled another wagon, this time cluttered with bottles and bandages, scissors and tapes, sticks and gauze. Walking on either side of it, as they rolled it through the doorway, came two young French nurses. Each, at first glance, looked exactly the opposite of the other.

The older, in her early twenties, lacked any physical appeal whatever. Her name, he later discovered, was Annette. She was short and heavy, yet without seeming fat.

Yvonne, on the other hand, was about two years younger. It was obvious from the moment she entered the room that she enjoyed completely the little world in which she lived, and, best of all, herself. She was deceptively attractive, for the greater part of her striking appearance was achieved somehow by her unshakable belief in the certainty of her loveliness. She wore her beauty as if there were no other gift a girl might own that could possibly please her more. She delighted in the special attention of men and their endless attempts to please her and make her laugh. She loved the compliments that were spoken to her to remind her how she looked—as if she could ever forget. She enjoyed the envious stares of other women and the dry-throated silences of some of the men. But she was pleased most of all by the confidence it gave her, for although she had not yet done everything she had secretly planned for herself, she knew in her heart that when the right time came, there would be nothing in the world she would be afraid to do.

Hers was far from a classic beauty. Above her waist there was nothing out of the ordinary to draw attention, and even her arms, though smooth of skin, seemed a little too thin. But below her waist was where the beauty began. Her long, lovely cheesecake legs were advertised most effectively by what could be seen of them below her white nurse's skirt. Her hips were wide, and the snugness of her skirt, which had been purposely taken in at the seam, displayed with subtle care the unusual fullness of her young buttocks. Wearing a long-sleeved sweater, with padding at the chest, she would make a fine, off-beat photo subject. Yet it was her face that put the stamp of success on her appearance. A slight hollowing of the cheeks made her full lips more prominent and disturbing. When she smiled, she appeared to be pulling her lips apart with an unusual effort, as if her teeth were about to bite into something.

This smile, Andrew discovered, was directed right at him. A strangely beautiful girl was smiling straight at him suddenly and he didn't feel the slightest anxiety at all. This in itself was unusual. In fact, he was surprised to find himself, with ease and enjoyment, grinning right back.

"You're the American," said Yvonne in French, and as she spoke her eyes had that lack of expression which meant she was paying the strictest attention. Annette absent-mindedly adjusted some of the jars in the medicine wagon. Both girls seemed to be waiting for someone.

"Yes, I am," he answered, amazed at how well his French was holding up, but wishing she would speak a little more slowly just the same.

"The one on the motorcycle," she continued, not asking but simply showing that she knew.

"The one no *longer* on the motorcycle," he corrected.

The pretty nurse laughed joyfully and nodded her head in agreement. Annette, on the other hand, did not look up, but on her white, expressionless face a ghostly smile appeared and vanished.

Before they could speak further there was a rustling at the doorway and in swept two faces disembodied and enveloped in black. The one leading the way was old and proud, but yet in such a happy rush that she almost came in on the run. The only thing about her that did not seem to be in a hurry was her engulfing, cheerful smile. This was the face of Sister Héloise, the Sister Superior of the hospital. She was the nun who had spoken to him in the emergency room the day before. When she entered, the two young nurses already in the room made an almost imperceptible move to attention. Though Sister Héloise, as well as everyone else, took her orders from the doctors, there was actually no higher authority in the whole hospital than the Sister Superior.

Right behind her, walking less swiftly, trying to be less obtrusive and yet somehow more prominent, was a Sister whose face immediately struck Andrew as one of the loveliest he had ever seen. It had the kind of beauty one did not associate with a living woman, but rather with a painting of a young girl by an old master. There was no need for her to smile to stress its joyfulness and when her features melted into deep seriousness the world of contemplation became a most appealing place indeed. For a time it was almost impossible for him to take his eyes from her. If he ever got his camera back, he would try to capture this face first of all.

To the young man's surprise the nuns swarmed to his bedside like a band of cheerful gossips surrounding a good story. Sister Veronica as well as the Sister Superior spoke perfect English. What they both wanted to know, after they had with kindness and patience asked him how he felt, was how it had all happened. But their enthusiasm came to an abrupt halt when they found that he knew no more than they; that, in fact, he knew nothing at all.

"Could that really be?" asked Sister Veronica, her eyes wide with amazement. "Oh, dear, now I don't know if that is good or bad."

But Sister Héloise was not one to waste time. She immediately ordered Yvonne to remove the bandages from about Andrew's neck, and breathing hard with attention and responsibility the Sister Superior leaned close to him and carefully supervised. He saw the now stern face of Sister Héloise glaring at his neck wounds as if confronting an old and hated enemy.

"Young man," she announced, "you are lucky to be alive."

The skin uncovered by the bandage felt cool and tender in the morning air. With a grunt Sister Héloise had given another order, and Annette came forward with new bandages for Yvonne. The

Sister Superior, with her engulfing smile of friendship to show him that everything would soon be all right again, mumbled something to him about the doctor coming later to look at his arm, and then hurried over to the other bed. Sister Veronica stepped into the Sister Superior's place and watched as Yvonne began wrapping up his neck again. But after a few rolls of the bandage, with Yvonne's lovely hands passing around and around him beneath his head, Andrew noticed that Sister Veronica was directing her eyes right at him.

"How long have you been riding motorcycles?" she asked softly, her eyes fascinated by the topic and perhaps even a little frightened by it.

"Oh, for a long time."

"Are you a very, very good driver?"

"Until yesterday I thought I was terrific."

Her eyes seemed to glow and her mouth opened slightly as if in anticipation of a smile.

"Maybe you still are," she said encouragingly. "Maybe it isn't your fault that you are here."

"I only wish I could find out."

"Do you go very fast?" her voice asked gently.

"Like the wind."

He, too, was speaking softly but he didn't know why. It was as if he were telling a story to a child. She sucked in a gentle stream of air and her eyes widened as far as they could.

"Oh, that must be wonderful," she said.

She was a most attentive audience. He had completely forgotten Yvonne and the fact that her arms were still working on him and that she was probably listening with puzzled interest at their strange and odd-sounding language. Off to his left he half-heard the Sister Superior talking in quiet tones to his indolent roommate.

"If I ever get the cycle back in one piece," he said to the young nun, "I'll take you for a ride."

At this she almost jumped back with fright, as if he had presented the cycle to her right there in the room at that moment and were about to help her climb on. Her face became as animated as a child's at a circus and she made a loud sound resembling both a laugh and a cry of excitement. Then she pushed her fingers against her mouth and sneaked a sheepish glance at Sister Héloise, who had turned to see what the noise was all about.

"He wants to take me for a ride," Sister Veronica said in breathless French and with a pretty blush.

"He will kill us all," announced the Sister Superior, and she promptly turned back to the other bed beside which she was standing. Into Andrew's surprised left ear poured the joyful little laugh of the girl who had just that moment finished bandaging his neck. Then Sister Héloise called to the two nurses and the nun to join her.

"*Oui, ma Sœur,*" sang the voice of Yvonne as she answered the call of the Sister Superior.

But Yvonne managed to delay long enough to challenge him with a mocking glance of exclamation, warning him that she was still right there in the room to be reckoned with, and scolding him for being so oblivious to her. After all, Sister Veronica was, he must be reminded, a Roman Catholic nun.

Growing tired from sitting up, Andrew leaned back to take a few minutes rest, when all at once he was startled by a full-throated scream which ceased as abruptly as it sounded. Annette was standing by the other bed as if she were deaf and had heard nothing. Yvonne was crouching on the floor beside the medicine wagon searching for something on the bottom shelf. She didn't look up at the sudden sound but her lips wrinkled as she strained to withhold an odd, self-satisfied grin. She remained below the level of the bed until she had composed her face and then she rose to her feet with a toss of her head. Sister Veronica, meanwhile, had rushed to the door in fright and closed it to keep further noise within the room.

The covers at the foot of the bed had been turned back. The leg was exposed, completely wrapped in bandages. The fingers of Sister Héloise froze in the air, inches from the leg, but not quite touching it. Her hands made no further movement. Her back was turned to the others, but they could see her head swinging slowly and rhythmically back and forth in obvious displeasure. She looked up at the ceiling to seek guidance and then returned to her job, her fingers reaching out once more in another attempt to remove the bandages. The man whose leg she was working on had lifted himself to one elbow. The look of beautiful melancholy was still on his face, but his eyes were terribly alive and when he saw her hands moving toward his leg again his features contorted with fright. Once more the room filled with that abrupt scream bursting from his throat. Then there was silence. The face was tranquil again, but the eyes were wild.

"I didn't *touch* you yet," Sister Héloise flung, in disgust, her hands angrily on her hips. The man did not answer. He seemed fascinated by his own leg.

"What is it?" Andrew whispered.

"This one's more trouble than all the others put together," Sister Héloise said in English, without turning around, her voice flat and oppressed. "It is sad ... sad for him and for the others who try to help. And sad most of all ... for his wife."

"What happened?"

In the background he heard the quietly hopeful and half-scolding voice of Sister Veronica. There was no sign that the melancholy face was even listening.

"It was an auto accident," the old nun told him quietly. "His leg was caught, became burned. An ugly thing to happen. He's been here a long time. He is much better now but he still carries on the same as when they first brought him in. Of course the leg must be treated anyway. Then it is war."

"But if he lets no one touch him ..."

"No one ..." And she tilted her head in the direction of Yvonne "... but her."

"Ohhh," the young man said with a drawn-out sound of revelation, but actually he didn't understand at all.

"He won't even let the others stay and assist." She shook her head as if the entire situation was so tangled with intolerable behavior that she couldn't get herself to speak of it any longer.

"How come he gets his way so ..."

But the answer came in the form of a loud scream and Sister Veronica tried vainly with hushes to silence it. Sister Héloise had commenced work again. This time she continued on his leg uninterrupted, and as a result the screaming gave them no mercy. He seemed unable to sit up and defend himself, so he reached out toward his leg in a frail and futile gesture, yelling at them all the while. But Sister Héloise brought an end to this by suddenly throwing up her arms in a gesture of utter helplessness. She turned and swept from the room. She was followed by Annette and then Sister Veronica, who walked very slowly, apparently staggered by regret and sorrow, and whose face was colored by the first traces of shame for a man who had no shame himself. Only Yvonne was to remain behind. As she watched the others leaving, she turned down the corners of her mouth in a slight, inverted grin as a woman will when her vanity has been touched.

"Wait, what happens now?" Andrew said to Sister Veronica who was just about to step out into the hall.

"You will see," said the young nun.

He found himself gazing at the closed door even after she had gone. The delicately featured man whom he later learned was Jean Lazare was leaning back enjoying the ministrations of the young French nurse. She passed her fingers through his hair several times and in a low pliant voice, such as one would use on a small frightened child, she murmured words to calm him. Her face, or at least what Andrew could see of it, was a constantly changing study in female animation. She would frown at him in mock reproach, then smile confidently as her eyes asked the unnecessary question: was she pleasing him? Then she would cluck her tongue loudly and wrinkle her forehead at him as she fastened a button of his pajama top that had accidentally come undone. The gradual metamorphosis of Jean Lazare's expression, from staunch melancholy to complete rapture, appeared almost comic. When she felt that he was sufficiently under her spell, she took up the thermometer and held it by one end with the two fingers of her right hand so that he could see it. He immediately shook his head no, and a part-whining, part-complaining voice escaped from his lips. But Yvonne insisted with such a defiant lift of her chin that he gave in immediately. In an effort to make up to her and hoping to erase any possible traces of anger, he lifted the sheet near his waist to help her with the job. Andrew saw a brief glimpse of skin and realized that Jean wore no bottoms to his pajamas. Yvonne reached under the covers and with her left hand on his waist she helped him roll away from her slightly onto his side. The Frenchman, stretching his neck, peered into her eyes intently while she stared back at him. On each of their faces was that momentary lapse of expression that often comes when complete concentration is devoted to a task that needs but a few more attentive moments to get it done. Her right hand was moving slowly beneath the blankets. Simultaneously both their faces became alight with a sly but triumphant grin; then time, which seemed to have stopped, began to move again. She withdrew her hand from the bed and he settled into position onto his back but suddenly stiffened with discomfort. Yvonne gave a little laugh of understanding and shook her head up and down, her face saying with a pleased smirk that it certainly served him right. After that she pulled back the sheets to uncover only his damaged leg and began unwrapping the bandages with great care. Afterward, with a pair of scissor clamps, she started peeling away the gauze paddings from the discolored leg. She moved the clamps with painstaking gentleness, talking to him all the while as she would to a frightened little baby. Many times she had to lean close, stroke his cheek again, and place her face near his as she made soft pitying sounds to silence his little noises of fear. Then she would return to her work once more, her right hand removing the bandages while her left hand disappeared under the covers to help relax him by fondly stroking, in a slow circular rhythm, the soft white flesh of his stomach.

At one point, when his fearful whimperings reached a new high and she in turn had soothed him with a flurry of attention more affectionate than usual, having reached over and kissed him once on the forehead, she turned her eyes at that moment toward the young man in the other bed. It was as if to see whether he had noticed the lavish attention she, Yvonne, was capable of giving and how far she would go for the comfort of a patient once it became her whim to do so. Her glance was intended to be fleeting, just a glimpse over her shoulder. But once she had looked, she couldn't turn away. To her complete astonishment Andrew was not in bed at all. He was standing next to it facing her with a secluded little grin. It was a smile directed at no one in particular, rather at some undefined point somewhere in space.

When the performance by Yvonne had first begun, Andrew watched it with revulsion and fascination. The tearful behavior of Jean Lazare was so foreign to him that it seemed, not the action of a living being, but, rather, the frightening and unfathomable gyrations of a creature in a dream. If she ever tried such a thing on *him*, he would do everything he could to get out of her reach. It was not affection or devotion that he was watching; it was simply a display of great conceit and power solely for the titillation of her own vanity. On the part of the man, it was the worst case of self-indulgence he had ever seen. No, he would not wait for her to try her selfish soothings on him. He would get out of the room now. That is, if he had enough strength.

Throwing aside the blankets he drove several flies scurrying into the air. The bedspring squeaked as he brought his legs dangling down over the side of the mattress, letting them hang in the air. He sat there looking at the floor, which now appeared to be a great distance below him. His head was throbbing, as was his left arm. Then all at once he was standing. He had slid off the mattress without giving himself time to think. He wobbled briefly, but remained on his legs. To stand alone, without leaning against anything, seemed an incredible feat. He decided it was the most tremendous performance he had ever achieved. And that was the very moment Yvonne chose to turn around and look. She found him displayed full length before her, a little grin bending his lips to celebrate what he had done.

He had an audience now of two. Yvonne had let out a delightful little sound of exclamation, and Jean Lazare, with a puzzled expression, also turned to see. Andrew ignored them both and began to make for the door. Walking was like a lie which, once begun, had to be continued. He grasped the knob and then turned back to look. Only when he had stopped did he realize how much effort he had been using. Yvonne was now looking at him with that enticing feminine expression of approval which, when directed at a man, was invariably less a compliment for what he had accomplished than a new awareness of and interest in the man who had accomplished it. This, he thought, was going to be the greatest damned exit he had ever made.

Closing the door behind him, he stepped out into the hallway and found it surprisingly dim even in the middle of the morning. On his left, around the corner of a stairway, he imagined the presence of a door. All he saw of it, though, was a long white block of sunlight falling on the floor from an open passageway that probably led to the outside. Down the hallway to his right, past several doors leading to rooms such as his, was a large dormitory with two long rows of hospital beds. Men could be seen moving about. Some had gathered together to talk, while others lay in their beds reading or doing nothing. The huge room seemed drained of any noise except the mute atmosphere of repose.

Behind him was the rustle of skirts, and then a gentle voice which could belong only to Sister Veronica.

"*Goodness.* Please be careful."

She came up to him quickly, as if he were about to need her physical support. He often smiled, afterward, remembering this moment, for had he actually fallen, as she feared, she would certainly have gone down with him, under his weight, and would probably have been hurt more than he. She appeared to have no physical strength at all—just a face of rare innocence. At that moment, as he looked at her, he saw what it was that gave her beauty that look of unreality. Her features seemed to be those of a lovely, healthy child, but there was also that fullness and maturity which could belong only to a woman. The blending of these two qualities, without one diluting the other, created a face so enchanting that it was impossible not to stare. And for the first time in his life he became aware of the immense power of selfless love and of the fact that he had been searching for it from the very beginning, though unaware that he had been searching at all.

"Are you all right?" she asked softly, as if there were some secret peril for them to share.

"Just trying to find out if I'm really alive," he smiled.

"You must be awfully strong to get up and walk the very next day."

The very next day? This came, not as news, but as shocking confirmation of something he had feared but did not quite understand.

Needing instant proof, he asked: "Was it raining yesterday?"

"Almost all day," she answered, studying him curiously.

"And for several days before that?"

"Yes."

A casual wave of his right index finger and then: "I think I'm going back to bed now," he explained.

Reopening the door to his room, he began the long journey. He had the feeling, when he finally reached his mattress and leaned against it for support, that if it had been a few feet more he could not have made it. Across his back and underneath his arms was the unpleasant dampness of his own sweat. A wave of self-pity came over him and he knew then that his strength was almost gone. Climbing into a high bed with only one arm seemed more than he could manage, and for a moment the effort made him feel sick. Somewhere in the background, the voice of Jean Lazare groaned in complaint; but then gliding in right on top of it, covering it, drowning it, flowed the smooth, tender, anesthetic sounds of the lovely Yvonne. Fifteen seconds later Andrew Williams was asleep.

18

For the fifth time he held his hand rigid in the air ready to pounce. His eyes rolled in their sockets as he watched. Then he brought his hand down hard on the blanket where the fly had landed. But for the fifth time it got away. Now, as it hovered near the door, Andrew waited. The door suddenly opened and the fly vanished into the evening-dimmed hallway at the same moment that a tall, dark-haired Frenchman came in. With white teeth gleaming and hand extended, he introduced himself as Dr. de Lyese. He appeared to be an illogical blend of impatience and self-control, with an obvious case of nerves. Using imperfect English, he began talking too loudly and too fast about things that had little, if anything, to do with medicine. At last, almost as an afterthought, he began questioning Andrew about his condition, but with none of the professional manner of a doctor examining a patient. It was rather as a casual acquaintance met accidentally in the street. Soon the doctor was off the subject again, talking now about America and how he would some day like to visit there.

Finally he touched on a topic that Andrew found of burning interest.

"I was given some information about your accident," the doctor said at last. "They tell me you remember nothing."

"That's right. The way things have been going lately, I guess I'm lucky to remember my own name."

"No, no, it is not uncommon. After such an accident it happens very often. Do not be concerned." While clearing his throat, he pressed his fist against his mouth. Then he came closer, his hand leaning against the bed and his voice softened slightly. "So…let me tell you…I phoned the police. They want to talk with you, later…later when you are able. You understand? Do not hurry. But I phoned them. They say this…they say you drove off the road and into a side wall of a restaurant. Yes. Luckily there was a large window and the force, you know, sends you right through into the restaurant. Luckily you weren't going very fast and luckily no people were eating." Then he added, as if he were giving the most important information of all: "It was not dinner hour, you know."

"Well, thank God for that," Andrew said bitterly and without thinking. "Wouldn't want to burn anybody with hot soup."

But Andrew's annoyance was actually his anger turning against himself. How could he possibly have allowed such an accident to happen? And after all the years he had spent on cycles and despite all the dangerous things he had learned to do on them. He must have looked like a fool. The whole thing was almost beyond belief. But he was surprised to discover that the doctor was enjoying his remark about the soup.

"Ah, *oui, oui, oui*," flew the sound of his voice. "This is good. You are funny."

"If you think that's something, you should have been there when I went through the window."

He watched as the doctor went off into another gale of laughter.

"But really," the Frenchman said when he finally was able, "it is something serious, no?" And he took on the air of a man revealing a hitherto unnoticed calamity. "It could have been very bad. You lose a lot of blood, a *lot* of blood. How you do not…split your neck in two…I do not know."

"What I can't understand," Andrew said, "is how the whole thing happened. What caused it?"

"Ah, *oui*. I am coming to this. There has not been time to look into it and the police they do not really care. You know? They want to be done. That is all. But I was told this: I was told that you went off the road to avoiding hitting a child. Yes, a child. My own opinion is this: The streets they are wet. You knew you could not stop in time. So, at your own risk, you steer the motorcycle off the road so as not to hit the child. You do not remember? But you are a hero, no? Today in this hospital we have a hero!" The doctor's face beamed with celebration. He clasped the young man's leg as if he were enjoying an off-color joke. "I have told the others, too. Why, you are even in the local newspaper. I tell you, you are a hero. The nurses may even give you special watching." At this his eyes widened enticingly. Then he laughed. Warm with excitement, he leaned back to observe how the young man reacted to all this news. But even during this moment of calm it appeared that it was the doctor and not the patient who had suddenly come into possession of some glorious honor and was therefore finding it impossible to defend himself against his own immodest glee.

"Huh!" Andrew said quietly, looking at his knees, "and I don't remember a thing...not a single damn thing." He brushed away a fly that had landed on the back of his hand and once more a little grunt of amazement escaped his lips. "But the cycle," he asked looking up suddenly. "Is it O.K.?— No, it couldn't be, could it? Did you hear anything?"

"It is ..." And the doctor moved the palms of his hands together with his elbows up and out. "It is finished."

"I see," Andrew said quietly. Once again in his life he felt himself understanding the concept of irretrievable loss.

While they were talking together, preparations were being made in the room for the doctor to examine the two patients. The medicine wagon was wheeled in, but this time only Yvonne and Sister Veronica were standing by. The doctor appeared reluctant to begin his work, but since Andrew was only the first patient in an evening of examinations that would take him through the entire hospital, the time to start could not be put off any longer.

"Well," he said, with the air of a man beginning a drudgery, "let us take a look at that neck."

As the bandage was being undone, the young man exchanged glances with Sister Veronica. Her usually genuine expression of cheerful understanding and sympathy was now joined by a look of awe and respect that took Andrew a little by surprise. It was the look of someone who had never faced a hero before and who was now looking at this phenomenon with all the admiration that she could muster. The expression was the kind one somehow never captured on film. Was all of what the doctor had said true? he wondered. But true or not, to be looked at in this way was extremely pleasant. He peeked quickly at Yvonne in an effort to see if she too had come under the spell of his unremembered deeds. Yes, he could see that she had. But there was no outward sign of awe or respect. What highlighted her face instead was the entire absence of expression. Gone was the confident, almost arrogant strut of self-pleased beauty, for a woman is only too aware of her own unworthiness in the presence of someone who has gained, even if just for that moment, her total admiration and respect.

"Where in America do you come from?" the doctor asked as he peered at the newly uncovered wounds.

"New York."

"Ah," the doctor exclaimed, and nodded his head. "I am going to New York some day. Yes, really." And he took time out from the examination to fix on Andrew's face a look expressing the extent of his determination on this point. "It is my…ambition. No? It is the same word in English as in French. Ambition?"

"That's right."

From Yvonne the doctor took another roll of bandages and began redoing the young man's neck. "You are very lucky to be alive, no?" This he added almost as a second thought, aware that perhaps at this point a comment was required of him.

"But first I must get to Paris. There are good positions there in hospitals but they are difficult to win. Ah, things are always happening there. It is the center of all Europe. You know? It is where the money is. It is where you can find life."

"The way you talk," said the young man with a grin, "I wish I were there right now."

"Me, also," the doctor beamed, and it was as if they had secretly joined in a conspiracy.

"Ohhhh," came a gentle, surprised, female voice, "you don't really mean that."

The doctor turned with a jolt, as though he had forgotten she was in the room. His handsome face changed and his eyes softened and filled with longing. It was a look Andrew recognized and understood. But to Andrew's surprise, Dr. de Lyese wasn't looking at Yvonne. Instead, he was looking directly at Sister Veronica.

"Ah," he said, "but I do really mean that."

"You want to leave?" asked the young nun with a forlorn voice touched by the sadness of anyone leaving anywhere. She paused for a while and then declared softly: "But the people here are so wonderful." There was a note of rapture in her voice. "Really, so wonderful."

During a moment of silence the doctor looked at her without saying anything. Then slowly and softly he spoke, and his words carried with them the burden of anxiety.

"It would be very, very easy to be wonderful to you," the doctor said. It occurred to Andrew, as he listened, that those were words a man does not use in speaking to a nun.

At that moment Yvonne came alive and made a slight movement of warning. It had nothing to do with what was being said, for she possessed no knowledge of the language they were speaking. The warning concerned a woman who had just entered the room and, nervously noticing that no one had seen her, had gone straight to the bed of Jean Lazare. He met her without a sign of recognition, but with eyes that stared directly into her face somewhat in the manner of a man who believes that the next few words spoken to him may decide his entire life. The woman, without uttering a sound, reached out her hand with uncertainty to caress his cheek, but the man rolled his head away with disgust and she swiftly pulled her arm back to her side. Her features colored briefly with embarrassment, but then she became stoical again. She was slim and simply dressed and there was an elusive quality in her face that made it seem born for the art of expressing love. But this was the remnant of a life no longer being lived, for now nothing could be seen in her expression but a terrible lifelessness. It was difficult to approximate her age. She seemed about the same age as her husband, possibly a bit older.

At the signal of warning from Yvonne, Dr. de Lyese looked around at the woman who had come in, but he said nothing. He exchanged a glance with the nurse, giving a nod to indicate his wish that she move the medicine wagon to the other bed. Instead of going about this immediately, her eyes remained on his face longer than was necessary and in her now energetic look there appeared signs of the birth of a smile. Then, with a sharp toss of her head which resembled a shiver of delight, she turned away and went about her work.

"Well," the doctor said as he secured the bandage under the young man's ear. "Here is where it all starts again." His face seemed to grow slack with fatigue. "But you are doing fine. Just rest." With a weak flash of teeth he slapped Andrew four times on the leg. "Just rest." And then he went to the other bed.

Mme. Lazare gave him a hopeful look, but the doctor simply nodded and, with his hand, directed her to take a position at the head of her husband's bed. The screaming had already begun, but the doctor appeared not to have heard. He pulled the covers back from the mattress and exposed the damaged leg. Sister Veronica was at the door, hurrying to seal in the noise. Leaning over him, pleading, trying to hold him down, placing her hand on his head, putting all her young desperate effort into quieting him, was the frantic Mme. Lazare.

"Shhhhh," her voice hushed loudly. "Shhhhhhh." But even this simple sound exposed to the whole room how nakedly embarrassed she was.

But nothing could be done. If her beseeching had any effect at all, it only made matters worse. At last the doctor signalled her away, and Yvonne took her place beside the bed. Since the signal was given with just the slightest movement of his hand, it was clear to Andrew that this scene must have been enacted many times in the past, because the wife and the nurse changed places immediately.

The screaming did not die out, but when Yvonne began to use her low, consoling voice, filled with the inarticulate sounds that one would use to soothe a crying child, the frantic yelling that had been heard throughout the hospital became confined to the room. Her fingers passed again and again through Jean Lazare's unruly hair and slowly she drew him into a world where just the two of them existed. Occasionally, when her pretty hand touched his cheek, the contorted look of terror paused for a moment and he simulated what might have passed for a hideous grin.

The doctor worked steadily on the leg while Sister Veronica stood near by to hand him whatever he needed. At the foot of the bed, with her hands holding the thick cold bar of the bedframe as if to give herself support, was M. Lazare's wife. Andrew was spellbound by what he saw in her face. She was watching, not her husband, nor what was being done to his leg, nor the doctor who was doing it, but, with terrible attention, the dangerously handsome face that was attending so skillfully to the needs and fears of her husband. Mme. Lazare stared at Yvonne for an immeasurable period of time with an intensely motionless, expressionless, bottomless absorption that only exists in the private and deadly world of female hate. But deep under the surface there was also the pain—the crying hopeless pain that lies below all anger—and the young man felt it and shared it and then wanted to hide from it. He climbed cautiously off the bed and walked out through the door and into the unlit empty hallway.

19

"COME IN. I'm in the mood for a talk."

It was a voice neither cold nor warm, and the accent that molded the words was definitely German. The door to the room across from his was wide open, and Andrew saw a gray-haired man seated in bed with a book propped firmly against his knees. He looked about fifty. His stern face with its cold, intelligent eyes, cruel mouth, and abrupt mustache was dominated by a pince-nez balanced precariously on the straight square nose. The room was small, but he shared it with no one else. There was a broken-down armchair beside the window, and a straight-backed wooden chair near the door. Attached to the head of his bed was a bright spotlight for reading. On a large table, to the man's right, was a scattered pile of old books, a large typewriter, a ream of paper, pencils, a bottle of ink, a fountain pen, several untouched chocolate bars, an assortment of magazines in various languages, a small apple, a penknife, and a pile of letters that had obviously been opened, read, and replaced in their envelopes. Andrew paused at the doorway. It was almost like the private study of someone's home. To enter seemed an intrusion.

"Take the wooden chair, if you will, and move it to the bed here," said the man, placing his book (open and face down) on the table, after which he pointed the lamp at the ceiling, to keep it out of the boy's eyes. "How are you feeling? I understand you're a bit of a hero. Come in, Mr. Williams, come in."

"Thank you, sir."

"Let me introduce myself. My name is Anton Kanka. That's it— sit right down."

"You seem to know all about me," Andrew said pleasantly as he leaned back in the chair.

"You must understand that you're quite an event here," said the host, talking in slow, dignified speech. Then his voice took on a quality that Andrew thought might possibly indicate the hint of a jest. "We don't often have young men from America visiting us with motorcycles…. As a matter of fact, if we did, I fear no window would be safe."

Andrew grinned. "Was that window, or widow?" he asked.

"If I were referring," replied Kanka cheerfully, "to women whose honor would be endangered by the presence of an American, I certainly would not limit the reference to widows."

"Let me plead innocence."

"To 'women,' perhaps; but as to plate-glass 'windows,' I conclude you must own up. Especially since you are wrapped in the telltale manner of a mummy. I suppose people have already told you how lucky you are?"

"Constantly."

"People do have a tendency to do that, don't they? As if you could never quite figure it out for yourself."

"My only good luck was that my bad luck wasn't fatal."

"Well, now—" said Kanka, producing two steel cups with a reach of his hand, "upon that well-turned phrase let us drink a toast."

Leaning over the medicine table to his left, he tilted the pitcher of wine until both cups were filled. The manner in which he moved seemed to require great effort. Andrew rose to take the drink held out to him and was surprised to find that it was not as heavy as the expression on Kanka's face had implied.

"And now for the toast," said the German, lifting his cup with both hands. "To the first American in three years to visit the *Hôpital Mixte de Lannemezan.* May all of his wounds heal quickly, and may he always have the good luck to have none of his bad luck be fatal."

The young man gestured in the air with his cup and then swallowed some of the tasty wine. He leaned back again and for a moment reveled in the calm and well-being that settles over the body during times of convalescence.

"Ah," he said, touching his bandaged neck and glancing at his sprained arm, "if only my draft board could see me now."

"Well, if you remain in this town, not only won't they ever *see* you, but even if they *looked* they'd never find you."

"I'm getting to appreciate this place more and more. But tell me, what is there to do here?"

At that moment, from across the hall, loud enough to reach them through a closed door, came a violent scream louder than all the rest that had preceded it.

"I mean besides listening to Mr. Lazare."

"One mustn't forget," Kanka said thoughtfully, "that a hospital is not really a healthy place. To get used to it is even more unhealthy."

"Yet the people are so friendly."

"It is my experience that it is sometimes more cheerful in hospitals than in other places in the world, because in hospitals there is hope. You can see it on the faces in the wards. And also courage. It is all the same thing. Cures are only temporary; only hope is permanent. To cure the mind, one must occupy oneself with the body, and to cure the body, one must occupy oneself with the mind. And there is where we come in. By a Hobson's choice it seems that *we* must occupy ourselves with the world of the mind—the infinite, indeterminate mind. A place, I have found, in which it is quite comfortable to live. That's what there is to do here."

"But for how long?"

"If necessary... forever."

He drew up his knees underneath the blankets and rested his arms and his chin upon them. His eyes seemed to be contemplating "forever" and finding it not too unbearable.

"Then," said his guest, "I should think a person would find life here quite flat."

The man in bed removed his pince-nez, which left a red mark on the base of his nose, and placed them carefully on the table.

"On the contrary," he said, and then he held up a triumphant finger and wiggled it in the air. "It is round." The heavy voice pronounced this melodramatically, with a tinge of humor. "I have sailed it in circumference. I know. It is round."

"Well..." Andrew began, his voice pitched in doubt. Then silence.

"The problem is that most people don't sail far enough. They refuse to be interested; they only want to be entertained."

"I still say..."

Sudden activity in the hallway interrupted him. The medicine wagon was being removed from the other room. Yvonne was wheeling it, with Sister Veronica helping. Close behind them strode Dr. de Lyese. All three, though not walking fast, gave the impression of hurrying. The doctor looked up from some deep invisible pit into which he had thrown his thoughts and noticed Anton Kanka seated in bed. The handsome teeth flashed into a smile and his arm swung forward and up into a greeting.

"Hello, hello," the doctor called, and then all three of them were gone. The door to the room from which they came was left partly open and the light inside had been turned off. Mme. Lazare had not yet come out.

"I thought they came in here next?" the young man asked.

"No. When you have been here as long as I have they no longer find it necessary to come in every day and examine you.... They come to talk, though, and sometimes that is quite rewarding." He lifted the shiny metal cup to his lips and then placed it back on the table. "But I was about to inform you that unless you brought along a suitcase of reading material—which is highly unlikely considering your mode of travel—or unless you send away for books—which will take time—you are forced to fall back on the hospital library. I think for you this will be particularly disappointing, for it contains only one book in English: *Romeo and Juliet.*"

The momentum of speech carried the German even further into his playful monologue.

"I have often suspected that the characters of Romeo and of Juliet are so insipid as drama (a girl of fourteen and a boy of sixteen) that if an actor and actress were to perform their parts properly...I believe it could ruin their careers.... My, you have a most contagious laugh."

"No, it is your humor that is contagious."

"Ah, good, we are going to flatter each other," said Kanka, shifting his position in the bed. "First I will say that you are very intelligent for an American, and you will say that I am very intelligent for a German, which of course will bring us to an impasse—whereupon we shall share another toast."

Kanka reached for the pitcher again and beckoned his guest to bring forth his cup.

"To which are you most trying to commit me," Andrew asked as he climbed to his feet, "a compliment, or a glass of wine?"

"Compliments preferably," Kanka answered, allowing his guest to help in the job of filling the cups. "Here in France we foreigners are offered too few compliments and too much wine."

But most infectious of all was Kanka's way of speaking.

"If it be your wish to rid your wine on me," Andrew said, after he had taken a full swallow, "then go to it. In fact, the more wine consumed, the more inclined am I toward delivering compliments."

Kanka was drinking at that moment and nodded his head slightly in approval.

"Are you aware," the young man went on, already feeling the first cup of wine, "that I am beginning to speak like you?"

The host leaned back and placed his head against the mountain of pillows behind him. He peered upward, as a man might when he suddenly discovers an answer he has long overlooked.

"I *knew* there was something pleasant about you."

"If it ever happened to me," Andrew grinned, "I think it might make me nervous."

"No, no, no," said Kanka in his most playfully dramatic tone, "I can think of no one I would more gladly have you resemble."

"Well, so far I haven't said a thing of soberness or value, if that's what you mean."

The conversation came to an abrupt halt. Briefly, but only briefly, Kanka looked as if he were about to laugh. Then he changed his mind, and with a roguish air he returned to Andrew's happy assault.

"Ah, you've lost it. You're speaking like yourself again and not like me any longer. I would never have fallen so low or displayed such bad taste as to devastate my guest with a remark as clever and pointed as that. Yes, you've lost it.... A pity."

There was a touch of seriousness in Andrew's smile. For, as sometimes happens during casual or even flippant moments of talk, something is said which, like a flash of light, reveals the strength and scope of the mind of the man to whom you are listening.

"But you are right," said the host. "This conversation has been lacking in wisdom. Do you suppose we will go on like this all night, uttering nothing but irrelevancies?"

"Let's not lose hope."

"True. From even the most trifling conversations there have been known to grow mighty oaks of thought.... Let me see. I will try to say something of soberness and value...Let me see. Humnnnn.... Ah, I have it!...Were you aware that a great, great grandfather of mine was a lawyer to Beethoven? True! As a matter of fact, for a long time that was my only claim to fame. Perhaps it still is. My brother sincerely believes that inheritance is what made me a critic of the arts—a form of family tradition that specializes in the mishandling of genius."

"You are an art critic?" asked the young man.

"To three newspapers in Germany, to a weekly in Italy, and to a monthly in Switzerland, I am a book critic. To a large but rather pompous publishing organization in Frankfurt which has put out four volumes of mine on art and music and is about to print a fifth, I am alternately either an art or a music critic; but to my brother, who honors me occasionally with a letter, I am no more than a mercenary lawyer of the arts."

Andrew sensed that his host was enjoying himself. He appeared to be one of those men who seem never to get angry, who seem forever in control, forever calm.

"I will venture to say," continued the thick German voice, "that after my next volume appears I won't hear from my brother for about six months."

With this, he laughed for the first time, but it was barely audible; more like a violent grin that had gotten out of control and from which had come a sound resembling a purr.

"What is the title?" Andrew asked, wondering if with this question he was imposing.

"*The Three Geographic Lines in European Art.* It is due in September."

"I hesitate to ask, but can you outline a little of what it's about?"

"Don't hesitate. I will tell you."

And so, for the next twenty minutes, Anton Kanka talked without interruption.

At first he spoke in broad terms and rather slowly, and the young man followed him with attention and interest, but afterwards the monologue became specific and esoteric, and it leaped from one art form to another with bewildering speed, never once even considering the possibility that the listener might be having trouble following. Now eloquent, now burdened with details, at times involved, but always driving relentlessly toward an elusive conclusion, the discourse eventually left the young man far behind. It was filled with an endless rosary of names in music, literature, and fine arts. Most of these Andrew knew about and understood; but others of whom he had never heard kept cropping up, over and over again. Andrew followed as best he could, while the narrative seemed to swarm over Europe in all directions at once. But at the end, the young man was not listening. Instead, he was going back in his mind to try to find where it was that his understanding had lost its way. When the lecture at last came to an end, Andrew found himself confronted by a wall of silence.

Six months? If I were his brother, Andrew thought to himself, he wouldn't hear from me for six years! But what he said was: "That *is* interesting."

"They will say that it covers too much ground," Kanka went on, as if he hadn't heard. "They'll say the scope is too large...and they will be right." His eyes danced playfully. "But it will be two volumes of one thousand, five hundred pages each; and it does the job. It does the job."

The young man was bewildered. The mind of Anton Kanka made him feel weak and worthless. If it had not been for the wine, Andrew would have been depressed, but he had drunk enough to give his body the illusion of perfection and strength. He looked up from his wine to say something cheerful, but he saw on Kanka's face such a surprising expression of pleasure and warmth that he found himself stopped even before he had begun. The young man turned to see, but the forgotten bandages on his neck restricted him. Pivoting in his chair, he found Sister Veronica standing right behind him. She placed a hand gently on his shoulder and her eyes contemplated him in that special way she had which made you feel that you and you alone were her real concern.

"I think now it is better for you to sleep," she said. Her voice had nothing of command in it.

He smiled up at her. "I feel very good."

"Attribute that to the wine," said Kanka playfully. "But mark my words, you will wake up tomorrow and find your arm still in a sling."

"Now, there," said Andrew, "is a safe Nostradamic pronouncement."

But the compassionate mood of sympathy that dominated the young nun seemed to make her oblivious to any quick changes of temperament in the conversation.

"I'm so glad you're feeling well," she answered, and then, glancing up at Kanka: "He is amazing. Yesterday afternoon he was nearly killed, and now look at him."

"Is his neck badly cut?" the German inquired.

"Yes, quite deep. But, luckily, at the side."

"I would like to know," he asked his guest, "how you avoided having both your throat cut and your neck broken? I had heard of

American ingenuity, but I can see now that I have vastly underrated it. How did you do it?"

"It wasn't easy." He grinned.

"It is God's miracle," the nun said timidly, and for a moment she looked frightened. Then her beautiful face softened with delight. "Will you do me a favor?" She smiled at Andrew.

"You have only to ask," he said with a gallant wave of his hand.

"Really?"

"Try me."

"All right," she said with an impish look, trying to build up suspense, "I would like you...to please...to...go to bed." Then she giggled and added: "Please?"

"I will be right in," he announced, and he wondered if it could be seen on his face how much she delighted him.

"Do you *really* mind? It *is* late."

"Not at all. I don't mind in the least," he said to her in the most convincing manner he could assume. "You are absolutely right. I will be in immediately."

She nodded her head, enchanting him again with her half-inquisitive look. Then she smiled once more, and swept out into the hallway. They both watched her go.

"Enchanting," Kanka began. "Simply enchanting." He was speaking to no one in particular. Not even himself. But his body, seemingly so devoid of energy, now almost throbbed with it. Then he turned to Andrew and began talking to him in the best of spirits. "Ha, isn't she both ludicrous and admirable all in one? Aren't they all? I ask you. They are struggling along like children, and all for a belief that no one in his right mind could ever be sure exists; like children obeying most a force they understand least. Ha, I ask you. In their confusion they try to abolish, on one hand, sex and self-enjoyment, and create, on the other, strength and human virtue. Then they attempt to join them all together in that sanctified place known as conjugal love. But enchanting, totally enchanting: especially she. Instead of teaching kindness with her religion, she teaches religion with her kindness.... Ah, yes.... Actually it is not hard at all to understand how the good doctor can fail to notice the robes she wears .... Yes. You see, when it comes to love, some men are satisfied with nothing less than the unobtainable."

A whispering of cloth, and in swept the face of Sister Héloise. She had a pill for M. Kanka and a word for his tardy guest and she delivered them both quickly.

"*Endormez-vous,*" she snapped, but there was no anger in her voice, just the need to get quickly done what was best for each patient.

Andrew bade his host good night and with an odd feeling of incompleteness, as if something had been left unsaid, he went back across the hall. He left the door to his room slightly open, as he had found it, so there would be enough light to make his way to his bed in the dark. A nurse would shut the door later when she came by.

He was just about to lift himself onto the mattress when he realized that someone was there standing in the blackness beside Lazare. His eyes had not yet become accustomed enough to the dark for him to see her, but what surprised him was that his own entrance into the room had gone unnoticed. Suddenly she began to speak, trying with every word to keep her tear-stained voice from getting too loud. Her swift, intimate French was overwhelmed with violent concern, and she seemed either about to cry or about to scream.

"Please, *please!* I've asked you not to think about it. I don't want to discuss it any longer."

"You are my wife," Jean Lazare said with tormented calm.

"Do you want me to know things I cannot know? Can any woman ..."

But she faltered into soundlessness.

"You are my wife," he said again with strenuous self-control.

"You will destroy yourself." Her voice was pleading with rage. "We *must* not *talk* about it. Please. I've got to leave now. *Please, please, please.*" There was a furious silence. Then she burst forth once again. "All I said was that I didn't know. How can I possibly know? How can I possibly guarantee?"

Her husband's voice sprang like an animal. "But you are *still … my … wife.*"

"Shhhh! … Oh, please. Shhhhh." Then her voice became drained of everything but stupendous fatigue.

"I will try to be as I have always been," she said.

"You will not!" The three words cut quietly through the dark.

"Let us talk of it no more."

"You are not sincere."

"I am," she hissed. "God knows I am."

"You are lying. I can tell. Then promise … go on, promise me that it will make no difference to you. You are my wife. Let's see you promise."

The elbow of Andrew's arm resting in the sling accidentally nudged the cup on the medicine table and all conversation drained away like water into sand. There was an abrupt silence like a clutch of pain. Then there came a faint memory of a whisper and a moment later, through the partially opened doorway, the shadow of Mme. Lazare passed briefly. Afterward a nurse came by, leaned in, and then closed the room into complete darkness. In bed, Andrew listened for a while to the exhausted quiet. Then, in French, he ventured two words.

"Good night."

But the answer he listened for in the dark did not come. The night was crucified by silence. Then some words of Anton Kanka's came back to him, for no reason at all. They had nothing to do with what he had just experienced, but the turmoil of his thoughts brought to the surface words from deep inside, as if he had heard them long ago. He listened to the thick German voice speaking once again. For a long while, as he lay quietly, he wondered again just why, when it comes to love, some men reach only for the unobtainable.

20

W HAT FIRST made Andrew aware of what was going on inside of him was his inability to get accustomed to the jostling. As the ambulance continued along the road, every movement bothered him. He wanted to breathe fresh air again, for the air in the ambulance was stagnant and infested with gas fumes. But the windows were not made to be opened. The further he got from the hospital, the worse he felt. He concentrated all his attention on holding his sickness quietly inside him as if it were an open bottle that he must not spill. On top of this his arm now throbbed. His clothes had been returned to him from the laundry only that morning and he had used his bad arm as well as his good one to climb into them.

The ambulance swung around a turn. The driver blew his horn at something, and then they began picking up speed again. Andrew heard nothing but the engine. He could feel it; he could smell it. There was nothing in the world he wanted more than for this journey to end. But the damned vehicle raced on heedlessly. He could do nothing but clutch with his photo-trained eyes at the briefly seen trees. He wished with all his heart that he could be with them—with the trees—standing firmly on the ground and sucking in air and seeing grass. Instead, he was caught behind the prison of the window, being taken where he did not want to go, and from where he would only have to return.

When it was at last over, and all movement had stopped, the relief came too late for him to find any joy in it. The two rear doors swung wide and he stepped down into the gray afternoon carrying his illness with him. There was a doorway inside **the** courtyard. The driver in the ambulance waited.

Police procedure may differ from country to country, but **the** attitude is always the same. With attentive unconcern, a bald, blue-uniformed sergeant faced him across an old barren desk. He sat on the other side as the sergeant recited a couple of dozen questions, listening with dead eyes as the young man answered each one in turn. For the whole time, even while the questioning went on, the room seemed strangely silent. At the end, Andrew signed a typed statement that gave his account of the little he knew about the accident. Then he reached into his pocket and took out his traveler's checks. They had been returned to him along with his saddlebags and his miraculously undamaged camera early that morning while he had still been asleep. Tearing out two checks, he signed them over. Only then did the grim-faced sergeant smile, and, for the first time, light and friendliness seemed to enter the room. In the manner of a man trying to win him over, the sergeant asked if he would now like to see the motorcycle. It was almost as if he were being given a special privilege. They took him into the courtyard, under a threatening sky, and led him to a doorless barnlike building where, inside against the wall, stood what was left of his German NSU. There was not much light, but he remained for some time staring with vacant wonder at the twisted and ruined machine. Later, as he walked back slowly and sadly across the courtyard, he became aware that his sickness had disappeared and in its place, curiously, was a most roguish feeling of immortality.

On the way back they stopped once more, and while the driver waited, he climbed out and made his way across the road toward the restaurant. The direction down which he had come ten days before was straight and lonely. The road curved where he was crossing it, but if it had not curved it would have led straight to the side of the building where a large window had recently been replaced with a new sheet of solid glass. At the foot of the wall were shattered pieces and slivers of the old window. Along the arid ground leading up to the side of the restaurant, there could be seen, occasionally, the straight tracks of a motorcycle. They were now fully caked and dry after that three-day spell of rain. Inside, the restaurant was empty except for an enormous woman seated on a stool at the cash register, reading a book. She put the book down as he came in, waddled out from behind the counter, and, with a genuine smile, waved a choice to him of any of the tables in the room. But halfway through her gesturing she came to a halt and inhaled quickly. Her smile vanished from her lips, but appeared again in her eyes.

"Edouard!" she called. The place filled with the sound of her high-pitched voice. "Edouard. He is *here*. Come!" And while she yelled in French with all her corpulent strength, her eyes looked at Andrew in a calm and curious way.

From out of the back room came a tall thin man who hurried without knowing why. He wore a dirty white apron with which he was feverishly drying his hands. When his wife explained to him who this stranger was, the man came alive with hospitality. Andrew was made to sit down. They brought out a glass of wine for him and then, for what seemed to him the hundredth time, he was told how lucky he was to be alive. By now he was beginning to believe it. Their ceremonious treatment of him was a surprise and he tried hard not to seem completely bewildered.

"I gave the police the money for the window," he said, hoping it would somehow repay their kindness.

"We know," smiled the fat woman who had seated herself next to him at the table. The man remained standing, looking down at him with a mixture of joy and amazement. He said: "The police just now phoned to tell us." Then he grinned also, and for a moment they were like two cats.

"I hope I haven't caused you too much trouble," Andrew said.

"Trouble? No, no!" said Edouard, earnestly.

"No trouble," said the fat woman.

"Many people come here afterward to eat," the man told him, nodding his head. He was holding onto the back of an empty chair and leaning over it slightly and then standing straight again in a casual rhythmic movement. "You got us into the newspaper. Many people come here to eat." He nodded his head with a foolish laugh. "For us it was good. Trouble? No, no."

"No trouble," said the fat woman.

Andrew shook his head in amazement. "Well, I'll be damned," he said in English, and then he took a sip of the wine.

"Drink up," Edouard smiled. "Drink up."

"You speak French very well," the fat woman said.

"Yes," her husband agreed. "You do."

"Thanks."

"Drink up," said she. "There is more."

"Yes," Edouard announced officially. "You can have more." But his face was blank and he shot a look at his wife.

The young man took another sip, but a twinge of conscience pulled at his sleeve and he remembered the ambulance waiting for him outside.

"Forgive me," he said sadly, "but I cannot stay. There is someone outside waiting.... But I came really to ask a question. Can you tell me...Well, what exactly did happen, anyway? Do you know?"

Their faces were baffled. He hurried to explain to them about the problem of his memory. There was a pause and then the fat woman began to speak.

"I was seated *there*...with a book. The place was empty. It had just stopped raining. No one had been in all day.... Well, all of a sudden there was such a...such a...sound my heart nearly stopped. I thought a bomb had landed. Oh, you should have heard it. But you were it! Oh, my! ..." And she shook her head apologetically, her lips quivering as she tried not to laugh at this accidental joke. "You came through that window *there* and like a cannon ball you went through all those chairs and tables until you stopped *there*." And she pointed to the opposite wall. "I didn't know what it was at first. I was so scared! Then, when I saw you lying there so still, I really got scared. I couldn't imagine what made you come through the window like that. Then Edouard came running from the kitchen and M. Fray ran in from outside. We called the ambulance."

"Did he see the whole thing?"

"Who?" they asked together like twin owls.

"M. Fray."

"Yes," said Edouard, "he was coming up the road. It had just stopped raining and he was going for a little drink."

"How much did he see?"

"All of it."

"What did he say?"

The tall Frenchman shrugged his shoulders. "He said you went off the road into the wall. That's all he said." It was as if he were reciting something quite elementary. "You went through the window, and the cycle bounced back onto the road. A few seconds later a truck came around the bend and ran over it. That's all." He shrugged again.

"A truck hit it afterward?" Andrew repeated stupidly.

"That's right."

"A truck, eh? ... But what caused me to go off the road? Did he say that?"

This time Edouard shrugged and said nothing.

"Wasn't there a child in the road? Something like that?"

"Child?" the Frenchman frowned. "Noooo! M. Fray said you went straight like an arrow. The road curved, but you didn't. You went right into the wall."

"But there was a child playing," said Andrew stiffly. "I was told that there was a child playing and that I was trying to avoid hitting it. That's why I left the road. Are you sure this is all he said?"

Edouard shook his head up and down slowly. His wife joined him.

"Nooooo," Edouard replied. "You went straight as an arrow. He said your head was sort of down all the while like you were looking at the ground below you. That's what he said. There was no child. There was no one."

The young man fingered the glass of wine on the table. "I see." The silence grew and seemed to warn him. "I see."

Afterward, as he crossed the unremembered road to where the ambulance was waiting, he took one last look down its gloomy stretch of trees. It wasn't until he was fully across and about to climb in that he realized it had again begun to rain.

21

BY LATE morning of the next day it had stopped raining, but to Andrew the reappearance of the sun was an event of little importance. He had become very quiet. When they arrived with the medicine wagon to attend to his neck he did not joke with them as he usually did. He remained inside himself, looked at no one, hardly spoke. Yvonne glanced at him questioningly, for she saw that something was wrong, but Sister Héloise and Annette went about their work as if they noticed nothing. For some reason Sister Veronica did not appear that morning. Since the Sister Superior was to be in the room with them for the entire examination, Yvonne behaved herself. When it was time for them to attend to Jean Lazare, Andrew left the room and went behind the wooden staircase to the open doorway, where he stood and watched the garden drying in the morning sun.

But his mind had gone back ten days to that wet road. Although he still remembered nothing, he now understood at last what had happened. He had begun worrying again to the point where he had fogotten what he was doing and had stupidly driven right off the road. He who had won motorcycle rallies on Long Island and had done hill climbing in Pennsylvania. It was too grotesque and foolish for words.

When his thoughts became too painful, he began strolling about aimlessly. But as he walked in the sun along a row of empty benches in the deserted garden, he realized that above all else he did not want to be alone that morning. Quickly he returned to the hospital, searching for someone he could talk to. He needed to distract his mind with the flippant pleasures of unimportant things. He went first to Anton Kanka's room and found the door open. He looked in with a smile, but the bed was empty. For a surprising moment there seemed to be no explanation. A quick search of the bathroom left him more puzzled than ever. Anton Kanka had died; that was it. The thought startled him. He walked through the dormitory without speaking to anyone, passed up the kitchen, and stepped into the sitting room. Two old, immobile men were frozen into a game of chess, and a small boy whose face was half-covered with bandages was seated at the other end of the long wooden table diligently drawing large faces on a huge pad with a big red crayon. Andrew went out through the other door and found himself in the rear yard of the hospital. Several men were seated near the wall, curing themselves in the sun. But Kanka was not among them. Off near the nurses' quarters, under a sheltering row of tranquil trees, he saw a number of shaded wooden chairs. Coming closer, he saw the back of a familiar head. The man glanced up from his book when he heard Andrew's metallic steps on the thickly covered, purposely pebbled ground, and when the man saw the look on the handsome face and the way the gloom was only half hidden behind a cheerless smile, he closed his book with a compact thud and asked the boy to sit down.

"I see you are not a sun worshiper," Andrew said, as he looked at the shadow of leaves on the austere face.

"Long ago," replied the thick German voice, "I learned that baking yourself in the sun produces on the organs of the body the equivalent of running for that same amount of time." He ran his palm gently across the top of the book in an almost loving gesture. "Since with *my* heart even walking is an adventure, I find it wiser to sit beneath a tree." He looked up into the branches cautiously. "I suppose the only danger now is falling fruit."

"Or a wood chopper," said the young man, but he was only pretending that his heart was light.

They spoke of casual things, but Kanka watched him with clinical attention.

"You appear depressed," said the German at last, and then he waited. But Andrew shrugged his shoulders and leaned his head against the back of the chair. "Don't tell me the screaming of M. Lazare has finally gotten you down?"

"I thought it got everybody down." Andrew said, as he watched the sunlit leaves moving overhead. "It's certainly loud enough."

"You know what the trouble is, don't you?"

"His leg got burnt."

"They didn't tell you? ... I suppose there was no point to it. Yet it does help to understand him .... You see ... he was castrated in the accident."

The young man lifted his head and there was shock in his eyes. Kanka returned the look calmly.

"Good *grief!*" cried the young man. Then he remembered the conversation he had overheard several nights ago and he thought about it for a while. "Jesus!"

"You know, I overheard him talking with his wife," Andrew said. "They were fighting, actually; not talking .... Then, I didn't understand."

Kanka removed the pince-nez from his face. "He is terror-stricken that he will now lose his wife. All sorts of things are going on in his mind. Slowly, he is tearing himself apart."

"But the way he's acting will surely drive her away."

"She will leave him anyhow. It is only a matter of time. I believe he understands this."

"*Must* it break up? Do *all* women run out at a time like this?"

"Yes, I suppose," said Kanka. "If the woman involved is really a woman. Marriage has become no longer a pledge to the death. Perhaps this is a good thing. She is still young, you know."

"And what becomes of *him?*" the young man said, and with his shoe he scraped aside a thick layer of pebbles until he could see a bit of the black earth.

"He will seek to put his life together again. And with the right attitude he'll do it."

"He hasn't got a chance," Andrew announced. "Not after a thing like that. At best he will just exist."

"And *there* is where we disagree."

Andrew looked at him again. "Remember, you are talking now about a man living without sex."

"Correct. It *can* be done."

"Impossible."

"Not at all."

"*Ah!*" sounded the answer of disbelief, and Andrew settled back into the slope of the chair as if in complete seclusion. He placed his legs on top of one of the flat wooden arms, and he appeared almost to be reclining. The white-topped Pyrenees, ragged and rocklike, seemed unreal in the great distant mist.

The young man's arm thrust into the air. "It just cannot be," he said with wide eyes. "It can't." But he became restless because Kanka remained annoyingly unconvinced. "I suppose you could show me someone who has performed this miracle?" the young man inquired, sarcastically. "I mean, not just a story about someone who knows someone who knows someone."

"I believe I could."

"All right... show me."

Kanka raised both arms slightly as if in a gesture of capitulation, his palms turned up and out. Into his eyes came a spark of intention that paralleled the movement of his hands, but its meaning was at first unintelligible. There was a frightening pause.

"*You!*" Andrew questioned him.

A feeble smile ebbed into the cold German lips and then was gone. He lifted the pince-nez and returned them to his nose.

"I assume you have already been told about my condition? My first heart attack came when I was about your age. Perhaps younger. I was always aware that I had a heart condition. I knew it ever since I was a child. But what I didn't know was that the day was coming when I would have to surrender all activities, both physical and emotional—everything that put even the slightest strain upon the heart. I don't want to give you a false impression. At first it was severely difficult. In fact, it did seem to me in the beginning that I was being forced to stop living entirely. But slowly I learned that this was not the case. It took me a few years. Then I had it beaten."

The young man carefully surveyed the other's face. He didn't know whether he felt admiration or fright.

"I cannot see," he said slowly, "how it can be done. You mean to say that with the same urges of other men you have found a way to give up women, physical activities, everything? My God, you have given up *everything*. The whole world!"

"And found another world in its place. You see, the urges of the human being are relative. But you do not dismiss an urge by satisfying it. It only returns stronger than ever. You must simply substitute a different desire in its place, one that you can deal with. Don't you know that you can eliminate desire just as you can eliminate fatigue? Energy thrives on activity. If you can find new activities, you can find new energies. As simple as that. The first step in conquering the problem of sex is to erase the submissive attitude that nothing can be done about it. This is the big victory. You see, it is all a matter of faith."

"Faith in what?" Andrew snapped.

"Ah, I can see disbelief growing in you. Don't worry, I am not an intellect without a soul. That would be a cliché. By 'faith' I mean faith in the superiority of the mind over everything else. That is the essence of the life struggle: the mind against all else—against the entire universe, in fact."

The voice of Anton Kanka revealed the sober excitement of a man talking on that one topic which means more to him than any other, which is the very crux of the man.

"But we are not getting down to the real problem."

"Have faith," Kanka said, holding up a finger. A playful look brightened his features. But then he became himself again. "Look at it this way: No matter what happens to a man—let it be anything—it simply gives him a new point of view, a new outlook. In that alone can be found reward more than enough. But it is up to the man. You see, the trick is not to try to consciously control one's emotions. Do you understand me? That's where so many go wrong. The trick is to exercise this." And he tapped his head at the temple. "You must go so deeply into the workings of your own existence that finally you discover that your emotions have become ideas, which is what they have been striving to become all along. Then to harness them will be easy. 'A complete life,' said Bernard Berenson, 'may be one ending in so full an identification with the not-self that there is no self left to die.' In fact, there it is in one sentence."

Behind these words was a meaning that Andrew found hard to penetrate. It was heavy, like the door of a prison, massive and difficult to move even during those moments when it was unlocked. His uneasiness turned to irritation, for he found himself still unconvinced.

"But each man is different," he told Kanka. "What might be possible for you..."

"Ah, but how do you know? I ask you? There are many jobs that look impossible until we finally do them. No man can know his limits unless he tries to reach them. The important thing to bear in mind is the attitude of faith. I know what it is to follow advice. It is sometimes hard even in the simplest of matters. The Bible tells us that Christ occasionally had trouble following his own teachings. Even Christ!"

"Now you sound like the Church."

"Ah, you have missed the point. Or perhaps it is I who missed it.... The Church is dying slowly and I am living slowly and that is about as much as we have in common. The Church thrives on the belief that it is you who need *it*, while actually it is the Church who needs *you*. Never forget that God is a rumor that has never been proven, heaven is a promise that has never been fulfilled, and hell is a bluff that has never been called." Then his eyes blazed brighter than Andrew had ever seen them. "And remember—above all else remember that the most important truth for a man to teach himself is that man does not need truth. He has been living without it for a million years and I suppose he will have to live without it for a million more. Whoever said that man wants the truth, anyway?

He loves generalities far too much for that. Truth and man are not really meant for each other, because man should not limit himself to knowing the impossible, and truth teaches him what is and is not impossible. Besides, the complete man needs nothing, not even people to understand him."

Here an exhausted silence settled upon them. Far overhead, out of reach, there floated an ornament of clouds. Andrew's arm hung uselessly over the edge of the chair. The tips of his fingers felt the pebbled floor of the yard. Without thought, he took up a single little stone and examined it. It felt sharp and indestructible between two fingers, and when he pressed hard it dug into his skin. His heart was whispering repeatedly: What did he just say? Did I hear anything for me? Was there anything there for me?

Slowly, so slowly at first that it did not seem to be happening at all, Anton Kanka moved himself toward the edge of his chair. His face was blank with self-absorption. He put aside the book, and then, placing a hand on the edge of each flat, wooden arm, he gradually, slowly, painstakingly lifted himself to his feet.

"You know, it takes me half the morning to walk out here," he said, almost cheerfully, "and then half the afternoon again to get back. If I wish to make it in time for dinner, I had better get started."

He moved his left leg forward and carefully placed his weight on it. Then, wearily, he dragged his other foot through the pebbles until at last it was even with the first. Now he had advanced one single step. After a pause he repeated this all over again, started forward once more with his left leg. Andrew watched his lingering, lumbering, nerve-racking pace with great concern. He was on his feet now himself, but he knew he would be unable to walk with Kanka at this pace. It would be too embarrassing for both of them. Yet it would be just as impossible for him to wait where he was and watch, or to walk briskly ahead and leave the German behind. With inexplicable repugnance he turned against this man and his weak heart, against everything about him, particularly the way he made him stand helplessly watching the foot drag across the empty yard, leaving a thick line throught the pebbles. There was no time for thought. Andrew was driven hurriedly into action.

"Wait!" he called to Kanka, who had covered half an eternity with only four steps. "Stay here. I'll be right back."

He was halfway across the yard before he had decided what he was going to do, and he was almost all the way across before he realized with surprise that he was running. He waited for danger signals from his legs, but when none came he kept on the run. Rounding the side of the hospital, he entered into the garden and there luckily spotted the very man he was looking for. Andrew had often seen him come and go through the hospital, but he had never given the man a second thought. Now it was different. The man was terribly thin and white and it was hard to tell his age except that he was over fifty. But all that really concerned Andrew was the wheel chair the man was seated in. After listening to the brief explanation of what the American wanted, the old Frenchman thought for a moment, considered what was being asked of him, and then agreed. Awkwardly Andrew helped him out of his chair and then lowered him onto a nearby bench. Running again and using his good arm, he pushed the empty wheel chair ahead of him and rounded the corner of the building. With his shoes churning loudly on the pebbled yard, he came up to Kanka and then, leaning backward, pulled the chair to a stop.

"Well, well," spoke the thick German voice. "Now why didn't I think of that?"

With Kanka in the chair, Andrew was unable to run with it. The weight was so much greater now that the wheels moved with difficulty over the pebbles. He had to exert more strength than he had expected. He placed his shoulder against the back of the chair and managed to keep it moving briskly until he could wheel it up the plank into the game room. The little boy with the bandaged face was gone, but the two men lifted their eyes from their checkered battlefield and smiled blankly at what they saw. Andrew pushed the wheel chair past the kitchen door and into the dormitory.

Kanka sat happily holding his book on his lap, and when several cheers rang out from the double row of beds, Kanka called in a gleeful voice: "You see, and all these years we used to laugh. American ingenuity! There really *is* such a thing."

The laughter rang louder than ever, but it was all behind them now, for he was pushing the chair rapidly down the hall. At last it reached the door of Kanka's room. The young man wheeled it in and then dragged it to a stop. Laboriously the German changed chairs, and when he was comfortably settled again he surveyed Andrew's face and saw it was aglow with the excitement of action. There was a pause, and it seemed to settle into the young man's blood and compose him.

"You were depressed a few minutes ago," Kanka said slowly, his voice housed in an odd silence. Andrew found the room soothing. Everything was strangely still. "But don't worry. You won't stay depressed. Not here. Not with this sun to suck up your energies and not with these simple, friendly people always at hand. Why, I would venture that even M. Lazare would find contentment if he remained here long enough." Into his eyes came that playful look that was generally as near as he ever got to a real grin. He added, "I mean, all faith aside."

Soon after this, Kanka reminded him that the owner was probably waiting for his wheel chair, and so the young man pushed it out and down the hall again, gathering speed as he went. He wasn't thinking now. It was easier that way. As he sped the chair through the dormitory, he noticed that some of the men were watching him with friendly attention. This gave him courage and he pulled the chair to a stop at the front of one of the beds where Yvonne was busy changing the sheets. He surprised her with a strong tug at her arm which made her stumble back against the chair and right into it. The girl screamed and the dormitory filled with the sturdy weight of male laughter. As he sped her down the aisle, she twisted around in the suddenly moving chair in which she was trapped and discovered Andrew's smiling face behind her. She was just able to put on a stern look of pretended reproach when the wheel chair dipped down the plank to the game room, and she squealed again. The men in the dormitory, though they could no longer see what was happening, heard her, and again responded with laughter. Keeping the chair going fast enough so she couldn't get to her feet, Andrew swung it out into the yard and around the building to the garden and Yvonne hung on with fearful pleasure as he sped up to the bench, and then, when she squealed once more, alarmed that he was going to run her right into it, he leaned backward and dragged the wheel chair to an abrupt halt.

"Here I am back again," Andrew said to the old man on the bench, "and look what I've brought you. M. Kanka asks you to accept this little offering as an expression of his thanks."

The pretty nurse had recovered herself by now and was on her feet standing in front of him.

"*Ou!*" she stormed with inarticulate fury. "*Oh!*" But her face became drained of all its sternness and he saw that her mouth was forcing back a smile. With a savage toss of her head she turned rearward, and with long and elegant strides which carried her disdainfully away from her kidnaper, she hurried back to her job. Andrew, smiling, helped the white-skinned gentleman back into his wheel chair. Then, after thanking him once more, he strode away leisurely along the path of the garden. But as if stored up and waiting, the result of all this running came to him now, and shapes of darkness began moving through his mind. With weakened legs he stepped to the nearest bench and slumped into it, covering his eyes with his hand. For a few moments he felt sick. Waiting, he did not move until the worst of it was gone. Only then did he lower his hand from his eyes and rub his face on his sleeve.

"Don't worry," Kanka had said, "you won't stay depressed. Not here." With ironic humor Andrew savored the sickening weakness inside his own body and then looked again at the hospital standing in the sun.

"Oh, I'm not depressed," he said to no one. "Hopeless, maybe. **But** not depressed."

22

B UT Anton Kanka was right. Not only did the pall of depression lift from Andrew's mind, but he slowly began to enjoy a sensation of such warmth and well-being that he couldn't remember when he had ever felt better. This sensation had been growing ever since he had entered the hospital, and, despite moments of remorse, it had continued to thrive and flourish until he suddenly became conscious of it and it was no longer a secret. When had he felt so confident? He could not recall. Must have been years ago when he, leading his friends on their cycles, laughed and roamed Long Island from end to end. The feeling meant more to him than he dared to think.

The kitchen was warm with mirth. He stood in the center, his body stiff, his head turned. With his bad arm (it was no longer in a sling, for it no longer throbbed) he gripped a limp dish towel and held the arm stiff and down across his body.

"Hu hey." His mouth hung open.

"Hu hey!" Yvonne answered. She stood proud and tall, like a dancer about to begin. At each hip she held a candle pointed at the young man in front of her. She took one step and paused. She took another and paused. Her body leaned forward, as if she were about to fall. Then she came at him with four quick graceful steps, and he made a *pase natural*. The candle on her left hip almost touched him as it went by. The cook, a chubby woman with a playful face, applauded, and called out, "*Olé*." Andrew made three more passes, feet together, standing straight and stately, while the girl flowed past him, the uplifted nose of her sensual face almost touching his each time. Then Andrew knelt in spectacular fashion on the floor of the kitchen and a chanting of "Ohhhh" filled the room. But as he held both ends of the dishcloth like a cape and swung it through the air, she lifted the candle near him and without removing her hand from her hip she bounced the candle on his head and continued past him. The cook screamed with approval, but Andrew snapped the dish towel sharply, like a whip, and before the giggling girl could get away, she felt the towel bite rudely into her rump. Annette roared with pleasure. Yvonne lifted a threatening candle high into the air and stepped toward him. But at the last minute she changed her mind. She pulled her lips apart and exposed her teeth in that sour smile of hers that looked so odd and evil, but which somehow left him indifferent. The young man heard the cook's whispering voice.

"Isn't he handsome?"

Turning on his knees, Andrew was just in time to see Annette nodding her head in agreement. But the cook noticed Andrew looking at her. The glint in his eyes made her fear that he might have overheard her. She quickly climbed to her feet and snatched the candles from the nurse's hands.

"*Now* let's play," she challenged, as she backed him furiously around the kitchen, using the candles like swords. The other two in the room became silly with laughter.

It was half an hour later by the clock on the wall when Yvonne glanced up casually and saw with fright that time had run ahead without her. She uncrossed her legs and started to get to her feet, but paused midway to jab her cigarette three times into an ash tray on the table.

"Ou, ou, ou, I must go," she cried, and in one bound she was out of the room and into the hall.

"Well," said the cook, noticing the clock, "there are still some dishes to be done." Then, turning to Andrew she added, "Now, if you really want to be of some help..."

"Oh, I'd love to," he answered, "but my arm, you know." And immediately he began to favor it. "It was the war. Did I ever tell you?

Well, you see, there I was, Paris had fallen, the Army was beaten and the German Air Force kept coming. It was terrible—plane after plane after plane ..." But he was moving toward the garden door as he talked because the cook had grabbed the candles again from where they had been lying idle by the sink. Holding them together like a single club, she came slowly and menacingly toward him. Her face was pretending the breaking point of exasperation. " 'Here comes a bomber,' the French major said to me. 'Fire at it.' And so I did. 'No, no, no,' he shouted, 'I didn't say knock it down. I just said fire at it. You don't want to get them angry, do you?' " At this Andrew had to run for it and he vanished through the door into the dark. Silhouetted in the doorway, she peered into the night, but was unable to see him. The candles were ready in her upheld hand. Then, before she went back in: "Americans!" she said, with a baffled shake of her head. "May the Lord have mercy on us."

There was no moon that night, but Andrew already knew his way about the hospital grounds without any trouble. The windows of the buildings were almost all bright with light, and as he went by he could see into some of them and watch for a moment the peacefully inert and lounging life of the sick. The blackness that engulfed him was friendly and peaceful, and he walked with ease, as if he were in his own bedroom. His mind was very still.

He thought for a while of Yvonne, and once again wondered about her with amazement. The girl had been flaunting her beauty at him constantly, yet not once did this frighten him or awaken in him feelings of anxiety. He did not stare at her or look away, unable to meet her eyes. A month before, he would not have believed this possible. His mind, when he looked at her now, remained clear and untroubled by desire. There were no signs of the usual gabble of sensual confusion. He had no idea why this was so, but it explained the pleasure he felt.

Looking through the windows into the men's dormitory, he was reminded of something that had happened that afternoon. While walking between the two long rows of beds, smiling cordially in return to cordial smiles, he had been overwhelmed by the vast harmony of kindness and good will. As one face after another warmed to him as he went, he felt his heart become flooded by a joy such as he could not remember except when he had been a foolish little boy during those simple years when happiness was much easier to find. And as he left the large room and went into the dim hallway, it seemed to him that worry was but a vicious little lie that really had no meaning at all.

Leaving the dormitory behind him, he walked through the blackness until he came to another building, of whose purpose he was not sure. Going around it on the right he found, on the other side, a large courtyard. At the far end of this courtyard was a wide gateway that let out into the cobbled streets of the town. Why not? he thought. A walk through the town appealed to him, and perhaps he would want to come back to take pictures of it the next day. But at the gate, as he was about to pass through it into the outside world, a voice from the guardhouse stopped him. He had no idea it was occupied at this hour, so he turned with surprise. Did he have a pass? No? Well then he really couldn't be allowed out. The man speaking to him appeared genuinely sorry, but rules were rules. If he could get the doctor to give him written permission, then it would be different. Otherwise he was truly very sorry.

"Who are you supposed to keep from escaping?" Andrew asked with a pleasant smile. "The sick, or the cured?"

"They never told me," said the gatekeeper. "Perhaps everybody."

"Even the nurses?" the young man added quickly.

"Ah, of course. They are the most important. It is they who really give the orders to the doctors. Did you know that?"

"And who gives orders to the nurses?"

"Why, the nuns, certainly."

"And the nuns? Who gives *them* orders?"

"Ah, if we only knew," sighed the gatekeeper. "If we only knew."

At last Andrew waved good night and turned his back on the town. He had been stopped at the gate, but somehow it failed to bother him. He was surprised at the ease with which he accepted the confines of the hospital wall. How willing he was to remain just where he was. Surprising.

The limitless freedom of the night beckoned his thoughts. As he walked and reflected, not conscious of what he was thinking, he suddenly recalled the idea of abstinence that had been expressed in his presence. It had aroused his anger because he had wanted very much to agree with it but couldn't. The idea was really an ancient one, but somehow he had the fantastic feeling that this very thought had survived to the twentieth century just so that one day it would be spoken in the courtyard of a small village hospital near the Spanish-French border and that he would be there to hear it. Perhaps it was the comforting stillness of the late evening, perhaps it was the feeling of well-being and completeness that was newly his, but the need of women in his private and most personal world—a need that he had always believed tremendous and all-important— had struck him now and for the very first time as perhaps not so important after all. Certainly at this moment there was no need. Then why must there *ever* be one? The everyday presence of Yvonne, which once might have been so disturbing, now made no claims on him at all. Perhaps he had changed. He had watched the movements of her beautifully sinuous legs and studied the dangerous lure of her young body, but he had come away profoundly content and untroubled by the greed of longing. Could a man do without love without giving up life? Standing secretly in the comfort of the dark and looking up with unseeing eyes at the silent black turbulence in the sky, he found he actually believed that it could be done. And more important, he believed that, in fact, it was he who could do it.

"Ah, here you are," The loud voice startled him. "You were not in your room when I came by."

Down the steps of the building that faced the gate came the graceful figure of Dr. de Lyese. He seemed to be in a great hurry and not really happy at having suddenly found Andrew standing there in the dark, but he stopped for a moment in the manner of one who is nervously about to rush off again at any moment.

The light from the tall lamppost at the front gate reached out just enough from across the wide courtyard to give life to the whiteness of the handsome teeth.

"What is that I see?" he asked. "Is that your arm out of the sling?"

"Yes," Andrew explained. "I removed it just after dinner. You see it felt so..."

"Good, good, good. So it is off. That is good. What I desire to say to you is this. You see? To tell you that the time, it has come for you to leave us."

The doctor smiled at the bringing of the news, but to Andrew the teeth gleamed insidiously.

"Leave?"

"Ah, *oui*." And then he laughed. "The time had to come, you know." Then he laughed again, but this time much louder.

"But I thought...I mean...at least..."

"But you must be happy? Now you can continue your travels, eh?" Again came the laughter, but it rang hollow in the night. He stepped closer, and in an intimate tone said, "You see...we need your bed." This was in a voice heavy with concealed meaning, but Andrew understood nothing but the nearness of a face and the scent of aftershave lotion.

"Ah, *oui*," the doctor cried, moving away. "The world is filling up with the sick. Every day they come. More and more, like an army. I tell you, the world is filling up with the sick." He was leaving now, walking backward. "I must go. *Vite, vite, vite.* Every day, more and more like an army. Nothing can stop them. Endlessly, endlessly." Heading along the wall in the opposite direction of the gate, his voice disappeared into the darkness along with the rest of him.

He had to get back to his room. That was all Andrew could think of. It was the only place he could go. To get there he had to proceed along the side of the building in the same general direction taken by the doctor. His mind was too shattered to make sense of what he had just been told. He realized only that he was frightened, without knowing why. Mechanically, his feet moved him forward through the blackness. Then, up ahead, small windows of light could be seen with eerie suddenness in the center of nowhere. The face of Dr. de Lyese appeared swiftly, and then with a thump the windows vanished. Of course, Andrew thought, understanding at last. His car. It's the doctor climbing into his Citroën. With every movement the young man expected the engine to roar and the headlights to be turned on. But there was only silence. In the dark he could barely make out the shape of the automobile and he wondered what the doctor was doing inside. Andrew came to the corner of the building and was about to turn and head down along the other wall when he saw something move. His eyes lost it immediately and then found it again heading toward the car. Again the windows appeared, for someone had opened the door on the side opposite the driver. She climbed through and dropped into the seat and into the curve of the Frenchman's arm. Swiftly the door closed once more, but in that brief moment Andrew saw smiling at the doctor a face he knew quite well. Intimate and eager, it had a bold grin.' The lips were pulled apart in an impudently exposed animal grimace, as if lust had eaten away the flesh to reveal forever the skeleton teeth.

Andrew was afraid to move for fear of being seen. He waited a long while for something to happen, but from the secret and terrible darkness within the automobile came no sound or movement. Then with stunning suddenness the motor retched and roared and headlights cut through the night. The Citroën leaped forward, and with a speed far greater than necessary it rushed down the drive, screeched into a turn, and, with a wave of an arm at the gatekeeper, the automobile disappeared. Now invisible on the opposite side of the wall, the car thundered down the street, grew weak and vanished. So it is the nurse the doctor drives off with, and not the nun. Failing to win the impossible, which he wants more than anything, he simply settles for less. And yet, Andrew thought, how very easy even that must be, if one is only given a choice.

The young man continued his way along the building, his head in a whirl. He reached with his hand and in the dark felt the symmetrical roughness of the bricks. When he came to where the two sides of the building formed a corner, he stopped. Above him the great silent turmoil reflected the presence of the moon. Somewhere far off, to his left, stood the tall Pyrenees. But now, as he looked, he could not see them.

He had been told that he must leave. He had not been prepared for such bad news. Now was not the time to leave. Certainly not now. He had to be sure—very sure—before stepping through the gates again and going out on his own. It was all too soon. Why did things like this always have to happen? Just because a man's body has healed, does that mean he is ready? He had only been in the hospital for about a week, but now they were making him leave. He wondered when. Tomorrow? God! There were too many things to settle before tomorrow. Kanka had said that it could be done. He had believed him, but now he wasn't sure any longer. He was being rushed out of believing. He was being rushed into doubt. There was only one thing to do.

Andrew hurried forward on swiftly moving feet. Each length of ground was a step toward deliverance. As he hurried along the gravel path he decided wildly that, even should the door be closed and the German asleep, he would knock.

23

THERE WAS a scurry of feet outside the door and then the quick, anxious knocking of knuckles.

"*Entrez,*" Kanka said at once. He seemed to sense a toll of alarm in the impatient noise.

The door burst open and in came Sister Veronica, as if escaping from a dying world. Her face was filled with apprehension and her words came clipped when she spoke.

"M. Kanka, if you please—do you speak Finnish?"

At this he threw back his blankets and began the job of lowering himself until his feet touched the floor. They seemed to understand each other perfectly.

"Would you help him?" said the nun to Andrew, who was sitting in a chair beside the bed. Then to the German she added: "Please, please be careful." After this she hurried out.

"What's happening?" the young man asked as he helped Kanka slide off the mattress.

"Another one of those inopportune opportunities, a chance to be a hero in my own small way. You are getting competition, my boy. Would you hand me my bathrobe? Thank you."

Kanka moved slowly toward the door. His pace was a bit faster than it had been the day before in the garden, but to Andrew it still seemed impossibly slow. Sister Veronica had opened the door on them, letting in the outside world, and now their interrupted hour-long talk was already slipping into the past like a distantly small and ever shrinking room.

"Look," Andrew said when they were both out in the hall, "let me hunt up that wheel chair for you."

But Kanka saw Sister Veronica appear in the distance of the corridor, and as she looked at him, her terrified eyes gave away the secret wish in her heart for him to hurry. She had no idea, though, that she had thus betrayed herself, and she even managed a smile before she stepped back into the emergency room.

"Too late now," Kanka said coldly and for a brief moment he simply stood and looked down the dark and empty passageway. Then, as if he had thrown away the chains of his affliction, he suddenly began to walk with the strides of a healthy man. Andrew felt himself tremble as he watched. He wanted to call out a warning, but the turmoil inside of him resulted in complete inaction. When Kanka at last entered the emergency room, the young man had to run to catch up with him.

But at the door he stopped, and there he stood. Two teen-age boys had been carried in out of the night and were being treated. One of them lay on a stretcher on the floor by the wall. An army blanket covered him to his head. He was more unconscious than awake, and occasionally he would moan softly to himself with the tone of someone deep in struggle with a bad dream. On the table was another boy, and it was to him that most of the attention was being paid. Half of his young face had been somehow reduced to chopped meat, and his clothes were entirely soaked with his own blood. But he did not seem to know that any damage had been done his face. Instead, he appeared to be terrified by the very fact of the hospital itself, and by the discovery of finding himself inside. There was a doctor standing next to the emergency table. He looked about thirty and was prematurely bald. He was staring about him in the manner of a man completely lost. Two nurses stood by, patiently waiting for someone to give them orders. One was a night nurse whom Andrew didn't recognize. The other was Annette. Her unattractive, unexpressive, uninterested face was the same as always. She looked at Andrew as he stood frozen in the doorway, but her eyes only seemed to be looking past him into the darkness.

As soon as Kanka had entered, he went directly to the boy lying on the table and began speaking to him in Finnish. Sister Veronica, at the other end of the room where she had gone to fetch something from one of the glass cabinets, was staring at Kanka with alarm. She had not missed the normal walking strides that he was now taking and her hand flew unconsciously to her lips. But the doctor in attendance was greatly relieved, for Kanka immediately took over the authority of the room.

"He is trying to say," Kanka informed them after he had spoken briefly with the boy, "that he is allergic to toxoid. He has been told that if he gets a strong dose of it he might die."

"But we weren't going to give him any," the doctor said with relief.

"Then that's settled. Is he bleeding anywhere but his face?"

"No," replied the night nurse.

"And the one on the stretcher?"

"A head concussion," the doctor put in.

"Take his pulse," Kanka ordered in a quiet tone.

"We did."

"Take it again," Kanka blurted out, "and keep taking it." Then he looked at the frightened boy on the table and his tone changed. Still speaking to the doctor, he asked: "How did all this happen?"

"Auto accident."

"How fast were they going? Does anyone know?"

"I don't know." The doctor turned to look at Sister Veronica, who was kneeling and taking the pulse of the boy on the stretcher. The nun felt his eyes on her.

"All I know, M. Kanka," she said without looking around, "was that they were racing with another car."

"Who was driving?"

There was no answer.

"Why don't you ask the boy?" the doctor suggested with a slight sting of annoyance in his words.

"Because, my dear doctor, he remembers absolutely nothing." Without looking at the doorway, the German added: "Something like your case, Mr. Williams. Not uncommon. Not uncommon." He adjusted his pince-nez. "Well, what remains to be done? I believe *that* one was driving," he said, indicating the stretcher. "Did you examine his chest and legs?"

"Not his legs."

"Go to it. And of course you intend to pick the glass out of this one's face? Do you not?"

"Yes, yes, of course," the doctor said as he went to the stretcher. He looked back for a second for approval but saw that Kanka was absorbed in another conversation with the boy with the damaged face.

"He says he's cold," Kanka explained, looking around. Annette took up a blanket from one of the chairs and came forward with it. The boy listened with tear-filled eyes as Kanka offered some comforting words. Then he patted the boy twice on the shoulder and was done with him. It was as if the boy ceased to exist. "I suppose that's it," he said looking about the room vaguely. A strange look came over his face.

"Oh, thank you so very much," said the warm and respectful voice of Sister Veronica as she stood up from the stretcher to look at him. But Kanka did not seem to hear.

"You are doing quite well," he said to the young doctor without conviction, but the doctor's face beamed.

"Both legs are fine," he announced happily. "But I did discover some deep cuts about the knees."

Again Anton Kanka did not hear.

"Yes, quite well," he said. "Keep it up." He was moving toward the door.

"Thank you," the doctor replied.

"Please be careful," called Sister Veronica.

None of the others could see his face now. Only Andrew watched how white and weary it was. The man coming toward him now possessed all of the hindered and brittle movements of the very old. He had returned once again to his slow, painstaking shuffle. Andrew held up the flat of his hand like a policeman stopping traffic.

"Wait!" he said in a wildly intimate tone. "I'll get the wheel chair."

Coming alive, he raced down the dark corridor, his legs kicking furiously behind him. The dormitory was heavy with the presence of sleep. Frantically he turned his head from side to side, searching between the beds while he ran. He felt his bandage loosening slightly about his neck, but it was of no concern to him. A dark shape between two of the beds caught his eye and in a moment he was running back in the direction he had come, pushing the wheel chair recklessly in front of him.

Kanka was just outside the emergency room, standing with his back against the wall. He appeared completely absorbed in thought, but Andrew didn't like the way his face looked or the way he seemed to be using the wall for support. Andrew had placed the chair into position and was about to help him into it when he noticed that Kanka was not even aware of him. The young man stepped closer and touched his arm. Kanka's face lifted slightly but his eyes were still lost.

"It is coming now, I think."

That was all he said, and Andrew watched with a slowly opening mouth. The hallway in which they stood hummed with silence. Anton Kanka looked as though he were trying to detect some specific sound, far off and almost lost, the very effort of which took all his awareness. Andrew debated what to do. He looked at the wheel chair, and with a little gesture was about to suggest that perhaps it would be best for Kanka to climb in when, with astonishment, he felt an arm being placed around his shoulders. Before he could really prepare himself he was supporting almost all of the man's weight. Kanka's face was digging into the young man's chest and Andrew had to circle his waist with both arms to keep him from falling. He was just about to call for help when Kanka's hand settled over his mouth and held in the frightened cry. The only sound in the corridor was the brittle breaking of glass as the pince-nez fell to the floor. The two of them clung together, Andrew leaning backward to balance the weight, and the stricken man circling his neck and clamping his mouth. Gradually Anton Kanka pulled himself up until he was again able to take most of his weight onto his own legs.

"Say nothing … to my room … hurry."

Only when he was seated in the wheel chair did he remove his hand from the young man's face.

"Don't worry," Kanka whispered, "I know what I'm doing… go on."

As the chair rolled along the smooth floor, a tiny squeak rose rhythmically from one of its wheels.

"Much obliged," Kanka whispered again after the young man had lifted him bodily into the bed. But he held Andrew by the wrist and wouldn't let him go.

"Let me call them," Andrew pleaded.

"But there is nothing anyone can do," the German explained with renewed strength. "Believe me when I tell you that. Besides, they are busy, anyway…. Don't look so terrified. You'll scare me half to death."

"Why the hell did you walk like that?"

A little glimmer was visible in the gray eyes of the stricken man's milk-white face. Slowly he said: "If a man is not ready to risk his life, where is his dignity?" To this, he added: "You know, I can't remember now if I made that up or read it somewhere."

The breathing was coming with more difficulty and Andrew knew the man was getting worse. But he could not run from the room as he wanted to. The grip of fingers on his wrist was amazingly firm. It seemed to chain him. He could not run. He could not move.

"Give Sister Héloise a message for me…. Tell her…not to worry about the world. Tell her that…that people who have been immoral will be punished by sin."

Here his mouth broke into an irrepressible smile, and it bloomed brighter than any smile the young man had ever seen Anton Kanka display.

"Tell her that for me, will you?" Kanka whispered, and for a moment he appeared to glow with pleasure at his sly little joke. "But tell…tell the woman I think highly of her…. Yes, tell her…I think very highly of her."

In the doorway of the small room appeared Sister Veronica. In her hands she held a pair of broken pince-nez. Her lovely face seemed to be quivering. Kanka immediately beckoned her to the other side of his bed. With his free hand he clasped one of hers and held it firmly. His eyes examined her face and saw that it was now even more beautiful because of its terror-stricken concern. Her mouth hung partly open, but it seemed like a bloodless wound rather than an organ through which one would speak.

"And afterward," he scolded them, "don't mourn for me, or for yourselves, which is really why people mourn." Then he saw how the tears were standing in her eyes. "Yes... it's all right to cry," he whispered to her. "It's good to have people cry for you.... Yet... I would rather have it be Mr. Williams," he grinned. "Women cry so easily."

From the darkness beyond the open door the stillness of the sleeping hospital moved in on them.

They saw Kanka grin once more. "I always had a fear," he said slowly, "that my death would be pure Lewis Carroll.... But it's all right. Everything has worked out fine.... I had always wanted to die in Italy. Italians are the people to die among... they understand. With them, crying is not a shame. It is an art.... But with you two youngsters... it is all right... it is fine."

An odd look settled onto his face. He stared for a moment at the ceiling.

"*Now*," he said to her, after making a careful study of her lovely, grief-stricken features. "*Now* you may go and get that doctor."

He spoke vigorously as if he had decided not to die after all. He released her hand. With a ruffle of her black skirts, she was gone.

"And you, Mr. Williams, will you do me a favor? Return that wheel chair to its owner, please. I can't help thinking he might need it and find it gone."

To protest seemed impossible, so Andrew performed the errand as quickly as he could and hurried back. He got to the door at the same time as did Sister Veronica. She had brought the doctor, who was hurrying along behind her looking more frightened than ever. They all entered the small room together.

His face was slightly contorted and the skin was an awful blue. It had happened while they were gone, and it was clear that he had timed it this way. They all stood without moving and each one watched Kanka's face as if awaiting some further word.

24

FACING SEAWARD at his morning table, he awaited breakfast by drumming with idle fingers and watching as the visitors to the city passed slowly in the streets. Beyond was the flat open sea of the Mediterranean. A bicycle glided silently along the curb, balanced by a family of three. The child, hidden in a bundled blanket, was held tightly in the mother's right arm. Down on the gray sand of the distant beach ran a group of bathers throwing a large volleyball. Out in the distant bay there floated, motionless as rock, a warship of the United States Navy.

Vaguely attentive to the pompous parading of people, he noticed two who stopped, deliberated a moment, and finally seated themselves at the open-air restaurant just one table away. The man was about twenty-three, with a crew haircut and a thin boyish face. He lounged with one arm sprawled over the small table top, carelessly clutching the hand of his young bride. They pressed their heads together as they leaned inward to share the single menu, and as they did so her tiny earrings chimed a brittle little ring. His legs were extended straight out, with his feet crossed at the ankles. The top two buttons of his sport shirt had been left casually open. He looked like a tennis player who had just returned victorious from the courts.

Andrew had seen them once before that same morning. They were checking in at the desk when he came down from his room. The hotel was a small inexpensive one, buried in one of the back streets blocks away. It struck Andrew as a pleasant coincidence that he saw them again so soon.

It was obvious that they were newlyweds. After they gave their breakfast orders she immediately and impishly moved her chair closer to his. He asked her something (probably, was she happy) and her eyes and mouth went wide with enchantment. She quickly pantomimed her feelings with inarticulate gestures. Finally, frustrated by her inability to find the proper words, her face bubbled into a sudden laugh and her head fell with a swoon of delight upon her husband's shoulder. He gave a lazy little laugh, but then she surprised him with a long, luxurious kiss.

The girl herself was striking. Andrew found himself observing her figure, her slim ankles, the white texture of her skin, and, most of all, her completely loving, vibrantly young, utterly married, sexually responding face. All this had struck a chord of longing in Andrew's memory and made him suddenly serious. Then, just as quickly, his mind became as calm again as the rippling sea.

Andrew finished his breakfast first. He paid the check and then the table was cleared. He could think of no way to stall without making it obvious. He wanted to remain and watch them enjoy themselves feeding breakfast to each other. He would have liked to go on looking in on them through their happiness as if it were a large, newly cleaned window. But he got to his feet instead, and, testing himself, took another secret appraisal of her from head to foot. But this time her beauty stirred no painful longing and so he left and went down the seaside street, hearing behind him her belled earrings softly shaking.

Time was moving in the sunlight in the way that it often does when it seems not to be moving at all. He was on the Riviera, walking through the city of Cannes, but the earth supporting him and the air feeding him all belonged to a brand-new world. It made such good sense. "Run after a new world, don't just run away from the old one." That was what Kanka had said. To hear it now repeating again in his mind made him joyful. He was determined to try. He clutched the air with his fists.

Anton Kanka. Strange, how a man's death can bring such permanence to his life. All the things Andrew remembered about him now seemed vividly and enduringly fixed in his mind. And that last hour they had spent together, with Kanka doing almost all of the talking, slowly built up in the young man's heart such faith in the world of the intellect that he became unquestioningly certain that whenever he wanted something but could not have it, he would dissolve his desire for it and dismiss it from his mind. "The mind is a wonderful place in which to hide," he heard Kanka saying, as if they were both together again. "The trouble is, not everybody can hide there. Develop your talent for faith. What you are attempting will not be easy. Achieve a lust for knowledge. This will transform everything. And with this you start your journey."

But the first journey Andrew took after having his breakfast was to the American Express to pick up his mail. There were three letters from his parents: one written at the Grand Canyon, and the other two at Yellowstone Park; he put these into his jacket to read later. There were also an amusing letter from D. J. Jones, two dull ones from other friends and one letter from Ted at *Graphic Globe* acknowledging his last shipment of film. From his sister Dominique, of course, there was nothing. Across the street from the American Express office he stopped for a moment and, leaning against the railing and facing the sea, read D.J.'s letter over again. There was an unconscious grin on his face as he finished it. Then he put all the letters away and began his first full day on the Riviera.

That afternoon he took a bus to Nice. It had none of the intimate quiet of Cannes, nor any of its charm. The beach was made up of rocks and stones, and the people sitting up above on the benches watched each other and tried to look as though they belonged.

Afterward he boarded another bus and made the journey to Monte Carlo. Here all the roads seemed to wind upward. As he climbed on foot he felt himself growing tired. He moved slowly, conserving his strength; but it really didn't matter how slowly he walked, for the entire place was asleep in the sun. Off in the distance he heard occasional gunfire, as if someone were making a last vain effort to stem the tide of silence. When he had finally gone as far up as the road would go, he came to the Grand Hotel. It seemed entirely deserted. All about him on the carefully manicured lawns and the geometrically clipped hedges roamed the uneasy quiet. The young man made his way among the cemented benches along the private concrete walk and came upon a fashion photographer and a model on location. Against a backdrop of blank wall, she posed white-faced, thin, and unreal, stubbornly grimacing a somber, haunted look of malnutrition. The headless photographer stood crouching beneath the black cloth that covered the ground glass while he groped directions in the air with a graceful left hand. They are alike the world over, Andrew thought, and he could also see himself squinting beneath the cloth, only he would never have taken a model all the way from Paris to the Riviera just to use a blank wall for a backdrop.

Andrew heard the whipcrack of a rifle and then the echo thumping into the hills. It was closer this time, and he walked on trying to locate the source of the noise. It appeared to come from the sea. He leaned against a concrete wall and saw below him a large semi-circular flat of grass resembling a golf green. It reached out like the turret of a castle. Far below was the solitary vastness of blue water. There were two small metal plates in the grass at the far end of the green. One of these plates suddenly opened and closed, and in that brief moment a pigeon appeared on the lawn. It paused for a time to examine the mystery of its freedom, and then it rose on rapid wings, gathering speed as it flew. The air around Andrew's ears exploded with gunfire, and the bird collapsed as if it had struck an invisible wall. It dropped back to the ground in an ugly ruffle of feathers. Leaning farther out, Andrew saw a man almost directly below him reloading a rifle and preparing for the next bird. On a small table stood a highball and a pack of cigarettes. When the dead bird had been removed by a colored attendant and the grass was clean again, the next pigeon appeared. When it got about ten feet off the ground, having escaped the first shot, the second caught it in the side. It spun around with one wing straight out and stiff until it hit the green and bounced. Desperately it flapped, but it couldn't regain the air nor even find its legs. This one too was removed while the man took a sip of his drink. Andrew watched several birds destroyed this way by the booming noise of the gun until finally one bird was struck but didn't fall. It made its way out to sea with an erratic working of its wings, occasionally halting all motion to glide for a while, then flapping again. Gradually as it grew smaller it lost altitude. While the man with the gun was firing at a new pigeon, the wounded bird was finally forced to land on the water far out from shore. A moment later it rose again working its way toward the open sea, moving along only a few feet above the rippling gleam of the sun. Then, when Andrew could barely see it any longer, it landed once more on the water and remained there for quite a while without moving its wings. But at last it went berserk, flapping wildly on top of the water until it finally sank out of sight and nothing more could be seen except the gleaming surface of the open sea. In the meantime, the man with the gun had killed three more birds.

When Andrew stepped back from the wall he found his clothes were covered with a strange rust-colored powder that gave him trouble when he tried to rub it off. He started away from the sound of the gun, and brushing his clothes with his hands, headed in the direction of the town. Somehow he no longer seemed to be walking with himself, sharing with his heart all of the things he saw. Now he walked alone through an oppressive silence, wondering what he would do next.

Late that night he found his way back to where the buses were and boarded one for Cannes. As he was carried along over the dark, winding roads, gently rocking, quivering, shaking from the vibration of the ride, he watched through the window the sprinkle of lights in the distant darkness; they were like ashes glowing on the hills. The long road wound slowly above the blackness of the sea, and then afterward Nice could be seen below them, dazzling the night with its glitter. As they rode down toward it from the hills, everyone in the bus who was still awake watched the sight in silence. At the depot they stopped to exchange passengers, and when the new people climbed on to take their seats, he saw the newlyweds again. The earrings jingled faintly. He lifted himself from his stupor and watched as they climbed into a seat across the aisle in front of him. Then the bus started up the hills again, and Andrew watched the shadow of the young couple as they braced themselves against the boring ride by softly huddling together in the dark. Occasionally her voice would break the quiet and its laughter would whisper its way to him, making it seem that they were the only two people awake in the slow, jostling caravan of sleep.

During the walk back to his hotel, and without knowing why, he followed behind them as they strolled. Holding each other about the waist, they studied whatever store window caught their fancy. Not far from the hotel they decided to step into a shop to buy some candy. Andrew left them there to go to his room, walking the last block and a half alone.

The accident, and now the full day of walking, had combined to make him very tired. Postponing his plans to write a letter, he decided to go straight to bed. The single bulb in the room, hanging by a wire from the center of the ceiling, switched off at the far wall by the door. He patted the floor with his bare feet as he crossed the room, then returned, lay down in the dark, and slowly stretched out. A lump on one side of the mattress forced him to lie near the unused door in the wall against which his bed had been placed. It had probably not been opened for years. He discovered he could reach up and let his arm hang as his fingers gripped the knob in the dark. Listening through the thin walls of the hotel to a medley of distant sounds, he heard the whispered scuffle of feet, garbled voices, the crackle of laughter, silence, then something falling, silence, the opening and closing of a door, a series of violent coughs, and then silence again. He lowered his arm from the doorknob, drew a deep breath, and slowly let the air escape.

Like a heavy, water-logged tree trunk gently breaking the surface of a lake, he discovered he had come awake. He felt that he had not been asleep for long. He shifted his position and closed his eyes, feeling his mind hold still for a moment just before beginning to wonder.

Then he heard it. From several feet away and from the other side of the wall it came. A brittle little ring, prissy and timorous, and before he knew why, he felt his heart leap. *They were in the next room!* It was a discovery that seemed to electrify the darkness. He sat up and found himself listening. First he was aware of movement, but he couldn't fit the sounds together to make a picture. For a moment, when they exchanged a few words, it sounded as though they were standing at the farthest end of the room. He frowned in concentration but was unable to hear what they said. Then there was a long gap of silence. Just when he decided that they had gone to sleep, he heard them climb into the straining bed; first her, and then him. He could tell that they were only inches away from him on the other side of the thin wall.

A stretching of limbs and a shifting of bodies finally settled into silence. But what did silence mean? It filled the air with terrible images. He waited. There was movement again and then a little titter of feminine laughter. This was kept down to a whisper, as if in respect to the night. But her voice was swallowed up by silence, a silence so heavy that it seemed their lips must be glued together.

Andrew was able, somehow, to recapture the look of her face. He saw her sitting at the breakfast table that morning with her eyes large and responsive and with lips that seemed always to be smiling, and with her whole attention absorbed with a love that made her oblivious to everything else. He tried to imagine himself as her husband. In the fancy of the moment, he was aware of a feeling of intense well-being. During that pleasant pause, while he dared daydream her love, he was at once released from the need to go on seeking. There was nothing more to seek. For if just such a daydream of dedicated affection and gentle understanding would only come alive for him, he felt sure it would bring an end to his plague.

The sounds that came to him through the wall in the dark seemed to be growing louder. But what he really heard was her heavy breathing. It seemed to drown out everything else. It was more than just breathing. It was the gasping of the Olympic runner at the end of the mile. It was the cry of a tongueless man calling for help. It was the sound of the animal in her breaking through the skin. Each convulsive gasp escaping uncontrollably from her throat pierced him with memory. Then, all at once, an old wound opened up in the dark labyrinth of his mind.

The snow, he remembered, had been falling steadily all that night. There was much of it on the ground and there was more of it still to come. They were parked on a dead-end street with the front bumper of the car against the wooden barricade that brought the road to a halt. On the other side of the fence were the Flushing Meadow swamps that had been, in 1939, the location for the New York World's Fair. Now it was deserted, and there was little left of the once great fair except for several concrete bridges which spanned Grand Central Parkway as it skirted the swampland on the west, or an occasional small wooden bridge near the center of the meadow which had once borne endless throngs of people over the small water inlets that joined the twin lakes of the old swamp. But now, as they parked on the side street against the barricade, the lakes were dead and frozen over and were being covered by snow.

But Andrew saw none of this, for the windshield of the car was also being covered, and all that could be seen was a thick layer of dark gray. They had been there for almost two hours with the motor idling gently, the heater turned on, and a window lowered ever so slightly for air. This kept the inside of the car warm enough so that they could remove their coats and dump them in the back seat. For two hours he had kissed her and had let his hands roam over her and had talked to her, and for two hours he had been as tranquil as the snow that had fastened itself to all the windows of the car, blotting out the rest of the world.

"Oh, I'm on fire," Pauline finally said, taking her mouth away from his. He felt her grow soft as if her body were about to liquefy and flow into his. Her eyes seemed to challenge him.

"I really am," she explained seriously, with an adult voice. "I'm on fire."

"You are?"

"Yes, I am."

Her words came with effort. She had been lying quite still, with her head against the seat. Then unexpectedly, she had kissed him as if she had just discovered what a kiss was all about.

"A little bonfire," she declared, with an exaggerated sensual movement of her lips. It occurred to him that perhaps she was not pretending.

"What are we going to do about it?" she breathed, drawing herself around on the seat.

"Well, we could cut a hole in the lake and go for a swim."

But she did not smile. Her seriousness was a reprimand. After a pause, she slowly announced:

"I think I'm going to rape you."

First there was dead silence and then, finally, "Oh?"

"I mean it. Don't you believe I mean it?"

"I don't doubt your word," he said. "You always seemed like a trustworthy sort of girl."

She took hold of the shoulder of his jacket as if the first step in her plan was to rip off his sleeve.

"I *mean* it!"

He could hear the very faint whisperings of snow as more and more of it came to rest upon the windshield.

"Well? Aren't you going to do anything?" The tone of her voice was punishing.

"You have new stockings on. I don't … I wouldn't want to …"

"Then take them *off*."

"You might get cold."

"Let *me* worry about that."

Pushing back her dress, he unbuckled the clasps of her garter belt. After removing her shoes, he peeled the stockings off her legs. She made no move to help.

"So slow," she scolded.

As she spoke the words, he became aware of how much she sounded like his sister.

"I'm waiting," Pauline said.

It had all seemed so frantically sudden. He had been going with her for a whole year, and their late evening intimacies had settled down, week after week, to an accepted repetition of "just so far and no further." Then, all at once, when he least expected it, she suddenly turned to him and demanded more. At the same time, the girl he had known all those months vanished. All her tender little female attentions that were meant to excite him and keep him coming back, all of the skillful promise of a loving look or a provocative smile—all of these things drained out of her, leaving nothing but the weight of her resting heavily against him.

"Will you come *on*," he heard her say impatiently. Her breathing seemed amazingly loud in the snow-stilled car. "What are you *waiting* for?"

He made no answer.

"All right, then..."

She climbed onto the seat with her knees, edged herself forward and then climbed over him. Her eyes kept watching him. Her hands held both sides of his head so he couldn't look away. After a while she shook her head wildly back and forth, growling like a wounded animal, until her hair was a shambles. In that moment of frustration once again she resembled his sister. Stopping, she looked at him and then pressed herself even more heavily against his body. But it was obvious she didn't know what to do. Finally, when he could take it no longer, he made her give it up. She waited for an explanation, so he said he was very tired, that he hadn't gotten much sleep. This always happened to him, he told her, when he was that tired. He was sorry. Perhaps next time. But as he talked he could tell from her face that what he was trying to save had already been lost. Afterward, with a dead expression, she sat back in the seat, became motionless and closed her eyes. Preparing to leave, he turned on the windshield wipers. They strained against the heavy snow and then swept it away from the glass in a thick arc. Through the mists of falling flakes, out as far as he could see, the white floor of the old fairgrounds stretched spotless and clean.

Andrew Williams hung between two worlds wishing he would not have to return to either one. In an old letter from D.J. there was a line that said: "I don't know what you did to that girl but she sure hates you!" The words were as clear as if the letter were still in his hand. But what had *she* done to *him*? She had found him out for what he was. She had carried the knowledge of it away with her, always looking at him through the anger of it when they met. *What had he done to her?* He had entered the exacting domain of female society and committed the worst crime of all. One that few women can ever forgive. But forgiveness was what he needed most. It was this torment that taught him the fear of knowing you will always be what you are and will never change; the defeat of winning everything in the world except the one thing you really want; and the love which is the one victory that makes all other defeats, even the final one, unimportant.

When Andrew Williams returned again to the night-filled room, he discovered that he was no longer in bed beside the locked door. He was sitting at the window with his foot at the sill. It had begun to rain and he watched it fall meaninglessly upon its own reflection in the street. It was falling everywhere in the darkness, upon the slanting roof tops of the sleeping city, upon the soft gray sand of the deserted beach, upon the high winding road leading down to Nice, upon the parapet of grass where the pigeons had been killed. It fell, slowly and steadily, in little ringlets, upon the flat, wide-open sea.

THREE

25

REACHING THE top of the long, high hill, he saw his own house and was home. The clothes pack hanging from his hand dragged a loose strap along the ground. Crossing the familiar street of childhood games and tireless running, he wearily wiped away with his sleeves the hot August sweat on his face. He saw the brown brick house, inanimate and old, and walking drowsily he wondered just what he would find inside. It would not be empty. That was more than one could hope for. But it was too hot to bother about that now. Whatever he would find, it was certain to be unpleasant.

As he moved up the short walk to the door, his hand reached into his side pocket for the key. For a moment he tried to remember the name of "the new one." Dominique had mentioned him in her letter. They had met during the summer and had quit camp together. The letter telling him about it was the only one he had ever received from his sister. It was filled with all the careful intrigue that she was planning and practicing against her parents. Funny he should forget. The name had occurred to him that very morning on board ship.

The young man closed the front door by leaning back against it until he felt it shut. The blinds were all drawn. Though the air seemed musty, it was almost cool. Anyway, he was home. Dropping the clothes pack near the wall, he went to the foot of the stairs. He was puzzled by what he saw. Could the house really be empty? It appeared to have been unoccupied for some time. This was so unexpected that he gave a soft little grunt of surprise and relief.

Then suddenly he realized with a jolt that he was being watched.

At the top of the stairs, someone dressed only in a pair of pajama pants was standing quietly and staring. It was a man he had never seen before. But for some strange reason, as soon as their eyes met, the name in his sister's letter flew back to him.

"Well, well, if it isn't Derek," Andrew said, as he began to climb the stairs.

The stranger made way for him, and for an uncertain clumsy moment they just stood and watched each other in silent threat. An expression of confusion made Derek's face seem slightly moronic.

"You're the brother," was what he finally said, but the remark was neither question nor statement, and it disappeared into the soundless summer air.

Behind the closed door of the bathroom the shower was running, and at last Andrew Williams knew where his sister was. The door to his parents' room was wide open, and in contrast to the murkiness of the rest of the house, it seemed flooded with light. Its brightness drew him in. Only one window was open, but the blind was lifted all the way. Immediately he knew why. It was the only window in the bedroom that opened over the unused drop of land behind the house that led down to the parkway below. No one in the neighborhood could see this window or know whether or not it was open. Looking out, he saw the Empire State Building standing in the far-distant mist. But it was the bed that really held his attention. The large double bed belonging to his vacationing parents. It had been slept in. So well slept in that it was only too clear that two people had done the job.

"We weren't expecting you, fella."

It was Derek who had spoken. He was at least two or three inches taller than Andrew and he had a massive hairless chest and huge shoulders. Now that his face had composed itself, it turned out to be one of those overgrown boyish faces so often seen on the athletic field at college. The perfectly short-cropped blond hair made the top of his head look wide and flat. Seeing the interest Andrew was taking in the bed, Derek stepped over to it and placed a large hand on the globed top of the bedpost.

"I sleep here, you understand."

The words explained nothing. Both men knew it. The silence that followed had an extra dimension, as if one silence had been added heavily to another. Both men became aware of this, too. Standing apart and facing each other, they waited. In the bathroom, the shower had been turned off. Then a door opened. After a few empty moments he heard his sister's voice. But so different was it from the way Andrew remembered, that at first he was not certain it was Dominique at all. The words seemed to slither through the air.

"Pussy," she called, imitating a spoiled child, "where are you?"

"In here, huh?" he answered.

"Don't be lazy."

"I mean it…. Dom?"

"Oh, are *you* lazy!"

Down the hall came the sound of bare feet. Both men continued to look at each other as the girl's voice grew closer.

"Derek Francis, you're getting lazier every day."

She wore no clothes, nothing, for she had come straight from the shower. She held a small towel in front of her which draped her thighs. It just about covered her in front, but was too small to do much for the rear. The girl, not seeing her brother, went directly to the other man and cuddled against him. Her voice was thick and full of reproach.

"Lazy," she said.

Andrew had kept still and secluded so that he might have the advantage of surprise. But in that swift entrance the advantage was all hers. For a terrible moment he wished he were somewhere else, somewhere the hell out of there, somewhere where he could send warning of his unexpected arrival, a warning he knew now he should have sent.

The rear view of the girl's wet body was entirely exposed. Andrew was unable to retrieve his startled eyes from her secret white skin. He could see her abruptly narrow waist, her full, protruding buttocks, and her long dancer's legs. Crushed against her man, her arms were now winding around his back, her nails testing his skin.

Finally Derek succeeded in distracting her attention. But all he could do was point. Dominique turned her head, her arms still around him. Andrew missed the first signs of shock on her face, for he was aware only of his own confusion and guilt. She spun around, holding the towel in front of her, holding it between herself and the sudden apparition of her brother. On the carpet beneath her feet there were little stains of shower water that had dripped from her body. Andrew watched as the expression on his sister's bleached face slowly began to change. He was familiar with that look.

"Get out!" she screamed. She swung her head, her eyes now blazing at Derek's face. "Why didn't you let me *know* he was *here?*" He began to lift his hands to explain but by then she was flinging words at her brother again.

"What are you doing here?" she cried. "*Well?*"

"What am I *doing* here? I've come home!"

"You weren't expected for weeks!"

"I changed my plans."

This seemed to anger her even more. She was trembling. Her words came in a rush. "You could have the common decency to send warning. Any idiot knows enough to do that!"

"I'm not in the habit of sending warnings wherever I go."

"Oh, you're so cute I could vomit!"

"How was I to know there was *reason* to send warning?"

"And to sneak into the house like a common thief!"

But she began to feel silly holding that little towel in front of her. With one hand she held the towel to her body, while with the other she reached over to the bed for the striped pajama top, the bottoms of which Derek was wearing.

"Turn around," she ordered, furiously.

Her brother obeyed. "And I didn't sneak in here," he said to the wall. "I used a key and walked through the front door. That's how I got in here. And why are all the windows closed pretending no one's home?"

"You know damn well why."

"I didn't, but I know now."

"Don't get cute! You're supposed to be in Europe. Why the hell didn't you stay there?"

"You're supposed to be at camp. Why didn't *you* stay *there*?"

"You know the reason for that, too," she said. "Or have you *already* forgotten my letter? Oh, for God's sake," she added, half in fury and half in ridicule, "turn around already."

She stood facing him, the pajama shirt buttoned to the neck. Almost a cheesecake shot, he thought. Just the length of her legs was showing. Her jutting breasts, for which she was locally famous, made the shirt resemble a maternity outfit. Derek was leaning against the bedpost enjoying the little family feud. The two lovers looked ridiculous as they stood there sharing a single pair of pajamas. If there was anything comic about sex at all, Andrew decided, it was perhaps such things as this.

"And how many nights has *he* been living here?" Andrew demanded, pointing his arm at Derek.

"He's *my* guest," she said, possessively.

"That I can see for myself. But what I asked was ..."

"I hope you don't think you're funny, because you're *sickening.*" She spat out the last word as if it had a terribly bitter taste.

"I asked how many nights."

"None of your damn business."

"Well last night was the last time. Today he's getting out."

"Oh, he is, is he? Well it's none of your freaken business what he does because he's my guest and he's ..."

Her lips paused. All three of them stopped to listen to the sound of the front door chimes. Her bare feet moving silently on the old rug, Dominique went quickly to a window whose Venetian blind was down and drawn tight. With one finger she lifted a slat and stole a look down into the street. To see the front door, she had to stand high on her toes. Stretching this way, with her two feet together and her heels in the air, her long dancer's legs looked their very best. More cheesecake; but actually not, for he could never have gotten her to smile.

"It's Ursula," she said, moving from the window. "Quick, go down and let her in."

Derek hitched up his pajama pants, reknotting the slip cord as he went. "I am on my way, beautiful one." The jolting of his weight could be felt as he bounced barefoot down the stairs.

Dominique was at the closet slipping on her father's bathrobe. Certain that his presence in the room was not wanted, Andrew began to leave. But his sister, head down and tightening the cord around her waist, began speaking at the open closet.

"Now that you're here," she said, her voice cold and familiar, "you can lend me the keys to the car. Derek and I are going to the beach tomorrow."

She turned and displayed a face that matched her voice. It had that vacuous prettiness which rarely changed except to permit the flow of anger or the occasional oddity of a little laugh. Her hair, unsettled by the removing of the shower cap, made her look a little wild, a little daring, as if she had just done some violent deed.

"To the beach? When did *you* learn to drive?"

"Tsh," came the petulant and barely tolerant sound from her lips. "*I'm* not going to drive it. He is." And with her head she indicated the room below, where already they could hear the gathering sounds of new voices.

"You're crazy."

Her face soured. "It's the family car and I'm part of the family."

"But the keys belong to me. Go ask father for *his* keys."

"Oh, you're a scream. I have as much right to the car as you."

"Only when you get a license."

"My dates have used the car before."

"When?"

"Herb Meyers used to get it quite often."

"Sure, when your ankle was in a cast and you couldn't walk. But afterward he could never get it."

"So what?"

"So you're not getting the car keys, that's what."

Dominique ground her frustration into a high-pitched squeal, gritting her teeth and furiously shaking her head back and forth with unutterable, uncontrollable rage. It was a demonstration

Andrew had seen many times before, and because anger came to her so easily and so often, he wondered once again how very strange it was that anger rarely seemed to come to him at all.

"And remember," he added quickly, feeling a moment of advantage, "he's getting out of here. No more free room and board for him."

Suddenly she settled into a calm, ugly fury. "Oh? Says who? Listen to me, young man, Mr. Smarty-Pants. He's my guest and he's staying as long as I like, and there's nothing you can do about it."

He was all set to answer when Derek proudly appeared in the doorway carrying a trim, yellow-haired girl relaxing in his arms.

"The greatest?" she asked, indicating the free ride she was getting. "Crazy?"

"You Jane, me Tarzan," Derek said to her.

"Uh, this guy's too much." Then with her thumb and fore-finger together to help express the explicitness of her meaning she answered: "Me Ursula, you elephant. *Comprende?— Don't you dare!*"

But Derek threw her into the air and she dropped down onto the large double bed. She shrieked once and bounced twice and then slowly sat up, pretending a resigned, disgusted face.

"You Jane, me Tarzan," he repeated working his bare chest with his fists.

"Oh, this boy's just got to go!" Ursula explained. "He's not well. But what's this? Hi! When did *you* get back?"

"Today," Andrew said.

"So soon? What shakes?"

"I just couldn't keep myself away from you."

Ursula looked around at the others. "For *this* he came back?" Then going along with the joke. "*Mama mia*, what a jerk."

"That's my *brother*," Dominique said, with disgust. She shook her head and gestured with her arm to indicate she was giving him away free to anyone who might want him. The bathrobe sleeve was too long for her arm and it swallowed her hand as she waved it. "Oh, sweet brother mine. He drops in like a plague. No warning. No letter. Nothing. Happy day."

"But, doll, that's what brothers are for," Ursula said, ignoring the bitter undertone in Dominique's voice. "Didn't you know that?" Then to prove she was only pretending, she threw Andrew a puckered little kiss. "And I want to see all those pictures you took in Europe. Don't you dare forget to show them to me. I bet they're great."

Folding her arms sullenly, Dominique abandoned the subject with a contemptuous turn of her body as she seated herself at her mother's vanity table. At the same time Derek leaned over the bedboard and stuck out his chin at Ursula.

"Tell me, baby, what have you done for men lately?"

"Go drown yourself," she said, kicking off her shoes so as not to dirty the sheets.

"You're looking O.K. in that dress."

"Mucho gracias, señor."

"Built for speed."

"Well, well," she said.

"Where is what's-her-name?" Dominique interrupted, to change the subject.

"Who's what's-her-name?" Ursula asked. "Oh, you mean Linda? She's coming. I told her to wait downstairs because I didn't know if you were decent, if you know what I mean. I left the door unlocked so she can walk right in."

"Why'd you tell her to come for, anyway?" Dominique complained, her face grimacing her displeasure. "She's so nothing."

"Oh, she's not that bad. And listen, doll, if we want to go sailing on her father's boat we've got to be friendly. *Comprende?*"

"Hey, I'm all for that," Derek put in. "When do we go?" And he rubbed the eager palms of his hands together as he leaned against the bedpost.

Dominique began to brush her hair violently. "The damn summer will be over before her stupid parents come back."

"So we still got to be friends with her, don't we? Anyway, I brought her here because I want to show you her new dress. The blue one I told you about."

"She's wearing it?"

"I made her put it on before we came over."

"And how are we going to get rid of her?" Dominique asked, peering at herself in the large, three-sided mirror.

"You worry too much," Ursula explained. "She's got to leave soon, and so do I. So get dressed, will ya? Hurry!"

"Must I?" Dominique asked.

"Come on, will you! Just throw something on. Tarzan, make her get dressed."

"That's not my line," he grinned. "I work the other way."

Ursula's mouth dropped open in mock astonishment. With extreme self-satisfaction, Derek began to laugh. But Dominique turned and threw her brush at him.

"You no-good bastard," she yelled. But she, too, was secretly enjoying herself.

Her lover ducked just in time. To avoid being hit, Andrew had to catch the brush in both his hands. He felt them sting, but his position against the wall did not change.

"Give it to me," Dominique demanded, when she saw him holding it.

Examining the brush, Andrew paused while everyone watched. Then, displaying contempt for his sister's behavior of throwing things about the house like a spoiled child, he lobbed the brush onto the mattress instead. It bounced and landed where Ursula was seated.

"Isn't he sweet," Dominique grimaced. "Isn't he just too sweet for words."

"Oh, good," beamed Ursula, pouncing on the brush. "Now you'll *have* to get dressed. Come on, doll. You, too, Tarzan. Get dressed."

Dominique stood up. A flap of her bathrobe, before folding closed, flashed a length of her leg.

"All right. Just to get rid of her, we'll get dressed." Then, to Derek: "Go on...Tarzan." She added this playfully, enjoying the new name for her lover. But then she glanced contemptuously at Andrew, her eyes going down to his feet and up to his head again.

"I'm waiting for you to *leave!*" She held her hands to her bathrobe as if preparing to take it off the very moment he was out of sight.

"We're both going," Ursula chimed. "Good-by, good-by."

"No, stay. I want to talk to you. I just want *him* to leave."

"But Derek has got to get dressed, too."

"This is your big moment," Derek said, fluttering his eyebrows at her wickedly.

"Oh, be quiet," Dominique replied, without looking at him. "He'll dress in the other room." Then, to Andrew: "Well?"

But her brother was already on his way. In that little struggle of theirs to see who could most often wound the other, he wanted to give her as little advantage as possible.

"And close the door after you."

He left them and descended the stairs. All was musty and dim again. A dead house with a numbing quiet. The third step from the top squeaked, as always; and farther down, the carpet was still loose. The front door seemed to be inviting him to leave, telling him that he would not find here what he was searching for. He wanted to walk out and never come back. But that would have pleased his sister, so it would never do. He was about to remove his clothes pack from the foyer and take it into the kitchen when, in the half-light of the living room, he noticed the girl for the first time. He had completely forgotten her.

26

"HERE, LET me give you some light."

He went to the large window and opened the blinds. There was a slap of dust, and the warm afternoon sunlight tilted into the room, probably for the first time in months.

Linda had been standing at the couch studying a painting on the wall. Her back was turned to him, but her posture made her seem ill-at-ease. Her long black hair smoothly outlined her head. It hung neatly down to her shoulders, but there it dispersed in clusters, some hanging straight down while others curled up or bent off to the sides. The rays of light were perfect across her face.

"Oh, please, no," she whirled around, startled. "I mean, you don't have to, really." But the blinds having already been opened, she smiled a bit foolishly. "I was finished looking at it, really. I was just waiting. Thank you, anyway." Then, she added: "I was just waiting. I really was." But her confusion remained. She gave an embarrassed laugh.

"Oh," he teased, "so you don't like our painting?"

"No, no..." Confusion became her enemy again. He was startled to see her blush. "I mean, I didn't mean that."

"Hey, wait a minute," he laughed, holding up his hand. "Hold on."

She looked down at her feet. "Yes, I talk too much, don't I?"

"Jesus. I was just kidding. I hate that painting. I always did."

She raised her head. "You do? You don't, really?"

"Sure. Look at it. It's awful. But just try to convince Mrs. Williams of that. She buys paintings like some people buy books: to fit the color scheme of the room."

"Oh, no."

"Oh, yes."

At this they both laughed, and Andrew was happy, for he had wanted, somehow, to make up for the embarrassment he had caused her.

"Why don't you sit down?" he asked, going to the opposite window and letting in more light. Now that he was in the house there would be no more hiding, no more drawing of shades or sealing of windows. Reaching through the blinds, he turned the handle, pushed the window, and it swung out. Noises of life came to him from distant streets and unseen people.

"That's all right. I've got to go soon. I'm just waiting…"

"Well, at least you can sit down. They're getting dressed upstairs. You might as well."

The fluffed and bloated pillows of the couch collapsed slowly under the girl's weight. Her body kept sinking gradually even after she had fully sat down. But the flow of conversation had come to a halt. For a moment it seemed to Andrew that nothing could get it started again. He busied himself idly with little things about the room, pretending they needed his immediate attention. The girl, whose hands were folded in her skirt, was staring steadily at the carpet. The way she bit her lip betrayed hidden tensions. At last she said:

"How … is Dominique?"

"All right, I guess."

"I think she's very lovely."

"That seems to be the popular opinion."

"No, really. She is very, *very* beautiful. You should be very proud."

"Well, let's not overdo it."

She pouted her regret at his tone of voice. "Oh, you shouldn't talk like that."

"Why not?"

"Because … well, I don't know if I should tell you …."

"Well?"

The girl lowered her head. "Because she says such nice things about you."

"*Me?*"

Linda wanted to smile sweetly, but she was puzzled by his outburst.

"Me?" he repeated, looking at her as if she had lost her wits. Then he laughed. "Are you crazy?"

"No, really." She had nearly climbed to her feet in a sudden effort at sincerity. "Oh, my. She said such wonderful, wonderful things. Really. She said ... well, she said how handsome she thinks you are and how much sex appeal..." At this she blushed and gave an insipid little smile which left her feeling more foolish than ever.

"*Me?!*" He stared. "Was she drunk, for crysake?"

The words stung her into complete silence. Her eyes seemed to withdraw in fright. Then something in the girl closed shut and she looked down at the carpet again.

Andrew was more puzzled than ever. "Look. Can you blame me? My sister hasn't said a civil word to me since Christmas."

She raised her head. "*Sister?*" Her hand flew to her lips. "You're not ... you're not Derek?"

"Uh, good grief, woman!" He slapped his forehead and fell into an armchair. Then with a grandiose wave of his arm he said to the ceiling: "Forgive her, oh Lord. She knows not what she does."

"I thought ... Oh, I'm sorry. I'm terribly sorry."

He found the amount of sincerity she could pack into a simple sentence remarkable.

"Oh, that's all right. Forget it! My name's Andrew. I'm Dominique's brother."

He tried to say this with equal seriousness, but toward the end, realizing what had happened, he began to grin. Her face became very pretty in its delightful confusion. She warned herself against laughter because she felt it coming. But then she saw his lips, and, remembering his indignation, she began to beam. It started softly in a little cataract of smiles, but at last they were both laughing like old friends.

"That *was* funny, wasn't it?" she said. "And I thought you were ... Oh, I *am* so stupid. But she never even mentioned you."

"See what I mean? See what I mean about Christmas?"

And they both enjoyed the joke all over again.

"Ho, ho, ho, what a riot!" It was Derek's voice bursting in on them. He stumbled into the room clasping his stomach and ridiculing their laughter. Pretending to be in a helpless fit, he dropped into an empty chair.

"They seem to be enjoying themselves," Dominique said.

"I'll say," Ursula agreed. "What shakes?"

The room fell into a resentful silence. For a moment, Linda faltered like one caught in the a¢t of stealing. Andrew was looking quietly at his sister. She had hurriedly put on one of her old dresses, but like all the others, it was cut square and low at the neck. Heavy mascara had been applied to her eyes, and her lips were bright with a new shade of lipstick. He had to admit it: she did look beautiful. Crossing the room to her favorite armchair, the one that made her feel like a queen, she let herself half-fall into the cushioned seat. Her partly exposed breasts bounced once like large soft weights and then came to rest.

"Come on, chum," Derek demanded. "Let us in on the big laugh."

"Just a private joke between old friends," Andrew said.

"I'll bet," Dominique said, suspicious of this infuriatingly clever brother of hers and of what he might be thinking; still begrudging him the admiration she had always hidden from him without knowing why.

"Do you two know each other?" Ursula put in.

"Well, *do* you?" Dominique insisted. "Or are you just trying to be cute?"

"Curiosity," he answered, "has killed better cats than you."

"Your sense of humor is just as pitiful as ever."

All this time Derek was eyeing the new girl as she sat sadly staring at her hands. "Well, isn't anyone going to introduce us?"

"Oh, I'm sorry," Ursula began. "Linda, this is Derek."

"Greetings," Derek said. "Glad to set eyes on ya."

"Look out." Andrew smiled at the girl.

"What was that supposed to mean?" Dominique flared.

"Hello," Linda answered with a weak voice, trying hard to smile.

"In fact," said Derek, "Hell-Oh!"

"All right," Dominique cautioned him coldly. "That'll be enough."

Ursula went over to the couch. "Get up, doll," she said to the girl, "I want them to see your new dress. Come on."

Linda got to her feet. She was at a loss about what to do next. Her hands became a problem. Everyone was looking at her. "It's just a dress," she apologized. "Really. Ursula made such a fuss. I don't…"

"Hush upa you face," said Ursula, playfully. "Now, turn all the way around. Make pretty for the people."

The girl quickly did so, hoping to get this over with as fast as possible. But Derek was not to be rushed.

"Whoa, Bessie," he called, "where's the fire? Turn slowly, slowly." His eyes were moving up and down with immense interest. "Shake it, but don't break it. Wrap it up and I'll take it."

Andrew watched as the girl suffered in the grip of her own laughter. She was trying to be a good sport, but her feet seemed rooted to the spot. Then the very thing she feared most began to happen: she blushed.

"My, my, look at that," said Derek. "Do it again."

She did.

"Let her alone," Andrew said.

But Derek wasn't listening. "Notice the way she fills it out in the rear? Yar, man. I like that."

"You would," Dominique said.

Linda continued in her weak, helpless way. "Oh, it's not a sexy dress at all," she fumbled, furious at the ease with which his rude words could make her perjure herself with laughter.

Ursula smiled. "It *is* a little tight across the hips."

Derek called to Andrew across the room. "Can you see what I mean?" Linda had turned her back to Andrew to escape from Derek's large dark eyes. "How does it look from there, chum? Good enough to eat?"

With this new burst of rudeness chilling her from all sides, she sat down on the couch as if stricken.

"Oh, you," Ursula said, waving him away with her hand. Then, to the girl, who was laughing, but hating herself for it: "Don't mind him."

"The dress *is* very nice," Dominique concluded. And finally, to her lover, who was still laughing: "Oh, shut up!"

Still fuming, she walked across the room to get a cigarette from the gold box on the center table. The conversation shifted to other things. Dominique made sure of that. She attempted to persuade Ursula to quit her summer job. It would give them free time to go shopping together. Everyone knew how Dominique loved to buy clothes. And the summer was nearly over, anyway. But Ursula said she couldn't. She needed the money for the winter. As it was, she wouldn't be making enough. At this point, Linda, who had remained quiet, suddenly got to her feet and announced awkwardly that she had to go. No one tried to stop her. But Andrew arose from his moody silence to say he would walk her home. Though the others commented on this to each other with gossiping glances he ignored them. Linda started to protest that she lived only a block and a half away, but he insisted. After a few half-hearted good-bys, they both left.

"Shake it but don't break it," Derek called after her, forcing her to laugh once again before they could escape from the house and into the hot summer sun.

27

D. J. Jones first looked to see whether his boss was watching. Then he dropped an extra scoop into each ice-cream sundae and winked at the two girls seated at the far end of the long counter. Next, a double spoonful of crushed nuts, and finally he buried it all beneath a curling white spray of whipped cream. Mr. Torodash insisted that the food from his soda fountain be used sparingly. But he was too busy ogling the girls to notice what was going on behind him. Beaming mischievously, D.J. walked along the wooden planks behind the counter and brought the two young ladies their order. Realizing what D.J. had done, the girls went off into a childish spasm of giggles. Mr. Torodash, whose 328 pounds engulfed the counter stool on which he sat, grew suspicious and, in puzzled self-defense, became playful himself.

"Should I give him a penny for his thoughts?" he roared, thumbing his hand at D.J.

"A whole penny?" D.J. asked. "Isn't that a little steep for you, sir?"

"Oh, we have jokes today."

"Working for you, sir, teaches a man the value of money."

"All right, funny man. Back to work." Then, under his breath, and lost among the convulsive sounds from the girls, Mr. Torodash added: "Clown!"

But as D.J. was poking fun at the fat man for whom he worked, another customer, who had quietly entered the store unseen, mounted a stool at the far end of the counter. In a few moments D.J. began working his way in that direction, wiping the counter lazily with a damp rag as he went. Suddenly a hand reached out and gripped his.

"Hey!" D.J. exclaimed, with wide startled eyes. "God damn it, buddy! When'd you get back?"

"Today."

"Christ, that's great. Say, I got your letter. How do ya feel? How's the arm? Hey, why you home so soon? The arm, huh? Christ, yar. I know what you mean. Listen, buddy, great to see ya. Bad arm and all." And D.J. leaned over the counter and banged Andrew on the shoulder with a big friendly fist. "Great to see ya. Oh, that your bad arm? Sorry. Sorry, man. Hey, boy, home, huh?"

"What's the order?" called out Mr. Torodash from the other end of the store.

"Listen, big one," D.J. said. "He's my friend."

"You ain't got any friends. What's the order?"

"He crapping about me?" Andrew asked, indicating the huge man with a tilt of his head.

"Ah, the old fart won't let anyone sit at the counter without ordering. You either buy something or you get out. Even if the damn place is empty." Then he yelled down angrily to where the man was sitting. "You're an old fathead, you know that?"

"Hey, careful," Andrew whispered. "He'll fire you."

"That's what I'm hoping for."

"Quiet, soda-jerk," Torodash answered with an unctuous grin, "or you'll lose your job."

"Can I count on that?"

But Andrew, afraid of trouble, ordered a small Coke just to make peace. D.J. concocted an extra large glassful with plenty of ice, three straws, and a slice of orange.

"This is a small Coke?"

"Drink, drink," D.J. said. "We celebrate your return."

The two friends began to talk, and their conversation quickly moved to things across the sea. Pretending work, D.J. lazily wiped the same part of the counter over and over again, while Andrew slowly sipped the giant Coke through the three straws.

"How's Madrid?" D.J. asked, beaming. "The greatest? Tremendous? Take good pictures? And Albina? Wonderful, isn't she?" Then his lips tightened into a wicked grin. "And how's what's-her-name, Bianca? Oh, man, what a pair of pontoons, huh?" For a moment he closed his eyes and cupped the air with his hands. "Almost as good as your sister—what do you think?" Then he laughed, for Andrew's sister was a running joke between them. "So tell me something. *Anything.* Bet you really made out there in Albina's, uh?"

"Sure did," said Andrew, telling the lie easily, naturally.

"Jesus, when I was there last year things were jumping. I mean it." Remembering it all, D.J. lapsed into a private daydream, shaking his head with disbelief. "God almighty, did things go on!"

"Yar, we had fun," Andrew said. "It was all right. No kidding. I'm glad you told me about it."

"O.K., glad you liked it…. Plenty of heads, huh? Lots of good-looking heads up there. That's how it was last year."

"Look, the place was jammed, really."

"'Cause I remember…"

"Hold on, now," Andrew broke in. "How are things with *you?*"

"Hell, you don't want to talk about me. You're the one fresh back from Europe, the one with a thriving travel career at twenty-four, the one with a satchel or two of great photo stories ready to be sold, the one…"

"All right, all right! Cut the smoke screen. You're hiding something. What is it?"

"What do you mean?" D.J. said, suspiciously.

"When I came in here you looked like you wanted to kill yourself. Come on, Big D. What's the story?"

Still eyeing his friend, Andrew leaned forward sipping his Coke. D.J. continued wiping the counter, his hand making lazy circular motions. "All right," he conceded. "All right." For a minute or two his hand continued moving. Then suddenly, in disgust, he stopped and threw the rag savagely into the sink.

Andrew removed his lips from the three straws. "So?"

"Boy, am I depressed. Wow! I'm the sort of guy, whatever I do, I do it wrong. I'm so depressed, I don't even feel like eating. Could you believe it? And you know me. Put a fork and knife in my hands and I don't look up for half an hour. Me. Not hungry. *Me!* I tell you I'm so depressed that if I should get laid right now all I'd think is, 'So why doesn't this happen more often?'"

Unable to restrain a sly smile, Andrew said: "All right, who's the woman?"

"The hell with that noise."

"So don't tell me. But don't knock yourself out about her. Tomorrow's a new day."

But the big voice boomed at them from the other end of the counter. "What's the order?" Another customer had entered the store.

This interruption had distracted D.J. He turned and asked: "What? Tomorrow?"

"I said there's always tomorrow."

"That's what I'm afraid of," D.J. said. Then he dismissed the whole thing. "Look, wait around. I get off in twenty minutes. I'll tell you all about it then. You had supper yet? All right, stick around and we'll eat in the back. Cheap."

"You mean inexpensive."

"Look, I work in this place. I mean cheap."

He hurried away to attend to his work while Andrew waited and took another sip. Several people came and went in the little side-street candy store and D. J. Jones was kept busy. When at last the hands of the clock above the magazine rack stood at six, D.J. undid the apron behind his back and, without looking, yelled: "Going off!" Then, carrying a stack of hamburgers and French fries that he had prepared on the boss's time, he led the way to a secluded wooden booth in the rear of the store. There he and Andrew began to eat.

The ponderous man climbed off the stool on which he had been sitting since early morning. His look was sour with the necessity of work. The great tragedy of his life at the moment was that the six o'clock replacement was once again late for work. She was a blonde he had hired just a month and one week ago, and if it weren't for the fact she was so pretty, he would have fired her days ago.

"All right," Andrew said, pouring out a quick stream of thin liquid ketchup over an open 'burger. "What's the story? Say, this stuff is all water."

"The old fart never misses a trick. Man, the things I could tell you about this place."

"Forget it, I'm eating. What's the story?"

As he began to talk, the eyes of D.J.'s crude and powerful face showed the gleam of attention. All the humor and gaiety in his world seemed to have vanished. The story, as Andrew suspected, had to do with a girl. She was the blonde for whom his boss was waiting so impatiently. D.J. had gotten to know her quite well, for whenever he remained to work overtime, he and this blonde would work together behind the counter. Soon D.J. found himself doing overtime three and four times a week.

"We get along great. Just great. She laughs at my jokes and sometimes when the old fart goes upstairs for a nap, we joke around with the customers and really have a ball. So what the hell, you know, I asked her out…. What does she say? She says she wants to stay friends. Doesn't want to spoil it. Wants it to remain—" and with disgust, he added: "platonic." For a moment he paused. "What a blow! Can't figure it. She keeps asking me to come and work with her. 'Come and keep me company,' she says. I swear, we get along great! I take her for a cycle ride sometimes. She loves it. But that's all. She won't go out." He lifted a 'burger to his mouth but then paused. "You know, I'm warm for her form. Man, oh man, it's murder!" He sank his teeth into the 'burger and finished half of it in one bite.

"So what do I do, buddy?" he continued, stabbing the French fries with a loosely held fork. "You're my manager. What do I do?"

"It's simple," Andrew replied, and he grinned as if he were about to laugh.

"Look, I'm serious."

"So am I. I tell you it's simple."

"So why are you smiling?"

" 'cause right away I know you won't believe me. You're a suspicious bastard. I tell you *it's* simple and right away you think *I'm* simple."

"Go on, I'm listening."

"First," Andrew said, shifting seriously in his seat and beginning that always enjoyable game of plotting the solution of someone else's social problem, "first, you stop seeing her. Stop working overtime, stop dropping around to see her, stop taking her for rides on your cycle ..."

"Why don't I stop breathing? It's easier."

"Let me do the talking, will ya? O.K., so as I was saying, you stop with her entirely. And you can't let up, or it's no good. But to begin, you first give her a little talking to. That's important. You tell her something like this. Tell her a platonic friendship is impossible. You thought about it; in fact, you've even been trying it, but it's no go. Throw her a few curves. Say her beauty is much too appealing to you just to forget about it. Don't be afraid; lay it on. That's got to please her no matter what she says. Tell her after all, you're only human. If you wanted the company of a man, you'd go to a man for it. But the company of a woman is unique, because it has everything. If you wanted just a friend, you'd buy a dog. Anything a woman can give you on a platonic basis, a man can give you more, and better, and with less trouble. Only by being a woman, tell her, can she be both a man and a woman at once. By holding back half of what she is, she can never hope to be more than half of anything. But if she wants to, she can be both a friend and a female. Whereas a man can only be a man."

"Is that true?" D.J. asked, with fascination.

"Who knows? But the job is to make her think so."

"Do you suppose she'll understand it?"

"What I'm worrying about," Andrew replied, "is, do *you* understand it?"

"Thanks."

"Then you soften her up again. You're sorry, tell her, but she's too beautiful, in your opinion, to be anything less than a woman.

Therefore she must either go out with you as a woman, or not at all. And if it's not at all, then you will have to stop seeing her."

"Suppose she says, O.K., stop seeing me?" D.J.'s eyebrows lowered with worry.

"That's fine. Then you stop seeing her like I told you. After a while you'll happen to accidentally-on-purpose bump into her, and then you ask her again. Casual-like. And if she's been missing you, she'll probably say Yes. See?"

"I don't know."

"I tell you this is the only move. Any other way you'll bleed your heart out, lose all your self-respect, and in the end it might get you a lot of nothing. *My* way you put yourself up at bat, you take your swing, and you get a base hit—or you don't. It's simple."

"What's simple?" a voice thundered. The enormous body of Mr. Torodash blocked the entrance of the booth. "What's simple?"

"Nothing, nothing," D.J. winced and his hand moved unconsciously through the air as if to wave him away. "Will you let us eat in peace?"

"You want to work a few hours?"

"No, thank you. No overtime tonight."

"Just for a few…"

"I said no."

"Simmer down, boy," said the big man. "Simmer down." Then his small eyes turned to Andrew. "He gets excited, this one." And he thumbed a fat hand toward D.J.'s face. "So worked up he gets."

"All right," D.J. complained, "what do ya want?"

"I don't want anything…. Where is she?"

"How should I know?"

"She's late."

"That's not my business. Listen, will ya let us eat in peace?"

"Simmer down, boy. He's always excited. Some case, this one."

D.J. remained silent in suffering patience, waiting for the huge man to leave. Slowly, Mr. Torodash turned his large body so that it faced up the aisle toward the counter. But his eyes glanced at the empty plates on the table. His lips bent into a small obese grin.

"Food good?" he asked.

Suddenly D.J. raised his head. "Good? I've eaten my heart out and had a better meal than this."

Sipping the last of his drink, Andrew nearly choked.

"Ach," bellowed the mountain of flesh, "funny man, funny man!" Then abandoning them to the folly of their young humor, he moved away.

"Let's get out of here," D.J. grumbled.

"Simmer down, boy."

"Oh, shut up. Come on."

Standing in the sunlight on the sidewalk in front of the store, D.J. began to feel better. He pointed a long arm toward the curb.

"Listen, buddy, how'd you like to buy a motorcycle?"

"No, thanks," Andrew said, but he came over to the curb where the Harley-Davidson stood. He ran his hand along the weather-worn Western saddle. "No, I don't think so." Then he paused a moment.

"Got to get rid of it," D.J. was saying. "This winter it's into the service with me. And you know, in the army you can't take it with you. You're in need of a cycle anyway, aren't you? I still think it was a mistake for you to sell that machine of yours before you left for Europe."

"Had to, remember? Needed the money."

"Well have you got any money left?"

"As a matter of fact," said Andrew, "I do."

"Great! Well what do you say? I'm sure we can come to terms, old buddy, old pal."

"No, I think not. But I'll tell you what you *can* do for me. Lend it to me for the evening." He rubbed his chin with an idle finger. "I guarantee I'll put it to good use."

"*You're* going to put *my* machine to good use? How do I lose out? I know I lose out somehow."

"This is going to come as a surprise to you," said Andrew, putting a hand on his friend's shoulder, "but this evening *I* have a date. Don't look at me that way. I really do. Her name is Linda."

"What's her last name?" said D.J., suspiciously.

"Who knows. I just met her."

"Just met her! My God! Here's a guy just gets off the boat, and in a few hours he's got a date. Me, I sweat all day for that fat bastard in there, trying for a month to get a base hit off this damn broad, and nothing. Nothing! Man, oh man! Some guys live right."

"So you'll lend me the machine?"

"And then what am *I* supposed to do?"

"Wait for this broad, why don't ya? Give her the pitch like I told you. Who knows? Maybe this is your night. Maybe…"

"Well," said D.J., "where have *you* been?"

"Hi, doll," Ursula said, as she scampered up to them. "Boy, am I late. What shakes?" But suddenly she saw Andrew's face and her surprised mouth gaped. "Hi, hi, hi!" Then as if they were both marionettes pulled by the same string, Ursula and D.J. both pointed to Andrew Williams, and, looking at each other in amazement, cried, "You know *him*?"

28

HE WAS afraid he was going to die. There had been an opening in the traffic moving slowly along the parkway. Putting on speed, he had raced ahead into the clear. A huge wall of night stood before him. Only the one-eyed headlight of his cycle parted the darkness and showed the road. Then, all at once he remembered. This was his first moment on a machine since that time in France which had almost been his last. It came to him like a letter he had forgotten to mail and remembered too late. He became a seated statue of fear. The one thing in the world that he wanted was to stop, but he couldn't. For if the end came, all that was no good in him would also be done with.

A voice whispered in the dark. It was shouting. But in the cascade of air buffeting his head it reached him only as a whisper. He yelled into the night. "What?!"

Again he heard the tumultuous whisper. This time he understood.

"It's fun," Linda was shouting at him.

"Frightened?" he yelled over his shoulder.

"Yes."

"Want me to stop?"

"Noooo," came the answer, as if it were traveling to him from miles away.

"O.K., hang on."

"What?"

"Hang on!"

This time she heard him, for he felt her arms tighten around him and her head press against the shield of his shoulder. Strange, that he should have forgotten her. The girl was hanging on to him as if her life depended on it. What could she know of his skill in using this machine? Yet her trust in him was complete. Her arms squeezed tight in the joyful danger of the moment, and behind him, through the thinness of his shirt, he felt her body pleasing his. The wall of night continued its retreat in front of him. Later he discovered he was bathed in sweat.

The sky had not a single star and so they placed their shoes where they could easily find them, beneath the cycle and up against the wheel. Along the enormous stretch of sand, invisible in the darkness, they saw the occasional fire of a beach party, nothing more. In the distance they could hear the crashing of the ancient sea. She took his hand and bravely led the way.

"Ou, feel how cool the sand is," she said, as they walked toward the sound of the ocean. Slowly and carefully they moved as if not quite certain whether the sand was their enemy or their friend. The wonder of her hand newly placed in his was enough to inspire his silence. He was beginning to feel that vague excited promise of the future whenever a girl, who was still a stranger, began showing the first harmless signs of liking him.

As they proceeded blindly barefoot on the beach, a tall trash basket suddenly came between them. Their hands were rudely separated. Andrew found himself standing alone, unable to see. The sea-rinsed air chilled him. She was gone. For a moment even the waves paused. He moved forward, arms outstretched, his eyes straining.

"Please," she said weakly, "where are you?"

He turned in her direction. "Right here. Take it easy."

"Where?" Her voice could not conceal her distress.

They were very close to each other now. With his arms out-stretched and his eyes closed, he felt his hand make contact with her soft breast. In a moment he was clasping her shoulders while the girl's head was pressed safely against his neck. She held herself close as if she were cold.

"I'm sorry," he said, meaning the way his hand had touched her. But she misunderstood.

"We couldn't help it. It was one of those baskets."

Then she added, "I was afraid. It was so stupid."

He wrapped both his arms around her. He knew it would make her feel better. But he felt foolish all the same.

"I bet you never thought Jones Beach could be so frightening."

"It's not that," she said. "It's the dark. Sometimes it gets the better of me. I know how foolish that must sound." The girl lifted her head to examine what she could see of his face. She tried to laugh. "Just like a little child." Then she shook her head.

"Are you afraid of the dark at home?"

"No, that's different."

"Then it *is* the beach you're afraid of."

"Maybe .... Listen .... It sounds terrible, doesn't it?"

"The waves frighten you?"

"I don't know. Listen to them. You can feel how strong they are by the awful sound they make when they hit the beach. Yet you can't see anything. I think that's what is frightening."

They had begun to walk again. His arm was around her waist. Occasionally he felt her bare foot touching his.

"Let's walk near one of those fires," he suggested.

"Are *you* afraid of the sea?" she asked.

"All depends. If I were out in the middle of it alone in a boat, sure. But just listening to it—that's something different. I feel awe, I feel mystery. In fact, it's almost a religious experience."

Her voice became happy. "You know? I think you're more frightened than me."

Her hand touched his cheek for a moment and surprised him.

"I'm only joking," she explained. "Really."

Then her voice turned sober again. "I'm such a coward."

"Just because of the dark? That's nonsense."

"No, I mean in other things."

"You're simply knocking yourself."

"They're just using me, Dominique and Ursula, you know that? They're looking to go sailing on my father's boat."

"I know," he replied.

"And I really shouldn't have spent my time with them. But I was a coward." After a pause, her voice began to weaken. "But Ursula isn't so bad, really. She changes when your sister is around. They get so silly when they're together. Sometimes it actually embarrasses me."

"They get silly?"

"Not really silly. They're always trying to be crazy or different. They're always laughing at other people behind their backs. They try to be different, but they end up doing what many people do who want to be different. They went down to Greenwich Village. You know, the dungaree group. They said they were protesting against snobbishness and conformity, but like some people in the Village they ended up conforming to each other and becoming the biggest snobs of all. It was just a phase, though, because they were really tourists and didn't belong. Anyway, they finally gave it up, but only after it had been going on all summer."

"Well, that's a side of my sister I never knew before. With me she's always the stiff-necked beauty afraid of letting herself go, afraid it might make her less beautiful."

"Yes, I know. She's very good-looking. But she has courage," Linda insisted, angrily, "and I haven't any. She can take it. She can take whatever happens. She's strong. But I keep falling apart inside. If I think someone dislikes me, or if I'm nervous about something, I get all confused or I become foolish and laugh too much or I cry. I cry a lot."

As he listened, he was becoming extremely fond of her. He wanted to tell her about it, about this new feeling of his, but he knew he wouldn't.

"Here," he said, pointing to a spot in the sand, "let's stop here."

They had come to within a dozen yards or so of the curling flame of the beach fire. Huddled figures were sprawled on blankets, but no one seemed to be moving, as if they were all asleep.

"Let's sit for a while," he said, noticing how the light of the fire played on her face.

They sank onto the softness beneath them and nestled their weight together. Someone near the fire moved to throw on more wood. The man's flame-lit face flickered in the distance.

"Nice and peaceful here, isn't it?" Andrew said.

She nodded without looking at him.

"Are you chilly?"

She shook her head.

"Look, you shouldn't think of Dominique as a mountain of strength."

"Your sister," she began, but could go no further. She bit her lip once more and waited. Staring at the campfire, she tried again, and this time achieved an entire sentence. "It's easy … when you're beautiful like she is."

"What are you talking about? You're very pretty."

But all at once, as if to prove how wrong he was, her face became incredibly ugly and she began crying to herself silently, just sitting there as if stricken, her head turned away from him to hide her shame. One of her hands clutched the blouse at her neck, the other hand fingered her cheeks uselessly. With his arm around her, Andrew was not sure what to do. Gradually he pressed her weight upon him. Her soft black hair ran against his cheek. Slowly he felt her accept the support of his body and begin to relax against it. His left hand slid up and down her sleeveless arm and her skin felt smooth and female. There was only waiting to be done now.

He was glad that she had begun to cry. If she hadn't, he would not be holding her so softly in his arms. The invisible sea crashed loudly somewhere off behind them. The sound of a woman's voice came laughing from the fire. Andrew placed his hand on the beach to support his weight. His fingers sank in and he could feel beneath the surface where the sand was cold. He worked his fingers even deeper and the sand became hard like dirt and he could go no further.

What if he should actually find something? he thought. Wouldn't that be strange? To reach with his hand at this one lonely spot upon the lonely endless beach, here at night in the middle of nowhere with a girl in the distance laughing and a girl at his ear crying; to reach at that very moment and uncover something of great value, a diamond, perhaps, or a thousand-dollar bill. Where on this great beach, he wondered, was there something hidden waiting to be found? One could search for a lifetime and never find it. That is, if there really was anything to be found.

She lifted her head and looked into his face. She had stopped crying.

"You see how I am?" she said.

"But all I said," he replied, smiling, "was that I thought you looked..."

He found himself kissing her. At first he was a little frightened. How good her mouth tasted. Some women you just kiss; others you also taste, as if kissing were not enough. Overjoyed, he felt her kissing him back. He kept hearing the sea and feeling the salt breeze from the ocean. The tears on her cheek, when he kissed them away, also tasted of salt.

29

Mambo Before breakfast! The entire second floor vibrates with moving feet. Dominique and her lover are dancing. Sounds from the record player swarm through the open doorway of her brother's room. On his disheveled bed, where Andrew Williams comes awake, he listens with annoyance to the orgy of music. He is ill at ease, for he cannot forget that there is now a stranger in the house. But the stranger is himself. As he lies there he finds it is easier to think of other things. He reaches for the pack of cigarettes and discovers there is only one left. This recalls that night on the beach three days ago.

She wiped from her face the tears that he had not completely kissed away, and then with a gentle voice, as if nothing had happened, she said, "Baby, do you have a cigarette?" As he reached into his pocket, he felt her lips press against his neck.

"Uh-oh."

"What's the matter?" she asked. "All gone?"

"One left."

"We'll share it."

"You take it."

"No, no," she smiled, kissing him, "we'll share it. I have spoken."

Then, with her nose almost touching his, she beamed to show she was only playing. They sat together in the sand and did not look at each other as they shared the last cigarette. Instead, they watched the distant, hypnotic fire. Her arms tightened around him and just when he had gotten to the point of realizing how contented he really was, it began to rain.

Later it became a joke, but at the time he was afraid everything was spoiled. Running with difficulty across the soft sand, they were followed by people from the beach party who were carrying blankets and baskets and were laughing hysterically as they made for the shelter of a nearby car. Standing first on one foot and then on the other, Linda slipped into her shoes while Andrew, kneeling in the dark, searched frantically through the saddlebags that hung over the rear wheel. Finally he fell backwards into a sitting position and slapped his forehead.

"It's not here. Oh, no. Oh, that no-good bastard! D.J., when I get my hands on you—" And he strangled the air with his fingers. "The rain cape," he explained to the girl, "it's gone. It should be in here at all times. Oh, that no-good..." And he slapped the ground with the palm of his hand and sent a rain puddle scaling in all directions. He even got some of it in his mouth.

"So we get wet," she laughed. "So what? I love the rain. Really." She threw out her arms and spun around in the mounting downpour.

Andrew sprang to his feet. "All right, you asked for it." Turning his face skyward he pointed his arm up into the blackness. "Listen to me, up there," he shouted. "The lady likes it, see? So rain, you understand? Rain, God damn it! Rain!"

In that wild calm just before the eruption of laughter, she watched him with fascination, as if suddenly, and for the first time in her life, she had found herself coming fully alive. At that moment, any photograph taken of her would have been beautiful.

"You're crazy." She grinned. "Do you know that?"

It took them forty-five minutes to get home. By the time they arrived at Linda's house, everything about them was drenched except their spirits. For the last kiss of the evening she sat herself side-saddle in front of him and he saw in the lamplight how her water-soaked clothes gripped her body. He saw as though for the first time the beautiful line of her breast, and when he held her against him, he felt the rounded curve of her hip, and in the rain he pressed his mouth to hers.

With a swing of his feet he is up. Crushing the cigarette into the ash tray near his camera on the table, he reaches for the cigarette pack without looking and works his finger inside to make sure it is really empty. Bits of tobacco at the bottom, nothing more. He crushes the empty pack with his fist and throws it at the basket, but misses. Going across the hall to the bathroom, he does not look toward his sister's room, where the dancing is still going on. He locks the door, drops the pants of his pajamas and lowers himself onto the toilet seat. It is still morning, but the air is already beginning to grow warm. He is thinking: Should I ask Dom to make me breakfast? I wonder? Just for the hell of it? Just to see her face? But he knows it is useless. She has cooked for him only once since he returned. And that was three days ago.

"You want some ham and eggs?" she had asked, when he came down and found them seated at the kitchen table. It was the first time they had faced each other since he had left them to walk Linda home. He had expected Dominique still to be carrying her hate because of his sudden arrival, but he was disarmed by the friendliness in her voice.

"Ham and eggs?" he said. "Why, that would be fine."

Dominique rose from the table, though her own breakfast was only half eaten, and side-stepped her way between the wall and Derek's chair as she headed for the stove. She was wearing a pair of shorts, and as she passed behind where her lover sat, he reached back and casually clapped a loose hand over the rounded calf of one of her bare legs. She pretended not to notice.

"From here your stems look all right," Derek said, as he watched her go.

They do, Andrew thought. Even he had to admit it. But to hear this other man say it only aroused disgust in him. Then he noticed she was also wearing high heels. High heels with shorts! And to top it off, a sweater as only she could wear one. The pin-up girl. That was his sister, all right. Always wearing the shield of glamour, just to be on the safe side. But to the compliment, Dominique made no reply. Before me, she feels uneasy, Andrew decided.

"Shake it but don't break it," Derek cracked, "wrap it up and I'll take it."

"Oh, be quiet, will you," she said, with a dead voice. She broke open two eggs and with the other hand reached for the package of ham.

Andrew felt himself being watched. He returned the stare.

"How goes it, fella?" Derek asked. "Sleep well?"

"Slept all right," Andrew said, wondering why he resented even being spoken to by this stranger.

"Good to hear it. Now as for me, I slept great. Let me tell *you*." And he slouched in his chair and folded his large hands on top of his head. Looking in Dominique's direction for a moment, he added: "Yar, man."

"Toast?" she asked her brother.

"Yes, please," Andrew replied, surprising himself with his own pleasantness. Underneath all that female armor, perhaps she *does* have a heart, he thought. When the idea, What does she want? entered his mind, he only half-listened to it.

"*That's* how I slept," Derek threw in. "Just like hot toast. Wow, I tell *you*." He laughed, trying as he did so to get them to join in.

I wish you would shut your mouth, Andrew thought. So this was the man he was going to throw out. And today was the day. Well, it would be a pleasure. Ulysses home from the wars. But what would his excuse be for slaughter? Could he find one? Would he really need one? Yes, he supposed he would.

"Have a nice time in Europe?" she asked, as she watched the eggs frying in the pan. The fumes had now begun to reach him.

"Yes, very nice."

Here's where it comes, he thought. Here's where she asks why I came home so early. Here's where it starts.

"Did you get to the Riviera?" she asked, looking up from the stove to do so.

"Yes, I spent several days there."

"It must be wonderful. I always wanted to go to the Riviera some day." She was envious of her own admiration for him. Oh, to be a man! She would exchange places gladly and take his camera and cycle and leave.

"Maybe father'll send you for a wedding present," Andrew suggested.

"Maybe," she concluded with a doubtful voice.

"Lot of good-looking heads there, I bet," said her lover. His eyes were filled with the dull envy of the nontraveler.

"Thanks," Andrew said, when she brought him his food. "That looks good."

"Nothing like home cooking, eh?" said Derek.

Dominique sat down. "Coffee?" she asked, and her brother extended his cup and saucer.

Something is wrong, he thought, as he watched her pour the black liquid from the coffeepot. We are all pretending, that's the trouble; and it's sad. All of us sitting domestically around the break-fast table, and yet only yesterday we hated each other. Now we sit politely sipping coffee.

"What are you going to do today?" she questioned him casually, as she handed back the cup and saucer.

"Gee, I don't know." He wanted to add, Why? but he didn't.

"We're going to the beach." The way she said it, it was almost an invitation.

Derek broke in. "Not that I love water. Just never saw her in a bathing suit before. Yar, man."

Dominique smiled at him reproachfully, but they seemed to be enjoying a vast, unspoken joke.

"And with that sweater she's wearing. I tell you she'll stop traffic before we get there." He turned to Andrew. "What do you think?"

"Oh, don't you know," she said, "that a brother never notices such things." Saying this she glanced at Andrew but found his face a blank. He was leaning forward scooping some food into his mouth and did not even look up.

"Is that so?" Derek said. "Boy, am I glad I'm not your brother."

She laughed, despite herself. Then her face stiffened slightly and she grew sober. Andrew could tell that under the table Derek had secretly put his hand on her leg.

He interrupted the silence with: "What were you saying about the beach?"

"Yes," she said, trying to put on her most pleasant smile. But to Andrew, at that moment, she looked sick. "Yes, would you be able to go with us?"

"I don't think so. There are a number of things I should get done."

He could not imagine what these things might be. But to spend a whole afternoon with these two would have been his idea of torture. They did not seem too unhappy at his refusal, either.

"Well, then," Dominique began, and as soon as she did so, Andrew suddenly understood her smiles, her invitations, and, of course, the breakfast. "Well, then, you *will* let us borrow your keys, won't you?" She laughed as she added, "It's an awfully long walk to the ocean."

"The Pacific, that is," Derek said, with uproarious laughter.

"You know the old joke," Dominique explained.

"Yes, I know the joke," Andrew said, "and you can laugh yourselves sick over it, but you're still not getting the car."

Dominique's face whitened. For a moment it looked as if she might go into another of her frustrated, high-pitched rages.

"Derek," she said, calmly, "would you mind?" And she indicated the door to the living room. "Just for a few minutes while I speak with my kind, dear brother. No, better still—would you run down to the corner store and pick up a bottle of sun-tan oil? Please? Thank you. We'll need it for the beach today, anyway."

When Derek climbed to his feet, the sudden size of him was startling. Andrew had forgotten how tall this intruder really was. The thin boyish face seemed to be toying with the idea of grinning, but nothing came of it. They waited, the sister and the brother, until they heard the front door slam. Then they were alone in the big house and the silence was like a falling vase that one watches helplessly, knowing it is about to smash.

"I want those keys, damn it," she yelled. "I have as much right to the car as you. You don't even use it, anyway. Yesterday you were on some Goddamn cycle all night. It was even raining, but you didn't take the car. No, you took that motorcycle and got drenched. But we had to stay home. And with the car parked right outside all night." She was on her feet now, storming at him with all her anger displayed on her distorted face. "What are you going to do, sit on your ass all summer? Don't you think it's about time you started taking your camera and hunting up a few jobs? And if you came home just so you can spy on me, then that's your sad mistake, because I'm not going to change my life one single bit. Do you hear me? And don't think you can threaten me, either. If you go to mother like a little cry-baby telling her stories about me, I'll just deny them, that's all. Understand? I'm *speaking* to you."

It was Andrew's intention to talk quietly against his sister's onslaught, but the first time he opened his mouth he found himself boiling with rage.

"Do *I* hear *you*? Do *I* hear *you*? Do *you* hear *me*! I want that guy to get out. Pack his bags and send that bastard on his way. Out! What do you think this place is? A brothel?"

"He's my guest!" she screamed, her finger tapping her chest like a furious woodpecker. She leaned over the table so she could bring her face closer to his. "He's my guest and he stays right here!"

"I'll throw 'im out!"

"You just try it."

"Don't worry, I will."

"Go on, just try it!"

"What the hell do you see in that bastard, anyway? He's a conceited ass and he reeks with phony smoothness."

"What do I *see* in him?" she returned. "He's *beautiful*. That's what I see in him." And she stiffened with an almost evil pride.

Silence. He was so astounded by this answer that he couldn't think of a single thing to say. He kept hearing the passionate way in which she had shouted the word "beautiful."

"And he's none of the things you say he is," she went on bitterly. "He has a lot of good qualities. But I wouldn't expect *you* to notice them. You don't even *know* him. How do you come off making judgments? For your information, Mr. Smarty-Pants, he loves me. *That's* how much you know about him."

She lifted her head in triumph, unconsciously throwing back her shoulders, which in turn caused her breasts to thrust out at him.

"Love?" Andrew cried. "That guy? Ha! He doesn't know what love is."

Her voice became ominous with its quiet. All her anger vanished and in its place was a subtle, mysterious self-assurance.

"Do *you?*" she said, and the words hung in the air and did not go away as other words do.

What does she mean? his heart whispered wildly. What does she think she knows? Who has been talking to her?

They heard the front door open, and in a few seconds Derek was standing in the kitchen, a bottle of sun-tan lotion visible in his fist. He was breathing hard, having run all the way.

Dominique greeted him by going over and taking hold of him with her hands. "He says you don't know what love is," she smiled. Then she snapped her head around to glare at her brother and inform him that he was definitely alone now, definitely outnumbered. "That's what he said," she continued. "Isn't that a scream?"

The little grin which Derek had seemed to be toying with, became visible now in a sly bend of his lips. He began to recite:

> "*A wanton young lady from Wimley,*
> *Reproached for not acting quite primly,*
> *Answered, 'Heavens above,*
> *I know sex isn't love,*
> *But it's such an attractive facsimile.'* "

Dominique was overcome with delight. "Isn't he wonderful?" she cried out as if the room were filled with people. She threw her arms around her lover's neck, tilted her head and kissed him.

Seated on the toilet seat, Andrew studies the ceiling. Good paint job. After all these years, and not a single crack. A few wrinkles, nothing more. Funny how you can still hear the music right through the walls. Too bad Linda has to see her aunt today. Could have gone to the beach. Could have gone for a walk. Shouldn't be greedy, though. Seen her now every day so far. In fact, every day for three days and three nights.

"Every day?" D.J. had asked on the phone. "You mean it? And tonight too?"

"Right."

"That makes it day and night for three straight. Man, oh man. What's the bit? When was the last time you saw a girl six times in three days? Better still, when was the last time you saw the same girl six times in *two months*? You're holding back on me, buddy! What's her name again?"

"Linda Jeffers, and that's the third time you asked me."

"I forget, I forget.... Wait a minute...Linda Jeffers. Wait a minute. She go to camp last summer? Near Lake Monhegan somewhere?"

"Yes, I think so."

"Wait a minute. She plays the guitar?"

"That she does."

"That's right. Linda Jeffers. Jesus, I think a friend of mine used to go out with her. At camp. Let's see. As I remember, he said she had long dark hair. Sort of a gentle-type person. Attractive."

"Cries easily," Andrew put in just for the hell of it.

"That's her. That's her," came the excited voice, louder than ever. "What a memory, huh?"

"Yar, what a memory. It took you three days just to remember the name, let alone place it.

"Slow, but sure."

"So what did this friend of your say about her?"

"Well..." Then there was nothing but silence.

"Come on. Spit it out."

"Tell me something. Do you think... I mean are you in love with her?"

"Oh, for crysake!"

"All right. All right.... He didn't say anything much. He just told me he did pretty good with her. That's what he said. It seems he did all right."

"Meaning?"

"Meaning, I don't know. Meaning I guess he shacked up with her for most of the summer."

"What does that prove?"

"*Nothing*," D.J. protested, and Andrew could almost see him shrugging his shoulders. "Nothing at all. Doesn't prove a thing." There was another silence. Then he added hesitantly: "How you doing with her? I mean any action so far?"

"Nothing to speak of. I was over her house last night. Her folks are vacationing. Just a little necking. I didn't push it."

"Uh-huh... uh-huh," he said while listening. Finally he burst out, "Listen, this guy could be wrong, you know. I mean, he could have been telling me a whole story."

"Relax, will ya?"

"I mean, you said it. What does it prove?"

"That life is to be lived. That's what it proves."

"Yar, I guess so."

But the air still had not cleared, so Andrew changed the subject.

"What's new with Ursula?"

"That's what I called you about," said D.J. eagerly. "It's going great. Just great. You're a genius, buddy. I swear. She dropped that platonic crap as soon as I put on the pressure. I told you about that, didn't I? Thought so. Well, yesterday I took her for a ride on the cycle just like you said."

"With or without a rain cape?" Andrew questioned him pointedly.

"Hummmmmm! Look, I told you I was sorry."

"I'm only kidding. What happened?"

"Guess what? We smooched it up."

"Oh, happy day."

"So far so good, right? Now what do I do?"

"If you don't know, I can't tell ya."

"No, I mean how do I get her in the mood? Look, you're my manager, aren't you? So manage."

Andrew resigned himself with a long exhale of air. "All right," he said. "Let's see. So far you've been playing it rough. That right?"

"You said it. Listen to this. Last night she says to me, 'Doll, aren't you going to give me a kiss?' 'Another one?' I said. 'What happened to the one I gave you an hour ago?' Smooth?"

"Oh, that was smooth.... Listen. Jerk. Before you smooth yourself right out of the picture I suggest a change of plans. You're on first base, right? Now show a little consideration. A little understanding. Got it? Play it casual. Sex is the furthest thing from your mind."

"It is?"

"All you want to do is get to know her better. It's a pleasure to be with her. To talk to her. Know what I mean? Get her confidence. Take your time. Remember: you're adult. You're experienced, you're understanding. You know the score, but you're not trying to win the ball game the first time at bat. If no one is home some night soon, bring her over. But don't do anything. That'll shake her up. Take your time. Got it?"

"Got it. And then the first moment she drops her guard. *Wam!*"

Andrew could tell that his friend was playing games again.

"Look, D.J."

"Warn, warn, warn!"

"Hey!"

"What a blow. Great move, great."

"*Hey!*"

"What? What'd you say? Wait a minute."

"Now what," Andrew smiled.

"Only this. You want to buy a cycle?"

"No, I don't."

"No?...Oh.... Well, in that case I have only one thing to say."

"What's that?"

There was a click. D.J. had hung up.

The mirror hangs above the sink. Back and forth over the top of his head go the strokes of his brush. A pleasant throb develops in one of the muscles of the upper arm. The toilet takes a long time to stop flushing. In the toothbrush rack on the wall two brushes are missing—his father and mother vacationing in California. The house seems terribly empty. Yet he does not miss them. But for the first time in his life he feels he really understands his mother, understands why she has been worrying all these years and will go on worrying for years to come. She is a warden, fearful that her only prisoner will escape. The prisoner is Dominique. Ever since he can remember, his mother has kept watch over her with an obsession dedicated to keeping his sister from sharing a bed with a man —*any* man. Little else of Dominique's activities have really interested her. Yet as only Dominique can tell and as Andrew suspects, this tireless diligence has been outwitted long ago. But Mrs. Williams does not know this, and so the standing of the guard continues as before, and the daughter continues to frustrate each new effort to restrict her with all the solemn patience of an adult being pestered by a spoiled child.

He began to wish his parents were home. They would at least have taken this burden from him. Now he understood some of his mother's feverish concern about his sister and her men. He understood as he watched their Mambo dancing and their intimate smiles and their lazy kisses. He understood when he heard Derek tiptoe through the hall at night on his way to Dominique's bed, or heard him tiptoe back again at dawn. Or as he watched television in the living room with them, when all they did was sit in one chair together, making the soft sullen sounds of love. Or saw

Derek smooth his hand over her hip as they walk slowly upstairs. Or watched the thousand and one little ways in which a couple can make themselves all alone in a room no matter who else is there. And then suddenly heard his sister's impatient voice say to him: "Well, and why are you so insulting with your silence?"

He wished his parents would return soon. Yet he knew that that wouldn't help, either. For what are parents but the familiar faces of strangers to whom we can no more bare our hearts than we can to the first person passing in the street. The Williams household on any typical day consisted of four people who carried the great love they had for each other so tightly locked within their hearts that it was as though they had no love there at all.

Perhaps what they needed, his sister and he, was to get away, to escape. For Dominique, the answer was marriage. The great American happy ending. Then her parents could wash their hands of her for good. But what about himself? He often wondered what it would be like if all his friends got married and he did not. In a way it would seem as if he were being left behind on some deserted ocean island, watching while the last boat pulls away and grows small.

Years ago, when he first found out about himself, when he first discovered what the word impotent meant, he spent a lot of time trying to think up an erection, trying to convince himself that he was all right. He would try it when alone at night, or even during the day while seated in the subway, or in a classroom, or even while at the movies. But whether or not he succeeded, his attempts only made things worse, because soon he found himself thinking of little else.

He had never realized before how much the sex act is taken for granted in everyday life. In posters, movies, on the radio, in television, in novels, in poems, almost everywhere. Many phases of love in society were touched upon—problems of money, security, morality, infidelity, indifference, separation, even death. But none of these mattered to him. And each new day was filled with a thousand new reminders of his unhappiness. These reminders came from friends, as well as strangers, and they were all accidental, for no one knew what was going on within him, and no one could be told. Finally it got so bad that almost every man he met in the street, or saw in the movies, or watched on TV, would set him to thinking: How is it with *him*, I wonder? Sometimes he would single someone out in a crowd and imagine that this man was like himself. Just stare at him and imagine it. And each time he did so he was amazed to discover how the man's face changed and became blank, lumbering, almost stupid. The contempt he felt for these men horrified him, for he soon realized that it was actually contempt for himself that he was feeling.

30

FOR A moment his finger pressed the doorbell and held it. He had climbed the stairs for nothing and was now waiting for nothing. The house was as dark as death. Not a single light in any of the windows. She had forgotten their appointment. He was sure of it. He was beginning to dislike her. How easy it was.

"Oh, here you are," Linda cried. She threw her arms out and hugged him tight. "I was so afraid you wouldn't come. I even phoned, but your sister said you had gone out." Her lips went warm and wet against his. He was familiar with her kisses now, but he still marveled at how they tasted. She pulled her head away and then kissed him again quickly, grunting as if he had squeezed her.

"Guess what?" she laughed. "The lights are out. The fuse blew or something." And he watched as she became a child again in her excitement. Then, stepping back for a moment, she vanished from the dim fringe of the street light into the blackness of the house.

"I don't have any matches," she called happily, and then she returned and he could see her again, dimly, as before. She was holding a candle. "I've been sitting in the dark for an hour like a goof," she admitted with a smile. He felt her delicious mouth again and again it was gone. "Do you have matches? Oh, please do. Please, please, pretty please! Have matches!"

"Yes," he said, reaching into his pocket, "I think so."

"Oh, please, please." Her eyes were closed as if she were wishing with all her heart.

"Ah, here," he exclaimed with a grin of triumph and he dangled them before her nose. "But you know, you could have used the stove."

"Oh, God. I never thought of that." She hid her face for a moment. Then she peeked between her fingers. Then she took her hands away. "Oh, Jeffers," she said, "what a brain you are." But Andrew only laughed, and in a moment the candle was lit, and by its light he discovered for the first time how very deep and pure was the darkness of her eyes.

"Can you fix a fuse?" she asked. "I can't."

"Ah, but you can blow them out. Now I couldn't do that if I tried. Anyone can fix them."

"That's right," she agreed with pretended pride.

"Come on, you, let's go downstairs."

"Wait." And she moved to the dining-room table and returned, holding a bottle. "For you," she said, holding it out with a sheepishly inverted grin.

"Ah, good, you bought more wine."

"It's open." Then, in baby talk, she added, "I took already. I sorry."

"What's a mouthful between friends."

"Just what *I* thought . . . so I drank the whole thing."

"Oh, swell," he said, and then after she kissed him again, "Let's go before you blow another fuse." Grinning directly at him, she allowed herself to look flattered.

With one hand on her waist and the other gripping the bottle, he led her through the kitchen toward the cellar steps. Linda held the candle. As they moved, it flickered as if it were going out. An eerie light danced all about on the walls.

"How did it go with your aunt today?"

"God, I don't even want to think about it," she said, shaking her head back and forth. "Just because my folks are away she takes it upon herself to be my sole guardian and protector. She's always asking me questions to find out if I'm behaving myself. 'Mustn't let any young men into the house, Linda, dear,' " the girl mimicked. " 'That wouldn't be proper, you know.' "

"Oh, she sounds delightful."

"And what kills me, I have to see her at least once a week. Can't avoid it. Andrew, you couldn't believe how she is. Remember when

Ingrid Bergman went to Europe and fell in love? Well, my lovely old aunt wrote letters to every newspaper in the city and to a dozen congressmen, too. She demanded that Bergman have her citizenship revoked and that she never be allowed in this country again."

"You should have written letters also. Demand the same thing for your aunt."

"That would have been justice, wouldn't it? Oh, she's a beaut."

At the top of the stairs they held each other firmly. Then in the shimmering candlelight, and with slow and awkward steps, they began to descend.

"When we fix the fuse," she said, "let's keep the lights out. All right? This is fun. You want to?"

"Good idea," he agreed, hitting his head accidentally against the overpass. The whole earth seemed jarred with pain. For a moment he did not move.

"Oh, baby, your head. Oh, I'm sorry. Guess I should have warned you." She kissed his brow. "Does it hurt?"

He touched himself and examined his finger for blood. "Now what were you saying about the lights?"

"Oh, I'm sorry. Really."

"Not at all! In fact, to show you what kind of a guy I am, I still think it's a good idea. In fact, let's drink to it."

They each swallowed some wine and then, putting the bottle down on the nearest step, she once again asked him about his head. Assured that all was well, she smiled and pecked him on the brow. Then she came close and held him tight. Everything was still for a moment. He felt his body begin to want her as if new blood, hot and thick and slow moving, had suddenly entered his veins. She was resting her head on his shoulder and with his hands he felt the softness of cashmere.

"I feel so very happy," she whispered. It was as if she had read his mind. He held the candle for her as she nestled against him. The flame, steady as stone, silently gave off a small ribbon of gray smoke that vanished upward. His head throbbed softly, a beacon winking in the night. Almost like a warning.

He whispered into her ear: "You know, we're not getting that fuse fixed this way."

The girl pulled away from him. "True," she said. Taking his free hand she led the way through the dark cellar to the fuse box in the rear. Her voice seemed a little sharp and he wondered whether she had been offended. He took a quick look, but her face was closed.

In no time at all he located the blown fuse. Luckily, there were a number of new fuses lined up along the wall resting on a two-by-four. As he worked, he noticed out of the tail of his eye how steadily she was watching him. Not watching what he was doing, but studying his face with that all-encompassing passive attention that a woman uses only when the face she is looking at is not looking at her.

"Well, that should do it," he said, closing the door to the fuse box. But she wasn't listening.

"Baby?" she whispered in a soft saturated voice which sounded more like an exhale of air. "Baby, I have something important to tell you." She came forward, her hands clasped behind her, her hips undulating subtly as she moved. She spoke to him again, and this time there came no sound at all. But he saw "baby" appear slowly and gently on her silent lips. As he watched her, his body began to generate heat. It was so strong and it had come about so quickly that he grew cautious. Several emotions seemed to be consuming her at once. As he studied her deep black eyes, he saw they were on the verge of tears. The more he watched, the less he understood. Her lips, very near him now, again moved silently.

But it was his own voice he heard. "Ouch! God damn it!"

The little candle-flame danced violently. A glob of hot wax had dropped onto his hand and the harmless sting had startled him. He examined his hand quickly, scraping off the wax with a finger-nail. Then he became angry. Holding the candle high, he rummaged among the dusty shelves of a nearby cabinet until he found what he wanted. He held up a small metal ash tray and examined it. With puffed cheeks he blew the ash tray clean of dust. Then, tipping the candle above it, he waited as drops of hot wax fell onto the metal dish and gathered in a tiny pool. "Come on! Come on!" The entire progress of his life had now been reduced to the slow and occasional dripping of the solitary candle. He stared at the tray with dedicated grimness. The tiny pool gradually began to thicken. At last there seemed to be enough. He took the candle and pressed it into its own wax until it stood upright by itself. "Ah, success."

"All right for you," she pretended. "If you don't want to listen to me..." And she walked briskly away. The mock injury in her tone was put on to conceal how hurt she really felt.

"Hey, wait a minute," he called, and he lost sight of her in the darkness. He heard her climbing the stairs. She was leaving.

"Hey, look, I just wanted to fix the damn candle. Oh, come on."

But she was gone and he no longer heard the sound of her feet. At the stairs, he looked up. There was nothing to be seen except the bottle of wine standing on one of the lower steps. He grabbed it with his free hand and began to climb. She would be waiting in the kitchen, hidden away in the darkness. She was only playing games. But standing in the center of the kitchen, holding the flame higher than his head, he could not see her anywhere. He thought of turning on the house lights, but decided against it. She wasn't in the dining room, either. The living room was next, and he examined all of its four corners. But no Linda.

"Hello there," he said loudly. He heard nothing. "Hello." The house remained silent as a tomb. "Anyone home?" he called out, trying to make his voice as light and carefree as he could. "Ready or not, here I come." But the words seemed to fall stupidly into the void. Had she left the house? No, she would be upstairs. Surely she would be upstairs. He began to climb the carpeted steps one after another. The dancing glare of the candle led the way. "Tap, tap, anyone around my base is it." And then: "I'll huff and I'll puff and I'll blow your house down." Silence. "'Out, out, brief candle! Life's but a walking shadow, a poor player who struts and frets his hour upon the stage, and then is heard no more.'" He had hoped to hear her laugh and he was ready to laugh along with her. But his voice rang empty against the silence. Standing now at the top of the stairs and feeling sure she was somewhere near him, he began, as a last resort, to recite a limerick he remembered hearing Derek quote:

> *"There was a young man called McLean,*
> *Who invented the damnedest machine.*
> *Concave or convex,*
> *It would fit either sex,*
> *And was perfectly easy to clean."*

Then from within the darkness of one of the rooms he finally heard it. A soft, secret, almost inaudible stifle of laughter. It was gone even before he had a chance to listen. He went in and found her standing in a corner, watching him like a guilty child.

"Hello," he said.

"'Lo," she answered impishly. The sound of her voice told him that all was well again. He could feel himself relax. Putting the candle and the wine bottle down on a nearby table, he looked curiously around him. It was her bedroom. Why, he wondered, had she hidden herself here? She left the corner where she was standing and started toward him. But she sat down, instead, on the edge of the bed and looked at him. He saw only one chair in the room, over by the window.

"No," she pouted. "Sit here." And with her hand she patted the blanket next to her. Their combined weight made the mattress sink, which pressed them closer together.

She kissed him on the cheek. "I sorry," she whispered.

"What were you about to say down there? Before the candle interrupted us?"

Smoothing her thin skirt over her legs, she looked down at her lap and did not answer. Her long straight hair fell forward, blocking his view of her face. She shrugged her shoulders.

He spoke with awkward gentleness. "No? ... You don't want to tell me?"

Again she shrugged.

"I'd like to know…. I have a feeling it was important…. Was it?"

She nodded. With his arm around her, she leaned against him. For a few moments nothing happened. Across the room the candle-flame was motionless. In the dead August night, miles away, came first the slow and then the frantic rataplan of a locomotive beginning to move. With a toss of her head, Linda threw back her hair. Her eyes were staring at him now, and once again, though free of sorrow, they seemed about to cry.

"Is something wrong?"

She rolled her head on his shoulder and he saw that she was hiding her face. Then she lifted her eyes again. The pretty face swung back and forth as if trying to shake off whatever it was that bound her tongue.

"Oh, there are so many, many things I want to tell you. No, nothing is wrong. It's just that… I like you so very, *very* much. I think…

"I think I love you," she brought out at last.

For a moment he thought she might reach out and touch him.

"Are you sure?" The words went dry in his throat as he said them. Not knowing what to say, he was sure he had said something stupid. But she took no notice.

"I love you *now*, anyway," she said, in answer to his question. Then she shook her head as if once again to fight down her emotions.

"Oh, Andrew. I haven't loved anyone in such a long time. A year almost. But now, when I hear something that makes me laugh, I think, Andrew would like that, or, I wish Andrew were here. Does that seem foolish? I mean, that we know each other only three days, and yet I feel that way?"

"Well, we saw an awful lot of each other in those three days and…"

She broke in quickly, knowing what he was about to say: "…and if instead we had seen each other for six Saturday nights in a row then…"

"…then it would add up to a month and a half."

"A month and a half that we would have known each other," she smiled.

"Wait, don't forget this evening."

"That's right. Oh, if we only had seen each other this afternoon too, then ..."

"... then it would be two whole months."

"Two months." Her eyes were wide with enchantment. The evening seemed to pause while she sat motionless, absorbing the wonder of it. "The same as knowing each other for *two whole months*."

"At this rate," he grinned, "we'll be getting divorced by October."

"And who will take custody of the children?"

"If we work it right maybe they'll take custody of *us*."

She fell against his chest to support her gentle laughter. Her arms were around him now and she was rocking him back and forth. With his hand he caressed her soft dark hair and then touched her cheek. She turned her head slightly and pressed her lips to his fingers.

"Are you happy?" he heard her say.

"I don't think I fully realize how happy I am."

"At parties I try so hard to have a good time and I'm always laughing. But inside I know I'm sad."

"Yes, I've done that too."

He ran the palm of his hand up her wonderfully smooth arm and then down again. She is right, he thought, we *are* happy. It seems almost too easy.

"Oh, think of all the things we'll do together. We will, won't we?"

"We will if I can help it."

"Think of all the times we'll walk together and talk together and laugh together." She looked up into his eyes with that look of a child that he found so exciting. "And all the times we'll make love together." She said these words without the slightest pretense or embarrassment, and he remembered later thinking to himself how rare and wonderful it was that she could do this. Once again, as had happened so many times in the past, he felt his body beginning to come alive inside.

"We will, won't we?" she asked.

301

"We will," he said.

"Many times?" She was smiling now.

"Many times."

They were kissing each other. Two long kisses and a long embrace and his need for her grew, a need for this girl whom he did not yet really know.

A gust of Long Island wind, coming through the open window, punched at the drapes, and the flame of the candle wavered dangerously.

"Oh, baby, close the door," she said softly, "or the draft will put out the candle."

Yes, he too did not want the darkness. He wanted to see her, to look at her. The darkness was too insistent. When he closed the door and came back she was stretched out on the bed. Room had been left for him beside her. With her feet she squeezed off her shoes and let them fall to the floor. It was good to stretch out, he thought, good to rest. Yet he felt a little tired. He tried not to think.

"Doesn't this feel wonderful?" she said as she snuggled against him. It amazed him how much at ease she was. "I could just go to sleep this way," her voice whispered into his ear. He reached his arm around her and pulled her closer. It was the thing to do. It was expected. Turning to say something to her he found her lips working against his like a warm, growing plant. Her arms were like giant vines that tightened about him slowly and dangerously. He felt his hand moving down her soft cashmered back, moving across her waist and then, as he held his breath, moving over her beautiful rounded rump. It was the thing to do. It was expected. And yet as much to his joy as to his sorrow, nothing happened. He could no longer taste her delicious mouth for now he was thinking too hard. Do not think, he counseled himself. This is what you wanted. Do not think. There were buttons up the side of her skirt and his fingers fumbled nervously with each one. She seemed half asleep. God, she must not leave me now. She must not go off into indifference and leave me.

He was waiting for desire to take possession of him. Perhaps seeing something ugly would prevent this from happening. But he looked at her anyway and it was as if he were seeing her for the first time. He had never realized before what a mature body she had. In clothes she appeared almost thin. But how different she was now!

She reached up and playfully ran her fingers through his hair. Why doesn't it come, he was thinking, why doesn't it come? And also, where was that look of hers, that childlike look that had always been so exciting to him? And that expression of hers of love so strong that she seemed almost to cry from it? Why was she so lazy? All the little things she did when her clothes were on—where were they now? At least she could speak to him, couldn't she? To share a few words of her love. As time passed he felt her need become eager under the gentle sliding pressure of his hand. He could tell by her breathing, by the way she closed and tightened her eyes, and by the way she kissed with her tongue like a secret part of her inner body gliding into his mouth and straining to go even deeper. Her arms clutched him. He must not fail her, he must not think negative thoughts.

"Baby," she whispered and then she gave him a look that said: We must not wait any longer.

"Listen, I have something…" But her lips coming close stopped him for the moment. Then she put on a smile that was very weak and he noticed for the first time how sickly white her face seemed.

"Look," he said, "something is wrong. I mean I can't, not just now. Not tonight." She was watching him, studying him. Her white face was puzzled.

Somewhere far off in the house there came the sound of chimes. Linda sat up suddenly. Her shoulder struck Andrew in the cheek. She sprang off the bed and sneaked to the window.

"It's my aunt," she cried, holding her hand to the side of her head as if she were in pain. "Oh, my God." Then looking suddenly at the man lying naked on her bed: "Quick! Hurry! Oh, God." She ran to the closet and pulled on a bathrobe.

"Pretend you're not home," he called to her.

"I can't. She has a key. If I don't answer she'll come in. Hurry. Oh, why the hell does she have to bother me. Damn her!"

Andrew was climbing furiously into his pants. Her panic was contagious and he became numb with frenzied activity.

"Oh, the wine," she cried. "Don't forget the wine." She swept up her clothes and underthings from the floor while her eyes darted about for further signs of sin. "Oh, the candle too. Take it. *Oh, please hurry!*" With her robe hanging open, she ran to hide her clothes and he saw her breasts bobbing as if they possessed a frenzy and panic all their own.

She pushed him barefoot into the hall while he juggled his shoes, socks, underwear, shirt, and the bottle of wine so it would not spill, and the burning candle so it would not set fire to the house. "Blow it out or my aunt will see." He became engulfed in darkness. "Where the hell is the stairs?" "Here, this way." "Look out, don't push. I'll break my neck." A wicked shot of pain crippled his foot as it struck against the bannister post. He danced like a one-legged blind man while a shoe came lose from his arms and in three jumps bounded noisily down the stairs. "Shhhhh," came a frantic hiss behind him. With her two cold hands on his shirtless back they staggered downward through the void and finally another shoe was dropped. Like a drunk he staggered his way through the maze of the strange house until he felt the kitchened coolness chill his bare feet. Frantically she picked up after him all the things that he had dropped, and at last, when he stood with his back to the rear door, which was now open and streaming moonlight, she piled his lost belongings back into his arms and begged him to leave. But the moonlight on her face and the terror in her eyes welded together his affection and his pity for her. He wanted to take and hold her. But his arms were bundled with stupid objects and he could not move. He wanted to stay beside her and calm her wild confusion, or take her with him and escape. But of course he could not, for she would not let him. All he wanted to do was kiss her, and all she wanted to do was make him leave.

"Oh, please go," came her whispered cry. "Pleeeeease!"

Finally, abruptly, the door was shut against him. He stood with his bare feet on the damp grass of the back yard. Moving slowly rearward, he watched as lights went on one after another in different rooms. The aunt was inside now, and just for a moment he glimpsed the two of them together through one of the windows. Then with all his things in his arms, he fell backward over a marble bench. Sitting on the ground in disgust, he pointed the bottom of the bottle at the moon and drank. He stared at the house for a while then drank again. At last he pulled on his shoes and shirt, and bolting one fence after another, he ran like a thief across unknown back yards.

31

"WHAT'S WITH you?" D.J. complained. "I want to go home."

"The night's still young."

"It's three A.M. for crysake. I'm tired, I'm tired."

"Come on," Andrew said, throwing an arm around him. "I want to show you something."

"You're drunk," D.J. said as they stumbled together down the deserted street. "And on wine yet."

"What's wrong with wine?" Andrew reached up with Linda's candle and swatted a low hanging leaf. "It's the greatest. Good for all occasions. Take a regal sip of it during meals, or get stinko with it afterward. Seduce a woman with it, or quench your thirst with it. You can get it cheap. It tastes good. It looks classy. And if the water in some damn Spanish town is no good, you can even brush your teeth with it! How's that?"

"You're drunk all right."

"But so are you," Andrew protested. A wine bottle hung from the hand that was draped around D.J.'s shoulders.

"I know. That's what hurts. Look, let's call it a night. What do you say? We've been stumping all over the neighborhood since God knows. How much wine did we buy tonight anyway? And we've even been kicked out of a bowling alley. I mean, that's the worst. Out of a bowling alley! What a blow!"

"So a couple of times I ran down the alley after the ball. He was just sore 'cause we were drunk. That's all." With his candle Andrew thrust at a lamppost, parried, and struck home.

"Sure, sure. Look, let's you and me call it a night. What do you say?"

"First I want to show you something," he said, steering D.J. around the corner and up the street. "I want to show you the way life ought to be."

"What are you talking about?"

"And speaking of seducing women, tell me again about Ursula."

"Who was speaking about seducing women?"

"The wine, remember?"

"Oh, yar."

With this Andrew rapped his friend playfully on the head with the candle, making a hollow knocking sound with his mouth.

"But I told you about her already."

"Tell me again," said Andrew gesturing ecstatically. "It's so beautiful. Especially that part when you had her on the ground in Cunningham Park at night and the ants were crawling all over you and you were trying to take off her bra. Ah, that's poetry. Sheer poetry." D.J. went into a sputtering little drunken laugh that bent him over nearly double. Andrew continued: "Go on, tell me. Tell me how she knows what's going on but she doesn't say a word. Silence is golden." Then Andrew began to laugh himself and he doubled forward in a wheeze of laughter. He stayed bent over and walked that way for a few moments using the candle as if it were a cane.

"Man, oh man!" D.J. said, now lost in memory. "That night I nearly made it. Damn. For a while there she was too hot to handle. She was scalding me. Warn, warn, warn." He began to rap his fists on the top of Andrew's head. "*Mama mia.* And then suddenly, like someone rammed a needle in her, she jumps a foot and it's all over. Couldn't do a thing. That's when I got sore. By now she's fighting like the devil. Her nails are like claws and she's trying to bite any-thing she can get her teeth into. Anything of me, that is. I figure any minute she'll cry out, you know, like what a big brute I am and so forth. But not a sound comes out of her. Almost like she's guilty or something. Then she gets me with her knee. Probably it was an accident. Who knows? I let go of her and she jumps up and stands there like a real bitch. A little worried, like maybe I'm dead and she killed me, you know, but smiling triumphantly. There I am half ruined on the ground and she's smiling. God, did I get mad. I waited a moment, like I haven't decided whether to pass out or not, then suddenly I let her have it with my fist. Everything I own right slam in the thigh."

"Ah, beautiful. The whole story is just beautiful. Isn't sex wonderful? Just grand. So what happened?"

"I can see I really hurt her. First she hobbles around making a strange wheezing sound. Then she goes down on the grass holding her leg with both her hands. I can't see her face but she lays there strange-like."

"What'd she say afterward?"

D.J. swung out his arms to show how completely baffled he was. "Not a thing. I half kill her and she doesn't say a damn thing. Who knows? So an hour later, after I drive her home on the cycle..."

"Yar?"

"She lets me kiss her good night." Again he swings out his arms and lets them slap back to his sides. "See what I mean? Strange! But I'll make that girl yet. Don't you think?"

"My friend, you'll make her or break her."

"I've been doing just what you said. Seriously. I've been playing it casual and everything."

"Well, let's drink to it," said Andrew. "Let us drink to the subtle and understanding way you are seducing this young lady, and let us hope you hurry with the job before she buys a pair of brass knuckles and lays you out."

"Hear, hear."

When they each had taken a mouthful from the bottle they found themselves at last in front of Andrew's house.

"My friend, you see before you the house of Usher."

"Look, I'm tired."

"All right, *go* if you must. But if you do, you'll miss the big fire."

"What?"

Andrew held up the candle in his hand and winked.

"Let's drink to it," he said, and with the bottle in his mouth and his head thrown back he walked up to the front door.

D.J. spoke to his friend in a cautious voice. "Hey, what are you going to do?" He followed Andrew up the path.

"Answer this one if you can. Ready? What is heaven going to be like? In twenty-five words or less. Plus a box top. Plus a box top and fifteen cents for handling, mailing, and graft. Just finish this sentence: 'Heaven is going to be...' O.K.? Well, what do you think?...All right, I'll answer it myself. Let me see...Heaven is going to be a place without women or the need of them. How's that? Huh?"

"What are you talking about?"

"I'm going to show you something. Follow me, Big D."

"Then will you go to bed? And no burning the house down!"

The door was open now and Andrew stood waiting. "Well?" he asked. "Coming?" He stuck the candle into the wine bottle and lit a match to it. There was no breeze, and the flame in the doorway held still.

"Christ, what are you doing?" D.J. said. "Just how drunk are you? In all seriousness. I don't trust you."

But all he got in answer to this was another wink.

"What do you want to show me anyway?"

But Andrew put a finger to his lips and then beckoned to him. There was nothing to do but follow. Inside, in the candled dimness, they made their way to the foot of the stairs and began to climb slowly and silently upward. Each time D.J. tried to ask a question or make some remark, a finger would fly to Andrew's lips. "Shhhhhh!"

"But all I want to know..."

"SHHHHHHHH!"

And so on they went in silence.

The door to his sister's room stood closed. With his hand on the knob he turned it slowly, almost not moving it at all. D.J.'s voice came in a scratching whisper. "What are you..."

"Shhhhhh!"

They waited a moment, listening, and the silence seemed to hum in their ears. He began to turn the knob again. Finally it would go no further. D.J. was about to whisper, but again Andrew's lips curled at him like the petals of a flower, and a thin little hiss escaped through his teeth. For a while the door seemed stuck. At last it gave way, and, with even greater caution than before, he carefully, silently, began to push. At last his entire head was able to fit through. Although D.J. was trying to hold him back, he pushed his way in, and D.J. found himself following.

His sister's room was small and the head of her bed was right near the door. Breathing the air, Andrew found it warm with lack of circulation. At the far wall a window was open, but it was not enough. The two in the bed were breathing heavily with sleep. Holding the bottle by the neck and tipping it a little so the wax would not fall and burn his hand, Andrew stood as if transfixed. There was a strong tug at his arm, but he did not seem to feel it. D.J. was becoming frantic under the burden of silence. For Andrew could not be persuaded to leave.

"You see that," Andrew said.

D.J. fumed a whisper between his teeth. "Let's get *out* of here? Will ya?"

"You see that? Look at them. *Look.*"

They did look, and no one moved. The candle-flame danced impassively, sending a glow of yellow against the dark walls. The lovers lay still. Derek was stretched out on his back, his massive chest easily supporting Dominique's head. Andrew examined the man's face and decided that even in sleep it looked proud with female conquest. On her side, leaning fully against him, Dominique nestled comfortably in the curve of his arm. A single white sheet covered them but only to their waists. The high roll of Dominique's hip was barely covered by the smooth sheet.

Noticing all her visible folds and curves, he wondered what D.J. was thinking at that moment. Most likely he was missing the whole point of their venture into the room. It would be just like him to do that. The point was that they were in bed together, these two, spending the night together—that it was his sister doing this, and doing it while her own brother was in the same house. She did not care if he found out, nor even care if he suspected. In fact, she did not seem to care about him at all.

Yes, D.J. was undoubtedly missing the point. He probably saw only her long body on the bed, only the half-uncovered wealth of woman stretched out like an offering before them, only the blind lust deep in his own eyes as he studied her closely. This was what D.J. saw, while Andrew alone could look at her as only a brother should. He was very certain of this. As much so as he was of anything. And even though it became an effort to turn his eyes away from her, he was still certain.

Then suddenly he noticed that all this while D.J. was staring not at Dominique, but at him. Catching the puzzled and curious look his friend was giving him, Andrew felt a chill.

With a wave of his hand he signaled to D.J. to leave. Andrew paused just long enough to take one last look at the face of the sleeping girl. The cheek she was resting on was squashed by the weight of her head, forcing her mouth into a sensuous pout. Even in sleep she appeared to be able to outwit him. He left the bottle with its candle standing upon a nearby chair. He stuck out his tongue at her and left the room.

Downstairs in the kitchen Andrew flipped on the light and slumped into a seat. The silence betrayed tension. D.J. said nothing. He just sat, watching.

"All right," Andrew warned him, pointing his finger across the table. "All right. You want to know what's wrong with me? Huh? You want me to tell you?" D.J. nodded his head. "You promise not to repeat it? Not to anyone? Not to a single soul?" D.J. nodded his head once again. "All right, then." Andrew paused a second.

"All right," he continued, rubbing the table with his finger. "The worst thing in the world. That's what happened to me." He placed one fist on top of the other and rested his chin on them. "I'm in love. How's that? I've fallen in love."

"That's bad?"

There was no answer. Then slowly, the expression on D.J.'s face began to change. He lifted his eyes and made a slight motion toward the ceiling.

Andrew let his arm fall to the table with disgust. "No, you idiot, not my sister."

"Linda?"

"That's the ticket."

"So what was the bit with going upstairs?"

"Ah, isn't she sweet? My sister? A regular pastoral scene, that was."

"Sweet she's not. She never was."

"That I know."

"She's got the kind of looks could suck your guts out."

"So I'm told."

"So what was the idea of us going into the room?"

"Wanted you to see what kind of sister I've got."

"What kind?" D.J. shrugged. "She's the female kind."

"She's the slut kind."

D.J. studied his friend with surprise. "Am I hearing right? In all seriousness. Is this old Andy Will talking? The guy who used to attack censorship and the double standard and the obsession with virginity and all the quote narrow-minded moral mania of this country unquote? Do I hear my old buddy talking?"

"What is this *un*holier-than-thou attitude?"

"No, honestly. You're not going to change all your ideas just because Dominique…" He made a vague wave of his hand and said no more.

"Just because Dominique dumps herself into anybody's bed, you mean?"

"Oh, it's not as bad as all that, is it? So you *don't* like the guy. So what? So maybe your sister doesn't like Linda. That's life, buddy."

"It's not what she *does*," Andrew said with annoyance, "it's the way she does it."

"So what way does she do it?" D.J. asked, with his hands out and his palms up and with an exaggerated shrug of his shoulders.

"What the hell are you defending my sister for, anyway? You never even liked her."

"What's that got to do with it?"

"Forget it," said Andrew, climbing to his feet. "I want some beer." He went to the refrigerator. "You want some beer?"

"On top of all that wine? You crazy?"

But Andrew brought back two cans. "Here, have some beer," he said, sliding one across the table.

"Look, I'm tired. I'm tired."

"Have some beer."

With a long, resigned exhale of air, D.J. lifted the can and looked at it. "Say, just what I wanted. Beer." Then he glanced at his friend and made a face, but Andrew was already drinking.

The house seemed unnaturally quiet, strangely empty. High on the kitchen wall the electric clock churned on into the night.

"Mo Schwartz. Ever hear from *him?*"

"They sent him to San Antonio," said D.J. "Poor slob, and you know how he hates the heat. Got a letter from him just last week. Says he met a guy from Pennsylvania who was out there that day last summer watching us hill climbing. That was the time Big Mo finally beat you out after you had taken him six times in a row. Remember?"

"Oh, yar," Andrew smiled, and for a happy moment he was remembering how it happened.

Behind him as he starts the climb up the slope he can feel the spectators watching and the women preparing to shriek. The rear wheel chews into the earth and spits out dirt. With thunder and dust his machine rushes him roughly toward the peak of the blue-sky–topped hill. He hugs the gas tank with his legs. The steepening hill fights the machine, the machine fights the hill, and he fights them both. Almost at the top, the cycle suddenly bucks, and like a wild horse on hind legs, it spins and thunders, and all at once Andrew is thrown hard on his back in the weeds. But his leather wrist thong comes free and the "dead man's switch" fails to turn the engine off. Down the hill goes the runaway cycle and one of the officials, fat Mr. Van Bursten, warning away the crowd at the bottom, prepares his lasso, and advances on the runaway engine. But the cycle swerves and he is almost hit head on. As he awkwardly stumbles away to avoid the charging machine, the handle bars accidentally hook the rope, snapping it tight. Like an overstuffed scarecrow, Mr. Van Bursten is pulled off his feet and dragged in the dust for many yards. Next it is Mo Schwartz's turn to try for the top. His mouth is clamped with determination. Andrew has beaten him six times in a row. Up the hill he rides, thundering, balancing, battling, while D.J. and Andrew watch and smile. But suddenly victory and the hilltop come too easily, too unexpectedly, and going fifty miles an hour, Mo and his machine fly roaring into the air twenty-five feet above the ground and then drop like a plane and pilot shot from the sky.

"Remember fat Van Bursten and his lasso?" D.J. asked.

Andrew shook his head and laughed.

"…and how Mo couldn't sit down afterward for a week!"

They grinned together happily for a while, thinking of Mo, now in Texas, and what had happened to him even in victory. Then D.J. spoke about the women in the crowd who had stood watching them that day.

"Remember that one in the knitted dress? Wow! And that friend of hers, the one who was so crazy about Belafonte? Oh, and then there was—what's her name? The one you drove back to Jersey?"

"Gladys."

"That's right, Gladys… Christ, the way they used to knock themselves out trying to get a ride. Remember?"

"You had to beat them off with sticks."

"You said it."

Then for a while there was only silence while each of them slowly got around to thinking the same thing.

"So, on the level," said D.J., "this thing with Linda. Are you really serious?"

"I have a funny feeling I shouldn't have mentioned it."

"Why?" D.J. frowned, slightly hurt.

" 'cause you'll keep reminding me." He took a slug of beer with comic soulfulness. "And I'm trying to forget."

"Oh, get off the pot. Does *she* love *you?*"

"I don't know."

"Did you ask her?"

"No, no .... But that didn't prevent her from telling me."

"What are you *talking* about? She told you? Then she does love you?"

"Ah, her love is like a hill of grass, like a crow gliding high through a summer sky, like a ..."

"All right, all right. Does she know you love her?"

Andrew's fingers began to rotate the beer can.

"I think," he said, concentrating on his drink as he spoke, "I think by now she knows I could never love her."

There was a moment of stillness during which Andrew felt his friend's eyes upon him.

"You want me to tell you something?" D.J. finally said. "I think you really *are* drunk."

"I wish that were true. We're both failures, you know that? We've been trying like hell to get drunk all night, and look: *nothing.*"

Andrew went for two more beers, opened them and returned to the table.

"But I still don't understand about Dominique," said D.J.

"Dominique who?" Andrew replied.

"I guess you're right. Let's forget it."

And so they sat and drank beer, talking more and more about less and less, until finally, when Andrew found himself laughing easily at almost anything, he knew the beer was working. A dozen beer cans were standing empty on the table when Andrew suddenly noticed his sister watching him from the doorway. Her lips were clenched in anger and her eyes squinted at the light. She had wrapped herself in an old winter bathrobe. In her hand hung the empty wine bottle. The flame of the candle had been blown out.

"Well, D.J.," Andrew said. "Something tells me it's about time we call it a night."

Six cans of beer had given him a lighthearted sense of caution toward the coming crisis. But his uneasiness emerged in the form of a peculiar little grin.

"That's like you," D.J. complained. "Just when I'm first getting comfortable, you want to break it up."

Hoping to bring things more quickly to an end, Andrew got to his feet. "Teach you to take so long getting comfortable."

D.J. looked up, unaware of the girl standing behind him. "So you're throwing me out? What a blow." With a big final swallow he finished off the last can. Then, taking his time, he shoved back his chair and with a great effort climbed groaning to his feet.

"You're absolutely sure, now?" he said. "You're positive I can definitely go home and go to sleep? No more problems, no more drinks, no more sneaking into strange bedrooms? I can definitely go home?"

"Will you go already?"

"All right. I can see I'm not wanted. I am going home."

"You are staying right here," Dominique said.

D.J. turned to look.

"Go on," Andrew said. "Go home."

"Don't you dare," she snapped. Her eyes were now fully accustomed to the light. She stepped into the kitchen. "I want to know the meaning of this." She held up the bottle and then brought it down firmly on the table, knocking over several of the empty beer cans. One rolled from the table and bounced noisily to the linoleum floor. "Start talking."

"You'd better take off, fella," Andrew suggested.

"Were you in my bedroom too?" Dominique said to D.J., her lips twisting with the hatred she had always felt for him. "Were you?"

"Use the back door," Andrew said.

"Don't you dare," she stormed. "Answer me. Were you in my bedroom? You and my filthy brother? Answer me! Of course you were. It's written all over your filthy face."

Andrew took D.J. by the arm. "Come on, fella."

"You stay right here, young man." Her voice was growing louder.

D.J. backed his way across the room, awkward and grotesque in his effort to be polite. With a face childlike in its helplessness he looked from brother to sister, bowing his head and biting his lip.

"I think I'd better go," he said weakly.

"What were you doing up there?" she cried.

"I'll see you tomorrow," Andrew said, as he opened the back door.

"Did you hear me?" Dominique yelled as she followed them. "I'm waiting for you to answer."

"I'll see ya," D.J. said timidly.

"Go already," said Andrew.

"So long."

"Get out then," she flared at him. "Coward! Run away like a filthy coward. Get out of this house."

But D.J. was gone and Andrew had shut the door.

"And you," she said, after a wave of silence had passed over them. "You're *disgusting*. What were you *doing* in my *room*?"

"What were *you* doing?" he returned quietly. "That's a better question."

"That's none of your business," she snapped.

"That's what you think. I want that guy to get out."

"Are you jealous? You're like a broken record. You must be *sick*." She spoke the word sick as if it were the hissing of a snake. Suddenly her eyes reminded him of the eyes of Señora Albina and the way she had looked at him that night—as if he had been a slide under a microscope, as if he had been some puzzling ugliness that had fouled her home. "I want you to answer," Dominique cried. "How dare you go into my bedroom? Do you hear me? How *dare* you?"

"Don't yell at me," he yelled back, suddenly furious. "You forget what I saw in there. You forget that I know just what you are."

Her face became hard. She feels superior, Andrew thought. I am dirt and she is looking down on me.

"What's with the noise in here?" It was Derek. He was standing in the doorway wearing only the bottoms to his pajamas, just as he had been that time when Andrew had first seen him. His eyes were twitching in the light.

"You know what?" said Dominique, hurrying to her lover's side. She looked with contempt from her brother's feet to his face. "He was in our room. He sneaked in like a thief when we were asleep. He and another one. A couple of Peeping Toms. A couple of dirty sex perverts. The police are looking for people like that! They're *sick!*"

Derek tried to grasp what she had said but he was still half asleep. "What?"

"Ask 'im," she cried. "He even admits it."

Andrew gathered up the empty beer cans and took them to the sink. Every one of her words and gestures irritated him. Even the swimming of the beer in his head had become unpleasant. His sister's voice continued, but as he contemplated this new feeling within him, he forgot to listen. It was Derek's voice that brought him back. He was speaking as if Andrew were a wayward child.

"You shouldn't have done that, chum. That wasn't clean living."

"It's the filthiest thing I ever heard of," Dominique broke in, her lips again twisting with uncontrollable contempt. "It's degenerate, it's simply disgusting. I knew you were *sick* but I didn't know you were *that* sick. A sex pervert. That's what I have for a brother. A sex pervert."

"That wasn't right, chum."

"Shut up and get out," Andrew said, beginning to be frightened because his anger was draining away. He became desperate as he felt himself sinking into indifference. A slight feeling of illness kept him from going completely numb.

"He's staying right here," Dominique was saying, "and there's nothing you can do about it." She lifted her chin and gave him one of her triumphant snoblike looks.

"He's getting out," said Andrew, trying to lift his voice. But it rang like a wild lie. The pollution inside of him continued to spread and it seemed as if his body was beginning to rot.

"You're becoming worthless." She was beginning to enjoy herself now. Her lover was near her. He gave her strength. "Worthless! You can't even hunt up a few jobs!"

"I didn't try," he managed to say. It terrified him that he couldn't set fire to his voice. He couldn't bellow at them as she was bellowing at him.

"You didn't try!" she said viciously. "So why didn't you?"

"Why don't *you*?" But now there was nothing left of his indignation but its sound.

"I don't have to." Then she looked at her amused lover with a coquettish grin. "I might get married any time."

"I wish to hell you would," Andrew replied quickly. The air seemed to be thick with illness as he talked.

"And you wish you *could*!" she snapped, turning on him fiercely. He noticed on her face a peculiar expression of triumph. A wave of anxiety passed over him as he wondered what it was that she saw. "A woman wants a *man*," she continued, venomously. "A *man*! But I suppose that's too much to ask."

What in hell does she mean? raced through his mind. What does she know? Frantically, he stoked the ashes of his fury but nothing happened. Then he had to tighten his lips to avoid choking on the strange illness that saturated the room.

"Come, honey," she said to Derek, "let's go." She gave his mouth a quick kiss.

"And keep your dirty nose out of our lives," she warned, staring narrow-eyed at her brother. "You should see a doctor." She took her lover's arm and was about to leave.

"Be a good boy, chum," Derek said. "Don't ever try nothing like that again."

At last the anger that Andrew had been searching for swept through him like a flash fire. For a moment it even made him forget the pollution moving through the room. It even made him forget the rot now gathering inside until he thought he might burst.

"*You!*" he screamed, and he pointed his arm like a sword. They both turned around. "You've had your last lay in this house. Get out! *Get out!* Or I'll *throw* you out!"

Derek's face seemed to hang in a void of illness, staring. When he finally spoke it was with too much calm to be natural.

"That wasn't nice. Not in front of a lady. You better take that back."

"Get out," Andrew repeated, his head vibrating with the outlandish volume of his own voice. A tremendous pressure was working inside his stomach. The rot inside of him moved up through his narrow neck. It filled his head, it pressed against his eyeballs, it clogged his nose.

"You better take that back." The words began to move in a whirlpool around him. He saw Derek stepping closer.

"Don't fight," came a woman's frightened voice.

"Get out," came another voice which reminded him of his own.

Get free, his heart whispered repeatedly. Get free. But he could not escape from the decay expanding inside of him. That was now the only thing he feared. The disease in the air and in his body began to flood as if a dam had given way. He waited for the room to explode. The vibration of a noiseless humming was everywhere. Suddenly the rot filled his mouth and he swirled to the sink. The empty beer cans were like signs of sacrilege at the bottom of a clean white world. In a warm easy flow, the brown and yellow liquid gasped from his mouth. While he was being sick, he heard behind him the whispered indecision of voices.

"Drinking! Serves you right." Dominique's voice was suddenly lecturing. "And stay out of our room. Get your cheap thrills some other way."

Later, when he was almost alive again, he looked around and discovered they were gone.

32

Kneeling On the high slanted roof under a September sun, D. J. Jones worked slowly and solemnly, repairing shingles. A black-and-yellow sports shirt hung unbuttoned and loose outside his pants. In the Sunday silence of early afternoon, his hammer rang steadily through the empty street. Down below, a woman had just dropped some trash into a battered garbage pail, jamming on the cover loudly. At the end of the block ran two boys lobbing a football. One raced into the lead, but the other threw beyond his reach. The ball bounced an eccentric dance in the road until it was snatched up again. Two floors above the street, D.J. returned to his hammering.

After a time Andrew's head appeared in the opening of the trap door.

D.J. grinned with surprise. "Hey, buddy. Didn't hear your car."

"I walked."

"Oh. How come?"

"Felt like it." He climbed onto the roof and stood up.

"Don't fall."

"Give me three good reasons."

From where he stood, Andrew could see the towers of Manhattan reaching up clear and sharp. Even the street seemed impressively far below him.

"Look out. Don't stand near the edge."

"Say, you can even see Brooklyn from here."

"Not quite. Careful, those shingles aren't safe. Why don't you sit down?"

Andrew pointed. "What is that out there? The Triborough Bridge?"

"The George Washington."

"Really? Can you see as far as that? You know something? A camera wouldn't get any of this."

"Will you sit down before you slide right off?"

"Yes, sir," said Andrew, giving a grotesque little salute. But in a few steps he had climbed up to the angle of the roof, and holding out his arms for balance, he tight-walked along the top.

D.J. gave up and selected another nail. "Christ, where were you yesterday? I didn't dare call the house."

"I was around. I went driving."

"With Linda?"

"No, just driving." He was at the far end of the roof and could walk no further. Looking down, he saw the pattern of back yards. "Linda wasn't home, anyway."

"What?" D. J. called.

"I said Linda was with her aunt."

"Oh, really?" He drove a nail into the roof. "What about your sister?" he asked, without looking up.

"What about her?"

"What happened after I left?"

"Big hassle. Same old thing."

As he stood with his hands behind him, facing the emptiness, he noticed a little boy below standing at a back fence looking up and watching. Andrew held out both his arms as if he were about to plunge off a diving board.

"She blow her top?"

"Doesn't she always?" said Andrew, with absent-minded calm. He moved closer to the edge of the angle of the roof where there was nothing but space. A breeze cooled his body. Muscles hardened with fear. The little boy was staring at him with open mouth.

D. J. said, "I swear, you shouldn't have brought me into her room like that." He shook his head. "Man, oh man!"

"Good for what ails ya," Andrew said, as though he were not really listening to his own words. He saw the boy grip the fence post with his fingers. The boy's mesmerized attention was directed high on a roof where a madman, standing against the sky, was about to dive to his death. Suddenly Andrew did a deep knee-bend.

"So what did she say about us going into her room? She must have really flipped her lid about that."

"What?"

D. J. looked around from his work. "Hey, what the *hell* are you doing?" He got to his feet. "Get back from there, will ya? Jesus."

Andrew's body was chilled by the pleasure of self-imposed fear. The nearer the edge he moved, the more alive he seemed to come. But the words of warning from behind him were enough, and he moved back.

"You crazy kid," D. J. said, "you want to kill yourself?"

"Crazy mixed-up kid," Andrew said, as he tight-walked back along the top of the roof.

"Look, if you're going to jump, *jump*. Don't just get me nervous!"

Climbing down to where his friend was sitting, Andrew stretched himself out and stared at the herds of clouds, his head resting comfortably on one of the shingles of the roof.

"Would you miss me," he asked, "if I jumped?"

"I don't know," said D.J. "You've got to jump first before I can tell."

"Thanks."

"So just what did happen after I left?"

Andrew rubbed his face with his hands. He began to yawn. "Nothing happened," he said, with a gaping mouth. "I told you."

The hammering started again, and as a nail was finally driven into the roof, Andrew felt the vibrations through his head. Neither of them spoke, but D.J.'s question seemed to hang uneasily in the air.

"Tell me," Andrew said, picking up an unused shingle as he lay on his back and tried to think of some way to drop the subject. "Tell me. About Ursula. Ahhhh, how *are* things."

D.J. gave a wicked little grin. Saying: "*Toujours l'amour*, tonight for sure," he gave the roof a pound with his hammer.

"You're seeing her tonight?" Andrew examined the shingle in his hand.

"Yar, man. My folks'll be out. The house'll be empty. Everything set up. Say, did I tell you about last night? Sitting in her living room? I got her bra off. Yar, but I cooled it. Went no farther. Really shook her up." Now he stopped work altogether and took out a pack of cigarettes. There were only two left and he handed one to his guest. "Tonight it's in like Flynn." He pounded the roof again.

"Great to hear it," said Andrew, reaching into his pocket for matches. A wind over the roof brought with it renewed memories of autumn. He lay quiet and felt the stillness bathe his face. But it chilled him and made his body twitch. He lit his cigarette and blew a close-lipped stream of smoke at the sky.

"You're doing fine," he said. "Just fine."

D.J. betrayed himself with an immodest grin. "What do you think," he asked. "Should I take her out first and then bring her home? Or should we spend the whole evening at my place?

Andrew gave an unconcerned shrug of his shoulders. He was up on one elbow now looking down into the street.

"Come on. What do you think? Everything you've said so far's been right."

The wind tumbled a page of newspaper along the gutter. The sun had gone behind a cloud and the world seemed sad.

"Spend the whole evening," Andrew said, but again he was thinking of other things.

"What's with you today?"

"Autumn fever."

"That anything like spring fever?"

"Worse.... Things begin to die. Yet it's never ugly."

"You've been drinking again?"

Andrew rolled over and faced his friend. "D.J.," he said, slapping him on the leg, "you're always good for a laugh."

"But you're not laughing. You're not laughing."

"Never mind that. Holy Moses, where did you get that shirt? Never mind that either. Listen. I'll tell you what we're going to do."

"What are we going to do?" D.J. asked immediately.

"We're going over there and throw the bastard out."

"What? *Who?*"

With a vague movement of his head, Andrew nodded in the general direction of his house. "Him. That guy living in my home like a king."

D.J. looked at him doubtfully. "When?"

"Tonight."

"Ah," D.J. smiled, greatly relieved, "no can do. *Toujours l'amour* tonight for sure. Remember?"

"Hell, you're right."

"Sorry," D.J. said, unable to hide his relief. "Perhaps another time." He rapped his hammer twice against the roof. "Meeting adjourned."

But before he could reach for another nail Andrew's hand took a viselike hold upon his wrist.

"Tomorrow then," said Andrew ominously.

"Tomorrow?"

"*Tomorrow.*"

"Both of us?"

"*Both of us.*"

"But there's only one of him."

"Now look, you. I want no arguments. You're my friend, right? So I want you around. My sister isn't going to just sit there and watch. He's going to be trouble enough. But there's two of them over there. And I don't want to break up the place. We'll try to bluff 'em. If that doesn't work, so then we'll throw the bastard out."

D.J. asked, "If there's a fight, which one do I take."

"My sister."

"Say, I'm beginning to like this idea!"

"Very funny."

"You're serious about this?"

"That's *it*." Andrew flicked his cigarette over the edge. The wind was no longer warm, yet not really cool, but again he felt another tightening chill. "So you're having Ursula over here this evening. Damn, I was going to ask if I could sleep over. I don't want to spend another night in that house. Not while that guy's still around. Well, that's life. I think I'll take off." He rose and stood at an angle on the roof.

D.J. pointed at him with the hammer. "Wait a minute. What about Linda? Her folk's aren't home. Go, man. You don't want to sleep here when you can sleep there! That's the move!"

"I don't know if she'll be home or not."

"So where would she stay? At her aunt's place? Fat chance."

"Yar, I suppose so. Guess I'll drop over tonight. See if she's there."

"That's the action. Live, man, live!"

With balanced steps Andrew moved toward the opening in the roof.

"You're walking home, huh?" D.J. asked.

"No, I don't want to buy your cycle."

"How'd you know? How'd you know?"

Andrew sat down at the edge of the trap and felt with his feet until he touched the ladder.

"And don't forget," he warned, "tomorrow."

"Oh, yar. Tomorrow. How big is this guy, anyway?"

"You saw him."

D.J.'s face settled into impatience. "I tell you, Mac, I was watching your sister."

"Well, he's a large one. Real big. See you tomorrow."

"Yar, tomorrow."

"Take it easy."

"Two hundred and fifty plus the rain cape?"

"Forget it."

33

T HE MOMENT he saw her face he knew something was wrong. There was no kiss at the door this time, not even a smile.

"Is anything the matter?"

"No."

But the tone of her voice warned him. He questioned her again.

"No, nothing is wrong. Please don't keep asking me."

She went back into the kitchen to finish the dishes.

"You can keep me company if you like," she called.

If you *like!* The words jabbed into him. She did not appear to be angry. But it seemed to him that female indifference could sometimes be far worse. He wanted to punish her. It would have been a pleasure at that moment.

"May I help?" he asked, as he watched her running the dishes under the hot water.

"No, I'm almost through."

"I could dry?"

"No, thank you. I just let them drip. The lazy man's way."

There seemed to be nothing further to say, so he just watched. She was dressed in a sloppy white housecoat and on her feet were a battered pair of gray slippers. They looked too big for her. Perhaps, he thought, they belonged to her mother.

"I phoned you today," he said, leaning against the tiled wall.

"I was in the city. I had to help my aunt do some shopping."

"What happened that time after she took us by surprise? Was she suspicious?"

"She's always suspicious."

As the girl spoke, some water sprayed off a plate that she was holding beneath the faucet and it wet her housecoat. "Tsh! Shit!" And she took a towel and wiped herself.

"What happened?"

"Just some water."

"No, I mean with your aunt."

"Oh, nothing. Nothing happened."

This is not working out, he decided. Being together like this is worse than being alone. He found himself fighting off an urge to take her in his arms, to try to wipe away her indifference, to touch her in a way that would somehow make her his again. If he could only put his hands on her, her affection would begin to flow as before. He was sure of it.

"Come," she said, "let's go into the living room." She was finished at the sink, but before he could get near her, she had whipped the towel over the doorknob and walked from the room.

"It's hot in there," she said. "I had the oven on. Do you have a cigarette?"

She was heading away from the couch to an armchair in the corner. Lengthening his stride, he caught her by the elbow. She turned to look, as if truly surprised. Grasping her other arm, he then tried for her lips. She turned away. "Please," she said. "Don't." And she continued to the chair alone.

As he went to the couch and sat down he felt like the clumsiest of fools.

"Ah, here," said Linda. She had just discovered some cigarettes in a leather box near at hand. "I forgot they were here. Right under my nose." She smiled at him so that he might share her little joke, but his face remained stern.

Oh, no you don't, he thought. You're not going to cover this up with cute little smiles. From across the room she held out the leather box to him. He shook his head, and then with an angry silence he watched as she went through the beautiful, sensuous, female performance of lighting a cigarette. But now it had all the repulsiveness of a moving snake. As soon as she had finished, he began to talk.

"Now that we're settled, I want you to tell me what's wrong. And never mind telling me it's nothing. Is it something to do with us?...Look, remember me?"

He waited for her to say no. But her head did not move. She did not speak. Holding an ash tray before her, she suspended her cigarette above it. The smoke curled slowly toward the ceiling.

"It *is* something to do with us, isn't it?" He was beginning to detest the sound of his own voice. He waited, and finally she nodded. Then abruptly she looked at him. Because he could not read the message in her eyes, he became uneasy.

"Perhaps I'm making too much of it," she began, studying the ash tray again. She shook her head. "No, that's wrong. That's not fair to you." She stopped and for a few seconds he thought she might not continue. "I just don't know how to put it," she finally said.

He studied her face with concern. Each time she finished speaking he could not seem to remember what she had just said. Her next words seemed never to come fast enough.

"When my aunt was here, you know? Well...well all that evening...after you left...I felt sick. Awful. It happens like that. I don't know. Even my aunt noticed something was wrong. She kept asking me why I looked so white. But we must never do that again. Not like that. Not halfway."

Looking at him no longer, she held herself with both her arms as if she were cold.

"You said you loved me." She did not answer. "You did, you thought you loved me."

"I don't know."

"If it should happen again, then what?"

Shaking her head: "I don't know."

"Would we be through?"

"I just don't know. Please, I don't want to discuss it." She turned away from him and put her cigarette gracefully into her mouth.

Only the length of the living room was between them, but it seemed to him that they were moving further apart.

"But we *must* talk about it," he demanded. "It's important to me."

With a touch of her finger she unconsciously flicked some ashes into the tray. Her face looked grim in the silence.

"I said it's important to me."

"I heard you."

"*Well?*"

"Please don't raise your voice. My neighbors will hear. Yes, it's important to me too."

"You're not sincere," he blurted out.

She climbed impatiently to her feet. "I am. God knows I am."

It was growing dark very slowly, and though he could still see her, everything in the room appeared dim and unreal. She strode to the table and crushed her cigarette into a bright-colored shell. Then she slumped into another chair. Her restlessness betrayed the anxiety she was trying to hide.

"Are we through?" he asked, in a lost voice.

Outside, an army of leaves scraped through the street in the wind. It was the sound of a summer dying. Then against his cheek came something soft. The surprise of a woman's hand. The weight of her body was beside him on the couch. "Oh, my poor little boy. So lonely." On his forehead pressed a moment of two pitying lips. Afterward, their dampness remained on his skin. In her eyes, all at once, he was startled to see the tender offer of love. Yet its power and unrestrained emotion seemed strangely familiar, not at all like something that had been eluding him for years.

"Oh, forget what I said," she was saying. "I was just feeling sorry for myself." He watched her smile now so near to him. "It's just that sometimes I get fed up." She looked down at her lap. Her hand touched his leg timidly. "It's not going to happen again, so why even talk about it." She kissed him quickly, once on the nose and once on the cheek. Then he was pulling her down and kissing her slowly and mutely on the mouth and she did not stop him. His nerves, after all that had happened, had gone dead, and during those first moments when he touched her he felt nothing. But suddenly there was something else. She was trying to be neutral. That was it. She was not participating.

Her eyes had opened to discover why he had stopped. Just the thought of finding anger in them brought back to him the memory of humiliation. Getting to her feet she began to pace up and down. Perhaps one look into his face was all she had needed. Her face frightened him. It was awfully white. Could it have started so soon?

"Well, *talk* at least," she snapped. "Otherwise I might as well go to bed and read."

That was how it began. With an urge to punish her, to shake her up, to surprise her. He reached out and hooked his hand around her thigh. With one brief effort he pulled the girl down beside him. Her eyes were wide with the pleasure of surprise. Her lips were impish, not angry. There was no attempt to get away. She waited, leaving the next move up to him.

It came suddenly, almost viciously, and was not what she expected. He had begun to tickle her and her face became clenched in silent, breathless laughter. She wrestled playfully, thinking it was only a game that would soon end or give way to better things. But his fingers assaulted her ribs steadily and though she now fumbled to clutch them, she could not stop the havoc they caused. Her laughter spilled out in a wild uncontrollable flood. It seemed to him that the movements of her body had become wonderfully free, spontaneous, almost beautiful in their completely uninhibited expression. Soon she began to resist desperately. She tried in every way possible to escape. She would swiftly draw her knees up to where they almost touched her chin and then she would kick out, her exposed legs pounding the pillows furiously and sending her slippers flying. She tried to crawl, climb or wriggle away. But all her efforts did not move her more than a few inches. Her face was now half-pain, half-pleasure. He was fascinated by every provocative movement of her body. The volcanic lava of his loins was coming to a boil. It began to flow up through dusty passages of his body and engulf him. With her laughter swallowed, the girl was lost in a multiple display of grotesque contortions, thrashing and lurching while her strength slowly slipped away. She was half off the couch now, writhing and dangling helplessly, and then she was suddenly dumped onto the carpeted floor. But the merciless hands stayed with her, continuing to work feverishly over her body. Almost too weak to move, she lay face down wriggling uselessly. The whole room had gone into a wild rampage of male pleasure. He could feel the lava burning and cleansing his body until he was no longer Andrew Williams, but a new and stronger person. Everything was forgotten but the nearness of her. His hands became urgent. They began squeezing and caressing. He needed to kiss her skin, he needed to crush his weight against her, he needed to ...

But then he saw her as if for the first time. Pushing at him feebly, struggling to rise, she was gasping in the terrible manner of a half-drowned swimmer. He was no longer touching her but still she groped to her feet, her throat gasping, eyes wet with tears, arms outstretched to hold him off at all cost. No real sound yet. Just a terrible rasping from a mouth that was like an open wound. And he kept looking at what he had done.

"Don't touch me," she screamed. "Don't come near me."

She ran crying into the kitchen, her bare feet slapping the linoleum in the almost dark. He heard the bathroom door pound shut. Run after her! But he could only walk. The erection straining to tear through his clothes kept him from moving easily, naturally. The light had to be turned on as he entered the kitchen. He rattled the door to the bathroom, but it was locked. "Linda? ... Linda, I'm sorry." From behind come nothing but the urgent panting of subdued tears. He rattled the knob again. "Baby, please." He knocked. "Honest to God, I'm sorry." But her crying didn't stop. "*Linda!*"

Then all at once: "Leave me alone. Oh, God, let me alone," she cried. "Go away and leave me alone." Her sobbing grew worse. Unthinking, he moved in a nervous little circle only to return again. He listened and then rubbed a hand over his eyes. But nothing happened, nothing changed. More and more he was becoming aware of just how pointless it was to stand there alone while she remained locked out of reach.

Once in the street, he found he was able to run. She would be just another girl he would never see again. It was as simple as that. One block up the hill and another to the right and he would be at his house. In the darkness his feet sped over the pavement with a rhythmic tapping sound, light and furious. Its cadence faltered for a moment as he jumped a little wagon left out on the sidewalk by a careless child. Then later it ceased altogether as he took a short cut across the lawn on the corner. The lights were on in his house, and when he had unlocked the front door, he could tell from the voices that his sister was having company. He hurried past the living room without looking in and ran the stairs, two at a time. When he reached his room he stopped, but his heavy breathing would not. He had paused only to think, to remember. In a drawer of his desk he found at last what he wanted. Opening the blue leatherette cover, he tore out five of the rectangular pages and signed his name on the space provided. Only a few left, he thought. Before he could put the five pages safely into his shirt pocket, he was out of the room and hurrying down the stairs again. Kneeling beside the liquor cabinet, fishing out his keys, he put the wrong one in first before he finally got it open. On the top shelf were two bottles of rye, one almost filled and the other nearly empty. He grabbed them both, and placing everything down for a moment on the table by the door, he snatched a jacket from the closet and pulled it on. With the liquor in his arms again he began to fear she might call to him before he could get to the safety of the street. He could just imagine someone asking, Who was *that?* after he had left, and his sister answering, Nobody, just my *dear* brother.

Under a tree on a neighbor's front lawn, he stopped in the dark to drink. Kill the almost empty one first, he thought. He walked swiftly, turned the corner and continued on. But halfway down the street again he stopped in the dark. With a clenched face he waited for the unpleasant sting to leave. Then he lifted the bottle again.

There was no more left. Swinging it loosely in his hand like a club he looked for some place to smash it. The wall of a nearby garage looked tempting. Behind him, though, he could still see his own house. Someone was upstairs. There was a light in the second-story bathroom. Placing the heavier bottle safely on the curb, he clutched the empty one tightly in his right hand, took several running steps forward, turned sideways, continued for two more and then heaved the bottle into the night. In the wild silence he waited, holding his breath. A distant lamplight traced the bottled shadow against the dark sky. Fear came awake when he saw he had given it too much height. Sailing silently over the roof, the bottle disappeared. He thought suddenly of the family car at the curb or of someone walking nearby. His eyes closed as he listened to it drop and shatter like a gunshot in the street. Lucky.

Hurrying on, he paused now and then only to help himself to some more of his father's warm whiskey. At D.J.'s house the cycle was parked out front and a light was on in the upstairs bedroom. Cupping his free hand to his mouth, Andrew called several times.

D.J. said, "Who is it?" as he stuck his head out and squinted down into the darkness with a worried face. "Oh, it's you. Whatdoyasay, champ?"

"It's a deal," Andrew shouted up, waving five traveler's checks in the air.

"What's a deal?"

"For the cycle."

"Hey, buddy, now you're talking! Say, what's that you got there, a bottle?"

"*Que paso, chico?*" It was Ursula now who had thrust her head out of the window. She waved, her arm and shoulder naked. "What shakes?"

"Quiet. We're talking business," D.J. said to her.

"Oh, shut up," she answered. Then, to Andrew: "How are you, doll?"

"So you want the cycle?" D.J. asked.

"Throw down the key. I'm sticking the money in the mail slot."

He went up and slipped the traveler's checks through the door. He felt the whiskey rolling around inside his head.

D.J. called down to him: "That Linda must be in a real hot hurry for a ride."

"That's it. She's real hot for a ride."

Ursula was laughing. "I hope you don't mean it the way you say it."

He twice snapped his fingers, impatiently in the air. "Let's go," Andrew said. "The key, man, the key!"

"Look, why don't you just borrow it? We'll talk tomorrow. No sweat."

"No dice. Now, or not at all."

"All right, all right," D.J. said, preparing to pull in his head. "The key's here somewhere."

Ursula, who had disappeared, now appeared again, thrusting out her hand. "I got it." Held by her fingers, he could see the key. Her bare arm stretched upward and outward, clean and slim.

"Let it drop," said Andrew, moving to a spot on the lawn directly under the window.

"First, tell us what's the rush?" she smiled, looking down at him coquettishly, and he could see there was going to be trouble. God damn women, he thought. Don't they ever do anything but give you trouble? He ignored her and lifted the whiskey to his mouth, the bottle jarring his teeth.

"Oh, I want some whiskey too," Ursula said.

D.J. accused her with a look. "And when *I* offered you some you didn't want any."

"Come down, I'll give you some," Andrew called.

Ursula leaned a little farther out, as if to get more confidential with him. The arm with the key was dangling down against the brick wall. "I'm not quite dressed for it," she whispered impishly.

"She's not kidding," D.J. smiled.

"What do you mean?" she said, pretending to scold him. "How would you know?"

"I have ways. I'm not so dumb." And as he spoke he did something with his hand inside the window that made her jump.

"Don't you dare," she squealed, pushing him away.

Andrew placed his hand against the wall. "I'm waiting for the key."

They did not seem to hear. The two heads, sticking comically out of the window, were engrossed in a happy world of their own. D.J. whispered something to her and she answered him by sticking out her tongue. But at the same time the nonchalant and naked arm of the pretty girl continued to dangle the key like the teasing of an animal with a piece of meat.

"Hey *you*," Andrew snarled.

"Who, me?" She looked down with surprise. "Oh, you still want this." And she held her arm straight out again as if she expected him to do tricks for it.

"Listen to me, you no-good, worthless, syphilitic little bitch, throw down that damn key or I'll put this bottle right through that damn window."

Her face went blank.

"Give him the key, will ya?" D.J. demanded softly.

"He doesn't have to speak like that," she whined. Then she turned to D.J. "You going to let him speak to me like that?" She studied him carefully.

"Let *go* of the thing, will ya?" He shook her arm until the key fell. Andrew missed, and it bounced against the wall behind a bush.

"That wasn't nice, him speaking like that." She was complaining now to no one in particular. There were tears in her voice.

"Oh, get inside already."

"Now don't *you* start up," she flung at D.J. angrily.

"It was your own fault," he said.

"Oh, yar?"

"Yar."

"Well I like that," she stormed. "Well I like that."

But this was all Andrew heard, for the motor was roaring now, and in a moment he was thundering up the block.

34

THE HUNGRY hands of the wind were pulling at his clothes once again. Outrageously loud and raucous, the noise of the engine gave back to him a long-lost sense of strength. Two young women paused on a street corner to stand and watch. He gunned the throttle and left them far behind. He felt powerful, he felt destructive. This Harley-Davidson, now all his own, could roar, could fly, could tear open the night. And mounted on top, and going like the wind, was a colossus.

His left hand, while clutching the handle bar, also held the neck of the bottle as it swung in the wind. That was how it happened. Speeding around a corner, the bottle was suddenly free, gone from his hand, and with all the engine noise he did not hear it fall. Slowing down, he circled back and stopped under the street light. Lifting his goggles and letting the engine idle, he studied the sadly broken pieces, the torn label, and the lazy stream of liquor making its way toward the curb. As if burying an only friend, he climbed off and swept the shattered tinkling glass several feet with his shoe until it all fell softly splashing to the bottom of a dark sewer.

His wallet revealed only one dollar. He knew that if he wanted to get more whiskey he would have to go home and get it. The whiskey that had begun to take hold of him beneath D.J.'s window had now vanished from his head.

Entering his own street, he idled up to the curb and cut the engine. The family car was standing in front of him, dead and cold. Slipping off his goggles, he went up the front walk, wondering if they were still in the house. At the door he reached into his pants pocket and abruptly his stomach felt empty. He stood still. His hands slapped his trousers at each thigh. Then they did the same in back. Frantically he began searching through his clothes, trying every pocket several times. But there was no longer any doubt. His keys were gone. Quickly and secretly he tried the door, but it was locked. Where could he have lost those keys? The liquor cabinet? No. The table! That was it. The table, where he had put everything down for a moment in order to get his jacket. Now what? He'd just as soon leave them there. Perhaps he'd be lucky and never need them again. But the key to the car was among them, and that was the one thing he did not want to let fall into his sister's hands. And still he could not get himself to ring the bell. While he stood there debating the problem, the door suddenly opened and there was Dominique.

Calmly, fashionably, she was leading her entourage into the evening. The world of night clubs and laughter awaited them. Derek, inside a sleek blue suit, was touching her arm and guiding it. Two other couples followed, the men also in blue serge with white ties and white shirts, and the women, their hair flowing loose, their gowns fitting tight, slowly on parade.

"What are you doing?" Dominique demanded, her proud and painted face hard with disapproval. She spoke in hasty fear which he attributed to her annoyance at meeting him while she was with her friends.

"This is my brother Andrew," she said, speaking now to her guests. Then with obvious effort she introduced him to the four people who were with her. He did not bother to catch their names. He was looking instead at his sister and at the way she was dressed. With her hair pinned up and with her strapless dress cut low, she seemed at sudden glance to be all skin. The long female neck, the high, proud prominence of her half-hidden breasts, the painstaking perfection of her red lips, the dark mascara hardening her eyes, and the long, slim sinuous arms reminding him of Ursula: all skin— all naked, curved, faultless skin. How many men, he wondered, over how many years had used his sister in their most private thoughts?

How many thousands of masculine eyes had caressed her secretly while she stood in the subway, or walked through the city, or came into a night club with her cold, snobbish parading face? And on how many street corners had his sister's name been rumored with informed confiding smiles?

"That your new motorcycle?" she questioned with surprise, as she caught herself admiring it. "Thought you left it in Europe?" The image of her brother as a fully grown man suddenly sprang up and frightened her. The independent traveler, the successful free-lancer, the skilled cyclist—he stood for all the things she could never be. It wasn't fair. She swept the image away with the ferocious force of spite. "Andrew, when are you going to grow up? Riding around like that." Then turning to the others. "Am I glad he's going into the army! Maybe *they'll* make a man of him." She shook her head and began leading the procession once again.

"And who's to make a woman of *you?* Who's to do that, huh?"

She turned, and with exaggeration, placed her hands on her hips. "If you don't think I'm a woman," she said, "then you're even less of a man than I thought." This got a slight laugh among the others. They had all been standing about rather uncomfortably but were nevertheless enjoying it. "Oh, go on inside," she said, laughing at her own joke now that the others had found it funny. "Go on and get your keys already." She waved him away with her hand as if she had finally grown tried of him and had given him up as hopeless.

Derek touched her a warning nudge with his arm. She realized the mistake she had made and studied her brother's features for signs of suspicion. But finally she got tired of this, too.

Turning to her lover: "Oh, what difference does it make?" she said in a petulant voice. She proceeded once again down the front walk, the others following her. But so did Andrew.

"So you found my keys?" he asked.

"Yes, I found your keys," she said, still walking and without looking back. "As usual, they were just where you had thrown them. Right on..."

"Right on the hall table. I know."

She had reached the sidewalk now and had turned to face him. Behind her was the family Buick parked at the curb. The other people in the party were milling about, but the brother and sister stood as if they were entirely alone. Out of the corner of his eye Andrew noticed the face of one of the other women. A blonde with an upturned nose. She was watching him with a distant and critical air of interest and amusement.

"So you *know* where they are?" said Dominique. "Well, we won't keep you. You can run off like a good little boy and put them safely in your pocket."

At first her brother did not answer. He went to the car and lifted himself into a sitting position on the front fender. "And *I* shan't keep *you,* dear sister."

She studied him. "Are you going somewhere on your motorcycle?"

"Maybe yes, maybe no."

He leaned back on the hood of the car and waited. Derek, his hands in his pockets, kicked some pebbles with his shoe. For a few seconds no one moved.

"Oh, come on, Dom," said the third girl, with a very bored and impatient face. "Let's take the subway."

"No," Dominique snapped. She was staring at her brother now with great annoyance. They all waited again and no one spoke. Andrew was deliberately studying his fingernails under the street light. The leaves were stirring in nearby trees, but there seemed to be no wind.

"All right," Dominique admitted at last. "So we *are* going for a ride. So what? I have a right. You haven't even touched the car in two days, Mr. Smarty-Pants. So there."

"Let's go," she said, turning to her friends. Then, to her brother again, she said: "And you'd better climb off there. You'd look pretty silly riding down Queens Boulevard that way."

Andrew slipped off the fender and stood up. Everyone was gathering near the doors.

"Okay, let's have it," Andrew said stiffly, reaching out his hand.

Dominique trembled. She spoke to him in a high-pitched, frustrated growl. "Drop dead!" She turned away, but then turned right back again. "You have your motorcycle. Don't be a hog. You're just being a hog."

His hand indicated he was still waiting. "Come on," he said quietly. "Hand it over."

"Tsh," said one of the women.

"What are you?" Dominique erupted. "A mental basket case? I told you. We're going for a ride. Keep your hands off me."

"Give me back my key." He tightened his hand on her wrist.

"Take your hands off, do you hear? I don't have it, anyway."

"This what you're looking for, chum?"

Derek, standing alone on the other side of the auto, was holding the key in his hand. He bent over to slip it into the lock. Andrew circled the car and came toward him. But at the last moment Derek smiled and threw the key over the roof of the car into the hands of one of the other men. So it was to be a game, Andrew thought. But he already knew he was beaten. The man on the other side who had caught the key was about to use it in the door. Everywhere there were smiling faces. Andrew circled the car on the run, knowing as he did so that it was a stupid thing to do. The same trick was played on him again. This time Derek missed, juggled, and then had it. Andrew was growing silently furious. The faces were making fun of him. The one who had just thrown back the key was standing only a few feet away and grinning. Calmly enraged, Andrew wanted to smash his face in. There stood his sister, too. Her look of pleasure annoyed him more than all the others. Now someone was actually laughing. It was Derek. He had unlocked the door on his side of the car and was holding it open to torment him. Running wildly, his leg scraping the bumper, his hand on the fender to help him turn, Andrew rounded the car and rushed at him. Once again the key was lobbed away, but this was no longer of any importance. There was only one thing now that mattered, and that was the violence of his own fury. They came together suddenly, one of them running hard, the other still smiling and realizing too late. Each of them knew only that his head had struck something hard. Pain came later. There was now only a numbing discomfort, a moment vivid with tiny flashes of light. Andrew swam backwards. Beneath him his feet were sluggish, reluctant, and then finally they were not there at all. Down he went, stretched out in the middle of the street. He was trying to think, but thoughts didn't come. His hand was touching something odd, something sharp, and he knew he ought to worry about it, but worry didn't come, either. He saw that Derek was down also. But he was getting up again, angry and sober. Climbing to his feet, Andrew accidentally kicked some pieces of glass and then remembered the bottle he had thrown over the roof. People were milling about, but by now he had wiped all their smiles away. Walking forward, carrying his pain secretly and stubbornly inside his head, he searched for his enemy. People were speaking, but he pushed by them. Derek held up the palms of his hands. With anger he rammed them against Andrew's chest.

"You looking for a bruise, chum?"

"Tsh," said a girl's frightened voice, "they're fighting."

"Derek, don't!" It was his sister.

Angrily Derek stepped up again. Two arms rammed against Andrew's chest. He was so shaken up he had to step back a few feet. Over Derek's eye there was a dark blotch.

"What's the story? Huh, Andy?"

The enemy now assaulting him appeared more angry, more powerful than ever. Again Andrew got pushed, thrown back. Unfriendly eyes were all around him, carefully watching.

Don't call me Andy, he thought, as his fury returned abruptly. He stepped forward and threw his fist hard into Derek's face.

"*Andrew!*" His sister's voice was scandalized, unbelieving. Someone strong took hold of his arms from behind.

"Stop them!" a girl cried.

"Tsh," said another.

"Hold him!"

"I've got him."

These were men's voices and one spoke almost into his ear. Derek was removing his hand from his mouth, noticing blood. Coming up to him quickly, Dominique showered her sympathy. Andrew was trying to get loose, for he could see Derek silently fuming. No one was holding *him*. Then he came, attacking. "Look out," someone yelled. Andrew struggled and finally got free, but it was too late, and Derek flew into him, leading with his right. Hurt, Andrew fell off balance against the fender of the car, his head numb, his lip beginning to sting. The worst is still coming, he thought. But he wanted revenge. He wanted to kill this man who was killing him. He wanted to gouge his eyes, choke him, kick him in the groin. But someone threw herself on top of him, holding him down, shielding him from the pain.

"Don't touch him," the voice screamed. "Stop it!" And the storm suddenly vanished.

Her hand reached out, feeling timidly where his cheek was damaged, where his lip was cut. The fingers were light, fearful, almost not touching him at all.

"All right, come on, stand back."

"Look, chum, he hit me first."

"Tsh, is he hurt?"

"What the hell do I care?"

"All right, come on. Stand back."

These voices, spoken as if at a distance, meant nothing to him. He barely heard them. The woman now pressing against him stood back and let him get to his feet. The moment had a wonderful awkwardness about it. Not in years had Andrew seen such a look on his sister's face. She seemed ashamed of it now. She was pulling herself together. But it was too late. He had seen it all, felt it all, even down to the little touch of her fingers against his damaged cheek.

"Give him back his key," she said, turning away. Her voice was almost inaudible. One of the men handed it over as if he did not wish to get too close. There was still a feeling of caution in the air.

"No, give it to *him*," Andrew announced, pointing to Derek, who was examining the knuckles of his right hand. Dominique turned around again. Andrew held up his arm. "All right," he said. "You wanted it? You've got it." Then to Derek: "Go on, take it. Unless you're too chicken." His sister was about to speak. "Shut up," Andrew said. "I don't want to hear a sound from you. You've said enough. Now get in." People began moving awkwardly toward the car. Derek looked puzzled. No one spoke. Finally even Dominique climbed in, her face closed and hard. Derek was sitting behind the wheel, adjusting his tie. The last door slammed. The car moved slowly, almost doubtfully, down the street. At last, with a loitering, painful turn, it was gone.

Dizzy, and a bit sick to his stomach, Andrew went to the curb and sat down. For a few seconds he did nothing but listen to the mute voices of pain coming to him from different parts of his body. In the lamplight he noticed the palm of his left hand. It was smeared thick with his own blood. Looking out into the streets he studied the shattered pieces of bottle glass.

She was coming slowly toward him from across the road. She had always looked a little lost, like a child; yet, somehow, by the way she walked he sensed at once an almost indefinable change, as though something young inside of her had gone, and something older had taken its place.

35

THE DIM street lamp, steady among the moving branches, revealed on both their faces the telltale stain of embarrassment that each of them thought was hidden. He sat on the low curb and looked up and watched her come forward.

"What happened?" she asked. "Your face...you look terrible!" Bending slightly forward, squinting, she inspected a bruised lip and winced; she saw a discolored cheek and reacted as if the pain were her own. He did not want her looking at him this way.

"Andrew, what happened?"

Watching as she spoke, his eyes resented her. Meanwhile, under cover of darkness, a detachment of leaves began moving somewhere up the street.

"Why are you here?"

She shrugged. "I just came."

"Oh, you just came."

An automobile with one headlight dimmer than the other motored toward them. The tires ground harmlessly over the broken glass. In a few moments all was still again.

"Were you in a fight?" She knelt down beside him in the street, her dress touching the road. "Were you?"

"What the hell do *you* care?"

"Don't *be* like that. I care!"

He turned his head away and glared at the darkness. A feeling of agitation was coming to the surface and he tried to hold it down.

Opening her mouth, she suddenly sucked in a draft of air. "Look at your hand! It's bleeding! What happened to it?"

"I repeat. What do *you* care?"

Brought on by the injustice of his own words, he felt in his heart the mounting pressure of tears.

She stared, listening to what she had just heard. "Don't *say* things like that!" Her voice wavered. "I wouldn't ask if I didn't care. Why are you like that?" She became silent. But she couldn't keep from looking at his hand. Then, abruptly: "Andrew, it's bleeding something awful." She took hold of him by the wrist and stood up. Between his feet in the gutter, as he sat, he saw the stains of his own blood. She pulled at him. "Come on. We've got to make you all better.

"Why do you just *sit?*" she asked him. "You'll *bleed* to death." Her voice was deep. It seemed to caress. And in some distant corner of his stubborn heart he felt the secret warmth of longing. He hoped he would give in.

When he got to his feet, his hand was still bleeding. The blood left spots along the concrete walk. He took out his handkerchief and held it against his palm. The door to the house was standing open; the light in the hallway was still on.

"Where are the bandages kept?" she asked as she opened the medicine cabinet of the upstairs bathroom.

He sat down on the edge of the tub. The rude signs of pain were still with him. The lip felt grotesquely large, but when he tested it with his fingers it was still just a lip. His cheek was throbbing and he still felt sick. He decided that the accident in Europe had taken more out of him than he had thought.

Hunting among the bottles on the glass shelves, Linda said: "And where is the—ah, here." And she lifted out the iodine.

First she rolled back his sleeve for him as if he were a little boy. Then she took his hand and submerged it in the hot water of the sink.

Andrew studied her silent face as she worked. It pleased him the way her long hair hung down and the way she suddenly tossed her head to throw it back. Occasionally she would sneak a quick smile at him, but he would turn his eyes away. The bandaging proved to be a bigger problem than it looked. She pulled up a small hamper to sit on. Their knees touched. With his hand in her lap she struggled with gauze and plaster and scissors until finally a bandage was achieved.

"There," she said when she was done, and they sat looking at each other. The room filled with silence. "Does it hurt?" she asked. And he answered, "No." And now they sat and they did not look at each other.

In a gentle voice, she asked: "Who were you fighting with? You don't have to tell me if you don't want."

Uncomfortable on the edge of the tub, he got to his feet. Gently he pulled his hands free, for she had taken hold of them. His face in the mirror offended him with its discolored, swollen patches. He did not feel good.

"Nothing to tell. It was interrupted before it started. Look, I think I'd better lie down for a while. I don't want to keep you."

"If you wish, I'll leave," Linda said. She was on her feet now cautiously touching his arm with her hand. "Don't you feel well? Maybe you'd *better* lie down."

His parents' room was close by. It was good to stretch out on the big bed. He felt her removing his shoes. Then she stood looking down at him with polite uncertainty. Nothing seemed real. What had happened between them earlier that evening appeared far more vivid, though now it lived only in his memory and in hers.

"How do you feel?" she asked.

"Soso."

"Did your sister go out for the evening?"

Ah, he thought, so she was prepared to talk about anything except what was really on their minds. Yet, in that summer dress, he admitted, she does look good. A little sad, though, as if she were remembering something.

"Do you want me to sit down beside you for a while? Or should I leave?"

"You can sit down." He shifted his weight slightly to make room.

"Maybe you'd rather I leave?"

"If I did, I would have told you." He patted the blanket. "Sit down." But she remained on her feet. He thought he knew what was on her mind. She wanted to tell him that he didn't sound convincing, that she didn't want to stay where she wasn't wanted. But once again she surprised him. The bed dipped slightly as she added her weight to it. No word was spoken. And that was the wonder of it.

"It's been a tough day," he said, trying to smile. It was the best he could do. She nodded and for a moment looked as if she also wanted to smile. He patted her hand as she sat beside him. Then he hated himself for touching her. She looked as uncomfortable as could be. He was tired. Too tired even to pretend. The sooner she left, the better. Then he could be himself again. She reached out and smoothed his hair. But her expression showed that she was miles away. The overhead light made her cheek bones even more prominent and gave her a beautifully tragic and worldly look. All thoughts and feelings seemed to be locked away in silence. All he could think of was what a strange thing it was that such a lovely girl should be sitting beside him. That she should be stroking his hair this way, as if she had really found something worth while in him.

"So why are you here?" Listening to his own voice, he found it pleasurably cruel.

"What do you mean?"

"You know what I mean. Why are you here? An hour ago you told me to leave. Didn't you? I don't understand. One minute it's 'Get out,' and the next it's hair-stroking time."

She took her hand away. Her face was a protest. "I didn't say 'get out.'"

"You said, go away. It's the same thing."

"I said, 'Leave me alone.' I was afraid. I thought you'd never stop."

"But what about before that? When you were walking up and down and getting sarcastic. When you said you might as well go up to bed and read."

She looked down at her hands and silently pleaded guilty.

Suddenly words poured out and he did not bother to stop them.

"Women, hell! Underneath all that moonlight-and-tenderness everything is cold, hard, and selfish. And, damn it, I swear every sacrifice is for a gain, and every impulse is with a plan, and every submission is a demand."

"You're all wrong," she cried. "That's just not true."

"Oh, no?"

"No."

"Well what about you? 'Talk to me,' you said, or you might as well go to bed and read. And you were supposed to be in love?"

"Oh, that's not fair." She was close to tears now. But it won no pity from him. He wanted to see her cry. He wanted to see her shed the tears that were welling up inside of him. If she failed to cry, he toyed with the idea of tickling her again. He wanted to reach her, to take hold of her raw feelings as if they were part of her body, and squeeze them. But the idea was frightening. It reminded him of what he had been trying not to think of since he had fled, running from her house. You're becoming perverted, he announced silently to himself.

He saw that her tears were about to come. Her head kept shaking back and forth.

"So it isn't fair, is it?" he declared. "Well, I couldn't care less. Because it's true. Every single word..."

"Please don't."

"...of it is true. I needed your help but..."

"Please."

"...I suppose that's too much to ask from any woman. I needed some love..."

"Don't."

"...but I suppose that also is too much to ask."

Her face became ugly as she began crying gently.

"I didn't understand. At that time I just didn't know."

Her hands covered her grief and she began to sob helplessly. Yet once it began he found that this, too, was not what he wanted. When he saw what he had done, he despised himself. He could not get his hands to touch her. Bending forward, he rested his face on her leg and rolled his head back and forth. "Don't," was all he could say. He wanted to weep, but inside of him there was nothing. It was like retching on an empty stomach. He had nothing to give. He felt he was not suffering enough. Even at being a failure, he had failed.

"Don't," he whispered. "The fault isn't yours. None of it is yours." His eyes were tightly shut to keep out the rest of the world. He felt the material of her dress against his lips as he whispered to her. Inside his own darkness he was numb. But he had found his voice. "Baby, please. This thing has nothing to do with you, believe me. God, don't cry. Not like that."

Linda saved him by placing a hand on his head. At first it was like a blow, but it was only her fingers softly touching him, gently moving, caressing his hair. Now, more than ever, she knew what was needed of her: a kind of sustained, durable patience. She held her own face with one hand and continued soothing him with the other.

"I should have known." For a moment that was all she could say. She uncovered her eyes and her face was smeared with grief. "I'm so stupid."

"No."

"Yes! Because I should have seen what was happening. Because I was thinking of myself only." With these words finally spoken and out of her, she found herself all at once in repossession of her self-control. Her surprise was that it had returned so soon, as though it had never really been lost at all. A tear suddenly slid down her cheek and she brushed it away, not with shame, but with anger. She was furious at these tears, unaware that she was no longer that same girl whom she herself had always reproached. "Who knows?" she continued. "The trouble might be with me instead of you. It's so wrong to take on all the blame alone, or even to blame someone else. All my life people have been impatient with me. They wanted me to be more like them, while, oh, how I was wishing it could be the other way around! They were forever doing or saying things that would crush me. Yet I always felt that if only they had just shown a little patience…And so now, when the tables get turned, what happens?

I catch myself doing to you what I always hated them for doing to me. Now I feel more crushed than ever."

"Listen," he insisted, holding her hand. "It's all right. Believe me. Since when are mistakes not allowed?"

She looked at him as though noticing, for the first time, a new dimension in his face. Then she said: "You're very kind, do you know that?" Her hand touched his cheek. "And I *am* in love. You'll see. I wasn't just a silly girl when I told you that." She continued to look at him with her wet eyes, and a river of warmth ran through his body. It was amazing how this girl had become so fully a woman.

"But what about... you know." He labored the words, wishing he did not have to say them. "What if we try again and it doesn't work?" She watched him. "Being in love," he continued, "doesn't always make things better." She was still watching him speak. "Christ, I don't want a guarantee. But I'd like to feel... to feel that for a little while, a month, a week even, that I won't be run out on.... I guess that's selfish. And I can't offer much in return. But it's hard to be unselfish. It takes too much pride. It takes too much lying. I saw my sister today. Just for a moment I saw her. The frightened, friendly little girl she once used to be. But it took a near riot to bring it out. She'll do anything, my sister, to avoid being herself. She thinks she's truthful. But when people think they're being truthful with you, they're simply giving in to their annoyance."

Here her dark eyes looked oddly at him as she listened. A change was coming over her, but he had no idea what it was. Now I lose her, he thought. I talk and talk, but I lose her.

"Be honest," he said. "Will you be honest? Don't say one thing and do another. If you want to go, then go."

The pretty mouth opened, then closed. There was something like sorrow in her eyes. Then all at once, with a helpless shake of her head, she got to her feet and made for the door. Resting on one elbow, he watched her go. The gentle, familiar rhythm of her hips commenced as she moved. The memory of Arpège stayed with him. How miserable to be left behind, he thought calmly. To feel the desperate security of being all alone.

Then the lights went out.

In the moonlight, a pair of feet moved across the carpet. After a moment of fumbling, the small lamp came alive at the table near the bed. The edge of the mattress dipped again beneath the added weight.

Leaning forward, she, the woman, placed a hand on either side of his head. His face puzzled her. She paused with a smile. Then she let him taste her mouth. The room was being flooded with her warmth. "Baby, don't worry. We'll do the best we can." Then she smiled. "You can even tickle me a little if you like. But not too much." Happily, she kissed him again. "But now I don't want you to worry. Everything will be all right."

"And if it isn't?"

"Please, I don't want you to worry, you'll see."

"But if it *isn't?*"

But the look on her face sobered him. It was then he realized not only that she was a woman, but that now she seemed, some-how, even more mature than he. She had let her hands drop to her lap, bent her head to one side, and let her shoulders sag. Then she reached out and held him close, her arms as far around him as they would go. "What *is* it, then? What do you want us to do, make a contract? ... That's it," she said quickly. "We'll make a contract." She forced him to sit up straight and look at her. She was trying to cheer him up. "I'll stay. Let me see, I'll stay ... until Christmas. How's that?" Despite himself, he grinned.

"O.K.?" she asked. "At least until Christmas?"

"Make it New Year's Eve," he said with a wry smile. "At least that way I'll have a date for a change."

"Silly," she laughed.

But he had taken her into his arms. Outside was the endless hum of the parkway. It was such a pleasure to touch her, to be touched by her, and to feel her softness through her thin summer dress and not have to think. Pain still throbbed secretly beneath his bandage. His lip bothered him as they kissed. But it did not matter. The smell of her body was all around him. One small corner of the bed was bathed in lamplight. His hand curved confidently up her long, smooth leg, not just unresisted but welcomed, until her tender firm thighs opened and sheltered him. The four walls of the room had vanished. There was neither darkness nor light.

Later, time began to move once more as the room came to rest. On the savage field lay the exhausted dead. The phone near them became suddenly rude with ringing. He waited a few drowsy moments and then reached up. It was D.J. complaining about Ursula. They had fallen into an argument right after Andrew had left. One thing led to another, and Ursula had thrown on her clothes and walked out. In a slow, sleepy daze, Andrew tried to pay attention. Reading her lips, he watched Linda say: "Who is it?" They placed their ears together and listened. A few strands of her hair were in his mouth. The words pouring desperately from the phone into his head seemed vaguely peaceful. The warmth of her flesh was like a blanket. Becoming playful, she began to kiss him while he listened. Every so often he had to pull his mouth away and grunt to prove to D.J. that he was still there. She made her hand into a little man who with two-fingered legs walked across the plateau of Andrew's chest, up the cliff of his neck and chin to where her fingers began dribbling his lips. He pulled his face away, and with his arm around her, he reached down and pinched her rump. She was kissing him again, but he quickly freed his lips to say: "Yes, I'm listening." But finally he convinced his friend that they should talk about the whole thing tomorrow. Even holding the phone was becoming an effort. He told D.J. to forget about Derek and forget about Dominique. Forget about everything. They would talk tomorrow.

"Oh, and listen," Andrew said, "very important."

"Yar?"

"You want to buy a motorcycle?"

"*What.*"

"Cheap."

"Oh, for crying out loud." And D.J. was gone.

A car was passing again in the street. Patterns moved on the ceiling. Must remember to sweep up that glass, he thought. They were alone in the big silent room and he held her close, for she was the whole world. His slow breath gently lifted and lowered the weight of her head on his chest. He was aware of feeling peaceful Neither the pleasure of success, nor the glory of escape from humiliation. It was as if everything else had been forgotten. He had not the slightest wish to remember. He did not even think of trying.

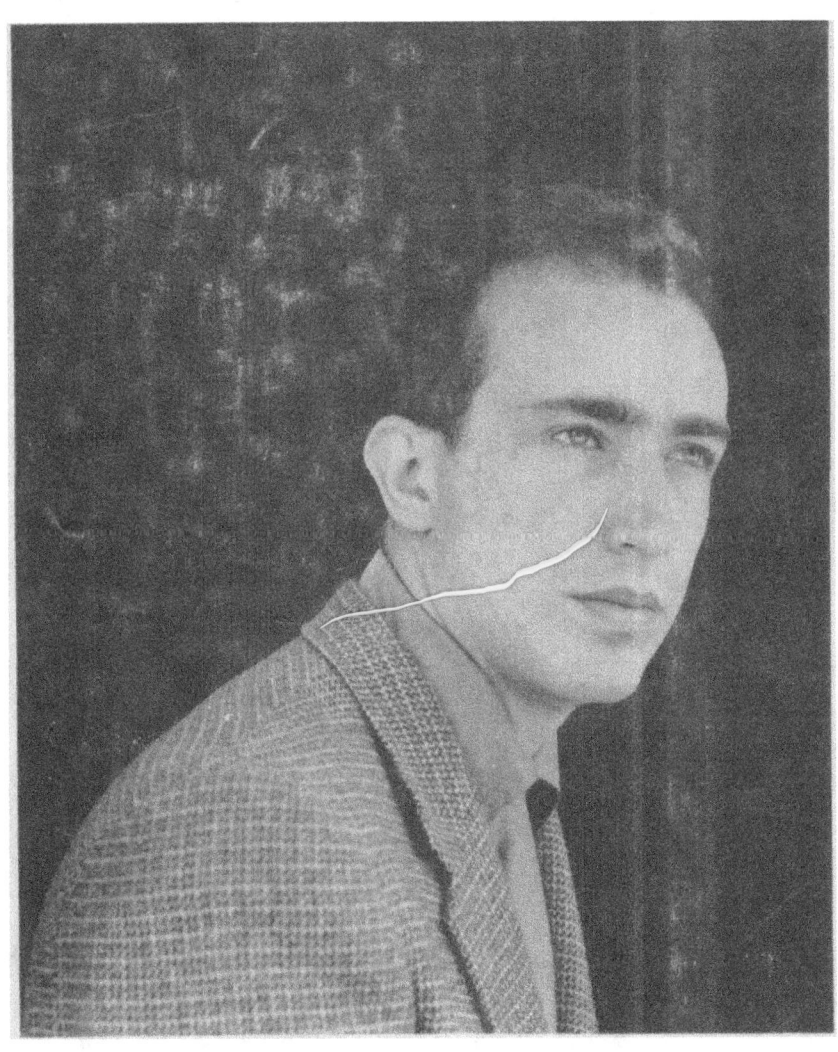

A native New Yorker, Leon Arden attended Columbia University, became a free-lance photographer and went to Europe where he photographed festivals, bullfights, and anything else of interest to editors, in Madrid, Barcelona, Valencia, Nice, Paris, and, on the other side of the world, in Mexico City, Patzcnaro, Oaxaca, and Monterrey.

He has traveled halfway around the world by track, bus, train, auto, plane and boat as well as on burro, horse and foot. And in his adventurous career he has had several narrow escapes: once while spear-fishing near Acapulco; another time in Madrid, when a wounded bull jumped the barrera and charged some of the photographers. Less exotically, Mr. Arden has also worked as a salesman in a large New York bookstore and as a dark-room attendant in an art and photo studio.

Now he devotes his full time to writing and pays this tribute to his native city as a workshop: "New York City is as good a place to write in as any because, for one thing, it can isolate you without cutting you off. The city bustles without distracting. You might get lonely, but you should never get bored."

www.ingramcontent.com/pod-product-compliance
Lightning Source LLC
Chambersburg PA
CBHW070622260626
47161CB00007B/2547